Stronger Than the Storm

Stronger Than the Storm

By Debbie Mura

Cover Design By Jimmy Mura
Cover Photo By Weiesnbach/Shutterstock
Back Cover Photo By iStock.com/Shannon Ruvelas

© 2019 Debbie Mura
ISBN: 978-1-7923-0231-2

For my parents, my husband and my children:
I am so blessed to have never lived
a single day without unconditional love!

Prologue:
Evening, Monday, Oct. 29, 2012

"Are we safe?" fifteen-year-old Lacey Freshet shouted to her friend as she spotted him outside the neighborhood Beach Club.

MacGyver heard his best friend's voice and looked up, smiling widely, even though he couldn't quite understand what she was yelling. The wind was howling, and the cyclone-fence gate was squealing as it swayed violently back and forth, clanging against its post.

"What? Can't hear you?" MacGyver shouted through the rain that was attacking from every direction. Raindrops seemed to defy gravity and pelt them not only from the sky but from the left, the right, front and back, and even bounced up with a fury from the ground.

As MacGyver's words reached Lacey's ears, she giggled when she realized he was wearing a green lawn and leaf bag over his gray hoodie.

Even though they'd hung out the night before, they ran to each other as if it'd been days with MacGyver covering twice the distance with his long strides.

Just as the teenagers met and threw their arms around each other, a loud boom filled the air, and the night sky flashed green.

"Hmm, electrifying," whispered MacGyver, bending over nearly a foot so he was speaking directly into his petite friend's right ear. Dimples bloomed on the brown-haired teen's cheeks, and her brown eyes lit up as bright as the explosion in the sky.

"There goes another transformer," Lacey's mother, Polly Freshet, called past the two teens to MacGyver's father, who was standing at the water's edge, which right now was several feet beyond the high-tide mark as the Barnegat Bay water inched its way toward the clubhouse building.

"Transformer? Is that what that is?" Richard Anderson said, gazing up at the green-glowing sky. He broached the distance to Lacey's mom, stepping past the two hugging teens, whose embrace lacked any actual human contact as Lacey was dressed head to toe in a bright blue rain suit she'd made from an old pool tarp and Velcro, and MacGyver was pretty well covered with his garbage bag raingear.

"This is less water than Irene. Wouldn't you say?" Mr. Anderson said, dismissively comparing the current battering by Superstorm Sandy with a hurricane that had largely fizzled out a year ago.

"Definitely," Polly said, surveying how far the water had risen past the bulkhead and onto the sandy beach. "They were calling for a huge storm surge, but this is high tide, and the water hasn't even reached the building."

As MacGyver walked with Lacey toward their parents, the sixteen-year-old said, "I didn't expect to see you here."

"Like a little wind and rain is going to keep us away from the beach. Pft," Lacey said, playing the tough guy. But her lifelong friend only smirked as he watched her struggle to remain upright as a wind gust tugged at her slender, less-than-five-foot frame, nearly sending her airborne.

"Most people have the good sense to stay inside during a hurricane. You should have known *we* would be at the beach," Lacey's mom added.

"They've been calling this the Frankenstorm, but it looks like we're safe," Mr. Anderson said. "Still, you better hold on to Lacey. She's so tiny; she might just blow away."

"No problem. I'll tie a string to her and fly her like a kite," MacGyver said, laughing.

"He's right. I'd say wind was our biggest problem with this storm," Polly Freshet said.

"Do you have any damage?" Richard Anderson asked.

"Part of the fence and a couple of trees came down. One broke a window. We'll have to call insurance tomorrow. How 'bout you?" Polly asked.

"No, we're good. By the way, I helped the Kanes move and cut up..." Mr. Anderson started before being interrupted by his son loudly clearing his throat.

Rather than be annoyed by the interruption, Richard Anderson quickly corrected himself. "I mean MacGyver and I helped the Kanes with that tree that came down last night. We can take care of yours tomorrow."

"Oh, you don't have to do that. I'll call a tree-removal company," Polly said.

"Don't be ridiculous. That's a waste of money. Besides, it's the least we can do for all the food MacGyver eats at your house."

"Hey, I don't eat that much," MacGyver protested.

"Do too," Lacey said and gave MacGyver a playful push that almost knocked him off balance and into the encroaching bay water.

As Lacey grabbed MacGyver's sleeve, the foursome could hear a voice from about half a block away calling out to them.

"Polly! Richard! What do you guys think? Are we..." Laura Peterson yelled over to them from a short distance away, but her words were swallowed by the wailing wind.

"What? I can't really understand what you're saying," Polly called back.

"Are we safe?" Laura Peterson repeated as she drew near the Beach Club entrance.

"I think so," Richard Anderson shouted. "According to the news, it's high tide now."

"Yeah, that's why I came down," Mrs. Peterson said as her neighbors pulled themselves away from staring at the tide line, past the clanking gate and back onto the street.

"Yeah, us too," Lacey and MacGyver said in unison before their parents had a chance to respond.

"That's what we do with every storm," MacGyver said off-handedly.

"I know," Lacey said with a smile. "We do, too. Half the time, we see you here."

"True," MacGyver said. He touched the sleeve of her homemade rain suit. "Nice getup."

"Better than yours," Lacey said, pointing at the garbage bag.

The five neighbors met in the middle of the road with no fear a car would come by. No one was out driving around since the governor had declared a state of emergency.

As she made her final approach, Mrs. Peterson fought with her red-and-white, polka-dot umbrella, which kept blowing inside out, until she surrendered and folded it away.

"Where's Ashley?" Lacey asked.

"She didn't want to get wet," Mrs. Peterson said.

"Wimp," MacGyver said.

"She's painting a pumpkin by candlelight," Ashley's mother continued. "This wind's been crazy. I was at ShopRite this afternoon, and the parking signs were slamming against the blacktop and then popping back up."

"That's why you weren't around when the fire department came through announcing a voluntary evacuation," Polly Freshet said.

"Exactly," Laura Peterson said.

"You should have seen people packing up their cars and heading out like a bunch of Okies," Lacey said

"Yeah, there was traffic on Silver Bay Road for the first time ever," MacGyver agreed.

"We had to wait through four lights just to get out of Silverton when I brought Jake over to my mother-in-law's up in Monmouth County," Polly Freshet said.

"Your mother-in-law's?"

"Ex-mother-in-law's," Polly clarified.

"I didn't think you spoke to her," Laura Peterson said.

"I haven't in more than a year, but she called this morning, worried about the kids. She said every weather report talked about Toms River like we have a bull's eye painted on us," Polly paused and looked over at the flooded Beach Club property. "I guess we got lucky. It's still supposed to be bad for a few more hours, but if this is high tide, we're good."

"Just a whole lot of panic for nothing," Mrs. Peterson agreed.

"We haven't flooded since '92, the year I got married. That was crazy. People were rowing boats right down Silver Bay Road," Richard Anderson said, referring to one of two main roads that connected their mile-square neighborhood to the rest of Toms River Township.

"That'd be so cool," MacGyver said. "I'd love to take a WaveRunner up to CVS."

"You don't have a WaveRunner," Lacey said. "Besides, all I want is for the electricity to turn back on. When the power went out about an hour ago, I was just finishing our costumes, which are gonna be sweet," Lacey said, mostly to MacGyver.

"You can do it tomorrow morning. Brittney's party isn't till seven-thirty," MacGyver said. "I can't wait to see them."

"You may have to hand stitch them," Polly said. "Transformers have been blowing all night. It might take a day or two for the power to come back." Polly's sentence was punctuated by what sounded like fireworks booming around them and the sky lighting up with a blue-green glow. As if in response, the wind picked up, and the rain's assault became fiercer.

"We better head back," Mrs. Peterson said.

"Yeah, see you tomorrow," said Mr. Anderson. "And Polly, hang on to her in the wind." They all laughed as the three families headed in different directions toward their own homes.

Forty-five minutes later, while Lacey and her mother played a game of Othello by flashlight, Lacey's cellphone rang.

"You guys need to get out now!" MacGyver yelled into her ear as soon as she answered.

"Very funny, MacGyver," Lacey said, while continuing to make a move that turned a row of discs from white to black.

"No, seriously! The water's rising! We just barely got our car out. We're passing Silver Bay School now."

Chapter One:
Nine Weeks Later, Wednesday, Jan. 2, 2013

Blue!

Lacey's thumbs flew over the keypad without thought, but before she pressed send, she stopped to consider whether she needed to add :) or perhaps ;). No, too flirty, she thought.

Blue! is enough. Send.

As the seconds passed, she hated herself for staring at her phone, ignoring six other texts while she waited for MacGyver's response.

Two minutes later, still nothing.

I'm such an idiot, she thought. *I shouldn't have sent that. What the hell was I thinking? I never text first. And, if anyone knows that, MacGyver does. He's going to think I'm desperate.*

Five minutes. She watched as the digits changed on her screen. Still nothing.

Ten minutes. Nothing.

She was so glad she had settled on "Blue!" and not the infinitely more personal "Hey." He would never know she hadn't actually seen a bright blue car drive by.

One hour. Nothing.

"Lacey, you need to come down and watch your brother while I pick up the pizza." Lacey heard her mother's voice echoing through the empty first floor of their home as if she were making an announcement on a faulty PA.

"Pizza again," the high school sophomore said, groaning, certain her mother couldn't hear her complaints. "She's got to be kidding."

Rolling over on the air mattress that currently served as her bed, Lacey shifted onto her elbows so that her voice would carry through the hall and down the stairs.

"Can't you take him with you?" No answer. "I'm busy."

The answer came swiftly in the form of her mother's heels advancing toward the staircase, followed by the sound of her voice, sharp and insistent.

"Lacey, honey, I can't hear you. Could you please come here, so I know what you're saying? Lacey, how many times do I have to tell you don't speak till you can see the whites of their eyes."

"Isn't it, don't shoot until..." Lacey countered as she arrived in the second-floor hallway.

"You want to find out?" Polly answered stone-faced. Then, her tone softened as she asked, "What are you so busy doing anyway? Sleeping?"

Lacey instantly felt as if she were being accused.

"No, Mom, I wasn't sleeping."

"Were you doing homework?"

"Okay, sure, that's what I was doing." Lacey frowned, then quickly decided to use her mother's nagging to her advantage. "And that's why I can't watch Jake right now. It's geometry, Mom; I really need to...

"Focus," they said together and laughed as they both poked fun at Polly's daily admonishment to her "flighty" teen.

"All right. I'll take him but try and finish up. I could use your help after dinner straightening up around here."

"Are you kidding? Really? Mom, how are we supposed to Swiffer raw plywood? You can't even take your shoes off downstairs anyway. And besides, nobody is going to be coming over....Shit, there's not even anybody to come over."

"Lacey, watch your language. I know it's hard, but we have to keep the place at least somewhat livable."

"It's not, Mom. It's just not."

"Whatever. Finish your homework." As she walked back toward her room, Lacey heard Polly's black leather pumps, the ones she reserved for the days she appeared in court, clicking loudly against the floor. Then, she heard her mother yell, "Jake! Jake! Come on, you're coming with me."

Hmm, Lacey thought. *I bet he's not in the same room, and why does she wear heels when she has a bad back? Maybe if she didn't wear those three-inch pumps, she wouldn't have needed my bed.*

Returning to her room, Lacey dove onto the air mattress, as much as anyone could dive onto an air mattress, and reached for her phone, which was chirping "You go Glenn Coco," her text tone.

Snatching it up, Lacey immediately read the screen.

I'm so bored.

Sorry, Brittney, I don't really care right now, Lacey thought, but she didn't actually finger a response. Her mind was stuck on one thing: No message from MacGyver.

Lacey glanced at her pile of notebooks – biology, English and geometry – and laughed aloud. Why was she still bringing the books home every night as if she were actually going to do her homework? It had been weeks since Lacey had done any school work at all, outside of the occasional worksheet copied in class. Yet, every day when the final bell rang, she rushed to her locker, reviewed her homework list and brought all the right books home.

Just under a thousand miles away, MacGyver stared down at the text and, at first, couldn't help but smile, knowing that Lacey was thinking about him. But the elation was short-lived.

Blue! Is she kidding? Was she just trying to be mean? Only Lacey could stab him from so far away.

He knew it was just the "electric car" game they'd been playing since they first got cellphones in sixth grade, where they texted just the color whenever they saw a bright-colored car. But come on! Couldn't she be just a little more sensitive? Didn't she have any idea what it was like for him being banished from all his friends? From her?

Blue! There was no "Blue" anymore, not since Sandy's sickening storm surge cut two new inlets into the Barnegat Bay.

MacGyver thought back on how Hurricane Sandy decimated the barrier peninsula at high tide on Monday, Oct. 29, and continued its march across the bay. Who knew the bay could overflow like a bathtub and basically wash away MacGyver's whole life?

MacGyver always felt so stupid when he thought back on that night. They were all so sure of themselves. *It was already high tide. The bay was nothing to worry about once high tide came and went. Ha!*

Sandy really was a Frankenstorm, he thought. *Undeterred by seawalls and sand dunes, she swept away houses like Monopoly board pieces. Even the oversized McMansions on tiny waterfront lots were simply tossed into the water. Who knew a storm could even do that?*

MacGyver thought about the thousands of vehicles, homes and businesses the storm recklessly tossed into the bay along with people's lives, and got mad. "It was after high tide!" he shouted alone in his room. Then more quietly he complained, "We were supposed to be safe."

But, of course, they hadn't been safe. The barrier peninsula breached, and the bay rose eleven feet in half an hour, leveling scores of communities, including the Silverton subdivision in Toms River where McGyver had lived all his life.

MacGyver shook his head. He hated to think about this crap. What was the point? He returned his gaze to his phone.

Blue! He looked at the word again and went searching through his pictures. At first, all he could find were shots of his new "friends" on the day they cut school.

That was a great day, he thought. *They asked me to go surfing but didn't realize they didn't have enough gas. Instead, we hung out in the swamps, smoking and mudding. Then, when a gator showed up, they took off and left me to fend for myself. Initiation prank, my ass! Who needs friends?*

Finally, he got past the recent shots and found the picture he was looking for. Staring at the two of them together, he wasn't sure which one he missed more, Lacey in her denim shorts and red bikini top or his electric blue 2003 PT Cruiser. He'd spent all of his life trying to win one and the last three summers fixing up the other, and one crazy high tide took both from him overnight!

Chapter Two:
Thursday, Jan. 3, 2013

MacGyver meant to respond to Lacey's text, but the next morning, he wondered if too much time had passed. What could he possibly say now? "Yellow?" "Hey?" Should he start a conversation? Things were so ridiculous between them now; neither one ever knew what to say.

For 15 years they shared a backyard, even convinced their parents to put a gate in the back fence so neither had to walk around the corner, and now they were lost to each other. Crap, he was just lost.

If he were in Toms River, he'd at least know where to go, what to do, when he needed to be alone with his thoughts. He'd simply take his bicycle and pedal around the neighborhood. He knew every house, every driveway and every dog. Hell, even the wild rabbits had names.

Or he could walk five houses down the road to the Rock Throwing Place and see if he could break his record of nine skips or at least Lacey's record of five. He laughed thinking about how much Lacey loved skipping stones – it was one of her favorite things to do – even though she wasn't particularly good at it.

Landlock, Fla., the Springfield, USA-maze his parents sentenced him to, had no such accommodations. Even if he still had a bike, it was definitely too hot. Who can ride around on hot pavement in ninety-five-degree weather? How could anyone live like this? He longed to be back in Jersey, where that afternoon was a balmy twenty-eight degrees, and no one had strung Christmas lights on any palm trees.

No one at school talked to him. Okay, that wasn't true. But no one worth talking to talked to him. Of course, it didn't help that when he first moved here last November, he only had a pair of jeans, flip-flops and two tee-shirts. One was of his friend's emo band, Harborland, and the other labeled him a victim for life, with its whining declaration, Restore the Shore.

He knew how absurd it sounded, but he just couldn't get past the thought that time had somehow fractured during that last October weekend before Sandy came for her unwelcome visit. One minute it was Sunday afternoon, and everyone was hanging out at the Beach Club, flying a kite in the pre-hurricane winds, and the next, it was two months later, and he was all alone. Nothing was going to be normal ever again.

On the Saturday before the storm struck, ten of them had squeezed into Lacey's mom's minivan and headed about twenty miles west, out to Jackson for Six Flags' Fright Fest. It had been a great day of riding roller coasters and an even better night of holding Lacey's hand as they wandered through dark and frightening, haunted trails inhabited by some pretty believable zombies. What is it about zombie chicks in wedding dresses that freaks everyone out?

When the dead bride tapped Lacey on the shoulder, she went ballistic, flinging obscenities her truck-driver grandfather would have been shocked to hear come from his Half Pint's mouth.

"You can't fucking touch me. It's against the rules," she shouted at the zombie.

As she regained her composure, Lacey turned to him for support as she always did. "MacGyver, you saw that, right? She flippin' touched me. They're not..."

But then she stopped, caught her breath, and suddenly forced out some laughter as her friends circled around in a show of support, and the creepy and unblinking actress slipped into the shadows.

"Are you all right?"

"What happened?"

"Do you want us to beat her up?"

Her friends' well-meaning entreaties made Lacey feel childish and self-conscious. She just wanted to move on. "It was nothing. Let's keep going," she insisted as they headed toward a maniacal zombie wielding a chainsaw.

As each of the girls latched onto someone in the group, Lacey whispered to MacGyver. "That bride-thing scared me so much I actually peed my pants. But just a little." Then, she added, "You can't see anything. Can you?"

While it was hard to get a good view of her butt – something he never tired of seeing – in the strobe-lighted cemetery scene they were walking through, MacGyver dutifully inspected his best friend and assured Lacey that her secret was safe.

"You don't mind that I said that to you, do you?" Lacey asked rather sheepishly, suddenly embarrassed.

MacGyver smiled and shrugged.

"Don't be silly. It's me you're talking to here," he assured her but worried as her hand slipped from his, only to be reassured as she flung his arm over her shoulder and leaned her head on his chest.

As the group creeped through the pitch black of the next trail, MacGyver wondered if Six Flags knew when they planned these haunted mazes just how much the jeering sounds of crickets and cicadas, heckling them through each step, added to the experience. As they weaved their way through the Pinelands, the teens remained on constant lookout for the escaped asylum patient said to threaten their very existence. Of course, MacGyver and his friends knew the real danger wasn't from the fictitious fiend Six

Flags had invented but from the "real" Jersey Devil who was said to have stalked the local Pine forests for decades.

As they climbed over hay bales and entered a small clearing, Lacey suddenly burst out laughing as they encountered a pair of giant headless corpses, standing about six-feet tall.

"What about them?" Lacey said, tugging on MacGyvers's shoulder so that he would lean down and she could speak into his ear.

"What about them?" he repeated, confused.

"The costumes?" Lacey said impatiently. "How 'bout we go to Brittney's party in those costumes?"

"I don't think they'll give them up," MacGyver said sincerely.

"No, I'll just make us costumes just like them. How 'bout it? I really like them," Lacey said as they slipped past the goons who were making grunting sounds, despite having no mouths.

"Can you?" MacGyver said.

"Of course," Lacey had said with little concern for the details, and that had settled it.

The costumes were never finished, and the party was never held. Sandy's arrival canceled everything – the Oct. 30th trick-or-treating in Toms River, the famous Toms River parade on Halloween night and trick-or-treating (on Oct. 31) everywhere else in the state.

Even though the governor had declared Halloween would merely be delayed a few days until Nov. 5, no one in Toms River and throughout much of New Jersey felt like celebrating when the nightmare they were living was far more frightening than any spooky pretend.

As the blackout continued on that fake Halloween, lucky New Jersey residents coped with the horrors of no electricity, hot water or cell service, while those most terrorized by Frankenstorm

Sandy adopted farmers' hours, using every moment of available sunlight to rummage through their soaked stuff and throw most of it out.

As MacGyver thought back on the holiday that wasn't, he remembered that in the days immediately following Sandy, neighbors would begin to fall into conversations commiserating with one another, only to cut the discussions short and return to work after uttering the suddenly popular catch-phrase, "Burning daylight."

As crazy as it sounded, some small part of MacGyver genuinely believed that time somehow split when the lights went out. The real world, the normal one, where Halloween comes every year and houses are permanent structures that aren't washed away by a mere rainstorm, continued somewhere else. Only MacGyver and everyone he knew had been doomed to take the other road, the one that swerved off into a bizarre Oz where grocery shopping takes place at a food pantry and Thanksgiving dinner is consumed among strangers at a church you've never attended.

Chapter Three:
Friday, Jan. 18, 2013

"Who are you going to Winter Formal with?" Britt asked Lacey, hounding her with the question for the twentieth time in the first fifteen minutes of their lunch period.

"I told you. I don't know, and I don't care."

"Really?" the raven-haired teen with the perfect complexion said, dripping with sarcasm. "I don't know him. Is he hot?"

"Oh, shut up. We were supposed to be going in a group. I don't even feel like going anymore now that you and Ashley have dates. I mean…" Lacey quickly caught herself before she pissed off both her best friends with one sentence. "I mean, I'm happy for you. I really am. It's just I don't…"

"You could go with Brian," Brittney said, cutting her off, obliviously assuming the issue was as simple as securing a date. Not that *that* was simple.

"It's just that I've never been to a dance without MacGyver," Lacey said, as she looked down at her hands and spied the blue shell friendship bracelet she'd worn for years. *Was he still wearing his?*

"I don't get you, Lacey. You weren't even dating MacGyver when he moved," Ashley said, scarfing down French fries while she cautiously scanned the cafeteria, hoping no one who mattered would catch her with food in her mouth.

"Yeah. The last time you two were actually together was in what? Sixth grade?" Britt added, as she took a metallic blue nail polish bottle from her purse and began touching up the nail she had chewed on during English.

"Seventh. But we were always together. Always."

"We know," Ashley and Brittney sighed in unison.

Lacey could tell both girls were doing their best to understand, but since MacGyver moved away two days after the storm, nearly three months ago, they had grown tired of her overwhelming melancholy. At times, they complained when she brought up his name. At others, she knew, they were making plans behind her back just so they didn't have to deal with her and the ever-lurking ghost of MacGyver Anderson.

What Lacey couldn't understand was why *they* weren't more upset. The four of them had seen each other pretty much every day since preschool. Now, while Lacey could barely go five minutes without thinking about him, she could tell Ashley and Britt went days at a time without sparing MacGyver so much as a passing thought.

"Y'know, it's kind of nice that the three of us get to hang out more now," Ashley said. "Y'know, just the girls."

"Yeah, what was it Connor used to call us?" Brittney asked.

"MacGyver's Angels," Lacey mumbled miserably.

Why can't I just move on? Lacey thought. Then, like a starlet slapped in a 1950s movie, she took action. She grabbed her flip-phone and headed over to Brian's table.

"Okay, yes," she said to the top of Brian's head as he and his friends stared at his iPhone, which was playing a YouTube video of a cat stuck on a ceiling fan.

"What was the question?" Brian responded before he looked up, his blue eyes meeting Lacey's steady gaze. "Lacey. Oh! Yes? You're kidding, right?"

"No. I mean, yes. Yes."

"Okay, good. I'll get the tickets."

"Just get one. I already have one."

"You do?"

"Yeah, we were all going as a group," she said, gesturing at Brittney and Ashley, who were staring over unabashedly as if

Brian were hosting an overcrowded Open Mic night and it was perfectly acceptable to strain to hear every word. "But, whatever. This will be good."

"Great. I'll get a ticket, and I'll see you…mmm," he looked at her shyly, his hand brushing back his sandy hair just to have something to do.

"In geometry next period," Lacey finished with a laugh and headed onto the lunch line. Grabbing just a hot pretzel and a bottle of water, Lacey pulled her student ID out of her lanyard, flipped it around and flashed the neon green S sticker at the lunch lady.

"You know you can get a full free lunch with that," said the frizzy-haired, red-headed lady who dressed like some retro rock star in pink tights and a short denim skirt with a huge cross dangling from her neck.

"Nah, I'm good," Lacey said, rapidly returning her ID backward to its holder so that the S no longer showed. "Thanks."

Back at her own table and the seat that might as well have been assigned to her the first day of freshman year, Lacey looked at her friends and said, "There. It's done. I'm going with Brian."

"We should go shopping this weekend," an extremely enthusiastic Ashley said without commenting on the sudden turn of events.

"Can't. It's the three-day weekend. I'm going skiing with my parents, unless they cancel again," Brittney said, pushing her chair back from the table and brushing her long black hair. "But, you two go. I already have my dress."

"It's a three-day weekend? Why?" Lacey asked.

As Brittney shrugged, Ashley provided, "Martin Luther King Day."

"Oh, yeah. I have a funny story about that," Lacey said, absent-mindedly braiding the fringe she'd cut into the bottom of the dollhouse jacket she'd rescued from a thrift store.

"Who has funny stories about MLK Day?"

"I do. Well actually my mom does."

"Of course she does."

"Anyway, it was the first MLK Day, and Polly was working for some big British law firm up in New York," Lacey explained.

"Wait. What do you mean the first MLK Day? The day he was born?" asked Brittney.

"Noooo. It was the first time we were celebrating it as a national holiday."

"Well, we weren't. I mean. We weren't born yet," Brittney interrupted again.

"Anyway, it was the first one," Lacey said, making eye contact with Ashley and exchanging the familiar if-she-cuts-me-off-one-more-time-I'm-gonna-hit-her look. "And well, Christmas and New Year's that year had fallen on Thursdays so the company had just given everyone off on Christmas and the day after and New Year's and the next day, and they were tired of giving out all these paid holidays."

"I can see that. My father would blow a gasket if he had to close down Dependable that many days," Brittney said.

"Annnny waaayyyy," Lacey continued, letting her annoyance show. "So the company made an announcement that all the African-American employees could have off for MLK Day, but everyone else had to work."

"What? That's ridiculous."

"Oh, come on, that didn't happen."

"Ask my mother."

"I would, but I don't want to sit through a ninety-minute lecture on the history of racism."

"Tell me about it."

As the bell rang, Brittney rushed off since her next class was literally a quarter-mile away through the endless alphabet-soup hallways. But Ashley grabbed Lacey's shoulder and leaned in. "You're not fooling me. I saw how you changed the subject. Let's go shopping this weekend. We can go to that new thrift store. Oh, better yet, Tiff said the People's Pantry has a ton of new designer dresses, Sandy donations from the fashion industry."

"Geez," Lacey said, frowning.

"Hey, there have to be some benefits to all this crap."

"Whatever."

Chapter Four:
Saturday, Jan. 26, 2013

Wearing the maroon Panthers tee-shirt, MacGyver felt like a fraud. He hated sports and had never been one of those rah-rah, go-school types. But his parents insisted he wear all the spirit clothes he'd been given shortly after arriving at his new school, so everyone would understand how grateful they were for the community's support.

Secretly he was, in fact, extremely thankful, and even shocked, at everything these strangers had done for his family. But why was he the only one who was required to wear his gratitude like a billboard? Mom and Dad could get away with sending little thank-you notes. How come he had to be his new town's Hurricane Sandy poster boy?

Holed up in his bedroom, MacGyver spent every afternoon and all weekend playing the Nintendo 64 he'd purchased at a garage sale. No matter how many times his mother insisted he "go out and get some fresh air," MacGyver wouldn't budge. And why should he? Even if he made some friends, they no doubt would want to go somewhere or do something, and that was clearly out of the question.

Hell, he couldn't even buy a $2 Chipwich from the ice cream truck, not that there were any ice cream trucks endlessly playing the annoying "Turkey in the Straw" here in Landlock, Fla. Who knew you could miss a sound you once hated so much?

It's not that money had been no object up until now. But, for the most part, whenever MacGyver or his parents wanted something – really wanted something – there was a way to get it. Not anymore.

When the storm surge came, it broke through every crack and seam of their once comfortable three-bedroom bi-level, toppled his treehouse and completely trashed his first-floor bedroom. Somehow, it also stole his once upbeat parents and left depressed, suddenly old people in their place – and that was before his father's back injury.

When MacGyver thought back on the Sunday and Monday when Sandy came for her unwelcome visit, he was always struck by how every tiny fiber of his life had changed. It was as if the blackout fell on his normal life, and the power was never to be restored again, at least not for his family.

Late on Sunday afternoon, Oct. 28, he and his dad had gathered and stored some lawn furniture and tied down heavier pieces like the wooden porch swing. They joined the parade of insanity with everyone buying what they must have thought would be the last loaves of bread ever baked and gallon jugs of water ever filled.

This ritual was not uncommon. The two of them had done the same thing for every major nor'easter or snowstorm that had headed toward the East Coast all of MacGyver's life.

They had been annoyed on this particular afternoon that they had to go to three stores before ending up in Lowe's getting flashlights and batteries. But the trip had been worth it for the comic value of watching people camped out in the aisles anxiously awaiting the delivery of portable generators.

"People are so spoiled," his father said. "We've never gone more than a few hours without power. Is that so terrible? What the hell do they need generators for? That's just people who have more money than they know what to do with it."

MacGyver agreed, and he and his dad were still laughing about this when they passed the local Wawa convenience store and saw the "No Gas" sign.

"Wow, people are going crazy," MacGyver said. "Don't they remember we went through all this last year for Irene and nothing happened?"

"Well, not exactly nothing. You did get to go swimming right in the driveway," his dad said, with a smirk.

"It wasn't that funny. I got stung by a jellyfish."

"Oh, yeah. I forgot about that."

"But, Dad, wasn't that the highest the water's ever come?"

"In your lifetime. Yes."

"And that was nothing. It didn't even get inside anyone's house."

"Well, a few houses flooded, but not many. But, you know the media's got to talk about something, and with everything closed down, they've got nothing better to do than scare people."

"I know," MacGyver said. "Did you see that weather reporter broadcasting from the Point Pleasant Boardwalk right before we left the house? She even looked bored and embarrassed, trying to make a big story out of high tide and a little wind," MacGyver scoffed.

After dinner that night, MacGyver went over to Lacey's where they nuked some popcorn and watched *Edward Scissorhands*. She had wanted to watch something scarier in keeping with the Halloween theme, but MacGyver knew those movies bothered him a lot more than they did his friend, and he hated to look like a wimp in front of her.

Getting her to choose the Tim Burton classic over *Insidious* was easy. MacGyver simply reminded her of two other times when they had watched the story of the hedge-clipping wonder during storms, and she picked it herself. She didn't know he was manipulating her or that MacGyver had long depended on her deep attachment to nostalgia and tradition to get his own way.

At exactly ten o'clock, Lacey's phone vibrated, and MacGyver groaned.

"Who is it now? Don't you know it's polite to turn your phone off when you have company?" he said, reaching for her cell.

"Hey," she said, swatting his hands away and trying to look at the display as she lifted her head off the pillow on his lap. "Last one. I promise. Just let me see who it is. Then, I'll shut it off."

"Ha. It's your mom," she mocked him as she read the message. "She wants you to come home early because of how hard the wind is blowing. She says the tree in the Kanes' front yard just came down, barely missing their car."

"Really? That's a pretty big tree, but is she kidding me? What does that have to do with me? She said I could stay till midnight. We already know there's no school tomorrow."

"Do you want me to text her? And where is your phone anyway?"

"I left it home. I know how to be polite," he said and tickled her.

"Stop. Stop. Mom, Mom, MacGyver is attacking me!"

"Again?" came a monotone, exaggeratedly bored response from the next room.

"Gee, thanks, Mom. You know most mothers would rush in to protect their daughter's honor."

"Sorry," Polly called without moving from the den.

"Should I text her?" Lacey asked MacGyver.

"No, I better go. See you tomorrow," he said before bear-hugging her for a full minute and then tickling her again.

"Mom!"

"MacGyver, do I have to come in there?" Polly teased. Neither Lacey nor MacGyver detected any movement in the other room, nor did they expect any.

"No, it's all right. I have to go, anyway," MacGyver called to the front of the house as he walked to the back door. "Goodnight, Polly. Thank you for having me."

###

"MacGyver. MacGyver? MacGyver!"

MacGyver bolted up in his bed, knocking the N64 controller to the floor.

"Yeah, Mom, what?"

"If you are not going to play that game, can you at least turn it off? How many times do we have to hear DINT, DINT. DINT. DINT-DINT. You know your father is trying to rest."

How long had he been sleeping? "Oh, sorry," he called back, pulling the controller up by its wire and ending the game. He rolled over on his side and hoped he could slip back into some dream. *Another one with Lacey would be nice,* he thought.

Chapter Five:
Saturday, Feb. 2, 2013

Lacey pulled up her pantyhose as gently as she could but somehow still managed to poke through them with one of the French-tipped nails that her grandmother had paid for after insisting Lacey get a manicure for the dance. After two years of radio silence, not even a Christmas card, it was weird having her grandparents back in her life, but also kind of nice.

"Shit," Lacey complained.

"Oh, who cares?" Ashley consoled her. "You hate those anyway. Go without."

"Yeah, you're right," Lacey agreed as she tripped out of the damaged stockings, balled them into a knot and threw them across Ashley's room. She missed the wastebasket, but Ashley reached down and provided an assist.

"Sit down on the bed, and I'll put your makeup on," Ashley instructed. As Lacey sat down, Ashley took the opportunity to get a good look at her friend's burgundy dress. "I love that dress on you. It really brings out your eyes."

"Thanks, but it's not as pretty as yours, and I would kill to have your blonde hair and blue eyes," Lacey said.

"Sure you would, and my twenty pounds of excess fat, too," Ashley said.

"You're being stupid. You're perfect."

"Right. Says the girl in the size two."

"That's only because I'll probably never reach five feet tall. Truth is I found this in the kids' department."

"Did not."

"Yeah, I did. And thanks to my completely flat chest. I didn't even have to alter it."

"I'm surprised you didn't anyway," Ashley said. "I love how you make everything your own, braiding your tank-top sleeves, replacing seams with safety pins and adding heart-shaped cutouts. How do you even think of these things?"

"I don't know. I guess nothing ever looks finished when I see it in the store."

"Except this dress?" Ashley asked.

"Huh?" Lacey said.

"You didn't change this dress at all. Don't get me wrong. It looks great, but it's not like you."

"Yeah," Lacey said. "I guess I just haven't felt very creative lately."

The girls fell quiet as Ashley applied Lacey's gold-hued eye shadow and jet-black mascara. The combination made her brown eyes sparkle against the shoulder-length frame of her honey brown hair.

After telling Lacey to hold still, Ashley took the opportunity to babble about Tyler and the deep significance of this, their first "real" date. After all, pizza at Vesuvius didn't count, and while Ashley had been making out with the Harry Potter-obsessed future chef every couple of days for the last two weeks, he still hadn't asked her out, and she worried he never would.

Lacey was thankful that while Ashley worked her magic with Mrs. Peterson's vast array of Mary Kay products, she could zone out. She had her own problems. She didn't really want to think about Ashley's love life; at least, she had one.

To Lacey, the ritual of dance preparation had always been way more fun than the dance itself, but prep day had lost its appeal without MacGyver.

Ever since middle school, she and MacGyver would start the day of a dance with a big lunch of breakfast foods -- especially bacon -- that he would make in the Freshet kitchen, always throwing out the first burnt chocolate chip pancake.

By the time they were done, the whole house would smell like fried foods and syrup, and nearly every pan and mixing bowl would be piled high in the sink. But because it was a dance day and Lacey had to straighten every last strand of MacGyver's thick, curly brown hair before getting dressed herself, her mother would inevitably volunteer to clean up, usually without even being asked.

"Ashley, Lacey, your dates are here," Laura Peterson called from outside Ashley's bedroom door.

"That sounds so funny," Ashley said, as she caught a final look at herself in the mirror and frowned.

"What?" Lacey asked, still a little lost in her revelry.

"Our dates. Ready?" Ashley asked as she reached to turn the doorknob.

"As much as I'll ever be," Lacey responded, running the back of her hand down the front of her dress.

Over the next twenty minutes, Laura Peterson took so many photos that Lacey thought she'd never let them leave for the dance. "Just one more" seemed to mean just ten thousand more.

"Oh, I wish I could get a picture in front of the fireplace," Ashley's mom complained as it became clear to nearly everyone why she couldn't quite get the shots she wanted.

"Well, you can. We can pose for more," Brian reassured her, looking around the living room to locate the all-important fireplace.

"Oh, shit," Ashley mumbled into Lacey's ear as her mother started to tear up.

"We can't. It..." Mrs. Peterson broke off and buried her face in a tissue.

"We can't. The fireplace is at our old house, the one that's being torn down," Ashley explained matter-of-factly, as if she were reciting times tables in third grade, as she walked over and hugged her mom.

"Uhhh, oh," Brian said, "I'm..." But he couldn't say anything more as Lacey made a zip-your-mouth sign behind the once eager photographer's back.

"Well, we need to go," Lacey said, practically pushing the boys toward the door.

"You guys head out. I'll be right there," Ashley said, making eye contact with Lacey.

Tyler didn't need to be told twice. He nearly bolted for the door. Lacey shoved Brian after him as he tried to end his first meeting with Ashley's mother with the usual polite niceties of "It was so nice to meet you" and "You have a lovely..."

As they walked down the few brick stairs of the garden apartments, Tyler glanced back toward the closed door.

"Do you think she'll be able to get out of there any time soon?" Tyler asked, loosening his tie just a little.

"Yeah, it shouldn't be too bad. Laura's getting a lot better," Lacey said. "She only asked Ashley to stay home from school and keep her company once this month."

As they approached Tyler's dad's gray SUV, Brian didn't say a word, and Lacey reached for the back door handle.

"Dude, don't you think you should open that for her?" Tyler teased.

"Oh, yeah, right," Brian said, rushing to pull open the door and nearly knocking Lacey over in the process.

Lacey's cheeks burned with embarrassment, and she wished Tyler hadn't said anything. Now both boys were staring at her as she awkwardly grabbed the door for support and practically did a high kick just to propel her short legs into what she considered a ridiculously tall SUV.

Lacey momentarily wished she hadn't discarded her pantyhose as her dress fluttered up nearly revealing her orange thong. But Brian didn't notice. His thoughts lingered on the mostly silent drama that had unfolded in the Petersons' apartment as he closed Lacey's door, then opened it again because he'd closed part of her dress in it, then, finally, closed it.

Just as Tyler and Brian settled themselves in the driver's side seats, Ashley came running down the steps, slipping once in the unfamiliar heels she wore. Tyler didn't get out again. He reached across the passenger seat and opened the door for Ashley, who climbed in.

"Sorry about that," Ashley said.

"Don't be sorry," Lacey said. "Is she all right?"

"Yeah, she'll be fine. The worst part was she kept apologizing to me, saying that she was trying really hard to make this a great day for me. She said she wanted to make it the first day when she didn't mention the storm."

"Wow, that's a tough one," Tyler said.

"I know," Ashley said. "I don't think that's going to happen for any of us for a least a few more months."

"Huh, hmm." Lacey made exaggerated sounds as if she were clearing her throat. "I don't talk about...about....that weekend in October."

"I know. But that's a problem, too" Ashley said, looking at her friend pointedly. "Anyway, I told her at least she'd have something to talk about at her support group this week."

"So who's ready for the Yule Ball?" Tyler said, turning up some tunes on his dad's stereo and picking up unnecessary speed.

"The what?" Brian asked.

"Nerd," Lacey said, laughing.

"Ignore him," Ashley said, at the same time. "It's a Harry Potter reference. He's full of them."

###

As soon as Tyler pulled into the school parking lot, Lacey and Ashley understood why Brittney and Connor had chosen to come on their own. Parked in front of the gymnasium door was a silver stretch limo, and Britt and Connor were getting out as if they were Kate Middleton and her prince. Britt even sported what looked like a diamond tiara and Jimmy Choo boots.

"She looks amazing," Lacey said.

"Well, yeah, but I mean it's only Winter Formal," Ashley said. "If she's coming to formal in a limo, what is she going to do for prom, rent Cinderella's carriage?"

Noticing Lacey didn't seem to agree, Ashley softened her tone. "Besides, she would have looked amazing anyway. She's a friggin' goddess."

"I know," Lacey said as she watched the chauffeur open the door for the high school royalty. "But so what? It's fun for her."

"Sure, it's great that her dad's failing business is now raking in literally millions, but it's all at our expense. Y'know? It kind of hurts."

"What?" Lacey stared at her friend incredulously. "You don't really mean that, do you? I mean it's not Dependable's fault that just about everyone in town needs a construction company right now."

Ashley shrugged and bit her lip.

"I know. It's just that my mom's still crying every day, and Brittney gets to run around in limos, all for the same reason. It's just not fair, y'know?"

"Ah, the wheel of fortune," Lacey said with a sigh.

"What? You mean that show with Vanna White?"

Lacey stared at her then said, "Just a Pollyism."

"Huh? Oh...Hey, Britt, cool ride!" Ashley said. "And you look amazing."

Brittney smiled, but leaned in between Ashley and Lacey and whispered. "Thanks, but I should have gotten something with a longer sleeve. Sleeveless tops make my ape arms stick out."

Lacey laughed. "How many times do we have to tell you that your arms are fine. They're not too..."

"Did you and Connor put the privacy window up on the way here?" Ashley teased, uninterested in stroking Brittney's ego.

Honestly, Lacey thought, Brittney and Connor looked like they stepped off the cover of a fashion magazine. If Connor didn't have braces, they would look absolutely perfect. Yet, Brittney never seemed to realize that.

As their circle widened, Lacey realized that Brian and Tyler had been standing off to the side waiting for them to finish their conversation since they'd arrived in the Autos R Us Arena at their school, which for just one night was masquerading as a castle-themed banquet hall.

"I hope you guys aren't mad," Brittney said as they headed inside. "My dad surprised me with the limo, said he borrowed it from a customer. I asked if you guys could come, but he said that would be taking advantage."

"No big deal. We get it," Lacey said.

"Limos always remind me of my dad's funeral anyway," Ashley said.

"Oh, this one wouldn't. It's got a large-screen TV, a DVD player, an amazing stereo, video games and a sun roof," Britt babbled.

"That's nothing. I've heard some limos have hot tubs," Brian said.

"Yeah, I was in Atlantic City one time, and I actually saw a stretch Harley Davidson limo. It was insane," Tyler said. "The only thing cooler would be a Thestral!"

"What?" Connor asked.

"Nerd," Ashley said.

"Oh, got it. I once saw a limo that was made to look like a tank," Connor chimed in.

"But you like this one. Don't you?" Brittney asked her date with a bit of a pout.

"Ah, yeah, I was just saying…" Connor didn't get to finish his sentence as the "Cha-Cha Slide" began to play, and the six classmates reported immediately to the dancefloor. The line dance mirrored Lacey's disposition not just that evening but for the last few months. She knew when to laugh, clap, hop, stomp, etc., but she was just performing the steps by rote. She wasn't really moving to the music. Meanwhile, the voice inside her head kept demanding an explanation for how everyone else around her could be having a good time in this storm-ravaged, ruined town.

Chapter Six:
Monday, Feb. 18, 2013

"MacGyver, you must have eaten a dozen ribs already. I can't believe you're still hungry," his mom said, sweat dripping from her face as she turned back to the charcoal grill in their backyard to take a stab at picking up a piece of meat before it was incinerated. Her lack of dexterity with the barbecue tongs reminded MacGyver of the time he and Lacey took Lacey's little brother to the Japanese restaurant. Everyone tried using chopsticks, of course, until Jake somehow managed to stab the hibachi chef with his.

"Why don't you use the spatula?" MacGyver groaned as he grabbed his plate and the jar of Saucy Susan.

"I don't know. Your dad says these are easier."

"Yeah, that's obvious. Exactly how many ribs did Darth Vader get already? I thought we were trying to save money, not cater for the dog."

"Stop being such a grump all the time," Dina Anderson said, scolding him in a tone that until a few months ago he thought was filed away under "the way Mom used to talk at me when I was a child."

Firmly and defiantly planting both elbows on the table, MacGyver lifted a sweet-and-sour-sauce-soaked rib to his face, only to have his mother swat at the offending joints with an oven mitt and demand, "Did you check on your father yet?"

"I will when I'm done."

"But then the food will be cold. Go see if he needs anything else."

"Give me a break, will you? I don't want to get all cleaned up just to come back to this, and besides, don't you care if *my* food gets cold?"

"You can take care of yourself. Don't you know how hard it is for your father, being stuck in that bed all day?"

"Sounds good to me," MacGyver grumbled and threw his food on his plate, but it bounced off and was caught mid-air by a ball of black fluff that quickly retreated to the other end of the yard.

"Darth Vader, you are the most annoying animal on the planet!" MacGyver yelled.

Stopping at the hose to rinse off his sticky hands, MacGyver headed in to see what his father might need, muttering to himself, "It'd be nice if someone cared about what I need."

"I wish I brought gloves," Lacey complained as she shoved her hands deeper into her pockets.

"I told you I'd buy you a pair before we left the mall," Brittney reminded her.

"I know. I know. It's just the restaurant is right at the end of the parking lot. Who knew you could get this cold, walking a few hundred feet?"

"Lacey, it's only fifteen degrees with the wind chill factor; it's not exactly a day for sunbathing."

"MacGyver could sunbathe. It's ninety-five in Landlock."

"Oh, were you texting him?" Brittney asked as she adjusted a gorgeous royal blue scarf that looked more like a fashion statement than a tool against the bitter cold.

Walking with Brittney wasn't always the best thing for Lacey's self-esteem. Britt was 5'10 and strutted with the confidence of a runway model, while Lacey practically had to run to keep up.

And why was it, Lacey thought, that when Brittney wore layers, it looked like a designer ensemble while Lacey merely looked like an overstuffed pig.

"Lacey, I asked you a question," Brittney said. "Where are you?"

"Sorry, what?"

"I asked if you've been texting MacGyver," Britt repeated, annoyed.

"Nah, not in a while. I just noticed the temperature on the Weather Channel this morning. Apparently a lot of people go to Florida for Presidents' Day weekend."

"Ah, huh... Lacey, you really should get a pair of Uggs. My feet are so warm. Between that and this Michael Kors scarf, I barely feel the cold."

Lacey turned her head and rolled her eyes. Fortunately, it was only a few more feet to the restaurant door. Had she realized the walk would be this cold, she would have insisted they get something at the food court, even if it was kind of crowded. At least, Brittney could call her mom and change the pick-up spot, so they wouldn't have to walk back.

Once they shucked all their layers of sweaters, hats and scarves, Lacey and Brittney settled comfortably into their booth. Lacey pulled her feet underneath her just to get warm and blew on her hands.

"We have to look at the menus," Brittney insisted, handing one over.

"Like you don't know what you want?"

"No, it's not that. They watch us. If we don't at least look at the menus, they think we're not ready to order yet and won't come over."

"All right." Lacey flipped open the menu, slammed it shut and placed it on the edge of the table. "Am I giving the proper signals now?"

"Sure, if you're trying to signal that you're a butt cake."

Lacey sighed and tried to change the subject. "What are you getting?"

"A cheeseburger with a slice of raw union, no tomato or lettuce, some French fries and…

"Brown gravy on the side," Lacey finished.

"Well, yeah," Brittney said with a laugh. "What about you?"

"I'm just getting fries and water."

"Oh, come on, you have to be hungry. Besides food will warm you up. Get a burger," Brittney said, placing a Visa card on the table. "My treat."

"Nah, you don't always have to pay for me."

"I'm not. Dad's credit card has this covered, get whatever you want."

"Britt, you know, a credit card isn't magic. Your father still has to pay the bill when it comes in."

"He doesn't care. The business is so busy. He never even notices what I spend anymore. Sometimes, I think about booking a cruise or buying a car, just to see if he's paying any attention at all."

A petite woman who looked too old to be anyone's sister but not quite old enough to be a mom approached the table. Sporting short brown braids and bangs, she wore a man's red-and-white striped tie, covered in kitschy buttons, fastened around her forehead.

"Get a load of this one. She thinks she looks like a teenager," Brittney whispered as the server neared.

"As if," Lacey responded and rolled her eyes.

"Hi, ladies. Today's drink specials are Hei... I mean strawberry smoothies and root beer floats. What can I get you?"

"I'll just have ice wa--"

"She'll have a Diet Coke and so will I."

"Is Diet Pepsi okay?"

"Is Monopoly money okay?" Brittney asked without a beat as the stunned waitress cracked a smile. Then, Britt added, "I don't know if you drink diet soda, but it's definitely not the same thing. Diet Pepsi tastes a lot more like regular Pepsi. It's too sweet, whereas Diet Coke is more refreshing and has a more palatable flavor."

The waitress who had been kneeling on one knee at the end of the table, pad at the ready, rocked back as she considered what to say next. "Mmm. I'm really sorry. We only have Pepsi products. Should I get you something else?"

"She's fine. Ignore her," Lacey said, reading the waitress' nametag. "Brielle. That's an unusual name. It's kinda like mine. I'm Lacey. I was named after the town. My parents lived in Barnegat and got caught in a snowstorm on the way to the hospital. I was delivered in the back seat of my dad's '88 Camaro at the Lacey rest area on the Parkway. Funny thing is you'd think they were unprepared 'cause I was a preemie or something, but I was actually two weeks late. Anyway, I was supposed to be named Autumn, but they decided Lacey made more sense. I love the story of people's names. My best friend...."

Brittney pretended to cough.

"My other – one of my other – best friends is named MacGyver after some TV character in the 1980s that his mother loved. The character apparently was amazing and could do stuff like stop bombs from exploding using a Snickers bar. The actor who played him has the same name as MacGyver's dad, which is honestly the only reason his mom agreed to meet him in the first place. Anyway, MacGyver's nothing like that..."

"Yeah, he has trouble unwrapping a Snickers bar."

Lacey frowned but turned her attention to the server. "True story. So what about you? Are you named after Brielle?"

"No. I don't know anyone named Brielle," the waitress said as she rose to her feet and started to play with the tail-end of the tie hanging at her shoulder.

"No, no. I mean the town Brielle. Were you named after the town? Y'know, like I was?"

"There's a town named Brielle?"

"Ah, yeah. It's about fifteen miles north of here," Brittney said incredulously.

"Huh. I didn't know that. I grew up in Rhode Island. My mom just picked it out of a book. She had no ideas and thought everyone should have a middle name."

"Oh," Lacey said, clearly thoroughly disappointed. "Wait a minute. Middle name? Why do you use your middle name? What's your first name?"

"God, Lacey, you are so nosy."

"She doesn't mind. Do you, Brielle, or whatever your name is?" She flashed a wide smile that revealed her dimples.

"No, it's okay. Actually, it's probably the kind of thing *you* would like. I usually use my first name, but people would get so angry and nasty with me that I just decided to put something else on my nametag."

"What? Why would people get mad because of your name? Is it FU or something?"

"It's Sandy."

"Uh."

"Oh," Lacey said, pushing the tip of her left thumbnail into the flesh of her left ring finger, a new habit she'd started doing absent-mindedly whenever anyone mentioned Hurricane Sandy.

"For the first few months after the storm, I just kind of took it, you know? People would come in and blame me for destroying their homes or for being out of work, and I would just say, 'I'm sorry' and laugh it off. But after a few months, I found I was coming home depressed and kind of miserable. Then, my brother suggested I change my nametag, and you'd be amazed what a difference it makes. The only problem is sometimes I forget to answer when someone is yelling Brielle across the room."

Lacey frowned, but said nothing, all the while, pushing her nail in harder till she broke the skin, and a little blood dripped out.

But, Brittney had a more appropriate response. "Serves them right. No one should be yelling across a restaurant."

"You have a point. I'll get your drinks and be right back."

Chapter Seven:
About 4:30 p.m. Friday, Feb. 22, 2013

"I don't know if I want to go. Brian is in Lexie's court," Lacey said somberly, picking a piece of pepperoni off her pizza and popping it into her mouth.

"So? What does that have to do with anything?" Ashley asked as Brittney stared across the table at Lacey, frowning.

"It's just that we don't really talk since…"

"Since you broke his heart," Brittney finished, leaning back on the orange metal chair she sat in at Vesuvius where the girls spent nearly every Friday afternoon.

"Yeah, right. I was going to say since Winter Formal," Lacey continued.

"Right. Since you broke his heart," Brittney insisted, tugging the sleeves of her green angora sweater down so that they covered her bracelets.

"Don't be stupid. He didn't even like me that much," Lacey said, frowning.

"Sure," Ashley said, wiping her mouth with a paper napkin. She covered her pizza crusts with the dirty napkin, then pushed her plate across the table into the empty space next to Brittney.

"Ashley, tell her," Lacey said. "You know he never even tried to kiss me or even hold my hand that night and basically hasn't talked to me since."

"Uh, true. But that's not exactly the whole story, Lacey," Ashley said. "I mean you did kind of ignore him all night. Y'know?"

"Did not."

"Lacey, you refused to dance and spent the night in the bathroom."

"Not true. I did all the line dances and can't help it if I got sick," she said while absent-mindedly twirling a wisp of her honey brown hair around her left index finger.

"Whatever. I still can't see why that would keep you from going to Lexie's Sweet 16. It's going to be amazing. They're having it at The Mansion, followed by a pool party and a sleepover for the girls at the Holiday Inn. Oh and her aunt who's chaperoning the overnight is only twenty-two," Brittney said.

"Yeah, my mom's not too happy about that, but she said I can go," Ashley said. "Besides this was supposed to be the year of the Sweet 16s, with parties every weekend, and we haven't been to one since last summer. Y'know?"

"It sucks that so many people had to cancel theirs," Lacey agreed. "I mean poor Chelsea spent all that money on that beautiful sequined dress she's never going to wear."

"Well, that's better than that girl in Point Pleasant who was buried in hers after getting that staph infection cleaning out her grandmother's flooded house," Brittney said as if relating the details of a boring tennis match.

"Yeah, that was so sad," Ashley said.

Lacey didn't comment, but she flashed Brittney a look of disappointment that said, "You know the rule: I don't talk about the storm." She couldn't understand why the hurricane still made its way into nearly every conversation.

Brittney gave a defiant shrug of her shoulders and continued. "Then it's agreed. As Polly would say, 'Life is short,'" Brittney insisted. "We're going to this party. Besides everybody's going to be there. We can't be the only ones who miss it, right?"

"I guess," Lacey relented.

"Good. Now that we know what we're doing three weeks from now, let's figure out what we're going to do tonight!"

"I don't know. Let's just have a sleepover and hang out at your house. How's that?" Ashley said, looking at Brittney for approval.

"Sure, but aren't you guys getting tired of that?" Brittney said. "It's like that's all we ever do."

"I know, but we're still living in just our upstairs bedrooms," Lacey said.

"And I'd have you over to my house, but the apartment is so small," Ashley said. "Wait a minute. That's it."

"What's it?" Lacey asked, wondering if she had zoned out on some important part of the conversation since Ashley looked so happy.

"My house."

"Right. You said it's too small," Lacey said.

"No, no. My house," Ashley said staring at her friends, her blue eyes gleaming. "Don't you get it?"

"Uh, no," Brittney said, annoyed that they were no closer to making plans for the night.

"We can have a party… at my house!"

"You just said it's too small even for the three of us to hang out."

"No, I didn't," Ashley said. "I said the apartment is too small. But my house."

"Is about to be torn down," Brittney said, pushing back her chair and brushing her hair.

"Exactly. About to be. It hasn't been yet. My mom is having all kinds of trouble getting permits or the mortgage company's approval or something. We can go there."

"How would we get in?"

"Uh, I have a key."

"Oh, right."

"I don't think your mother will let us," Lacey pointed out.

"I don't think my mother will ever know," Ashley said, lightly elbowing her in the ribs.

"Okay, I'm in. I think…" Lacey said before being cut off by Britt.

"I'm already texting Connor."

"This is great," Ashley said, excitedly. "I didn't think I'd ever be there again."

"When was the last time you were in the house?" Brittney asked.

"Christmas time. We had to get my grandmother's star for the top of the tree and some other things. I couldn't believe my mother, Miss Sentimental, was actually going to put up a tree with just the stuff that West Virginia church group brought us. Can you imagine?"

"Yeah, she would have been bawling all day Christmas," Brittney agreed.

"Well, she kind of was half the day anyway."

"But at least she was crying in front of a tree decorated with the macaroni wheel ornament we made in preschool and the ceramic igloo we made in second grade," Lacey said with a laugh.

"Exactly," Ashley agreed as she got up and cleared away their dirty plates.

While Lacey texted her mom, Brittney went into party-planning mode. "We'll have to go to my house first and get some flashlights and blankets."

"Won't your brother say something?"

"Nah. I'll bet Jared and Priscilla will be holed up in his room, and he won't even know we're there."

"My mother never lets me have guys in my room, even now, when there isn't anywhere else. When Brian came over that time before formal, we had to sit out in the hallway outside my bedroom watching videos on my laptop," Lacey said.

"We're not allowed to, either. But who's going to stop him?' Brittney said as she put on her winter jacket. "Jared says he's helping Priscilla pick a college, but I doubt that's why they need the door locked."

"What's so hard about choosing a college?" Lacey asked. "You apply to three, and you go to the one that's going to be the cheapest."

"Apparently, Priscilla applied to something like 20 schools and got in to all of them, except Princeton."

"Why would she apply to so many schools? That must have cost a fortune," Lacey said.

"Nope. All free," Brittney said.

"You must have that wrong. It can cost as much as ninety dollars just to apply to one school," Ashley said.

"Not if you can play the Sandy card. All application fees were waived," Brittney said. "But I do feel a little bad for her. When she wanted to visit schools last November, her parents told her just to apply to wherever, and they would visit this spring. Now, they've told her to stay on the East Coast and visit on her own. They're too busy with Sandy stuff to go on any tours."

"That does kinda suck," Lacey said, wishing she could think of a way to change the subject.

"Yeah, I heard her on the phone with her mom one day, yelling something like 'In a year, you'll be done with all this Sandy shit, but I'll be at whatever college I had to pick without any help for another three years!'"

"I totally get where she's coming from."

"Whatever," Brittney said, clearly bored. "Hey, I think my dad has an old boom box in the garage. We can take that, too."

"We'll need batteries," Ashley said. "I'm so psyched to go to my house for a change. No offense, Britt, but I am getting so tired of hanging out in your rec room. I was never that big a fan of air hockey or pool."

"Yeah, last time Polly saw your mom, she offered to pay child support," Lacey said to Brittney, laughing.

As the girls walked into Brittney's white two-story home, they slipped off their shoes and left them at the door, showing the respect the Martinez family always demanded. Then, they took off in three directions ransacking nearly every room of such things as Cheez Its, flashlights and sleeping bags and plopping their bounty into a pile on the living room floor. The only room that was spared their fury was the one where All Time Low was blaring behind what was probably a locked door. Brittney's brother and his girlfriend were definitely home.

Brittney took a minute away from marauding to call her mother's cell.

"Hey, Mom, just wanted to let you know that we're going to… What? Yeah, I will put some Fancy Feast out for Gato. Are you sure she's even still alive? I haven't seen her in…I didn't think you would….It doesn't mean anything. It doesn't matter. We just came from Vesuvius anyway….I had two slices. We're fine…Who are you with? … Do I even know them? …Okay …Okay….No problem. See you later."

"Did you say you were going to Ashley's?" Lacey asked.

"Hey, that's cute," Ashley piped in. "That isn't even a lie."

"I would have, but she never asked. They're on their way to AC with some 'old friends.' People I've never even heard of that they supposedly have known since kindergarten. How is that even possible?"

"I didn't know they liked to gamble," Lacey said.

"They don't. They're going to see Paul Anka."

"Who?" asked Ashley.

"I don't know. I think he's a magician or something."

"No, I'm pretty sure it's the dog on Gilmore Girls," Lacey said.

"I don't think they're going to see a dog," Brittney said, confused.

"I always thought your parents were homebodies," Lacey said.

"Yeah, when we were in Silver Bay Elementary and Intermediate East, I don't think they ever went out," Ashley said.

"They didn't," Britt agreed. "But I've been told it's because they didn't have the money for the nicer things in life. Oh, and get this, what money they did have had to be spent on 'you kids.' Like we asked to be born."

Brittney was slipping into her my-parents-don't-care-about-me funk, so Lacey brought the conversation back to their plans. "Well, did you tell her you were sleeping out?"

"Apparently they don't care enough to ask. So I guess we're good. I'll leave a note. Lacey get the batteries out of the junk drawer."

The girls stuffed their party-to-go into three Hefty Cinch Saks and headed toward the door. As they passed Jared's room, Brittney knocked.

"I'm going," Brittney called.

"So?"

"So, nothing. Just thought I'd tell you."

No answer.

"Don't do anything we wouldn't do," Ashley purred.

"And if you do, use protection!" Lacey added after seeing how dejected Brittney looked that her brother was ignoring her. "I never really liked Priscilla," she mumbled as her friends laughed.

"You don't still like him do you?" Britt asked Lacey.

"No. That was *so* two years ago."

Chapter Eight:
Thirty minutes later, Friday, Feb. 22, 2013

"Aren't you worried someone is going to see us?" Brittney asked Ashley as they turned onto the block of the Petersons' two-story home, lugging their Hefty bags over their shoulders.

"See me doing what?" Ashley asked. "Going into my own house?"

"Besides," Lacey said. "No one's living on her block yet. We Freshets are just about the only lucky people who get to live in post-apocalyptic Silverton, at least near the Beach Club."

After their quarter-mile walk down the oddly quiet and mostly vacant Silver Bay Road, the girls were anxious to unlock Ashley's door and relax before getting ready for their company, but as they swung the door open, the trio stepped back rather than inside as a noxious odor accosted them.

"What is that? It smells like a cabbage patch," Brittney said.

"It's nothing. Come on," Ashley said, but neither Lacey nor Brittney moved.

"No, really, it will be fine," Ashley insisted as she pushed her head back and took a deep breath of outside air before stepping over the threshold.

"Come on, let's at least check it out," Lacey said as her stomach turned just a little from the putrid, rotten-egg odor wafting from Ashley's once beautiful living room.

"We should just go back to my house. No worries," Brittney said. "We can still have people over since only Jared's home."

Brittney turned to head back down the front walk.

"No, wait," Ashley insisted, grabbing her friend by the arm and turning her around. "It's fine upstairs. We only have to walk through here."

Lacey shined a flashlight around the formerly cream-colored living room. The walls were covered in a haphazard variety of shades of gray, black, green and blue. "Wow, this looks like an experiment in mold proliferation."

"It's just the living room," Ashley said a little defensively. "We tore the Sheetrock out everywhere else downstairs before we knew we had to knock the house down. C'mon, let's set up in my mother's room."

"Great. I need to use the bathroom," Brittney announced rushing toward the stairs.

"Uh, no," both Lacey and Ashley responded immediately.

"What do you mean no? I have to go."

"Not here," Ashley said as she looked at Lacey with a knowing look that just confused Brittney.

"Ashley, I know your mother never wanted us using her private bathroom, but I don't think it matters right now."

"Yeah, that's brilliant, Britt. That's why we said no," Lacey said, shaking her head dismissively.

"It's not?"

"Brittney, the house has been prepared for demolition. The plumbing has been disconnected," Ashley finally explained as they climbed upstairs.

"So? Uh. Wait a minute. Then this is stupid. We can't have people over with no toilet, especially if they're drinking. Right?"

"Who said anything about drinking?" Ashley asked.

"Connor. He said he'd bring some beer."

"I don't know if that's a good idea," Lacey wondered aloud.

"I do. It's not, but neither is breaking and entering," Britt countered as they reached the top of the stairs.

"This isn't breaking and entering. It's my house," Ashley said, her voice rising with frustration.

"Right. The one without a bathroom. What are we going to do? I really have to go," Britt said, impatiently, as the girls entered Laura Peterson's mostly empty room.

"Can I just run to your house?" she asked Lacey.

"Sure. Then explain to my mother why you're there when we're all supposed to be at Ashley's."

Lacey and Ashley looked at each other and shook their heads.

"Brittney, follow me to the window," Ashley said, walking to her mother's bedroom window, which overlooked the street. "Okay. Now, what do you see?"

"A few empty houses, Lacey's house, some vacant lots where houses used to be. Shit, I didn't realize they tore so many down. Oh, and a couple of houses up 10 feet on cinder blocks."

"They're concrete blocks," Lacey said.

"What's the difference?"

"Concrete's a lot stronger," Lacey explained.

"And heavier," Ashley added, remembering the day she and Lacey helped their neighbor organize some leftover blocks on his property.

"Whatever. How does this help me? Come on. I have to go."

"What else do you see?"

"Nothing. A couple of seagulls and some squirrels? What?" Brittney said, as she started to wiggle a bit, doing the I-have-to-pee dance one usually expects of preschoolers.

"Mr. Bobs," Lacey said.

"And Johnny on the Spots," Ashley added.

"Huh."

"Portapotties. The neighborhood's crawling with them. Pick any one you want," Ashley said, handing her a box of tissues.

"And don't forget your hands," Lacey added, slipping her a small bottle of hand sanitizer.

As Brittney retreated out the door, Ashley turned to Lacey.

"She still doesn't get it," Ashley said.

"Why would she? Everything in her world is Juicy Couture bags and Jimmy Choo perfume. Who would have thought living just six blocks away would make such a difference?"

"Hey, I almost forgot to tell you. You're not going to believe this. My Aunt Sharon called the other day, and my mother got off the phone and was crying hysterically," Ashley confided.

"Well, that's not that unusual," Lacey responded a bit too quickly, wishing that for once she would have just listened.

"True, but get this. She called to let us know she and Uncle Jeff bought a summer house in Ortley Beach and, 'Isn't it wonderful that they got such a great deal at a foreclosure sale?'" Ashley said.

"Ew," Lacey said, accenting her disapproval by wrinkling up her nose and face.

"Yeah, she actually told my mom that they were 'lucky because of Sandy.' Can you *believe* that?" Ashley asked.

"Well," Lacey said, trying to channel some of her mother's positive attitude, but failing. "It is true. People from up north have no idea. To them, it was just two weeks without electricity. They don't think."

"Yeah, but come on. This is my mother's sister, and she called all excited, y'know?" Ashley said.

"Well, you will get to see them more," Lacey said, proud that she was able to find the bright spot.

"Yeah, but 'lucky because of Sandy.' That's as bad as that first week back at school, remember that?"

"Which part? The teachers telling us we had no excuse for not having homework done after a two-week *vacation?* Or the idiots complaining about how bad life was because they didn't have any power. Boo hoo," Lacey said.

"Yeah, Karney actually referred to the storm as 'the blackout.' Really lady? We lost our houses in that *blackout*," Ashley recalled, anger rising in her voice and flashing in her eyes.

"Oh and Nickens, with his Heroes of the Week. Ewww,' Lacey said.

Lacey mimicked her high school's morning announcements. "Good morning everyone. We want to tell you about today's Hero of the Week, Lindsay Montenegro, who helped two local families tear down their Sheetrock."

"Oh and the football team delivered hot chocolate to those poor people working on their flooded homes," Ashley added. "While the cheerleaders baked cookies. Oh that stuff makes me so mad. Did they really think we wanted to be called 'those poor people' all the time?"

"And where were our medals for sorting through everything we ever made or owned and drying it out or throwing it out?" Lacey added, realizing she'd been thinking this for months but had never voiced it.

"Or most likely, drying it out then throwing it out," Ashley said with a mirthless giggle.

"Yeah, I think we went through every card I ever made my mom and dad three or four times before Mom would let us throw them out," Lacey said.

"I know we had some things that were stuck together in a ball, and we couldn't tell what they were, but my mother wouldn't toss them until we had at least some idea what they might have been," Ashley said.

As they talked about things they never addressed before, the girls emptied their garbage bags and prepared the room for a party. As they worked, they connected in a way they hadn't been able to ever since the storm. And Lacey didn't even think to complain that they were talking about Sandy.

"We still have eight blue containers marked 'Sandy miscellaneous,'" Lacey said. "Our kids will probably still be going through those containers."

"No, Grandma said we can't throw them out," Ashley said, laughing.

"But, Mom, Sandy was fifty years ago," Lacey replied in a mock plea.

The girls found themselves lost in laughter and enjoying their surprising openness. They hadn't realized it, but somehow the storm had closed each of them off, even from each other.

Chapter Nine:
Immediately following, Friday, Feb. 22, 2013

"Ughh, I think I got hepatitis from that outhouse," Brittney said, stomping in and tossing the hand sanitizer back to Lacey.

"It's not an outhouse, and you can't get hepatitis unless you used a needle in there," Ashley countered.

"Whose did you use anyway?" Lacey asked.

"Whose needle? I didn't use any needles," Brittney said, shifting her gaze between Ashley and Lacey in confusion.

"No, whose toilet?" Ashley asked.

"Nobody's toilet. Toilets flush," Brittney said. She looked at the empty spot where she had dumped her garbage bag filled with loot, but regained composure when she spotted her purse and walked across the room to grab it.

"I used the one in front of the twins' house," Brittney said as she found her brush and began stroking her waist-length hair.

"I figured if someone complained, I could at least tell them I was looking for Donovan or Michael," she explained as she bent over, hung her head upside down and continued brushing.

"You should have used the one outside the Beach Club. Someone keeps it stocked with baby wipes and Lysol," Lacey said as she and Ashley finished placing the remainder of their supplies in their "appropriate" places.

"Yeah, and it's got a mirror," Ashley added as she balled up the three black garbage bags and shoved them in a drawer in her mother's now-useless master bathroom.

"Uh, great. I'll remember that next time." After returning her brush to her pocketbook, Brittney crossed to where Ashley was standing, doing a last-minute inspection of the room. "Ash, are you sure you want to stay here tonight? I mean, we can have people over my house. My parents won't be home till 2 o'clock at the earliest."

"We're good," Ashley said. "Besides, everyone can stay the whole night here. We haven't been able to do that since Connor's parents went to Hawaii last summer."

"That was awesome. I can't believe that video is still online, and no one's parents have seen it," Lacey said.

"Excuse me, but if you remember, my parents not only saw it, they gave me the third degree on how exactly we got up on the roof," Brittney said, whining a little.

"Yeah, but Britt, they only wanted to know, so they could try planking with their friends," Ashley countered.

"Don't remind me," Brittney said, lowering her face into her hands in pseudo shame. "They're so embarrassing. Forty- and fifty-year-olds pretty much playing dead up on their roof. Do you remember my mother? My mother…"

And clearly Ashley and Lacey both remembered, as the three of them doubled over laughing, thinking back on the day.

"My mother…." Brittney couldn't get the words out as she convulsed with laughter. "Had to be rescued by the fire department after she planked on the roof and then suddenly remembered that she's afraid of heights."

"How could we forget? They sent three firetrucks, and pretty much every volunteer in Silverton responded to the call," Lacey said.

"I know. It was like we were having a freakin' block party while my mother insisted any movement, and she would crash to the ground," Brittney said.

"Remember that kid Bryce from across the street started selling his Cub Scout popcorn to everybody who was standing around. His mother wanted to kill him," Ashley recalled.

"I thought he showed true entrepreneurial initiative," Lacey said.

"Oh, listen to her," Brittney mocked. "True entrepreneurial initiative!' You sound like Mr. Rittenhouse."

"I should. I'm called into his office pretty much every other day," Lacey said.

"Still failing chemistry?" Ashley asked, as a soft, almost motherly, tone creeped into her voice.

"And geometry."

"Crap," Britt said.

"Oh, but if I change for the rest of the marking period, I might scrape by with a D in gym. Whoopee!" Lacey said, surprisingly showing no signs of stress.

"How are you even allowed out?" Ashley asked.

"Pft. Mom has been very understanding. She has sent several e-mails explaining how difficult things have been being practically homeless and how busy she is with so many foreclosures on her plate."

"Your mother is playing the Sandy card?" Brittney said astonished.

"Sure, Britt. Think about it," Lacey scoffed.

Brittney just stared at her. She'd known Mrs. Freshet since preschool, and she wasn't one to make excuses for anything Lacey did. But Ashley caught on quickly.

"Lacey, you didn't?" Ashley asked with a look of both astonishment and admiration.

"What?" Britt asked.

"Lacey, are you kidding me? You'll never see sunlight again. When your mother finds out that you hacked her e-mail," Ashley said, starting to sound like the prosecuting attorney she hoped to be one day.

"I did not," Lacey said.

"You didn't? Then, how did you do it?" Ashley asked.

"Easy. I created a new e-mail account and then changed the emergency contact cards in the office."

"Are you kidding me?" Britt asked, as she brushed on a new coat of blue nail polish.

"No. Remember they kept bugging all of us that it was important to keep those cards up to date even…

"If your situations are only temporary," Lacey and Ashley finished together.

"What did you do about her phone?" Brittney asked, confused.

"Piece of cake. Sandy took out the house phone…And you know how you guys are always complaining that I have to record an outgoing message and get rid of that weird automated voice on my voicemail. Well, now you know why I never did…Polly answers every phone call or letter with an e-mail, using lots of big lawyerly words like litigation and pro bono," a contented Lacey proudly explained.

"Geez, Lace. This isn't going to end well," Ashley said.

"Who cares? Right now the school just thinks Pollyanna Freshet is just one of the hundreds of parents who stopped paying attention to their kids when the tide got high," Lacey said, brushing off her friend's concerns.

"Yeah. Who has time to talk about grades or Formal dresses when there's FEMA and the insurance to deal with?" Ashley said, thinking about her own situation.

"Not to mention the SBA," Lacey said.

"And RREM," Ashley added.

As the girls ran through a laundry list of alphabet-soup government agencies and programs, Lacey couldn't help thinking how ridiculous it was that kids at school were constantly talking about these things instead of bands and Netflix.

Brittney interrupted her revelry. "I get it. I get it. Still, Lacey, your mom will eventually find out, and it won't be pretty," she said.

"I'll worry about that when it happens. Right now we have a party to plan," Lacey said. "Ashley, are these night stands and this folding chair the only things you have for people to sit on?"

"Nah, drag the futon mattresses out of my room and the guest room. Mom thought they were getting kind of old, so she decided to leave them. Also, there's a bunch of old stuffed animals that will work. Remember my four-foot unicorn, and Pegasus?"

"You're getting rid of them?" Brittney asked, surprised.

"No room in the apartment, and I can' really complain too much. All of my mom's keepsakes were downstairs or in the garage, so she's not too sympathetic about stuffed animals I never touch anymore," Ashley said complacently.

As Brittney stepped out of the room, Ashley looked at Lacey. "Don't worry. Whatever happens with your mom, we'll get you through it."

"The thing is, I'm not worried. I just don't care. Not about anything," Lacey casually confided her biggest secret.

"Ashley, Ashley, come here!" Brittney called from down the hall. "Holy crap! Holy crap! Come here. Quick!"

As Lacey and Ashley darted down the hall, Lacey tripped but caught herself before she fell.

"We should have used the flashlights," Ashley said as she helped Lacey recover, and they both entered Ashley's childhood bedroom.

"Look," Brittney said, shining her cellphone light along the top of the walls, which were all dripping wet.

"That's all right, Britt. It's just condensation. Lacey and I already dried up my mother's room while you were going to the bathroom. It just happens 'cause the building's been sitting empty," Ashley explained.

"Are you sure? Maybe there's a broken pipe." Brittney barely looked at her friends as they spoke. Her eyes were fixed on the very wet ceiling, which had clearly rattled her.

"Britt, why would there be a pipe in the second-floor ceiling? Where would it be going?" Lacey asked. "Don't worry. It's fine. We'll drag over that futon and Uni and Pegsy, but we better hurry. People are going to be here soon."

Chapter Ten:
Later that night, Friday, Feb. 22, 2013

"Hey, nobody told me this was a Halloween party," Brian said, as the wavy-haired blond arrived and took a four-pack of Mike's Hard Lemonade out of his backpack.

"Halloween party?" Brittney asked, putting on a sweater over her Taylor Swift tee-shirt. "It's not a Halloween party."

"Oh, yeah. Then why is the whole neighborhood decorated for Halloween? I mean my dad's upset 'cause it's been too cold to take down the Christmas decorations. He needs to take a drive around Silverton. Then he'll chill out."

"Oh, don't be an asshole," Connor said, glancing over at Brittney with a is-this-guy-for-real look. "Do you think people are going to stand around taking down their scarecrows and skeletons when they're busy ripping out their Sheetrock?"

Lacey heard the anger in Connor's voice. Part of her wanted to protect Brian from the Silverton Crew's distaste for Toms River teens who don't understand what they're going through. But she had a stronger inclination to pile on instead, so that's what she did.

"Oh better yet. They're going to run over here with their keepsake boxes to rescue their family's treasured Halloween heirlooms just before they raze their house," she quipped.

Brian swiped at an errant strand of hair that had shifted out of place beneath the royal blue Mets cap he wore. He tried to move the conversation in another direction. "Hey, I've been watching them raise this one house in East Dover. Right now, it's up on pallets about fifteen feet in the air. It's really cool."

"I said raze, with a Z, not raise," Lacey said, feeling a little ashamed of herself for being so snide. She realized Brian had never been anything but nice to her, but she just couldn't help herself.

61

"Huh?" Brian said.

"Raze," Brittney jumped in. "She means tear down, not lift."

"Oh. Uh. Oh. Sorry, sorry," Brian said. "Does anyone want one of these?" He passed around the lemonades he'd swiped from his father's man cave. In his rush to get onto a new topic, he gave away all four drinks without keeping one for himself.

As he fumbled with the empty cardboard carrier, Brian tried again. "I didn't mean to insult anyone."

"Of course you didn't," Ashley said from her seat on a worn futon mattress, folded over, against the wall. "And Karney meant nothing by it Friday when she told the class she was tired of hearing people using Sandy as an excuse for late assignments. She said this to Tiff, when Tiff told her she didn't have access to a computer while she's living in her grandfather's basement."

"That's not exactly what happened," Brittney said. "Karney got pissed off when Tiff said she couldn't finish her homework because she's 'living in captivity.'"

"Yeah, well, that's what she calls it, and she's right. Her natural life is basically on hold," Lacey said.

"But she doesn't have to be so melodramatic," Brittney said.

"You don't understand," Ashley snapped.

"All right, all right," Connor said. He scooted his muscular butt off the night stand he was sitting on. As she watched him, Lacey wondered if you had to work out as hard as football players to get in that kind of shape.

Squatting down to remove the lid from a bright blue cooler with his last name, "Russo," scrawled across it in black Sharpie, Connor took command of the room. "Let's stop fighting and let's start drinking," he said, taking two Budweiser cans from the cooler and passing one to Brian.

"A toast!" Tyler shouted as he pushed the aluminum tab in, releasing the familiar and refreshing popping sound of a freshly opened can.

"To Sandy!" Connor shouted.

Seated next to Ashley on the futon mattress, Lacey raised her Mike's Hard and then hearing the tribute to Sandy lowered it again.

"Excuse me?" she asked pointedly. "Why would we drink to…to what you said?"

"Because before Sandy, my parents would definitely notice if I took two six-packs of beer and a cooler and left the house," Connor said, laughing as he and Brian clicked cans and white foam lightly drizzled down their arms.

"Now, my parents are so distracted that I can get away with almost anything," Connor said in a self-congratulatory tone as he downed a large gulp of his beer.

"I can drink to that," Ashley said, standing up dramatically. "Without Sandy we wouldn't have our own place to party, either," she said, pulling Lacey to her feet.

Reluctantly, Lacey stood and looked around her circle of friends eager to party. Defeated, she raised her bottle.

"To Sandy," she said, with a small sigh. Then, she clicked her beverage against Ashley's, then Britt's.

When the toast was over, Lacey grabbed Ashley's arm and pulled her blonde friend into the upstairs hall.

"You didn't tell me you were inviting Brian," Lacey said in an irritated whisper.

"I didn't," Ashley said, but Lacey just stared at her. "I swear. Tyler must have told him."

"This is flippin' great," Lacey moaned. "What am I supposed to do, especially now that the twins and Tiff and Lexie aren't coming?"

"Don't worry about it. Don't even think about him being here," Ashley said.

"Great. That's going to be easy with just the six of us. You four are going to hook up and leave us staring at each other."

"You don't know that," Ashley said.

Lacey twisted the left-side of her mouth in a gesture that said, "Yeah, right."

"Lacey, look, the way I see it. You've got a lot bigger problems than Brian Simons. Come on, let's just have a good time," Ashley said, her blue eyes begging Lacey to relax.

"Sure," Lacey said. "YOLO. Whatever."

By the time the girls returned to Ashley's mother's bedroom, all the tension in the room had dissipated. Soon everyone was buzzed and acting pretty silly.

"Let's play Truth or Dare," Tyler suggested.

"Nah, way too early," Brittney said.

"Too early?" Ashley repeated, checking her phone. "It's already ten thirty."

"Really?" Lacey said. "I thought it was earlier. Anyway, I'm in."

"Me, too," said Connor, and the group assembled in a circle like they were getting ready for a preschool game of "Duck, Duck, Goose," which four of them had actually played together many times back in the day.

"Who's going first?" Tyler asked.

Silence. Everyone cautiously looked around for a volunteer, trying not to make eye contact that could lead to an unwanted first-round draft.

"Lacey," Brittney said, crossing her arms. "You have to go first."

"Why me?"

"Your mom picked you up right before your turn last time."

"Oh, that's right," Tyler said.

"That game was already over," Lacey protested. "Everybody quit after you refused to eat that spider."

"I chose Truth," Tyler said.

"You did not."

"Did too."

"Did not."

"Did..."

"Lacey," Connor interrupted. "Truth or dare?"

"Fine," Lacey said. "Dare."

"Dare?" Are you sure?" Connor asked, displaying a wicked smile that somehow seemed even more charming with his wire braces threaded with blue rubber bands showing. Lacey might have found the look from the wide-shouldered football player intimidating if they hadn't known each other since they were in diapers.

"Bring it on," Lacey said, pushing back her shoulders and pointing her index fingers at one another like she were waiting for a wrestling match to begin.

One side of his mouth curled up in a mischievous smile. "Lacey, I dare you to run down the street topless."

"Are you serious?"

"That's illegal," Ashley said.

"No it's not," Connor said.

"I think it is," Ashley said.

"Well, I'm not 100 percent sure about Toms River, but I know it's not in New York," Connor said

"Really?" Brian asked.

"Look it up," Connor said.

"Check this out," Tyler said, showing Brian and Connor the gotopless.org website on his phone. As the boys scrolled through photos of topless women and made crude remarks, Lacey whispered in Brittney's ear. "Keep them distracted." She grabbed Ashley by the arm and the two headed down the stairs.

As they stepped out into the night air, Lacey quickly pulled off her sweater and tank top and handed them to her friend as she unclasped and yanked off her bra.

"Crap, it's cold out here," she said.

"I can tell," Ashley said with a smirk.

"Cute," Lacey said. "I'm going to run down to the corner. You take a video, um, from behind."

Then, she took off, moving more quickly than she had ever run in her life.

As Lacey reached the corner and pivoted around, she braced herself, half expecting all five of her friends to be staring down the block at her. Instead, she smiled when she saw just Ashley with her fists in the air, Rocky style, rushing to return her clothes.

Lacey was still panting as she and Ashley stepped into the party room and heard Brittney directing the boys' attention to another website.

"These women were protesting Sharia law during the Olympics last summer," Brittney said as Lacey sat down and pulled both a sleeping bag and a blanket around herself.

"Did you have any trouble distracting them?" Ashley asked, taking out her cellphone.

"Nah, it's true. Boobs are power," Brittney said, smirking as she high-fived Lacey.

"Hey, where were you two?" Tyler asked, barely pulling his eyes away from the revealing photos on his cellphone.

"Taking a little run," Lacey said.

"What?" Brian asked.

"Did it!" Lacey yelled triumphantly.

"Did what?" Connor asked.

"Ran down the block topless. Ashley's my witness."

"Yup, she did," Ashley said.

"Prove it."

"Right here," Ashley said showing a video of a topless Lacey running away from the camera.

"No fair," Connor said, running his hand through his thick black hair, as he watched the video and contemplated the defeat of his dare.

"Why?" Lacey said.

"We were supposed to watch you," Connor admitted, frowning.

"Nobody said that," Lacey said.

"But, we can't even see anything," Tyler complained, handing Ashley back her phone.

"Perv," Lacey said.

"You've got balls," Connor said.

"I think the point is. I don't," Lacey countered, and everyone laughed. "My turn...Tyler. Truth or dare?"

"Truth," he said.

"You remember in sixth grade. Did you really kiss Amber McGee?"

"Mmm."

"Tell the truth," Brittney prompted.

"No," Tyler admitted.

"I knew it," Ashley said.

"But if I had a Time Traveler, I'd change that now," he said.

"Would you?" Ashley said, making eye contact.

As Tyler looked away, Lacey said, "I knew he was lying! Ashley, you owe me a dollar."

"Wait a minute. You can't use this game to settle side bets."

"Who said?"

"It's just not right," Tyler said.

"That question was lame," Brittney complained. "I've got one."

"It's my turn," Tyler said.

"Go ahead," Brittney said.

"Ashley, what was the worst moment of your life so far?" Tyler asked.

"Dark," Brian said.

"Really?" Ashley asked.

"Really," Tyler said.

"You guys are going to think this is incredibly lame," she said, sucking in the cold air before she continued. "I guess it had to be when my mother realized someone stole our TV."

"Someone stealing your TV. That's it?" Brittney asked.

"Well, you see, after Sandy my mother was freaked out and worried because we didn't own our house. It was my grandparents' summer house, and they didn't have any insurance, and FEMA wouldn't cover it because it was a second home. But for Christmas, she decided to splurge and get us just one great present, a 60-inch flat screen TV for the apartment. It practically covered the whole wall. But then on New Year's Eve when we were at my aunt's house, someone broke in and stole it.

As Ashley paused, Lacey absentmindedly dug her left thumbnail into her left ring finger.

"That's all they took 'cause we didn't really have anything else, just some second-hand furniture and air mattresses. When we came in and found it gone, she just screamed and cried. She was wailing that there was no God. Now, some of this might have been 'cause she'd been drinking a little. But it broke my heart seeing her like that, and I'll never forget the sound."

"Wow, that's awful, Ash. I didn't know," Lacey said, reaching over to grab Ashley's hand.

"Yeah, I mean I knew about the TV, but I didn't know it was like that," Britt said.

"Hey, c'mon people, this is supposed to be a party," Tyler said. "Brittney, I dare you to kiss Brian."

"Is that all you got?" Brittney said. She scooched over in front of Brian and planted a kiss on his mouth that lasted about thirty seconds.

"Now, this is a party," Brian joked.

"Yeah, but that's not how the game is played. You never gave me a chance to choose," Brittney said.

Everyone stared at her.

"Choose whether I wanted a Truth or a Dare," she said.

"Oh, I thought maybe you wanted to choose a different guy, like maybe me," Connor said, joking, but it was clear he was half serious.

"In your dreams," she countered, then winked. They'd been dating for about a year, but no one considered it particularly serious.

"What about me?" Tyler said, and Brittney kissed the top of his head.

"How 'bout me?" Ashley suggested, earning a Brian-like, full-on kiss that drew applause from the guys and a disgusted "Pervs!" from Lacey.

As the friends slipped from buzzed into drunk, the game turned more and more into a kissing game, but nobody minded. Brian and Lacey deftly avoided each other, eventually retreating into their phones while Ashley and Tyler and Brittney and Connor cuddled up against one another.

Chapter Eleven:
Monday, Feb. 25, 2013

Hey

There. She sent it. Now it was up to him, Lacey thought as she lay on her air mattress waiting for the sleep that lately never seemed to come. If MacGyver didn't respond, then that's it. She'd move on.

I have plenty of other friends. I don't need to be crushing on someone eight states away, she thought.

After Lacey sent the text, she switched her phone to vibrate only and threw it down. Then, she headed to the bathroom for what her Uncle Paul called a "constitutional."

As she sat there taking care of business, Lacey quickly slipped from her euphoria over having taken command of her life to feeling like an idiot first for sending the text and then for locking herself away from her only contact with the outside world. What if she took twenty minutes in here and MacGyver thought she was ignoring him?

Lacey considered rushing back to her phone, but Mother Nature dictated otherwise, and her demands seemed to take an eternity. Yet, three minutes later, Lacey was back in her room, staring at a picture of Mr. Rodriquez's white standard poodle "Tiny" doing it with a stray at the Beach Club.

Damn, Lacey thought, she really needed to stop letting Connor use her phone. He always changed the background when she wasn't looking. And what the hell was it with all these strays lately? What kind of person just lets their dog loose instead of finding it a home or at least bringing it to a shelter?

As she reset the picture to the one of Ashley, Brittney and her in Britt's hot tub, Lacey blinked to hold back tears. MacGyver hadn't answered.

While she was swiping at her face with the back of her hand, Lacey jumped a little when her phone shuddered, causing her to drop the device somewhere into the heap of clothes on the floor.

Tossing aside two thongs that weren't dirty but didn't seem to fit right when she had put them on that morning, Lacey uncovered the elusive device beneath a purple pushup bra and a green sweatshirt she would never wear that read, "Restore the Shore."

Hey!

Hey with an exclamation point. Awesome! He not only answered but was happy to hear from her. Right? That punctuation can't mean anything else, can it?

Now what.

"I" she typed, then deleted it. She followed with "Just checking in" and erased that, too.

When she finished typing, *What's up?* she hit send immediately, so she couldn't talk herself out of it.

Nothing. The response came without hesitation.

Wow, she thought, *I must be the only one he's texting right now.* Okay, now what?

She giggled, and her thumbs typed. *You know, we never really texted when you lived here.*

The response came quickly this time. *I know. I liked coming to your door.* While Lacey was still staring at her phone, MacGyver added, *That way I got to see you.*

She knew exactly what to say, *I just thought you came by when you were bored.*

MacGyver's answer came immediately. They were off to a text conversation without any awkward pauses.

M: *Then, I was bored A LOT. LOL*

L: *Well, yeah. It made sense. You never can stand still.*

M: *Me. You're the one who always has to be doing something.*

L: *Better than you, always having to be doing someone.*

M: *What????*

L: *I'm kidding. Lol*

M: *Lacey*

L: *Yeah*

M: *I don't know*

L: *Yes, you do. What?*

M: *Lacey*

L: *You already said that*

M: *I miss you.*

L: *I miss you, too.*

M : ... (MacGyver actually typed the three periods, filling in the awkward pause in their conversation with an ellipse, which was the habit among their friends.)

L: *Lol*

M: *It's more than that*

L: *More than missing me?*

M: *Yeah*

L: *What?*

M: *I shouldn't say.*

L: *Why not?*

M: *I never have before*

L: *Never have what?*

M: *....*

L: *.... ?*

M: *Told you I love you.*

L: *Yes, you have. Lots of times.*

M: *No, I mean, yes. I mean*

L: *...*

M: *You are going to make me say it.*

L: *I'm going to make you text it.*

M: *Lol*

L: *…. What?*

M: *Lacey, I'm in love with you.*

L: *…*

M: *…*

L: *…*

M: *Are you there?*

L: *MacGyver*

M: *Yeah*

L: *I love you.*

M: *Yeah… Yeah, I know that.*

L: *No, I mean…*

M: *What?*

L: *I'm in love with you, too.*

M: *U R?*

L: *Yeah, but that doesn't mean you should start texting like an idiot.*

M: *Huh? Oh, sorry. Why didn't you say so sooner?*

L: *Why didn't you?*

M: *It seemed stupid.*

L: *Loving me is stupid?*

M: *No. telling you.*

L: *Telling me is stupid?*

M: *Yes. I mean no. Lol. I just figured you knew.*

L: *What am I supposed to be, psychic?*

M: *Well everyone else knew.*

L: *What do you mean everyone? Like who?*

M: *Everyone. Ashley. Brittney. Your mom.*

L: *How would they know?*

M: *I told them.*

73

L: *You told my mom?*

M: *Yeah, why not?*

L: *You told my mom, but you didn't tell me.*

M: *I thought you'd laugh.*

L: *What? Why would I laugh?*

M: *Well, you know. We haven't dated since middle school.*

L: *You haven't asked since seventh grade.*

M: *When you laughed...*

L: *No, I....uh...sorry.*

M: *Lol I can picture you right now with your head tilted a little to the left, the way you do when you are remembering something.*

L: *Lol. And you should wipe the hair away from in front of your right eye.*

M: *What? This isn't Skype. You don't know that my hair is in my eyes.*

L: *I do now.*

M: *What?*

L: *You just said 'that my hair is in my eyes.' Got you.*

M: *You do.*

L: *Do what?*

M: *Got me. I can't think of anything but you 24/7. It's crazy and I'm miserable.*

L: *You're lying. I'll bet you have a girlfriend and you're just playing me.*

M: *Lacey, I would never do that.*

L: *I know...But you do have friends, don't you?*

M: *Not really.*

L: *None at all?*

M: *A few, kind of, just at school. None like you.*

L: *Of course not. There's no one like me. Lol.*

M: *You're right.*

L: *I miss you. It's not the same without you here.*

M: *At least, you still have everyone else.*

L: *Not really. No one else lives here anymore. Lots of people, even people who are supposed to live here, just avoid Silverton.*

M: *Why?*

L: *It's depressing. There's still piles of garbage and Dumpsters in front of half the houses. And the banging.*

M: *What banging?*

L: *Constant banging. Everything is under construction. There's never a moment's peace, just lots of big trucks, power saws, nail guns and workers shouting at one another in a dozen languages, just not English.*

M: *Did you say constant banging?*

L: *Yeah, why?*

M: *Now, that's something I'd like to get in on.*

L: *What?*

M: *Constant banging...*

L: *Lol. MacGyver, you are such a guy.*

M: *That's what you like about me, right?*

L: *...*

M: *Right?*

L: *I'm not answering that.*

M: *You already did.*

L: *Yeah, I guess I did.*

M: *Ha!*

L: *Ha yourself!*

M: *Lacey?*

L: *Yeah?*

M: *What are we going to do?*

L: *I don't know. This sucks.*

M: *I know.*

L: *Could you do me a favor though?*

M: *What?*

L: *Try and make a friend, a real friend. I can't stand to think of you all alone.*

M: *I thought you wanted me all to yourself.*

L: *I do. But till we figure out a way to bring you home, I want you to try and be happy.*

M: *OK, I'll look for some girl to flirt with.*

L: *OK*

M: *OK?*

L: *Yeah, OK. Whatever will make you smile.*

M: *Um. OK*

L: *MacGyver*

M: *Yeah*

L: *I'm serious. I hate thinking of you sad and alone. Just don't forget about me. OK?*

M: *Couldn't if I tried... And I tried.*

L: *You tried?*

M: *Yeah.*

L: *Why?*

M: *You never texted or called. I figured you moved on.*

L: *YOU NEVER TEXTED OR CALLED!*

M: *Are you shouting at me?*

L: *No. Yes. You should text first.*

M: *Why?*

L: *Why? Because*

M: *Because why?*

L: *Just because*

M: *Oh, now I understand.*

L: *Good.*

M: *Hey, Lacey?*

L: *Yeah?*

M: *Let's text or call each other whenever we want from now on.*

L: *Can't*

M: *Why not?*

L: *Because*

M: *Because why?*

L: *It would be all day every day.*

M: *For me too.*

L: *Really?*

M: *Yeah. Hey, Lacey?*

L: *Yeah*

M: *I love you, but I have to go take care of my dad.*

L: *OK, love you, too! Talk to you soon?*

M: *Oh, yeah!*

L: *Lol*

Lacey quickly saved the conversation and reread it. And reread it. And reread it until she fell asleep.

Chapter Twelve:
Tuesday, Feb. 26, 2013

The next morning, Lacey was late for the bus simply because she couldn't take her eyes off her text screen. As much as it thrilled her to see the words, "I love you," she couldn't really get her mind off the rest of the conversation. For as long as she could remember, no matter what was going on, MacGyver was always smiling. Even when he was grounded, he would stare out his back window and make stupid faces at her until she was doubled over in the grass, laughing.

If she was going to be honest with herself, she'd spent the last four months picturing him hanging out with bikini-clad Florida bombshells draped over his outstretched arms. As much as the picture irritated her – all right, downright pissed her off – it also comforted her knowing at least one of them was living a happy, normal life.

In Lacey's mind, MacGyver had been spared the brunt of the storm when his parents decided to run away. That's how she and her friends always referred to the Andersons' moving just two days after Sandy hit, "running away."

To them, it was as if the Anderson family took off like bandits in the middle of the night. Who moves while their home is still full of bay water, without even trying to go through any of their downstairs belongings?

Lacey had sat on the very top of the Andersons now-useless Toyota pickup and watched as MacGyver and his dad sloshed through the water, packing their upstairs possessions into a U-Haul. She had heard Richard Anderson yell, "Leave it. Just leave it," when MacGyver suggested they sort through the first floor to find what was salvageable.

Knowing everything MacGyver owned was downstairs, Lacey kicked the back of her heel against the red Toyota as hard as she could but jumped a little when she heard the loud bang that exploded upon impact. The sound was much louder than she expected, but that's not what startled her. The quiet creaking of a spider web of destruction creeping across the windshield did.

"I'm sorry. I'm sorry, Mr. Anderson," she said as she scrambled off the vehicle and ran to MacGyver's side.

"For what?" Richard Anderson said as he and MacGyver shoved a queen size box spring into the U-Haul and slammed the tailgate closed.

"Your truck," Lacey said, pointing to the damage. "I'll pay for it."

"Oh, don't worry about it. The salvage company is coming for the truck and the PT Cruiser tomorrow. Don't think we'll get any less because of that nick."

"Nick? I destroyed the windshield."

"Not really, Lacey. A tree fell on it during the storm, and it had a small crack. You just made it a little worse," he said.

"Yeah, Lace, you didn't think you were that strong, did you?" MacGyver teased.

Later that night, Polly tried to explain that the Andersons' house was already "underwater" before the storm hit, but Ashley and Lacey had a very difficult time understanding this.

"Don't be stupid, Polly," Lacey had argued with her mother. "No one's house was underwater before the storm, not even the Beach Club, and that's the closest building to the bay."

"Lacey, first, I don't appreciate it when you call me by my first name."

"Mmmm. Hmm. I know," Lacey said, as she grabbed another brownie from the tray on the card table set up in their new "multipurpose" room, which used to be the guest room.

"Second, the term underwater refers to how much money someone owes on their mortgage. If they owe more than the house is worth, that's called being underwater."

"Polly, I don't need to know all your lawyer mumbo jumbo. All I know is no one was underwater."

"Lacey, let's say you own a car and you owe $5,000, but if you sold the car, you could only get $2,000. That's what they call being underwater," her mother said patiently.

"I get it," Ashley said, actually excited to understand the concept.

"Whatever," Lacey said, rolling her eyes.

"Honey, a lot of people in our neighborhood have been underwater since the real estate market crash a few years ago. That's why they abandoned their houses. They didn't have any equity," Polly said. "It's almost like they really didn't own them; they had nothing to fight for."

"Okay, whatever," Lacey said.

"Lacey, you have to accept that things change. MacGyver might have moved even without San-"

"Don't say it," Lacey said, pulling Ashley's arm and leaving the room.

Thinking back on that conversation and the words Polly used always upset Lacey. Didn't Polly understand that MacGyver was supposed to fight for *her*? She would never say that aloud because she recognized that it sounded pretty insane. MacGyver was just a sixteen-year-old kid, but inside, that's how she felt.

Still, for the last few months a part of her had been really happy that MacGyver had been spared living in people's basements, sleeping on couches, distracted parents and insensitive teachers. In Florida, he never had to face the relentless questions from dozens of organizations that first asked if you needed help but then pushed you to volunteer.

He was, as far as Lacey was concerned, the one who got to have the good life, the one teenagers were supposed to have – with friends and parties and maybe even some weed and sex, like in the movies.

Since the day MacGyver's U-Haul had headed up Silver Bay Road, part of Lacey had been living vicariously through the life MacGyver was supposed to be having in fabulous Florida, home of Disney World and the Wizarding World of Harry Potter. How could anyone be unhappy there?

MacGyver's melancholy was a huge disappointment for Lacey, who up until then was angry that he got through the storm unscathed. Was it only Brittney and Ashley's Aunt Sharon, then, who benefited from the rising surf?

Lacey didn't have time to think about all this as she trudged her way through Silverton, hoping to catch up with another High School North-bound bus, so she wouldn't have to ask her mother for a ride. Hitching a ride on a different high school bus would have been impossible last year, but this year everything was different. Four months after the storm, most of the normally packed Silverton buses had only a handful of riders, and all of the bus drivers were super considerate and concerned, having driven daily through what looked like Afghanistan or Iraq. It was so easy to play the Sandy card with them.

As Lacey waved her hands in front of the bus Ryan Sonders from down the street normally took, an unfamiliar driver pulled over for her.

"Could you please give me a ride to North? I missed my bus. My mother's already gone to work. And all of the neighbors I could usually ask for help aren't living here right now. Please?" Lacey pleaded, pretending to shiver a little against the cold for effect.

"Sure, honey. No problem," the female driver ushered her onboard.

"Thanks," Lacey said as she clambered up the stairs and searched the bus for a familiar face. But, there were none. Ryan's family was living at his grandmother's in Philadelphia, and most of his neighbors were still out, too. The bus, which normally would be so full that every seat, even the short ones, would have to be shared, offered Lacey endless accommodations. Better yet, this overwhelming privacy meant Lacey could reread, analyze and memorize her texts from MacGyver.

"Honey, I think this is your stop," the bus driver said with a laugh as she looked back at Lacey. Lost in her phone, Lacey didn't notice when the bus arrived outside High School North and unloaded its passengers.

Looking around the deserted bus, Lacey blushed, flipped her phone closed and slipped it into her pocket.

"I'm so sorry. I..." she said, grabbing her backpack and rushing toward the door.

"Are you okay?" the driver asked, suddenly morphing from an anonymous stranger into a surrogate-mother-type with soft blue eyes and a caring smile – everything Lacey didn't want!

"Fine," Lacey snapped and instantly felt embarrassed. "Sorry."

As she rushed off the bus, she walked straight into Vice Principal Rittenhouse.

"Miss Freshet, what a pleasure running into you," Rittenhouse said with a sarcastic, but not malevolent, grin. "It's so nice to see you somewhere other than my office."

"I agree," Lacey said, regaining her footing both physically and in the conversation. "I've been thinking if I'm going to spend so much time there we should really talk about redecorating the place. You know I took interior design last year."

"Actually, I did know that. It was back when you deigned to attend your classes."

"Hey, that's not fair. You know I go to all -- well, most of -- my classes."

"You're right. I'm sorry," the vice principal agreed. "Your problem is that you generally don't do any of the assignments." An electronic tone filled the air, and Lacey knew it would be her best chance to escape.

"Got to go," she yelled, rushing toward E wing.

Chapter Thirteen:
Thursday, Feb. 28, 2013

Ashley, get over here quick. Lacey's thumbs flew over her phone's keypad.

A: *Something wrong?*

L: *No.*

A: *Then what?*

L: *Just come.*

It had been fifteen minutes since their text exchange, and Ashley still wasn't there. Lacey realized she didn't quite live around the corner anymore, but come on. She was taking way too long, and Lacey didn't want to wait any longer to explore the thirty-five-foot-long mobile home that she'd come home to find starting at her garage and sticking out two feet past the end of her driveway.

Lying on her back on the trampoline in her front yard, Lacey considered sending a picture to MacGyver, but dismissed the idea.

"I'd look pretty lame bundled up in scarf and gloves when he's probably just wearing shorts and a tee-shirt," she thought.

Thinking about MacGyver, Lacey mentally thanked him for the sixteen-foot diameter trampoline she was impatiently waiting on.

Over the years, Lacey begged her parents for a trampoline like MacGyver's. But, her mother, always the practical lawyer, insisted trampolines are "nothing more than a lawsuit waiting to happen."

MacGyver, of course, knew all this, but it didn't stop him from having their friends roll his around the corner just before he left for Florida. When Polly asked him about it, he said, "I guess the wind blew it over here during the storm."

There was no way she could say no that day when the entire Silverton Crew was all on the verge of tears.

What is taking Ashley so long? Lacey thought as she reached for her phone. But before she could even open it, Ashley turned the corner on the purple bike she bought last month off Craigslist.

Huffing and struggling to catch her breath as she pushed down the kickstand, Ashley demanded, "What's so important?!"

Lacey leaped from the trampoline, and, of course, tripped and fell on her face. But she wasn't hurt, and she and Ashley dissolved into laughter, pausing twice in their hysterics, before they could both fully gain coherency at the same time.

As Lacey wiped the dirt from her face and her hands, Ashley ran past her, nearly knocking her down again.

"You got a mobile home? Where are you going? You're not moving are you? Please tell me you're not moving?"

"No, we're not moving. It's FEMA's idea of appropriate living space."

"What?"

"We're not allowed to live upstairs anymore. Proper living conditions require a kitchen, and apparently one with an Easy Bake oven is good enough," Lacey said, motioning toward the trailer home like a spokesmodel on *The Price Is Right*.

"What?"

"Come on. I'll show you. Polly said we get to keep this until the house is done."

"Sweet. You should take a trip, like to the Grand Canyon."

"That's what I said, too. Only I was thinking Florida."

"Of course you were."

Lacey frowned at her friend but chose to ignore the comment. "Anyway, we only get two hundred miles total, or it's like a gazillion dollars a mile. We only have enough mileage to get propane when we need it and to bring it back down to some RV place near Atlantic City when we're done."

"So you're moving in here? All three of you?"

"Well, that's what we're *supposed* to do," Lacey said in a sing-song voice. "But Mom said we don't have to as long as we don't tell too many people. We're still living in the house. We're going to use this for cooking and somewhere to do homework since the builders don't go home until around four-thirty. But, she said we can actually have sleepovers out here."

"Are you kidding? That's awesome," Ashley said as she made her way through the Winnebago into the master bedroom at the rear. "Damn, this is bigger than my room."

"Well, not your real room."

"True. Who should we call first?"

"Text every GES and tell them we're having a party," Lacey said as she led the way back through each tiny room, up a ladder near the driver's seat and into the queen-size loft.

As both girls flopped down, cellphones at the ready, Ashley asked, "Every guest? What guests? You have people staying with you…now?"

"No, not guest. GES," Lacey answered.

"What?"

"Don't you know that's what everyone is calling us GES? G-E-S?" Lacey said, spelling out the letters and expressing astonishment that her friend hadn't heard the euphemism.

"What are you talking about?" Ashley asked.

"Oh, yeah, I heard Hannah in gym the other day talking about how the GES are turning this year into a real downer. Nickens won't allow them to plan a class trip because too many of the GES can't afford it."

"Why are they calling us that?"

"Are you kidding? Ashley, come on, think!"

"I have no idea," Ashley said earnestly, turning on her side to face Lacey.

"Oh, come on. Seriously?"

"Seriously. What?"

"Our mailboxes."

"What about our mailboxes?"

"They're all painted with G-E-S."

"That's not true. Both the Allens and the Kanes had it spray-painted on their front picture windows."

"Exactly. Pretty much everyone who flooded has that scrawled prominently on their houses. And so now, we're the GES people."

"Geez, really? That's just stupid."

"Sweetheart, we're in high school. Everything is stupid," Lacey said.

"Lacey, what's it even mean?" Ashley asked.

"It means our classmates are butt cakes and blaming us for ruining their fun," Lacey said, stretching her legs up in the air to touch the RV's roof.

"No, not that. G-E-S? I never really thought about it."

"Oh. Gas and electric service shut off," Lacey explained.

"Oh, that's right. I remember when the rescue workers came by two days after Sandy. We thought they were bringing supplies. Y'know, water, towels, bleach. Instead, they came into the house, disconnected and took our power boxes and left. My mother was so pissed."

"I know. Polly lost it. She was screaming and threatening a lawsuit, and she doesn't do that."

"No," Ashley confirmed. "But this was different. All the neighbors were complaining about how they had to make appointments with the electric and gas companies. It took weeks even for those people who didn't have any damage."

"I forgot about that. Everybody was yelling and cursing about that the night of the big barbecue," Lacey remembered.

"Oh God. That was so much fun. The whole neighborhood and a potluck barbecue and bonfire in the middle of the intersection. We should do that ag..." Ashley let her words drift off without finishing her sentence.

"Okay, the next time we have armed National Guards blocking access to our neighborhood, we could probably do that again," Lacey said with a smirk.

"Yeah, I know. I heard myself saying it," Ashley said. "Anyway, it's funny, a lot of these houses have power now, but I don't think anyone cleaned off the spray paint."

"Priorities."

"Now, you sound like your mother."

"No, if I was my mother I'd be telling you to look at the bright side. At least they didn't have to paint numbers on our houses with the amount of dead bodies found inside, like they did in New Orleans after Katrina," Lacey said, remembering a conversation she had recently had with her mother.

"God, that's creepy."

"Feeling lucky yet?" Lacey asked.

"Shut up."

Chapter Fourteen:
Saturday, March 16, 2013

"Surprise!" Lacey heard what sounded like hundreds of voices scream as she walked in her front door after spending the day at Ashley's, not writing the paper that's due on "Of Mice and Men."

Looking around at a house full of teenagers, Lacey had a hard time understanding what was happening. All her in-denial brain would supply was: "Holy shit! My mother didn't really do this, did she?"

But, of course, she quickly realized as mascara-laden tears streaked down her face, her mother had ignored her assurances that no party this year was fine with her.

That's why Ashley suddenly wanted to play dress-up, fixing our hair and makeup, right before we switched houses. I knew that was odd, Lacey chided herself. *I should have figured it out.*

"Oh, honey. I guess we really surprised you?" Polly said as she hugged her trembling daughter.

"Yeah. Definitely," Lacey said in a whisper, trying to pull herself together.

"Are you surprised?" Ashley asked.

"We got you. Didn't we?" Britt insisted as she pushed to the front of what looked like three or four dozen teenagers. Lost in a cacophony of screams of "Happy Birthday!" "Surprise!" and "Did you know?" Lacey didn't know what to say and who to answer first.

Of course, she didn't know! If she had been paying attention, she could have stopped this insane catastrophe. Pretty much every kid at school, church or the Y that she had ever exchanged a word with was here in her house. Her unfinished, under-construction, *undone* house. It was one thing to have her Silverton friends over from time to time, but many of these kids lived in North Dover and Downtown. Most of them had already forgotten there was a storm. They didn't want to come face to face with Sandy. What the hell were her mother and friends thinking?

As Lacey struggled to don her party face, she didn't even realize she was pushing her left thumbnail just below the first bend on her ring finger. Then, the room erupted into Macklemore's "Thrift Shop," and the crowd shifted away from her and onto the purple-lit dancefloor as some guys called out that they were "gonna pop some tags."

Wait a minute, Lacey thought. Since when did her living room feature a dancefloor? In fact, how were they even allowed to be in there? Only the workers had spent any time in the downstairs rooms since the day back in November when she, her mom and some church volunteers tore the Sheetrock down.

Taking the whole picture in, Lacey couldn't help but be impressed. Still mortified, but impressed. Her mother had turned her own first-floor master bedroom into a kind-of indoor patio complete with lawn chairs, a porch swing, bright green fake-grass carpet and beach towels. It made sense since the outdoor chairs and tables were the only furniture the Freshets still had.

The dancefloor was actually the freshly laid plywood subflooring, and the drab newly drywalled, but not yet painted, walls were dimly lit with twinkling Christmas lights. Great, Lacey thought, maybe the kids from school will think HardieBacker is some chic new designer, rather than a drywall manufacturer.

Truthfully, the total effect made the place look fun and unusual, not trashed as it had the day before. Lacey admired her mother's ingenuity and appreciated the love that went into creating all this; yet, she hated every bit of it.

She was sure this party would be the talk of the town and not in a good way. While most of Toms Rivers' sixteen-year-olds were dressing in long sequined gowns and being toasted at gorgeous banquets that rivaled weddings, Lacey was wearing jeans and a tank top and dancing in her unfinished home. Why hadn't her mother believed her that it was okay that they couldn't afford the Sweet Sixteen at the country club that she had always dreamed of? Her mother was always trying to make things better. How come she still didn't realize that some things can't be made better, only worse?

"What time does this go to?" Lacey asked her mother as she watched her friends jumping around under what seemed to be a laser light show in her living room.

"All night. The boys can stay till midnight, but some of the girls are sleeping over in the trailer," said her mom, flashing one of her I-know-how-to-make-you-happy smiles.

"Great," Lacey said, flatly and too quickly. The sarcasm was a slap in Polly's face. The smile that Lacey hadn't seen on her mother in months vanished.

"Oh, Lacey, you don't want this. Do you? You're upset. Shit!"

"Mom!"

"Oh, sorry." They both started laughing. Lacey had never heard her mother curse before, and she hadn't imagined that the first time she did, it would be funny. She hugged her mother tight, pulled back and looked at her and almost died laughing once again.

"Lacey, I'm so sorry. I ju…."

"Shhh. I'm being a jerk, Mom. This is great. Thanks. You're the best," Lacey hugged her mom tight and whispered. "I'm gonna go talk to my friends. Thank you."

As "Don't You Worry Child" screamed through the house, the floor seemed to be bouncing up and down with the rhythm of the music. Lacey tried to lose herself in dancing. She tried to be happy that all of these people wanted to be at her party, but she just couldn't be. So, she faked it. No problem. She was getting really good at that.

After every song, she smiled and scanned the crowd to take in the faces. There were so many people here, but honestly, all she saw was the one who was missing: MacGyver.

Chapter Fifteen:
Sunday, March 17, 2013

"Lacey, you can't sleep at the table," Polly admonished her daughter, who was slumped over a bowl of Honey Nut Cheerios in the tiny RV kitchen around three the next afternoon.

"Well, technically, this turns into another bed. The table pulls up and a piece fits in between to fill it out. Britt slept here last night."

"She did? Isn't she a little tall for that. It's meant for little kids. You probably should have slept here and given her one of the bigger beds," Polly said, looking at the space and shaking her head a little.

"It was fine," Lacey said, shoveling a spoonful of Cheerios into her mouth.

"It seemed like everyone had a good time last night. What time did you get to sleep?" Polly asked.

"I don't know. Maybe seven. It was really tough on Ashley. She had soccer this morning. She didn't sleep at all. Yeah, that's right, we all decided to go to sleep after Laura picked her up."

"I was looking at your presents this morning. Looks like there's a lot of shopping in your future, so many gift cards."

"Well, I guess most parents don't think they're rude."

"Lacey, I can't help it. That's what my mother taught me. She said money and gift certificates showed a lack of thought."

"Gift certificates?"

"That's what they were called when I was growing up. Remember: Everything wasn't in a computer then."

"Oh, yeah, back in the dark ages before the Internet." Lacey said, yawning.

"Don't be so smart. It really wasn't that long ago."

93

"Umm. Hmm." Lacey pushed her finished cereal bowl aside and plopped her face on the table atop a small stuffed animal she'd gotten as a gift the night before.

"Lacey, don't. You're going to wind up with milk in your hair, and that bear is going to be all sticky."

"It's a rabbit."

"What?"

"It's not a bear, Mom. It's a stuffed bunny."

"Oh." Polly put down the garbage bag she'd been filling with empty soda cans and water bottles and sat across from Lacey, pushing her daughter's head up off the table and rescuing the squished rabbit.

"That's really cute, so soft," she said, stroking the bunny's fur.

"Yes, Polly. But it's not real."

"Good thing, too. Remember the mess Shelley used to make? I would find hay everywhere."

"Too soon, Mom," Lacey snapped and dropped her head onto the table again. Her mother blushed and reached across and grabbed her daughter's hand.

"I know how much you loved her, honey. I'll never forgive myself for what happened. I never imagined the water would get that high. I'm really sorry."

"I don't want to talk about it," Lacey said, pulling away from her mother and dropping her head on the table again.

"Hey, about your presents, I can't figure one of them out," Polly said.

"Which one?" Lacey said, lifting her head off the table.

"The stepladder. Who gave you that?"

"Oh. Umm. Connor."

"Why?"

Lacey got up and stepped into the tiny aisle between the table and the sink to wash her cereal bowl. "Why do you have to know everything?"

"What? Lacey, I was just asking. It wasn't a secret or anything. You got the present in front of a roomful of your friends."

"Right. My friends. Not my mother," Lacey snapped as she dried the bowl and put it in the doll-size cabinets.

"Lacey, you're being ridiculous. I was just asking. It seems like an odd gift."

Lacey sighed and sat next to her mother, leaning her head against her to break the tension. Then, she took a breath and plunged ahead. "Okay, here's the thing. It's a joke."

"A joke?"

"Yeah."

"What kind of joke?"

"You know Josh?"

"Josh Hamilton?"

"Nooo. The other one."

"Josh Brown. The really tall kid?"

"That's the one."

"Okay."

"Connor thinks I like him."

"And?"

"Connor keeps teasing me that I would need a stepladder to kiss him....It's a joke. You get it?"

"It's not really that funny. And stepladders are kind of expensive..."

"Polly, do you have to analyze everything?" Lacey said as she got up and started very industriously cleaning.

"No. But do you?" Polly asked.

"Do I what?" Lacey asked, looking at her mother confused.

"Like Josh?"

"Nooo." They studied each other's face. "Oh, please Mom. Don't read anything more into this. I told you. It's just a joke."

"Okay." They quietly finished cleaning. When two garbage bags were tied up, Polly turned to her daughter. "All right, now you have to throw out the trailer trash… Did you get it?"

"Yeah, but it's not funny. None of this is funny."

"Lighten up, Lacey. It's just life."

"Whatever." Lacey sighed heavily, grabbed the bags and headed toward the door. "I'm going in to take a shower," she said and walked out. A second later she was back for just an instant. "Hey, Mom, maybe it was a little funny. Anyway, thank you. Thank you for everything."

Chapter Sixteen:
Wednesday, March 27, 2013

Dear Mrs. Freshet,

I wanted to alert you that Lacey is having difficulty in several classes and may have to attend summer school. If she does not dramatically improve her grades during the next three months, she may be compelled to repeat sophomore year.

I know that you have said it would be difficult to come in and meet with her teachers. However, I want to extend the invitation once again. Please remember the school offers peer tutoring after school, and her instructors are also willing to work with Lacey to help her catch up.

I hope you will contact me to discuss this further. If an in-person conference is too difficult, perhaps we can set up a phone conference.

Thank you for your attention to this matter.
Tanya Jones
Guidance

Lacey stared at the e-mail and then reread it. What struck her most is that she wasn't crying or scared. She felt... Nothing. She didn't feel anything. In freshman year, even a low B might have been enough to induce a few tears. Now, the prospect of failing basically everything left no impression.

Is it time to tell Mom? she thought. *Nah, nothing good could come from that. Besides, next week is Spring Break, and Grandma is taking Jake and me to Disney World. I'm not screwing that up.*

She closed her laptop, pushed her desk chair over to her window, took in the view and sighed. She knew she wasn't supposed to be in the house right now because the workers were still downstairs installing cabinets in the kitchen, but she didn't want to sit in the mobile home right now. She wanted to be in her own room with her own familiar view of the world.

For Lacey, the coming of spring was always marked by lots of kids her age, older and younger, filling the street with longboards and basketballs. In a neighborhood that centered on family life, children and teens were everywhere on spring days, hanging out playing basketball on portable hoops left right in the street. Middle-schoolers dazzled grade-schoolers with new skateboard tricks, and everyone headed to the Beach Club to goof around on the sand and enjoy the sun. Her mother always said that their section of Silverton was a throwback to the 1950s where every neighbor knew one another's names and habits, but Lacey didn't really know what she was talking about. This was all she'd ever known.

As she stared down the street toward the waterfront, Lacey smiled thinking about how every year at this time, some idiot would try to be cool and jump into the bay even though it was only sixty-five degrees out and forty in the water. That fool – and at least twice that she could remember it was MacGyver – would then come running down the block screaming about the cold.

Despite being at the same window she'd always looked out from, Lacey's view so far this year was inconceivably different. A dull residue of mud still tainted every street surface, like a curse that had befallen them. Kids were nowhere to be found. Instead of skateboards, there were white contractors' vans and pickup trucks everywhere, and screaming teenagers were replaced by foul-mouthed workers cursing as they rebuilt what to them were just structures, mere buildings, not homes and a neighborhood.

The other day, when her grandmother took Jake to see "Wreck-It Ralph" for the third time, and the temperature soared to an unseasonable seventy-five degrees, Lacey ignored her mother's rule that she stay in and do her homework. *Homework, pft!* Instead, she slipped into her favorite jean shorts and a red bikini top and headed four doors down to the Beach Club.

Just getting into the liberating summer clothes was so empowering, as if what had been weighing her down were the layers of sweaters and scarves, not her mood and circumstances.

Lacey had even allowed herself to hope some of her friends had the same thought and would meet her there. She did not text and invite them as that would have broken the spring-day spell.

Slipping on her orange flip-flops reminded her of last summer, a time before Sandy. *Was there really a time before Sandy? It seemed so hard to remember.* With her mind returning to thoughts of normal life and normal Silverton, Lacey started to look around for signs of the bunny team, a litter of rabbits she and her friends had hand-raised a year earlier after their mother was hit by a car.

Lacey and her friends had successfully raised and released five rabbits. But the sixth rabbit, Shelley, had become too attached to Lacey. After the group tried several times to set her free, everyone agreed she was a "House Bunny," a term they'd adopted from a silly movie that was one of Brittney's favorites.

It took precisely five steps before Lacey realized she wasn't in Kansas, or in this case, Silverton, anymore. Workers lifting the house across the street spotted her and began whistling and catcalling.

Having never been exposed to such misogynistic behavior before, Lacey froze. She stood there staring at the construction crew, practically unblinking, just listening and staring. It really was as if she had gone from Kansas to Oz, but only if Oz were a dark and vile place where she was nothing but an object to be leered at.

After what seemed hours, but was probably only a minute, an older man, maybe in his fifties, who had been staring at blueprints on the front seat of a pickup noticed what was happening. "Shut the fuck up!" he yelled, and the men went back to work.

But Lacey didn't move. She just stood statue-still and stared until finally the apparent boss, a guy with a beer belly and gray hair, took a step toward her, calling, "Sorry, miss." And then, "Miss, are you all right?"

Lacey tried to smile and didn't know for sure if the effort was successful. However, the man's voice was enough to remove the Krazy glue from her feet and propel her toward the beach.

At the Beach Club, Lacey first headed to her favorite swing, which was really stupid since she knew the play equipment had been toppled and twisted in the storm. Then, she slogged across the sand to the two-room, white clubhouse with its weathered wood siding and flat roof that was home to nearly every family and community party she had ever attended. Every Saturday and many Sundays from May to October, the Beach Club grounds crawled with children jumping in the water, parents and aunts and uncles drinking wine and beer from aluminum cans and plastic cups and grandparents talking about the good old days. Lacey and her friends attended nearly every one of those parties and knew most of the players, even if they came from faraway towns. They often joked that from the Boat Slips, which flanked the channel leading to the swimming beach, every party looked exactly the same. The only difference was which family was going to have to stay and clean up.

Slumping against the locked door and looking up at where the canvas awning should have been, Lacey cried and cried until she slipped down into the sand. No one else was there. *Warm temperatures and the other wonders of spring aren't going to change a thing,* she thought as a stray dog came by, rubbed against her and whined as if it was crying along.

The rhythmic sound of the gentle bay waves lapping the sand tugged at Lacey, urging her to come closer. Eventually she and the sandy-colored dog could resist no longer as if pulled by the tide to the shoreline. Soon they were splashing and playing in the surf. The dog found an old ball on the beach and relentlessly nuzzled Lacey till she would throw it.

Buoyed by the companionship, Lacey left the Beach Club grounds with the chain-link gate swinging in the wind and headed to her other favorite childhood spot, the Rock Throwing Place, just a block away. The dog followed for a few steps then turned back to the Beach Club and the ball.

Lacey quickly strode to the sanctuary of her favorite place and cautiously propped herself atop a piling at the bulkhead. She realized two surprising things: She had not been here since the day MacGyver moved and this place seemed to be the one spot in town that was, in fact, unchanged.

Lacey hated to describe the Rock Throwing Place to anyone who didn't live in Silverton. To local kids, the Rock Throwing Place was a magical, waterfront oasis that parents never invaded, a place for quiet conversations, secrets and confessions, maybe a little fishing and crabbing and, of course, rock throwing, a place that was completely their own. *To outsiders*, she supposed, *it was just a bayfront street end.*

Lacey picked up and sorted a handful of the plentiful stones, searching for the perfect flat one that could skip across the water as if it were Jesus. When she found it, she fingered it absentmindedly as she gazed out at the horizon and the county park about a mile across the water, taunting Lacey and her friends to come visit. But, while the park and nature preserve that had been the site of many class trips seemed just a stone's throw away and could be reached in about five minutes by boat, on land it was more than fifteen miles across town, too far away to even contemplate the bike ride.

Thoughts of biking led to memories of MacGyver, who was always particularly frustrated by the distance to the park. As children, he had tried repeatedly to swim to the park or paddle across on a raft, but all his efforts failed miserably. She pressed her lips to the rock and slipped it in her pocket. Looking out at the horizon, she let the tears flow freely, making no effort to wipe them away.

Chapter Seventeen:
Wednesday, March 27, 2013

MacGyver stared down at his Algebra test paper, a burning sense of rage and injustice bubbling up within him. This is fucking math, not English, his mind screamed so deafeningly loud that he worried the words would slip out of his mouth. He looked at the paper again in disbelief and anger, ten word problems, each presented as a dense paragraph filled with words stolen from the pages of his *Vocabulary for the College Bound* book. Shit! Getting a good grade in math shouldn't rely on his reading comprehension skills.

He scanned the page for what looked to be the easiest problem, No. 7. He'd try that first. "Divide $80 among three people so that the second will have twice as much as the first and the third will have $5 less than the second." He knew this would basically break down to a simple formula, one side of which would be "= 80," but he just couldn't concentrate. It was just about 1 p.m.; the bell would ring in around thirty-five minutes, and he could go home and get something to eat. His stomach was growling because he could never eat when he first got up at six a.m., and he went to the library at lunch because figuring out where and with whom he should sit in the cafeteria was just a nightmare.

He scanned the page again, and his eyes fell to another quandary about trains going in opposite directions. That's enough of this nonsense, he thought, and began to write after his name and above the first question. "If students in algebra courses could demonstrate a proficiency with mathematical skills without having to spend 45 minutes struggling with the dsylexia that makes the rest of the school day torture, how many teen lives would be spared?"

He reread his words, corrected the spelling of dyslexia and laughed. Then, he handed in the paper, upside down in the stack on the teacher's desk.

When he returned to his seat, MacGyver put his head down on the desk and prayed the sweet release of the electronic tone would come soon.

"Mac, Mac. Hey, the bell rang," the guy who sat behind him said as he kicked MacGyver's chair to wake him up.

"Who? What?" a disoriented MacGyver said, pushing himself back into a sitting position.

"Dude, the bell rang," said a short, skinny guy wearing thick black glasses in an ill-fitting blue flannel shirt.

"Oh," MacGyver said, stumbling out of the desk into the aisle between the rows of chairs. "Thanks."

"So how'd ya do, Mac?"

"Um, good," MacGyver lied.

"Really? I bombed. I hate word problems."

"Right!" MacGyver said. "I mean they're not fair. This is fuckin' math."

"I hear you. By the way, I'm Kevin. You're Mac, right?" the kid said, though he seemed pretty sure of himself.

"MacGyver."

"Yeah, I know, but I figure, they probably call you Mac for short. Right?"

"Not really. No one's ever called me that. But, I mean, you can if you want."

"Okay, Mac," Kevin said.

As they walked out of the classroom, Kevin complained again about the test.

"Yeah, my dad's not going to be happy when he sees this grade. Hopefully, she won't post the grades on parent portal until Monday. That way it won't ruin the weekend."

"My parents never look," MacGyver said.

"Lucky," Kevin said.

"Yeah," MacGyver said, thinking this idiot has no idea what he's talking about.

"Hey, my dad and I are going hunting this weekend if you want to come."

"Hunting for what?"

"Small game mostly, maybe a hog or a pheasant."

"Don't you guys have PETA here?"

"Peter who?"

"Not Peter, PETA," MacGyver corrected.

"You mean like the character in the Hunger Games?" "What? No. I mean the animal-rights people."

"Never heard of them," said Kevin. "But my dad says nobody can criticize us 'cause we eat what we kill."

"Gotcha."

"So what do you say, Mac? Want to come hunting with us this weekend?"

"Uh, maybe," MacGyver said. He had absolutely no interest in hunting, but this was the first semi-normal kid to talk to him since his first group of so-called friends all got sent to the alternative high school. Sure, they were all off in the last-chance school for kids who cut classes too often, but they left behind his new yearning for cigarettes.

"All right, then," said Kevin. "You come hunting with us Saturday and then join us for a dinner of maybe some venison or rabbit."

"Rabbit?" MacGyver asked startled. He could feel the blood draining from his face.

"Yeah, they're the easiest to catch around here."

"Umm. Okay," MacGyver said. "But I've got to tell you. I can't…I mean, I'm, a…I'm a vegetarian."

Chapter Eighteen:
Late afternoon, Wednesday, March 27, 2013

As she stared out her bedroom window toward the Beach Club, Lacey reached into the pocket of her denim shorts and balled her fingers around the crumpled e-mail from guidance. Pulling it out, she compulsively reread Jones' message as if her eyes scouring the page for the fiftieth time would be enough to erase the words. Finally, the offending paper struck a chord in her. It was not the anticipated sadness or even worry: It was paranoia.

Why the hell did you print it out? she scolded herself. *Now what are you going to do with it? What if Mom comes by right this minute and asks what you're looking at?*

That's stupid, she argued with herself in her head. *Yeah, but what if? Polly has been acting weird lately. Has she? Sure, she has, always asking if something's wrong and coming in your room.*

Lacey bolted down the stairs, through her under-construction living room and out of her house. She ran past the Beach Club for once not even noticing the missing swing set and took refuge standing on the bulkhead at the Rock Throwing Place. She stared at the horizon beyond the county park and out to the spot where Seaside Heights' amusement rides no longer stood, her fingers reflexively tightening and releasing around the crumpled e-mail.

"What's up?"

Startled by Ashley's sudden appearance, Lacey nearly lost her footing on the bulkhead. "Geez, Ash, way to sneak up on a per..."

"Lacey!" Tyler yelled, slipping out from behind the Snobs' bayfront house.

Lacey had barely recovered from Ashley's sudden appearance from nowhere. Having a second person magically apparate on the scene totally shifted her balance, and she lost her footing. Fortunately, she was able to twist her weight landward. Unfortunately, both her phone and the balled paper she was holding flew into the bay, landing with a splash.

"Fuck!" she yelled, as her phone sank into the murky water.

"What's the big deal? It's just a little litter," Tyler said as he and Ashley came within reach.

"Litter? That was my phone!" Lacey whined, staring at the water as if some hidden porpoise or mermaid would pop out and return the device.

"Oh. Shit," he said. "I thought it was that paper you were staring at."

"It is...it was," Lacey practically whispered. "It's..."

Tyler was reaching out into the bay with his foot trying to kick the ball of paper that was bobbing along the surface. Ashley threw her arm over Lacey's shoulder. "I'm sorry," she said.

"Don't do that," Lacey said firmly.

"What? Hug you?" Ashley said, letting go and backing up a half step.

"No, not that," she said. "Tyler, let it go. It was...nothing."

"Are you sure?" he said, still waving his leg just a half inch above the water.

"Yeah."

"Okay," he said, straightening up.

"What are you going to do?" Ashley asked.

"I don't know... I don't know... maybe hide it from her," Lacey said with a shrug.

"Yeah, right? As if you could hide anything from Polly. You tell her everything," Ashley said knowingly, her blonde, curly hair bouncing around her shoulders as she shook her head.

"You're right," Lacey said, watching as the crumpled e-mail drifted out into the bay. "I tell her everything...So, what are you two doing here?"

"We like to come and sit out on the Snobs' dock after we..." Before Tyler could finish, Ashley punched his arm. He grinned up at Ashley before saying, "Do our homework."

Weird, Lacey thought. She hadn't realized the two had been hanging out.

"The Snobs' dock. Really?" Lacey said, glancing to her right at a six-foot scarecrow screwed to a wooden fence in front of the pink two-story home.

"Yeah, they haven't been back," Ashley said. "And their dock goes out at least 25 feet. It's great to sit out there. It's like being on a boat."

"I'm on a boat," Lacey sang. "I'm on a boat. Everybody look at me 'cause I'm sailing on a boat."

"Knock it off," Ashley said as Lacey started to throw her hands in the air, and Tyler chimed in. "Both of you."

"Come on. Let's show her," Ashley said, pulling Tyler's arms out of the air and grabbing his hand.

"Won't he yell at us?" Lacey said, mocking the scarecrow as they headed through a hole where three slats were missing from the fence. "The Snobs wouldn't like this," Lacey said and laughed.

"I can't believe their name is actually Snobs," Tyler said, furrowing his brow as his brown hair was swept back by a light wind.

"What?" the two girls said in unison, stopping and staring at their companion.

"Well, yeah, it's just such a crappy name," he said.

"You actually think their name is Snobs?" Lacey said, laughing, stopping, then giggling again.

"You're kidding, right?" Ashley said.

"What? You mean it's not?" Tyler asked.

"Of course not," Ashley said. When Tyler looked embarrassed she stroked his cheek and grabbed his hand. "No, silly," she added softly.

"We call them that because they used to always yell at us for hanging out down here," Lacey said.

"That's until Lacey told them off," Ashley said. "What was it? About four years ago?"

"Yeah, about that," Lacey said. "And I did not tell them off. I simply politely explained to them that they did not have any more legal right over the public street end than we do."

"Oh, that's right, your mother's a lawyer. Isn't she?" Tyler said.

Lacey nodded, and Ashley continued the story. "It didn't end there. The guy – Mr. Snob or whatever his real name is – said, 'Well, fine, but those rocks you keep throwing in the bay cost money, and I bought them myself."

Lacey mimicked the man's scolding as if she were Ashley's puppet, waving her finger in Tyler's face.

"So, I said, 'No problem. We'll bring our own!'" Lacey said.

"Then the whole neighborhood, every kid 10 to 15, helped bring a pile of lawn stones the Freshets had left over on the side of their house down here. It must have taken us two hours. Remember?"

"Yeah, and MacGyver," Lacey said, laughing too hard to talk. "He hitches up this wagon to the back of his bike and fills it up."

"But hits a pothole on the way over here," Ashley said, laughing too.

"And there he was, sprawled out on the street, surrounded by all these Jersey white stones. And we were all laughing."

"And he kept saying, 'It's not funny…

"My knee is bleeding," the girls finished together, laughing loudly.

"Wow, you guys in Silverton, you really know how to party," Tyler said.

Responding in unison once more, the girls said, "We do." Then Lacey said more somberly, "We did."

As if summoned psychically, Lacey suddenly turned to head home. "Look guys. I better go tell my mom about my phone."

"Do you want me to come for support?" Ashley called after her.

"Nah. Pft. I got this; see you later," Lacey called back as she put on a brave face. But as she walked past abandoned and sad-looking GES homes, her shoulders sagged, but not nearly as much as her mood.

Chapter Nineteen:
Friday, March 29, 2013

"So much for the big hunting trip," MacGyver muttered as he unzipped his backpack. He dumped a few notebooks, crumpled test papers and some notices that were supposed to have been signed and returned to school onto his bed. He only paused a second when the half-eaten granola bar joined them along with a gum wrapper balled and sealed with a wad of "ABC gum."

"Yuck," he said to his empty room, but he wasn't disgusted enough to get up and throw the gross items in his desk-side trash can, only three feet away. They could wait.

As MacGyver packed, he felt surprisingly torn. His mother had thought he'd be thrilled that his aunt bought him a plane ticket to spend Spring Break with her in New Jersey, and he was. But, he couldn't believe the trip came up on the one week when someone here had actually invited him to hang out.

As much as he was dying to spend time with his friends, and of course, his family, in New Jersey, he wondered if Kevin would think he was just copping out. They didn't really know each other, so MacGyver was unsure how he would take it. And right now, Kevin was the only person in Florida who had shown any interest in hanging out with him. "This'll teach him," MacGyver grunted.

He reached down next to his bed and pulled up clean tee-shirts and shorts from a laundry basket stuffed with clothes he was "expected to put away" himself and shoved them into the bag. Then, an idea that he considered brilliant occurred to him, and he reached into his bottom dresser drawer for some boxers to add to the mix.

Ha. I got this, he thought to himself. His triumph, however, reminded him of the last time he converted his "book bag" to a "vacation valise," which is what Lacey had called it.

The two of them were in his room two summers ago, getting his stuff together for a week at his grandmother's in Long Island, about 150 miles away. Lacey had come over so they could goof around on his trampoline, but MacGyver's mom wouldn't let him hang out until his chores were done, and that included packing. Lacey had really been a pain in the butt that day.

First, she tried to tell him that his backpack wasn't big enough for a whole week away. She even went so far as to insist they search his attic for a larger suitcase. After ninety minutes in the attic, during which Lacey played with all of his childhood toys and tried on his mom's, and even some of his dad's, old clothes, hats and coats, she conceded that there were no suitcases to be found.

Then, she wanted to go to her house and continue their exhaustive searching for this bag he only needed for the drive to his grandmother's a couple of hours away. But, by this point, MacGyver had gotten so hot and sweaty from the oppressive heat in the unair-conditioned attic that he put his foot down.

"Look, Lacey, I don't really need your help, and I don't need a suitcase."

"You're a guy. You don't know what you need," she responded with a laugh, a smirk and a pouty little smile that he normally couldn't refuse. But with sweat dripping from his face and his brown hair plastered to his head, MacGyver just wasn't having it.

"Lacey, regardless of the number of X chromosomes I have, I DO know what I want and need, AND WHAT I NEED NOW IS FOR YOU TO GO HOME SO I CAN SHOVE SOME CLOTHES IN

MY BOOK BAG AND THEN TAKE A SHOWER SO WE CAN JUMP ON THE TRAMPOLINE."

That's when she said it. Quietly and calmly, with no sarcasm in her voice.

"Vacation valise."

"What?"

"Vacation valise. If you are going to take out the books, you can't very well call it a book bag. It's a vacation valise," she said.

"Vacation what? What does that even mean?"

"It's an old-fashioned word my Great Aunt Anna uses when she means suitcase," Lacey said, handing him the backpack and heading toward his door.

"And while Polly is going to think it's weird that I'm showering before bouncing around on a trampoline on a ninety-degree day, I, too, will go freshen up and be back in about ten minutes."

He just stared at her. She was calm and composed. Her demeanor showed no sign that he had just yelled at her.

Then she crossed back to the bed.

"By the way, you can't just shove whatever you see in the bag. You have to think in terms of outfits. What shirts do you want to wear with which pants? Otherwise you wind up being away stuck with purple pants and a Mets tee-shirt, and royal blue and orange and purple just don't go. Believe me."

"GET OUT!"

"Okay, back in about fifteen. Okay?"

"Yeah, that sounds good. Unless…"

"Unless…"

"Do you want to go swimming instead?"

"Sure. My house or the bay?

"The bay sounds good."

"All right, but then I'm just changing, not showering."

"Did I ask?"

"No, you didn't, but I'm telling."

"Well, thank you," MacGyver said as he shoved a random pile of shirts into the bag. "See you at the Beach Club."

"Vacation valise," MacGyver muttered to himself. That girl is crazy, he thought as he zipped up his backpack. He gave a passing thought to his grandmother's house, which had also flooded in Sandy, even though it was so far away. Then, he returned to thinking about Lacey.

"Crazy," he said aloud and fell back on his bed and reached for his phone. He wanted to text her, but they'd had a fight about a week ago, and she'd basically told him not to text until he had a girlfriend. He wasn't positive, but he felt pretty sure that wasn't what she really wanted. *No worries*, he thought, *in a few hours we'll be together.*

Chapter Twenty:
About 10 a.m. Saturday, March 30, 2013

"Enjoy the rest of your day in Central Florida," the flight attendant said as the seatbelt light went out, and a plane full of restless snowbirds raced to be the first ones in the aisle.

"Get up, Jake," Lacey demanded as she shook her sleeping brother. "Get up."

"Let him be, Lacey. It's going to take a few minutes for everyone to get their stuff from the overhead compartments," Grandma Irene said as she took off her reading glasses and let them fall on her chest, dangling from turquois beads around her neck.

"We could have been first. Now we have to wait for everyone," Lacey complained.

"Honey, it doesn't matter. We all have to wait for our bags at the carousel anyway," Lacey's grandmother said reasonably.

"Carousel," a sleepy Jake repeated, bolting upright. "We're here. We're in Disney World?"

"Not exactly," Grandma Irene said, patting the boys leg. "But we have landed."

"And we're going to be the last ones off the plane thanks to you," Lacey said with a sigh, slumping back against her upright seat.

"Lacey, honey," her grandmother said. "I'll bet we won't even be the last ones to get our rental car. You'll see. Besides, what's the big rush? Space Mountain will be there no matter when we arrive."

Grandma Irene reached across Jake and brushed wisps of honey brown hair out of Lacey's eyes before adding in a whisper. "Though, I do wish they would hurry up a little. I have to pee, and old ladies can't hold it as long as you kids."

"I can hold it for hours, days," Jake said earnestly. "Lacey has to go at every rest stop."

"Do not," she said, looking at her little brother and noticing just how excited he was. His short legs were bouncing against the seat and his hands were wrapped around a Buzz Lightyear action figure. Lacey reached over to tickle him but accidentally brushed against a button on the toy.

"To infinity and beyond," Buzz said in what sounded like the distinctive voice from the *Toy Story* movies.

"Hmmm," she said, thinking about the play figure for the first time. "That really sounds like Buzz Lightyear."

"It *is* Buzz Lightyear!" Jake said, his ears turning bright red.

"No, I know, but it sounds like him," Lacey said.

"It is him," Jake said, pursing his lips and speaking through clenched teeth.

Lacey pushed the button again, this time intentionally.

"Evil never wins," Buzz responded.

"Do you hear that, Grandma? Doesn't that sound like Buzz Lightyear?"

"It *is* Buzz Lightyear."

"Lacey, why are you bothering him?" Grandma Irene asked.

"This is an intergalactic emergency," Buzz said as Jake held onto him tightly.

"See, doesn't that sound like Buzz? ...I mean, oh what's his name?...Tim Allen. Doesn't it sound like Tim Allen?"

"Oh, I don't know, dear. I can't imagine they hire the real actors to make the toys," their grandmother said as she started to get up, now that the plane was starting to empty out.

"Who's Tim Allen?" asked Jake, as he slipped his thumb into his mouth.

"It sounds like Tim Allen. Doesn't it?" argued Lacey as Buzz said, "Do you know these life forms?"

"I just don't think they would spend all that money to get Tim Allen," Grandma Irene said.

"Still. It sounds like Tim Allen," Lacey said, the last one of the trio to find her way into the aisle.

"I'll tell you a secret," said a short, balding man who was grabbing the final briefcase from the overhead compartments. "It probably is him."

Lacey twisted her head to look behind her.

"Huh?" she said.

As she heard the brilliant syllable escape her lips, she chastised herself that she was starting to sound like the straight-F student she was becoming.

"I work for Disney," said the man. "It probably is him. They make every effort to use the same actors. Although, since I'm divulging secrets, I'll tell you something else. Sometimes Tom Hanks gets too busy to record the Woody voice. Then, they use his brother, Jim. Sounds just like him."

"Wow, thanks," Lacey said. "This was going to bother me the entire vacation. I really appreciate your letting us know."

"You didn't hear it from me," the man said as he reached in his pocket for a pair of sunglasses. "Have a great vacation."

"Hey, one other thing. I mean, if you don't mind," Lacey said.

"Sure. What can I help you with?" the man said.

"Is it true that you can't point?" Lacey asked.

"Excuse me?" he said staring at her.

"Is it true that you're not allowed to point if someone asks for directions or something?"

"Oh, you mean in the parks," he said. "Yes, but I don't work in the parks, so I hadn't thought about that rule for a long time, not since my college internship, which was twenty years ago."

"Oh, I've heard about that program. It's supposed to be really fun. I'd do it just for a chance to go down in the secret tunnels," Lacey said.

Then she realized Grandma Irene and Jake had already deplaned.

"Crap," she said. "I'm sorry. I have to go catch up with my family."

"Of course. Have fun," the man yelled after Lacey, who was practically sprinting as she headed down the gangway.

Chapter Twenty-One:
Around noon, March 30, 2013

"Grandma," Lacey said as soon as her clothes were unpacked into the hotel dresser.

"Yes, dear."

"Can I borrow your phone?"

"Lacey, your mother said you weren't allowed to use the phone except to call her. Something about breaking yours."

"I didn't break it," Lacey said. "I dropped it. In the bay," she added more quietly.

"Either way, your mother said I should not lend you my phone, and you know I don't like to undermine her," Grandma Irene said, turning her attention to her grandson. "Jake, honey, are you ready to go to the pool?"

"Yup!" he said, grabbing a towel.

"Leave that here. We can get towels at the pool; these are for our showers...Lacey, we are going to take a quick dip before we head over to the parks," Grandma said. Dressed in a black and white bathing suit with a knee-length skirt that covered so much of her body she might as well as been wearing clothes, Grandma Irene walked toward the door with her card key and her cellphone in her hand.

"Oh, I guess I won't be needing this," she said, heading back into the room to leave her phone on the nightstand between the beds. Kissing Lacey on the top of her head, she said, "There's a hammock right over by the lake. It looks like a nice place to relax and chat."

"Thank you!" Lacey said, smiling so that her dimples appeared.

"For what? I didn't do anything," Grandma said and winked at her. "Oh, and remember we plan to leave in about ninety minutes. First stop, Fastpass for Space Mountain."

"Grandma, I think you like that ride more than I do," Lacey said.

"I know I do!" her grandmother said heading toward the door in water shoes. For some reason, she didn't like flip-flops.

"Are we going?" Jake called from the door he was holding open.

"Don't forget to use sunscreen," Grandma called back to Lacey as she grabbed Jake's hand and headed for the elevator.

Grandma was right. The oversized hammock was the perfect spot to try and get some color after months of tan-assaulting, frigid temperatures in their native Garden State. Lacey stretched out and stared up at the sun until all she could see were colorful dots dancing around, blocking both sun and sky. In her left hand, she gripped her grandmother's phone, weighing it as if it were a college acceptance/rejection letter. The answers were right there, but she was too afraid to look.

What am I waiting for? I have to call MacGyver. Won't it be great if he could get a ride over here? Or, maybe, I could go there and see where he's been living? He said he's less than three hours from the Orlando airport. This has to be doable.

How do I ask? What do I say? He's going to think I'm crazy. We haven't talked in almost two weeks. What if he's met someone? What if he's over me?

Don't be stupid. Nothing's changed in all these years. Why would it change now? Of course, he wants to see you. Sometimes, Lacey, you can be so stupid, she scolded herself, wishing she could stop the endless arguing voices.

Lacey lay on the hammock listening to her "little birds," as she called them, talk, argue and rationalize. She got so wrapped up in the quarrelling that she actually slipped the cellphone into her shorts pocket and brought both her hands over her face stretching high into the sky. Keeping her fingers tightly together, she pretended each of her hands was a bird, and the birds were chirping animatedly at one another. As her thumb and fingers on one hand met, the digits on her other hand responded in a coordinated fashion.

As the argument continued, Lacey started to get lost in the puppetry, and she giggled at the barebones Punch and Judy show.

"Knock it off. You're wasting precious time," the left "bird" squawked as Lacey actually voiced the words. Surprised to hear her own voice, she turned her hands so that both "birds" were staring down at her, silent, then fell like rocks, in a show of defeat, to her sides.

Grabbing the phone, she checked the time. In forty-five minutes she was expected to be dressed and ready to commence the coaster-riding extravaganza.

"Stop stalling," she snapped at herself, surprisingly loudly and began punching in the numbers.

"Hello. Hey…..What?..........Oh, I'm sorry you've got my voicemail. *That's* why I can't hear you. Anyway, you know what to do." MacGyver's voice was so warm, friendly and reassuring, but, of course, just a mirage. He wasn't really there.

"Really, God? Really?" she yelled to the sky after disconnecting the call. She got up and walked the perimeter of the lake at the Caribbean Beach resort where they were staying at Disney World, disciplining herself that she could only call back once, and not until she had completed the full circumference.

###

Even though she knew it was a sold-out resort during Spring Break, Lacey was dumbfounded when she returned to her hammock and found some hairy old guy lying there in a Mickey Mouse bathing suit that definitely should have been at least two sizes larger. It didn't really matter, though, as she was already five minutes late meeting Grandma. Still, she figured she was entitled to call MacGyver one more time. After all, she had completed a full lap of the lake, and that was the deal she had made with herself.

When Lacey heard MacGyver's voice boom, "Hello," her heart stopped for just an instant until she heard, "Hey…What?....Oh,…."

"Thanks anyway," she yelled sarcastically to the heavens and scurried up a flight of stairs to her room.

Chapter Twenty-Two:
April 1, 2013

As he pulled up the metal, horseshoe-shaped latch on the Beach Club's cyclone fence gate, MacGyver couldn't help but smile. For the first time in five months, he was home.

He paused to zip up his gray hoodie before pushing open the gate. He had almost forgotten how windy it could be by the water, not to mention how much colder New Jersey is.

Running over to the spot where the swings and slide no longer stood, he kicked at a piece of sand-covered wood before realizing it was the four-foot-by-two-foot wooden sign that normally stood at the entrance, reading "Beach Club," and in smaller letters, "Members Only."

"Damn," MacGyver said aloud, pulling up his hood to keep his hair from blowing in the wind and smacking him in the face.

It's like they're not even trying to put this place back together, he thought as he looked over at the Beach Club building, which sported missing wood paneling, one lone black shutter hanging at an awkward angle and a small group of teenagers standing outside.

"MacGyver!"

As soon as she saw him, Ashley screamed his name and came running at full soccer speed across the sand. When she reached him, the two hugged and squeezed each other hard with neither wanting to break away.

"Hey, wait a minute! Save some for me," Britt whined as she jogged over. She pulled MacGyver out of Ashley's arms and replaced her with her own full-body hug, the kind of embrace her mother had recently started to complain was "too intimate" at her age.

"Me, too," Ashley complained, feeling left out, and the circle opened up and swallowed her whole.

MacGyver had to look away when he saw tears fall from Ashley's bright blue eyes. He knew how she felt. The scene was so familiar, yet so foreign.

Tyler walked over then, somewhat breaking the spell, and the three lifelong friends each pushed back about a foot as Ashley dried her cheeks.

"W'as up, y'all?" Tyler drawled doing a piss-poor job of faking a Southern accent. "When did y'all get here?"

"My aunt dropped me off about ten minutes ago," MacGyver said, pushing off his hood. He reached out his right hand, and the boys clasped hands high in the air and pumped their joined fists like they'd won some championship.

As they walked over to the Beach Club to sit beneath the missing awning, MacGyver bent over and grabbed a fistful of sand, holding tight as he walked. The sand sifted through his fingers.

"Hmm," he said.

What?" Brittney asked, running her hand through her long black hair to straighten any strands that went astray during their hug.

"It's different," MacGyver said.

"Different from what?" Tyler asked.

"The beach sand in Florida is different. Thicker somehow," he said.

"You said you don't live near a beach in Florida," Brittney said.

"Class trip," MacGyver said. "Took forever on the bus to get there."

"How can the sand be different?" Tyler asked. "I mean, it's just sand."

"I don't know. It just feels different in Florida, not as soft," MacGyver said.

"That's weird," Ashley said.

"Yeah, it's kinda like our lives," MacGyver said, focusing his brown eyes on the sand that slipped to the ground in such a haphazard way it didn't even form a pile.

"What's that supposed to mean?" Brittney asked, nibbling on her blue pinky nail.

"The sand. Look at it. You can grab it and hold tight, but without your even noticing, it slowly slips away," MacGyver said, stretching out his arm and opening his hand palm up.

As he spoke, the sand slipped through his fingers, passed the blue shell friendship bracelet he always wore, and returned to the ground.

"That's depressing," Tyler said as he grabbed a seat on one of the plastic Adirondack chairs that had been placed around the beach, replacing the wooden benches that had stood for decades.

"Sorry," MacGyver said as he and Britt pulled up chairs next to Tyler, and Ashley plopped onto Tyler's lap.

MacGyver stared over at Tyler and Ashley, blinking.

"Oh. I see," he said. "I guess some things have changed since I've been away."

Ashley blushed. "Well," she said, as Tyler shook his head a little.

"Nothing serious, man. We're just messing around," Tyler said.

"Ouch," said Brittney.

"What?" asked Ashley, pretending not to agree with Britt's assessment of Tyler's comment.

A moment passed in silence, then Ashley said, "You know she's not here. Right?

"Who's not?" MacGyver said.

"Right," said Britt. "Like you're not about to ask where Lacey is?"

"Well, maybe," MacGyver said, taking out a box of Marlboro Black and offering his stunned friends each one before reaching into his pocket for a lighter and flicking it.

A torch-size flame grew instantly from the top of the blue Bic lighter, nearly scorching MacGyver's shoulder-length brown hair as it blew in the wind.

"Crap," he said, dropping the lighter and quickly picking it up again. "I was teasing my cousin, Ruthie, with it before I got here and forgot to turn it back down."

"You were playing with fire with Ruthie. What is she eight?" Britt asked, not bothering to hide her disapproval.

"She's twelve," MacGyver responded as he finally lit his cigarette. "And don't judge me. I wasn't playing with fire. I was just teasing her."

"With fire," said Britt, scoffing.

"She's twelve. I can't believe it. Twelve. That's how old we were when we used to play Kiss Stop O," Ashley said, pulling her shoulder-length blonde hair back into a loose braid as she spoke.

"Kiss Stop O?" Tyler asked.

"Manhunt with kissing," Brittney explained. MacGyver noticed she tugged down her sleeves to make sure her "ugly arms" weren't showing. Some things don't change, he thought.

"I know, but Ruthie's not like us. She's too young for that kind of thing," MacGyver said, flicking ashes off the end of his cigarette.

"Oh, sure," Ashley said. "That's what our parents thought."

"Yeah, but this is my baby cousin."

"Geez, I remember when she was born," Britt said.

"Yeah, she was the tiniest baby I ever saw," Ashley said.

"That's because my aunt was only five and a half months along when she had her. They say it's a miracle that Ruthie doesn't have any permanent disability."

"Yeah, except having you for a cousin," Ashley teased.

MacGyver shot Ashley a look, pretending to be indignant. Then, he asked, "What do you mean she's not here? Did she go to the store or something?"

"Nope. Florida," said Britt, placing a hand on her friend's shoulder.

"Yeah, right. Very funny," MacGyver said. But when he realized his friends were serious, he let out a sound that was half grunt, half scream and got up, ignoring the comfort Britt tried to offer. As he paced the beach, he complained, "Are you kidding me?"

"No. Sorry, pal," Tyler said. "She's off to the Land of the Giant Rat, though why they would go there when they can visit Hogwarts is beyond me."

"No way," MacGyver said. "But why didn't she tell me?"

"I guess she doesn't tell you everything anymore," Ashley said, recalling years of fighting over which one of them was really Lacey's closest friend.

"Guess not," MacGyver said. "When does she get back?"

"I think Saturday," Britt said.

"Shit. I leave on Friday," MacGyver said.

"Why didn't you tell us you were coming?"

"I wanted it to be a surprise."

"Well, surprise," Ashley said, holding out her arms to console MacGyver.

Before MacGyver could accept the hug, Tyler excitedly suggested, "Let's have a GES party."

"*You* can't call a GES party," Ashley said.

"What? Why not?"

"Because you're not a GES," both girls responded simultaneously.

"Hey, I'm the guest. And, I say let's party," MacGyver said, trying to sound upbeat as he looked around the Beach Club property and saw all the things that weren't there, the swing set, jungle gym and slide, several big trees, and Lacey.

"GES," Britt said.

"That's what I said. I'm the guest," MacGyver said, pushing his curly brown hair away from his face.

"First of all, you live here. Don't argue," Ashley said, holding out her hand as if it could stop reality from ruining their reunion. "And, the word is GES, G-E-S, and you are one. Or would be if you hadn't run away."

"What the hell are they talking about?" MacGyver leaned over and asked Tyler.

"Who cares? Glad you're home, man. We're going to have the best party ever tonight."

Chapter Twenty-Three:
Around 7 p.m. Thursday, April 4, 2013

"Lacey."

"Yeah, Grandma."

"Here it is Thursday night and the whole week you haven't talked to me once about the number one thing on your mind. Why is that?" Grandma Irene asked as they enjoyed ice cream at a Disney arcade.

"What do you mean? You made sure we got on Tower of Terror three times. That's my favorite."

"Mhm. Hmm."

Her grandmother didn't say anything else and just stared over as Lacey toyed with the green ice cream in her paper bowl.

"Honestly, Grandma. This trip has been amazing. Thanks so much for taking both of us, especially Jake. I think he really needed to get away from all the storm sh…stuff."

"But."

"But?"

"But something's still bothering you, and I think I know what it is."

"Oh, Grandma. No. You don't have to worry. I'm kind of over the whole Dad thing. He just wasn't happy. Honestly, it's okay. As Mom says, 'I hope he finds what he's looking for in Alaska.'"

Grandma Irene put down her spoon and reached over to touch her granddaughter's cheek. "I do, too. Still, I can tell you I'm not proud of how he's treated you, especially now. And, I'm not proud of myself either."

"Grandma, don't," Lacey said, trying to stop this conversation in its tracks.

"No, it's true. Your grandfather and I were just so embarrassed by how Jonathan up and left that we didn't know how to face the three of you. We were wrong," she said, looking down at her wrinkled hands. "We should have been there for you."

"You're here now, and this trip is amazing," Lacey said as she absently began twirling her hair around her index finger.

"It was all so confusing. If I could do it again..." The frown lines around her grandmother's mouth and eyes deepened as she spoke.

"Grandma, what have you always told me?" Lacey said, worried that her grandmother was going to lose it. She had never seen that happen before and didn't know how to handle it. "No regrets, right?"

"Yes, I know. I'm great with the advice, aren't I?" Grandma said. "But something's still eating you. I can tell."

"Please don't worry about it. It's not about you or the trip or Dad. I mean there's really nothing you can do. It's just...."

"It's just?"

... After a long pause, Lacey added, "Grandma, really, thank you. And I'm so sorry that we dragged you away from Grandpa. You must miss him."

Her grandmother laughed softly.

"Honey, when you've been married for as long as we have, a little vacation from each other now and then can be a really good thing. Besides you know how grumpy your grandfather gets when he has to wait for anything. He can't do these lines."

"I know, but I mean, you left him just so you could cheer us up."

"Is that what you think? Ouch!" Grandma said. "Damn, Rocky Road, I should know better than to eat anything with nuts with these dentures. Excuse me."

131

Her grandmother reached into her mouth and fished out a nut, which she tucked into a napkin she balled up and left on the table.

"Take care of your teeth. These things can be a real pain. Here I go again with the advice. Anyway, where was I? Oh, Lacey, honey, this is a treat for me, getting to spend time with my almost all-grown-up granddaughter and little Jake, especially having you all to myself."

"Thanks," Lacey said. On an impulse, she walked around the table, hugged and quickly kissed her grandmother on the lips, the way they'd done her whole life, even though she secretly hated the gesture and would have rather aimed at her cheek.

"Mmm. Minty," said her grandmother. "Maybe *I* should have gotten chocolate chip mint."

"Do you want to trade?" Lacey offered.

"Now you say that when you have what, a spoonful or two left? No thanks."

They laughed as Jake ran over to ask his grandmother for more arcade tokens.

"It's smart the way you don't give them to him all at once," Lacey said.

"It's not so smart the way you still aren't telling me what's really bothering you."

"It's just a boy."

"A boy or MacGyver?" her grandmother asked.

Lacey huffed a little in a fake, you-got-me, kind-of laugh. "MacGyver is a boy, Grandma."

"Not to you, dear."

"What do you mean?"

"He's the future you've always imagined for yourself. Not just a boy."

"What? No," Lacey said, blushing.

"Sure he is, honey. Since you were a tiny little girl just able to walk, the two of you have always been inseparable. I meant to ask this earlier, but I didn't want to intrude. Why haven't you asked if he could spend a day at Disney World with us?"

"What? Well..."

"Don't tell me you haven't thought about this. How far away does he live? About three hours away?"

"Only two-and-a-half."

"Mmm. Hmm I knew you had to be thinking of this. So why don't you call him? Maybe he can come out Saturday when he's off school. Our flight doesn't leave until midnight."

"I've been calling him, Grandma. He's not picking up."

"Oh, I'm sorry, honey."

"It's all right. I think maybe he's met someone and just doesn't want to tell me."

"Oh, I see."

"No, you don't," Lacey said as a tear slipped down her cheek and plopped into her ice cream bowl. "You see, he's been so miserable and talking to each other just made us miss each other more. And I didn't want him to be sad and all alone down there."

"Honey, he moved with his parents," her grandmother said, reaching across the table and patting Lacey's hand.

"You know what I mean. Well, anyway, a couple of weeks ago, I told him that I would be mad at him if he didn't go get a girlfriend," Lacey said, twirling her hair and looking down at her ice cream. "I told him not to call or text me again until he could send me a picture of him kissing his girlfriend."

"Really?" Grandma Irene said, forcing a smile to hide her confusion. "Well, okay."

"No, it's not okay. Since then he hasn't answered my calls or my texts. And now I'm here, and I could see him, but I can't."

Lacey began silently crying

"What's wrong with her?" Jake asked, running over with strands of purple prize tickets in his right hand and his left hand out for more tokens.

"Don't worry; she's fine," Grandma Irene said, handing over the coins.

"Lacey, honey, you're fifteen. Nothing is this important."

"Sixteen," Lacey said, sniffling

"Sorry, sixteen. There are going to be lots of boys and lots of friends," her grandmother said, wiping away her tears. "Honey, we are on Disney property here at Lake Buena Vista. I don't think it's even legal to cry on Disney property."

"Grandma, they call this Downtown Disney now," Lacey said, regaining her composure.

"It will always be Lake Buena Vista to me," her grandmother said and hugged her.

Chapter Twenty-Four:
Thursday, April 4, 2013

While his friends had adjusted to drinking over the last few months, until that week, MacGyver had never consumed alcohol except for a few sips of champagne on New Year's Eve.

He was stunned both by how much his friends drank and the vast assortment of new beverages they imbibed. One night they passed a bottle of wine around; the next it was vodka. It seemed his group of friends had expanded to include Jack Daniels, Johnnie Walker, Captain Morgan, basically whatever they could get their hands on.

The same Silverton Crew, which only last year thought Yoohoo was the bomb, seemed to choke down anything with alcohol in it without question, even if it tasted like lighter fluid.

The problem MacGyver found was that despite his height, when it came to alcohol, he was a lightweight. About an hour into each night, he was already slurring words and stumbling when he walked.

"Ash....Ashhhlllleeee?" The way MacGyver slurred the name, it sounded like a question.

"Yes."

"Why? Jusssst tell me why?"

"Why what?"

"Why does sssssshhhhe hate me?"

"Who?"

"Lacccccey. Why does she hate me?"

"She doesn't hate you. She just went on vacation. You just have really sucky timing."

"Nope. Nope. No. NO," he said, each syllable a little more emphatic than the last. "She hates me."

"Why?"

"Why? That'sss what I asked you."

"No, why do you think she hates you?" Ashley asked.

"I don't know….'cause I left her," he said, sucking down the last few sips of a bottle of Maddog 360 Blue. "This stuff is good," he said as he tripped over to a garbage can.

"Hey," Ashley said. "Take that downstairs to recycling."

"Not right now," MacGyver said opening a bottle of Maddog Red. "I'll do it later."

"Okay, but don't throw it in the garbage. Just 'cause you're depressed is no reason to comingle. You've got to worry about the environment."

"Why? It doesn't worry about me. Nobody does."

"What do you mean?"

"I mean nobody does. I swear my parents are hoping I don't come back home. They're probably praying I convince my aunt to let me stay up here with her."

"Why would you want to do that? Dude, you live in Florida, sunshine and swimming pools every day of the year, not to mention the beach."

"Ashley, I live in Landlock, Fla. Landfuck, Fla. There is no beach."

"Yeah, but Florida's just a tiny little peninsula right. I mean thin, not tiny. What is it, like an hour from anywhere in the state to a beach? That's got to be amazing."

"Asssshley, you live a few doors away from the beach. Whaaaat are you talking about?"

"Not anymore. Well, at least, not right now."

"Yeah, but you will."

"Sure, but sometimes, you know, it's snowing or twenty degrees. It never gets like that in Florida. You probably don't even need anything other than flip-flops….except for gym."

"They call it PE there."

"That's stupid. Why?"

"I'll give you five guesses."

"Pedophiles' exercise."

"What? No!"

"Physician's excuse."

"No. Nope."

"MacGyver, this is stupid. Why do they call it PE? Does it have anything to do with penguins?"

"Huh? No."

"Is it…"

"Wait a minute. Wait a minute. My phone is ringing."

"No it's not."

"Yes, it is. It's vibrating."

Ashley reached over and placed a hand against MacGyver's leg. "Tingly," she said, giggling.

"Watch out," he said, jumping up and spilling Maddog all over both of them.

"Geez, MacGyver. Nice job." Ashley complained as he tried to help her dry up the sticky liquid with his sweatshirt. Stripping off the hoodie, MacGyver abandoned it for Ashley to deal with and reached into his pocket for the phone.

"It'ssss nobody," he said, when he looked at the number.

"Nobody," Ashley said. "Nobody doesn't call."

"No, I mean it's an unknown number."

"Why don't you answer it anyway?"

"Nah, my parents owe all this money, and the collection agencies have started calling even my phone. Besides, it'ssss stopped now. Sssorry about this," he said, taking back his sweatshirt and tossing it in a corner.

"No big deal," she said.

"Hey, I know," he said. "We can Facetime Lacccey."

"Sorry, honey, no can do. She dropped her phone in the bay."

"Again?" MacGyver said.

"It's only the third time," Ashley said with a laugh. "But to be fair, it's no different from another person just dropping their phone. I mean Lacey is always down at the Rock Throwing Place or the Beach Club or the Boat Slips."

"Yeah, I guess you're right. I didn't realize how much time we all spent there until I moved. You know? I think I miss the Rock Throwing Place the most."

"Geez, thanks a lot," Ashley said, stiffening.

"What? Whhhaaaat?" he slurred.

"So you like a dirty street end more than any of your friends?"

"That's not what I meant."

"It's what you said."

"Ashley, no, wait," MacGyver said, and then, he started to laugh.

"What's so funny?" Ashley asked, indignant.

"Ha," MacGyver said, pulling himself together. "Lately I haven't been talking to very many kids. It's really nice just to be somewhere with friends and just talk, you know. And not to have to try so hard to fit in."

"MacGyver, trust me, you'll never fit in anywhere."

"Thanks. That's exactly what I'm afraid of."

"Aww, honey, I was just joking," Ashley said and reached over and pecked his cheek.

"Wow! You're the first girl who's kissed me in months," MacGyver said.

"Ah, honey," Ashley said and hugged her friend tightly. "It will get better."

"Hey, I just had an idea. Yeah, it's a good idea," MacGyver said. "Actualalally, a freakin' awesome idea."

"What?"

"Kiss me."

"What?" Ashley said, instinctively pulling away.

"Kisssss me," he said without a moment's hesitation. Then, he added, "Not for real or anything. Just so I can take a picture."

"What?"

"There's thissss girl at, um, at home, who um dared me. Yeah, dared me to send her a picture of me kissing someone."

"What for?"

"It's kind of a long story. I, um, want to make her jealous."

"Okay, but see, you do have things going on at home."

"You're right. I do, at home," he said and pulled out his phone.

Ashley pecked him on the lips as MacGyver held out his right arm and took a selfie showing the back of Ashley's head and some of MacGyver's face mid kiss.

"Got it," MacGyver said. "That will show her."

"Sounds like a weird girl," Ashley said. "Hope it works out for you... Though, maybe you shouldn't tell Lacey I said that."

She pushed her feet flat onto the floor parallel in front of her and prepared to stand up. She reached over and messed up MacGyver's curly hair and then leaned in for a brief hug.

"I've got to go check in with Tyler. I don't want him to think I ditched him."

"Hey, what's going on with him? Are you guys going out?"

"You heard him today. We're just messing around."

"Oh," MacGyver said. "You looked kind of tight earlier today."

"Oh, we are. It's not that we're not, you know, into each other. It's just that we don't want to put labels on it. Tyler thinks the terms girlfriend and boyfriend are too possessive. Y'know, like you own the person."

"Uh huh."

"He was so sweet, MacGyver. He told me he doesn't want to demean me by calling me his girlfriend. Isn't that so sweet, so sensitive?"

"Uh, yeah."

As Ashley started to walk away, MacGyver called after her. "Beee careful." But by the time he managed to slur the words together, Ashley was out of earshot.

Chapter Twenty-Five:
Late night, April 4, 2013

Why the hell doesn't he answer? Lacey had slipped out of bed, taken her grandmother's cellphone and was walking around the resort grounds. The lighting, which she assumed was meant to be mood-setting, kept everything so dark that she could feel panic welling up in her stomach like a little kid put to bed in a strange room without a nightlight.

There's no reason to be afraid, she told herself. *No reason at all. This is Disney World. Nothing bad ever happens here.* But, of course, she knew she was wrong. Lots of horrible things had happened at Disney over the years. For instance, an 18-year-old drowned when he and his 10-year-old brother hid on Tom Sawyer Island after closing, then got bored and attempted to swim off the island. And, a cast member was crushed to death at the Carousel of Progress back in 1974. Or was that in Disneyland?

Lacey had read these stories and dozens more on the long drive down to Florida one year when her parents were still together. That was about six, no seven years ago. She remembered the trip fondly because it was one of the last times she saw her parents laughing and holding hands, getting along really well together, not screaming and yelling like the participants on some reality TV show. *And why is it that they label something reality when it's really crass and disturbing?*

That's not my reality, Lacey thought. *You never see a reality show focused on hot breakfasts on Sunday mornings with pancakes and French toast or a family saying grace before they eat. It's always people screaming at each other flipping the bird and dropping the F-bomb.* Thinking back on that trip to Florida, Lacey started to calculate the math for the first time and became totally grossed out.

"Oh, my God," she said aloud as she headed out to what she now thought of as her hammock. Counting the months one more time she came to the very logical conclusion: Jake was probably conceived on that trip. "Ewww. Ewwww."

An actual shudder ran down her back. She wasn't sure if it was the thought of her parents having sex that sent the chills through her or if it was the fact she was wandering around in baby doll pajamas in the middle of the night. She wished Polly had allowed her to pack her normal tee-shirt and sleeping shorts. But her mother insisted it was inappropriate to wear a "Will Trade Virginity for Concert Tickets" shirt while on a trip with her grandmother.

When Lacey reached the hammock, she stretched out and then glanced at the phone for the time. It was only ten o'clock. God, her grandmother and Jake certainly went to sleep early. She called up her grandmother's list of recent calls and redialed MacGyver. Voicemail. Damn.

She repeated this disaster recipe three more times before ten-forty-five. Defeated she cried for about ten minutes before inspiration struck. She could call MacGyver's house phone – only one problem. She didn't know the number.

Now, what was the number her mother had her call to have someone else look it up. Six-one-one? No, that's the number when you're having phone trouble. Seven-one-one, no. *Well, I know it's not nine-one-one,* Lacey thought. Eventually, she remembered: four-one-one, and she placed the call.

"City and state please."

"The number for Richard Anderson."

"City and state please."

"Oh, oh, right. City and state," Lacey said.

Before Lacey could answer, an operator was on the line, replacing the automated voice. "City and state please." Lacey wondered if this really was a live person now; she couldn't quite be sure since this voice seemed just as mechanical as the previous one.

"Landfuck." *Goddamn MacGyver. Now he's got me saying it,* Lacey thought.

"Ma'am I'm sorry. I can't understand you."

"I'm sorry, Landlock, Florida."

"What listing?"

"Anderson, Richard. I mean Richard Anderson, however, you put it."

"So the first name is Anderson, like Anderson Cooper?" the operator asked.

"No, no. The first name is Richard. Richard Anderson."

"Oh! Like the guy who played MacGyver. Only he's Richard Dean Anderson, right?"

"Right," said Lacey. "Actually, this guy is Richard Dan Anderson. Close, right?"

"One moment please." Lacey wasn't sure exactly what happened next. Perhaps she accidentally touched the disconnect button, either that or the operator hung up on her.

After two more tries. Lacey finally had the number. Of course, now it was eleven-fifteen, well past the time when decent people make phone calls that aren't to say your Uncle Harold just died. Lacey never understood that either. She could remember at least five phone calls that came in the middle of the night to announce some distant relative had entered the Pearly Gates. Why in the world was this information so important that it couldn't wait until morning? Was each soul entering heaven required to have at least two to three dozen groggy earthly companions cheering them on in order to learn the secret password for entry to the Next World?

Lacey was so distraught that she decided to forgo proper protocol and call MacGyver's home.

"Hello."

"Hello, Mrs. Anderson. It's Lacey Freshet."

"Lacey, is everything all right? Is MacGyver all right?"

"Uh, what do you mean? I just wanted to ask if I could talk to him."

"Talk to him, honey. Isn't he sleeping over your house tonight?"

"WHAT?" Lacey screamed it so loudly that the light snapped on in the hotel room nearest her, but quickly was extinguished.

"Lacey, it's awfully late for a joke like this. Put MacGyver on dear and thank your mother for letting him stay there."

"Uh, oh, okay, Mrs. Anderson. Actually MacGyver just stepped away from the phone, so I'll go now. Sorry if we played this, uh, joke too late. You know how he is."

"Never mind. It's always nice to hear your voice. Good night, dear. Tell Polly I said hi."

With that, she was gone. Lacey couldn't believe what she had just heard. MacGyver was supposed to be sleeping over her house tonight? He was in New Jersey?! What the hell. The world was truly unfair.

Lacey tried to call MacGyver's cell again. Voicemail. Then she called Ashley and Britt and got their voicemails as well. She started to cry inconsolably – not that there was anyone around the hammock who could rush to console her.

After having walked around both Animal Kingdom and Hollywood Studios, which Grandma insisted on calling MGM, in the hot sun all day, Lacey was actually very tired, even though her desire to see MacGyver had kept her from sleeping. So as she cried and cried, her body started to relax in the hammock, and eventually, she was sound asleep.

Chapter Twenty-Six:
Very early hours of the morning, Friday, April 5, 2013

Hey I just met you.
And this is crazy.
But here's my number
So call me maybe.

MacGyver and Brittney sang together as he walked her down the pitch black street, past homes that ranged from left untouched since the storm to under construction and nearly done.

"See, you can sing," MacGyver said, as they made their way to the "good portajohn."

"Not really. You're just drrrunnnk, verrry drunk."

"Nah, you should take chorus next year. Lester would love you."

"Lester?"

"Mr. C."

"Huh?"

"Mr. Cavanaugh, the chorus teacher. His name's Lester or Lloyd. Maybe it's Lloyd. Yeah, it is Lloyd."

"Oh, yeah, you're not drunk."

"Nah, I'm sober now. It's just been a long time, and now I've got all these new teachers I've got to know, too. It's hard."

"Oh, poor baby, you've got it so hard living down in paradise."

"Oh, not this crap again."

"What crap?"

"You all do it to me. The whole your-life-must-be-so-great routine. You have it so wonderful down in the fuckin' beautiful Sunshine State. It must be all rainbows and unicorns!"

"Chill, MacGyver."

"No, I won't, and you want to know why?" he was screaming now. "My life sucks!! Do you hear that: It sucks!"

"Right," Brittney said with a smirk. "Sorry, bud, but this is my stop," she interrupted his rant. "Feel free to scream away while I pee. It's one of the great things about Silverton these day. You can scream all night. Nobody minds. There's no one here to hear you."

As Britt flicked on her flashlight and headed into the heavy plastic outhouse, MacGyver took her advice.

"And that's another thing!" he yelled. "I'm so tired of everyone putting Silverton down. You guys don't know what it's like to miss this place. You don't know how lucky you have it."

Brittney stepped out of the portajohn rubbing her hands together to absorb hand sanitizer. Just as MacGyver was about to shout additional complaints to the heavens, she interrupted. "Thanks for walking me down here, MacGyver. I know there's no one around, but I still find it creepy wandering around in the dark. I mean there's the streetlights, the ones that still work, but there's no lights coming from any houses."

"No problem," he said.

"Okay, now that we've got the niceties out of the way, shut up and listen to me. You think you're the only one who misses this place. We all miss Silverton. Look around. This isn't Silverton. This is an abandoned mud hole. All you do is whine and complain. Oh, Florida is so hot. Oh, my parents don't understand. Oh, I miss my friends. Well, I miss them, too. No one survived the storm, MacGyver. No one."

"What are you talking about? Your house didn't even flood!"

"MacGyver, you don't know what you're talking about. Living here is like surviving the apocalypse. Nobody's life was untouched. Nobody's. We're all changed, and none of it is for the better."

That was the last straw. MacGyver had heard how Brittney had gone to Winter Formal in a stretch limo. Who the hell was she to yell at him?

"Oh, really, Brittney? Having trouble adjusting to your chauffeur? Or is it too hard to pick out which new car you'd like for your seventeenth birthday? What the hell do you know?"

"I know that you get to live somewhere where things are normal, and the rest of us are stuck here where everything's all fucked up!"

MacGyver didn't know what to say. He felt bad for yelling at Brittney. He had never seen her so angry before. But, honestly, wasn't she being a little overdramatic and overemotional? Maybe she's on her period, he thought, knowing that thought was very sexist of him. But, c'mon, sometimes it was true, wasn't it? Still, they'd been friends for so many years, and this was his last night in Silverton.

"Hey, Freckle Face, I'm sorry," he said and he slipped an arm around her shoulders to pull her in for a hug.

"Freckle Face? Nobody's called me that since third grade," she said and leaned in for the embrace. "I'm sorry, too."

Chapter Twenty-Seven:
Approximately 7 a.m. Friday, April 5, 2013

"Lacey, Lacey."

Lacey couldn't believe how bright it was as she opened her eyes to Grandma Irene's voice. *Where the...oh my God...,* she thought.

"Grandma, oh my God. Grandma. I'm so sorry."

"What are you doing out here? And dressed only in your pajamas. Do you have any idea what could have happened to you?" Grandma asked as Lacey jumped down from the hammock and searched feebly for her orange flip-flops.

"What are you doing out here?" Jake asked, removing his thumb from his mouth just long enough to ask the question. "Couldn't you sleep with Grandma's snoring?"

"Jake, shh," said Lacey as her grandmother's cheeks turned pink.

"Grandma was crying. She thought you ran away," Jake said, but he was barely paying attention as he noticed a salamander and started chasing it.

"Oh, Grandma, no," Lacey said, reaching for her grandmother.

"Lacey, oh my goodness, what happened to you?" her grandmother said. Grandma Irene took a step back and opened her mouth wide but no sound emerged.

"What?" Lacey said. Then, she glanced down at her arms and legs and suddenly started to itch all over. Every inch of her was covered in tiny, but very swollen, little red bumps.

"Fleas," Grandmother and granddaughter said together.

A few years back when her grandmother was dog-sitting for a friend, Lacey had stayed over and slept with the adorable Yorkie puppy, after begging her parents to get her one of her own. But the next morning the puppy's magic spell was broken. Lacey had been bitten all over by fleas, and it turned out she was highly allergic.

Reaching up to scratch a spot on her chin, Lacey turned to her grandmother for confirmation of what she already knew. "They're all over my face, too, aren't they?"

"I'm afraid so, honey. We'll have to get you some cortisone," her grandmother said, taking Lacey's hand as if she were the six-year-old. "We'll have to find a doc in the box. C'mon, Jake, we need to go."

"But, wait. I've almost..." As the salamander slipped away, he stood up and looked at Lacey for the first time that morning. "You look like a monster. Grandma, don't touch her."

"Hush," their grandmother said, as they headed back to their room.

Chapter Twenty-Eight:
Sunday Morning, April 7, 2013

"You're home," Polly picked up Jake and kissed him before putting her arms around Lacey. "You don't look too bad."

"Not too bad? Mom, I can't go to school if I still look like this tomorrow."

"We'll see."

"The swelling's gone down a lot, and they're not as red," Grandma Irene said. "Otherwise, we had such a great time."

"And we brought you home a Tink," Jake said.

"Shh, we had it wrapped, Jake. You're not supposed to tell her what it is," Lacey scolded.

"Oh, sorry. It's a Tinkerbell music box," he blurted out in excitement without thinking.

"Geez," Lacey said and handed a wrapped box to her mother.

As Polly unwrapped the delicate trinket, and it started to play, "You Can Fly" tears came to her eyes. "Ma...Irene, thank you so much. You really don't know how much this means to us. They so needed some time away from here and all this," she said, motioning around at the still unfinished downstairs rooms. "I do have good news, though. The builder threw together a makeshift kitchen, so we don't have to go out to the trailer anymore to cook."

"What about for homework?" Lacey asked.

"Well, yeah, it's still too loud and probably dangerous to be in here during the day."

Lacey ran into the kitchen, her sneakers thudding against the plywood flooring. She couldn't believe her eyes when she saw their plastic laundry room slop sink hooked up right under the window and a slightly rusty oven range where her mother's double oven once stood.

Still she tried to sound genuine. "This is great, Mom."

"It's only temporary."

"I know. I mean it. It's great. We don't have to use the Little People's kitchen anymore."

"Yeah, and we got a free refrigerator from a church group. So we're in good shape, only have to go buy some ice cube trays."

"No ice maker?" Lacey said. "I didn't think they made refrigerators without ice makers anymore."

"Not only that, and Ma, ummm Irene, you'll appreciate this. It's not frost free."

"You're kidding," the older woman said. "Now, that's something I haven't seen in decades."

"I know. I was pretty surprised. Not that I mind. It's no big deal to defrost. I just didn't know. You'll think this is funny. I actually called the manufacturer as the freezer space started getting smaller. I said, 'I don't think the defrost is working.' And the guy, a real comedian, said, 'Well, I should hope not.' And I asked him what he meant. And he said, 'It doesn't have one.'"

The ladies laughed for a few moments more than the story really warranted.

"Well, I'll be going," Grandma Irene said. "Is there anything else I can do for you before I go? Anything you need, Polly?"

"No, you've done more than enough. I'm eternally grateful," Polly said, kissing Irene on the cheek.

Once she had said good-bye to her grandchildren, Grandma Irene slipped out the door calling back, "See you soon."

"Who wants to go over to the Boardwalk for some pizza?" Polly asked.

"The Boardwalk? We can't get over there without ID," Lacey said.

"Not anymore. They opened the bridge on Tuesday," Polly said. "You wouldn't believe the devastation over there. And all of the tourists. Everybody's rushing over to see the roller coaster in the ocean. The few open businesses are making a killing."

"I don't know, Mom," Lacey said. "I kinda wanted to catch up with my friends. Not that I'd let them see me like this."

"I want to see the roller coaster!" Jake exclaimed.

"Your friends can wait a little while, Lacey," Polly said. "I haven't talked to either of you in days. I get you first. By the way, you missed MacGyver."

"What do you mean I missed MacGyver?" Lacey said, trying to sound surprised.

"He was here the other day. He was visiting his Aunt Susan for Spring Break and was nice enough to stop by with Ashley and Brittney even though they knew you weren't here. He looked g.... Well, honestly, he looked kind of terrible. Tired and, you know, kind of unhappy, but maybe that was just because he was disappointed you weren't here."

"Did he say when he's going back?" Lacey asked hopefully.

"I think he left yesterday. No, Friday. I'm sorry, honey, but hey, you got to go to Disney World."

"Mom, you should have seen all the cool stuff they had," Jake interrupted. "They've got this Ariel ride with Sebastian, and oh man, you should have seen Ursula. She must be really scary for little kids."

"Oh yeah, right, for little kids," Lacey teased. "Like you didn't nearly piss your pants."

"She snuck up on me."

"Sneaked, and that's kind of impossible. We were the ones in the ride car, and *she* never moves."

"What do you mean? Of course, she moves. That's what makes her so scary."

"It's an animatronic, Jake. It's always in the same spot."

"An anima-what?" Jake asked.

"Jake, every time you go on the ride, she's going to be there in the same spot."

"Well, duh," Jake said. "Everyone knows that."

The conversation went on like that as Polly ushered them into the car.

"Mom, why do you have the Prayer of Serenity in the corner of your dashboard? That's new," Lacey asked as she buckled her seatbelt.

"I just got a new inspection sticker," Polly said matter-of-factly.

"So?"

"The back of it says, 'Stronger than the Storm,' and I just don't want to look at that every time I'm in the car."

"You'd rather look at the Prayer of Serenity?"

"You know I've always loved that prayer."

"Makes me wonder if maybe you're not a secret alcoholic."

"What?"

"It's the prayer of the twelve-step programs. Is there something you're not telling me?"

"I just like the prayer," Polly said, falling quiet as they drove across the Mathis Bridge to neighboring Seaside Heights on the barrier peninsula. Lacey felt a little nervous to be heading over the bridge as she had heard such horror stories of what it was like over there.

As she looked out the side window, Lacey watched the gentle waves lapping against a nearby fishing boat anchored in the bay.

"Well, the bay looks normal. Maybe it's not so bad over there," she said.

"Don't get your hopes up. I haven't been over yet, but I've heard it's pretty bad," Polly said.

"What's bad?" Jake asked.

"Butting into other people's conversations," Lacey snapped.

"Lacey, be nice. Jake, we have to warn you: The Boardwalk isn't going to look like the last time you saw it. It's going to take a long time for them to fix it back up."

"I know, but they're going to fix it up for summer. Right?"

"I'm afraid it's probably going to take longer than that."

"Mom, should we be doing this at all? It could be very upsetting. Y'know, for him," Lacey said.

"Lacey, I think it's important for all of us to see we're not the only ones going through this, and a lot of people have it a lot worse than we do. We're actually pretty lucky."

"Lucky," Lacey mocked.

"You might think so after you see what these poor people are going through."

"Don't say that!"

"Don't say what?"

"Poor people. I am so tired of being one of these poor people."

"I'm sorry."

"Do you think any of the rides will be open? Don't they open on Easter?" Jake asked.

"Open? They're at the bottom of the ocean," Lacey said.

"Even Stillwalk Manor?" Jake asked about the popular haunted house at the end of the Casino amusement pier. "I thought it was just the roller coaster that blew into the ocean."

"Jake, honey, I guess I should have warned you," Polly said. "Casino Pier was pretty much destroyed."

"Oh. They're going to put it all back, right?" Jake said, slipping his thumb into his mouth.

"I hope so. But it's going to take time, no matter what happens."

"Will we be able to see the mansion in the water?"

"I don't think so. The pictures I saw online only showed the roller coaster sticking above the waves."

"Are the stands on the boardwalk still there? I want fries from Curley's," Jake said.

"Some of them are there, I guess," Polly said, as she threaded the car around a large sand bar that took up half the road coming off the bridge. "But I don't think they'll be open. The houses and other buildings over here were hit a lot harder than our neighborhood, if you can believe it. Some were completely swept away by waves..."

"Was it what they call Sue-Mommy?" Jake interrupted.

Polly and Lacey both cracked up laughing. Between giggles, Lacey corrected, "Tsunami."

"And no," Polly said. "It wasn't a tsunami. It was a storm surge. You see the ocean kind of took a short cut. Instead of going around the oceanfront towns, it cut right through one of them. That's why the bay spilled over, too, and we flooded. But over here, things are a lot worse. Buildings are still falling apart, and they're surrounded by huge piles of sand."

"Aren't they being fixed?" Jake asked.

"Yes, but it's off to a slow start because the damage is a lot worse," Polly said. "Many areas still don't have the power back on yet, and there's so much debris everywhere that workers still can't go up some of the streets."

"I thought people came back here two weeks after the storm," Lacey said. "That was almost five months ago. What have they been doing all this time?"

"That was just so they could see what the situation was with their houses and to retrieve whatever valuables they could find,"

Polly said. "I read on the Asbury Park Press website that residents were brought in on buses. Some of them found stuff in their yards, like wedding rings and yearbooks, that came from houses a mile away."

"So we're supposed to consider ourselves lucky?" Lacey asked. "Like, at least we got to look at our stuff before having to throw most of it out?"

"This has been bad for everyone," Polly said. "Don't you remember? A lot of the families who have been going to our church lately came from over here."

"I get to be an ambassador at Sunday school," Jake said. "My partner is Joey, who said he used to be able to see the Ferris wheel from his bedroom window on Stork Island."

"You mean Pelican Island, right at the bottom of the bridge, on your way into Seaside," Polly said. "We just drove through there. Joey and his mother are staying with his grandparents over in Manchester until their house is fixed."

"Do you think Joey will invite me to a sleepover when they move back home?" Jake asked. "I want to see the rides from his window."

"I'm sure he will," Polly said. "But don't ask him about it any time soon. His mother was telling me last Sunday that it looks like their house will have to be torn down because it was too damaged to fix. Building a new house could take a long time."

"Great, so that means we're going to be stuck with all these extra people at church forever," Lacey said, groaning.

"Lacey, that's not a very Christian attitude," her mother admonished.

"I'm sorry," Lacey said, and she meant it. "It's just I used to know everyone at church, and now there are all these strangers. And I don't want to be an ambassador. It seems like all we do is talk about the storm."

"Well, that probably can't be helped, considering the situation," Polly said. "Just give it time."

"I guess," Lacey said. Without thinking, she stabbed her left thumbnail into her ring finger. "Do you really think Curley's will be closed? I was hoping for some fries. Last summer, I got them every Thursday when my friends came over for the fireworks."

"Cross your fingers," Polly said putting the car in park. "But just try to remember, Sandy didn't happen just to us. We're not coming here to sightsee. I want you to understand our situation is just a small piece of the puzzle."

"Yeah, I know," Lacey said, bored with the daily lesson.

Chapter Twenty-Nine:
Mid-Day Sunday, April 7, 2013

"Lacey, aren't you getting out?"

"What?"

"We're here. Aren't you getting out?"

"Oh, yeah," she said, releasing her seatbelt and reaching for the door. Her mother had parked in the municipal lot across from the water park in Seaside Heights where Lacey went a few times every summer. But as she looked at the park now, she wondered if she'd ridden those slides for the last time. Several tubes hung limply, cut off in midair, and others were rising out of sand piles like strange abstract sculptures.

"Shit," Lacey said.

"Lacey!"

"What?"

"Language."

"Oh, sorry," she said. Normally, she would have argued about her mother's prudish ways. C'mon, Jake was hearing those words from other kids at school anyway, and her mother knew that's how Lacey talked when she was with her friends. But, looking around first at the water park, and then at the collapsed bungalows, Lacey was too stunned to speak.

Crap, the storm had been more than five months ago and over here it looked like it happened yesterday. As they walked east toward the Boardwalk a block away, they passed what is usually one of the most expensive parking lots with its prime location just across from the backside of some Boardwalk arcades, but it looked like it might never see another tourist's dollar. The entire lot was piled high with miscellaneous business signs and local landmarks, like a 12-foot-tall Alfred E. Newman, a few oversized crane games and the cars of various rides, including a munchkin-sized motorcycle and a weather-faded red boat with a string bell that kept ringing as the wind blew.

"Lacey. Lacey. Lacey!" her mother's shouts cut through her daze.

"Yeah, Mom."

"I'm trying to talk to you. Jake wants to go see the Jet Star roller coaster over in the water. Are you coming?"

"Yeah, I'm… I'll meet you over there," Lacey said. "I just want to walk around a little."

"Okay, don't take too long."

Lacey wandered across the street into an arcade that was celebrating its anniversary with a giant "50 years" banner and for no reason that she could articulate began to bawl. She walked past some little kids playing Skeeball and watched for a while. She loved the game ever since a guy who worked there one time showed her how to get a forty or fifty with nearly every ball by rolling it down the side rather than the middle.

But she couldn't watch for long because the tears just kept coming. She passed a virtual-reality roller coaster simulator and headed to the front door and Boardwalk. But when she got to what was normally the business's main entrance, she was stopped by a large plate glass window with no entrances or exits.

At first, she was annoyed not to have access to the Boardwalk, but then she looked more closely. There was no Boardwalk. Damn. She'd forgotten that. The storm had ripped apart the popular oceanfront promenade board by board.

Now as she stood at the window, she could see only sand and the ocean in the near distance. The sand, which was supposed to stop about twenty-five feet away, just went right up to the window. There was no walkway, and even more surprisingly, no five-foot drop onto the beach. It was just smooth sand straight across.

Lacey stared out and cried. Rather than wipe away the tears, she balled her hands into fists and thrust them into her front pockets. Then, she looked to the left where the Casino amusement pier should be, but it was mostly gone. Looking right, she saw that the Funtown Park Pier about a half mile away was also in ruins.

It's no wonder they had a mandatory evacuation here, Lacey mused, thinking back to the day of the storm and the Toms River police cars announcing "a voluntary evacuation notice" in her neighborhood. As she stared at the devastation, Lacey remembered hearing Gov. Christie on the radio that day warning anyone under mandatory evacuation that if they stayed behind there would be no one to rescue them if they changed their minds during the height of the storm.

Lacey had later heard recorded 9-1-1 phone calls where people were holed up in their attics screaming and crying that they were going to die. They called in terror when the storm water rose above the second story and was still rising. She'd also heard a girl at school talk about swimming through the flood waters with her handicapped grandmother tied to a raft to reach a National Guard rescue truck.

Standing there, Lacey became aggressively angry with her mother. *Why did she bring me here? She knows I don't like to think about San...the storm. Let everyone else do that. God knows that's all anyone else ever wants to talk about. I'm just moving on.*

But, of course, staring at the missing Boardwalk, a staple of her life much like air or water, she couldn't push the storm out of her thoughts. She considered all the stories she'd heard of what people were going through since the storm, leaned her forehead against the unwelcomed plate glass window, and stood there, shaking and crying.

In years past, staring at the ocean always made her feel happy. After about 10 minutes, she reached into her pocket and pulled out a tissue. After examining it to make sure it was just crumpled up and not used, she wiped her eyes and headed back the way she came to go meet her mother and Jake.

She was surprised to find them in good moods, chatting wildly about what it would be like to ride the Jet Star in the ocean where it now sat and rumors that the mayor was considering leaving it there as a landmark.

"It's so good that they've finally opened it up over there, and people can start to recover," Polly said.

"Are you kidding me? Did you look around?" Lacey snapped, biting into a slice of pepperoni pizza back at a local Silverton pizzeria. They had planned to eat in Seaside but couldn't find an open business. The few that had been open earlier in the day had to close when they ran out of supplies.

"I know, but at least now they can get in there," Polly said. "A lot of those homes haven't been cleaned out yet. Nobody's done any mold remediation. It feels good to see that we're starting to make progress."

Progress? Are you kidding? That's the worst disaster I've ever seen. Lacey didn't voice her anger. She'd missed her mother when she was in Florida but now wondered why. *The woman is clueless!*

Lacey felt like the trip to Seaside had been a personal attack. In Silverton, if you didn't look at the mud in the street or the piles of garbage in front of peoples' homes, you could almost convince yourself that everything was fine. In fact, at night, when she would take walks through the abandoned streets, Lacey would look at the houses, knowing they were gutted inside and many had no drywall up to four to six feet, and think the neighborhood looked the same. It was as if people had up and left for no reason at all.

Sometimes she would tell herself that it was a poltergeist, not a storm, that had visited the area, and somehow that made her feel better.

As the day wore on, she equated their trip over to Seaside with an unwanted intervention. *Polly knows better than to make me face Sandy. How dare she!*

But as she ate her pizza and listened while her mother and brother shared stories of Disney World both from this trip and previous ones, she began to mellow.

Eventually, Lacey admitted to herself that she liked being out to dinner with them. She liked, even loved, her family. Actually, she was a pretty lucky kid. After all, she just got back from Disney World.

Instantly her alter ego fought back at the complacency. *Oh, yeah? Then why don't I feel lucky? That wasn't Disney World. It smelled like popcorn and cotton candy like Disney World does. It had rides that make your heart pound, bushes shaped like Disney characters and towels folded in the shape of Mickey like Disney World, but that wasn't Disney World!*

Disney World is an amazing, fun place where all your cares melt away, where you are always living in the moment for the next OOH or AAAHHH experience. That wasn't Disney World! It was some strange facsimile where you laughed and smiled with Jake and Grandma Irene. But, let's face it, if they weren't around, you weren't there. You were wherever you've been for the last five months... nowhere.

Chapter Thirty:
Dinnertime Sunday, April 7, 2013

"MacGyver, you've been very quiet the last two days. Didn't you enjoy your trip?" his mother asked over a spaghetti dinner they shared at the kitchen counter.

"Yeah, sure it was great. We had a lot of fun. It's just that I didn't..."

"Hey," his mother cut him off. "What sort of game were you and Lacey playing? Why did you have her call here so close to midnight? You know how important it is that your father gets his rest."

"What? I didn't..." MacGyver stopped himself from answering and pretended to be struggling to get a particularly stubborn strand of the pasta onto his fork. "Uh, we were just messing around."

"Well, next time you're messing around, do it earlier in the day. If I didn't know you two better, I might have worried about where you were. That's not a nice thing to do to your poor mother when you're so far away," his Mom mock scolded him. "How is Lacey anyway?"

"Ummm. Fine... Hey, are there any more meatballs?"

"Sorry, I only had a little meat, and Dad's disability check doesn't come until Wednesday," his mother said, looking down so that MacGyver could see the inch-long brown roots that supported her otherwise frosted hair.

"No problem. Can I please be excused?" MacGyver asked, afraid if he continued talking to his mom he would definitely blow his cover. The last thing he wanted to do was reveal that he never got to see Lacey, and instead of spending time with Lacey and Polly, he'd attended all-nighters in Ashley's condemned house.

"Sure, just check on your father please and make sure he doesn't need anything before you disappear into Mario land."

"Mario land? Never heard it called that before. Anyway, I've been playing Zelda."

"Glad you cleared that one up for me. Go ahead before I make you do the dishes."

MacGyver cleared his place and returned the milk and other perishables to the refrigerator before he left the room. As he reached for the butter, his mother touched his arm and looked up into his big brown eyes. "I know you weren't gone that long, but I missed you. You really are a big help around here."

Rather than answer, he shrugged and walked off to check on his dad. The growl-like sounds of his father's snoring reached him before he could peek into his parents' bedroom. But, rather than turn away, he slipped quietly into the room and stood frozen for a minute, wondering how his father could possibly get comfortable enough to sleep in the traction contraption that imprisoned him.

MacGyver and his parents had only been in town a few days when his father found a Craigslist ad under "labor" that promised $800 cash for two days of landscaping work. But the ad that sounded like a call to help some homeowner with heavy yardwork was placed by a tree-trimming company that needed an extra hand to tear out and cart away tree stumps weighing a few hundred pounds each.

After the first day, Richard Anderson was tired and stumbling around the house nearly crippled. MacGyver's mom insisted he not go back, but the agreement he signed was very clear. He'd only be paid minimum wage unless he worked both days, and besides, they needed the money while he searched for permanent employment.

Midway through the second day, as Mr. Anderson struggled to drag a 400-pound tree stump, he heard something snap in his back. The pain was too great to straighten up. His boss was very compassionate and never even complained that he could no longer work. In fact, he drove Richard Anderson to the emergency room – four hours later when the crew was finished with the day's work. As it turned out, his dad had torn his spinal erector muscles so extensively that doctors said it would take months of traction and bed rest for them to heal.

That was months ago. Since then, his dad had become incredibly depressed, hardly spoke and barely ate. As MacGyver stood silently watching the man who first taught him how to build a go-cart and then how to rebuild the engine in his PT Cruiser, he barely recognized him. His dad looked a lot more like his grandfather than the dad he'd always been able to depend upon.

As MacGyver was about to turn away and head to his room, he noticed his dad's blanket had slipped to the floor, so he bent down and gently placed it over his dad's emaciated form. MacGyver thought of all the times his dad had tucked him in over the years.

I guess, now it's my turn, he thought, before he turned and headed for the door.

Back in his room, MacGyver reached for his "vacation valise," instead of the N64 controller. In what he thought of as a very streamlined version of his mom's "getting ready for the school week" routine that had been a Sunday night standard for most of his life, MacGyver dumped his dirty vacation clothes on the floor and returned his never touched school books to their home.

Then, he lay on his back and thought about Silverton and his friends. The trip had definitely not gone as planned, and it wasn't just that Lacey wasn't there. First of all, the whole idea was that he would have a chance to be "home" for a while. But the Jersey Shore he returned to bore little resemblance to the place where he grew up. His block was deserted. Lacey's house was gutted. And his friends all seemed a little off.

Sure it was fun to party in Ashley's vacant house, but why did everyone have to drink so much? It was as if there were no joy there anymore. *What the hell happened to the world?* he thought. *Will things ever be normal again?*

He pulled out his phone, stared at pictures from his trip, and later, Lacey. Eventually, he fell asleep, spending the night in his clothes and on top of the bed his mother had made.

Chapter Thirty-One:
Around 9:30 p.m., Sunday, April 7, 2013

After Jake went to bed, Polly knocked on Lacey's door but didn't wait for an answer.

"I need to talk to you," Polly said, staring down at Lacey who was lying on her air mattress and talking to friends on Facebook.

"I'm kind of busy, Mom. I haven't spoken to my friends in over a week. Can this wait?"

"No, it can't," her mother said and folded down the laptop screen.

"Geez, Mom, you could at least have let me finish my conversation."

Polly eased herself down to sit on the air mattress next to her annoyed daughter. As she did, she noticed the red bumps on Lacey's skin were all but faded away. "Does it still itch?"

"Not, that bad," Lacey said, sitting up. "The prescription is really helping, but I don't think the lotion does crap except make me smell like tar and exhaust fumes."

"Lacey, could you please start watching your language?"

"What? Exhaust fumes?"

"Crap," her mother said patiently.

Lacey rolled her eyes. "That's not even a curse, but whatever. I'm sorry," she said, hoping her mother would then leave her room. When she didn't, Lacey added, "So what's up?"

"Why don't you tell me?" Polly Freshet said, studying Lacey's face as if the answer to some all-important question could be found there.

"Oh, we're going to play some sort of guessing game. Mom, if you're just looking for company, can you call one of your own friends? I really need to catch up on what happened around here while I was gone."

"Lacey, watch your mouth. Why don't you tell me what's going on with you lately? Is there anything you were supposed to tell me?"

Lacey thought for a minute. "Not really. But I was thinking, can I use the money I was saving to get a car to get a new phone? I really can't go any longer without one."

"Lacey, forget about the phone," her mother snapped uncharacteristically. "I got a letter last week that we need to talk about."

"A letter?" Lacey said, looking up at her mother and trying not to give her true fears away. Of course, she never had much of what Lady Gaga called a "Poker Face." Besides, her right foot started tapping uncontrollably as it always did when she'd been caught hiding something.

"Lacey, why don't you tell me what it's about?"

Lacey sat quietly twirling her hair with her left index finger for about twenty seconds. She guessed incorrectly that her best shot at getting off easy was trying to be cute. "You're the one who read it, Mom. Why don't you tell me?"

Polly sighed and blew out a stream of air. Her chest heaved, and she looked at her daughter with hurt eyes. That's what really got Lacey. *Why did they have to be hurt eyes? Why couldn't they be angry eyes? Angry was so much easier to deal with.*

"Okay, Lacey, let's get to it then. From what I gathered, you are not only failing three, possibly four, classes, you've been intercepting letters and phone calls from the school. And, you've been making everyone think that I am just too busy to what? To care? To notice? Is that what's been happening?"

Lacey jumped up and began pacing but didn't say a word.

"What the hell is going on with you? Why didn't you tell me? How am I supposed to help you if you don't even tell me what's happening? How could you make your guidance counselor and all of your teachers believe that I'm too busy at work to even come in for a conference?"

Lacey said nothing. It wasn't that she was being particularly defiant or standing her ground or anything. She just had nothing to say.

"Well, answer me."

Lacey stood still, looked at her mother and bit her lip. "Which question?"

"All of them!" her mother yelled.

"Shh, you'll wake Jake," Lacey said.

"Lacey, talk to me. What is going on?"

Silence.

"Lacey..."

"I don't know."

"What do you mean you don't know? What does that mean? How could you lie to me like this?"

"Technically, I wasn't lying," Lacey said, pacing again.

"How could you be so deceptive?"

"Now, wait a minute," Lacey stopped pacing and looked right into her mother's eyes. "You're the one who was being deceptive."

"What?"

"Yes, you're the liar!" Lacey screamed, hearing herself turn into a screaming maniac, and someone she didn't like being, but not knowing how to stop it. How dare her mother act like *she* wasn't the one playing games here? Did she think Lacey was stupid?

"When did I lie?" Polly said incredulously, standing up to meet her daughter's gaze.

"All day!" Lacey screamed. "All day! First, with Grandma and then over in Seaside and at the pizza place. We have this big family day. And, me like a jerk, I'm enjoying it…to a point. I don't even feel that bad that I'm not out with my friends. And the whole time, you're lying to me, just putting on a show for the kid you really care about, right?"

"What?" Polly was genuinely confused.

"I mean so little to you that you couldn't even bring this up when I first got home. You had to act like everything was wonderful for Jake. We always have to make things as normal as we can for Jake! Try not to upset Jake too much! You don't even really care about me, do you?"

"Lacey, you're being ridiculous."

"Am I? Are you sure? Would you even be so upset if it wasn't that the teachers all think you're too busy to come to school? You don't even really care how I'm doing; do you? This is all about how *you* look and your precious reputation."

"Lacey, that's crazy. Where would you even get an idea like that?"

"From you, Mom. From you!" she screamed as she ran from the room, crying. Flying down the stairs, Lacey called back, "I'm going for a walk. Don't follow me."

"No, you're…."

Lacey was out the front door before Polly could say "not."

Chapter Thirty-Two:
Immediately Following, Sunday, April 7, 2013

"Damn. Fuckin' shit," Lacey said as she headed toward her backyard then abruptly turned and began half walking, half jogging down the street. The night air was cool against her bare arms.

"How dare she!" she screamed to the empty street. The Freshets were the only people in a two-block area who had moved back in, so at night, once the workers had called it a day, the block was deserted.

"Fuck you!" she yelled. Her own angry voice made her stop in her tracks, feeling suddenly embarrassed and kind of stupid even though no one could hear her.

As if the comfort of the bay were calling her, Lacey resumed walking, slower now, taking special notice of the few homes between her house and the Beach Club. The place was such a mish-mosh. One house was nearly ready for its occupants to return; another hadn't been touched yet. A third was high up on pallets waiting to be lowered back onto its raised foundation. And, then, there was a vacant lot where the Connors had lived for sixty years.

Tired and confused, Lacey's first instinct was to sit on the familiar sands outside the Beach Club, but the gate was locked. Even though climbing around the fence end that jutted out over the harbor was something she had done thousands of times, she couldn't summon the energy.

Instead, she headed to the Rock Throwing Place.

I just want to go home, Lacey thought, even though she knew that made no sense. She was home. But she wasn't.

I just want... I just want, Lacey thought. *What the fuck do I want?* As she walked the unfamiliar, familiar street, she wished she had her phone and could call MacGyver. She wished she hadn't missed MacGyver's visit. She wished her friends were back home. She wished she wasn't disappointing her mother. Fuck, she just wished she wasn't such a disappointment.

At the Rock Throwing Place, she stood in the absolute darkness that comes from no streetlights and no neighbors, the kind of darkness one encounters on a camping trip in the Pine Barrens or deep in a cave.

The cold night air gave rise to tiny goose bumps all up and down her bare arms, but she ignored them. Climbing onto the bulkhead, Lacey paced the narrow wooden walkway as if she were an Olympic gymnast noodling around on a balance beam.

As she paced, her stomach clenched and her hands fisted up into balls. Her eyes began to sting, but no tears came. And then, she just stopped and stood still. She squinted across the bay toward Seaside, but, of course, there were no Ferris wheel lights, nothing to see. Here, like everywhere else, nothing.

She looked down where she knew the bay must be but couldn't distinguish it from the night sky. *Everywhere*, she thought, *nothing*. Then, she stepped off the bulkhead into the darkness.

Chapter Thirty-Three:
Immediately following, Sunday, April 7, 2013

"Owww! Shit! Oww!" Lacey screamed after clawing her way up to the water's surface and pushing her head up for air.

Her right hand grabbed the bulkhead, and she tried to pull herself up. But it seemed she had gained about a thousand pounds. She could barely hold her head above the water's surface. It was as if some sort of sea monster were pulling her down, and the grip was not only strong, it was painful.

Suddenly aware of a burning sensation in her left calf and ankle, Lacey tried to throw all her weight against the bulkhead, but she hardly budged and the effort caused her to scream out in pain. As she yelled, her right hand started to lose its grasp, and she clawed her fingers into the wood, sending a splinter under the nail of her index finger and causing her to lose her fragile hold on terra firma.

As her arm slapped against the water's surface, splashing her in the face, Lacey finally realized her foot was held in place by something really heavy. Every time she tried to free herself, she was not only wrenching her ankle but also pushing some sharp object deeper into the flesh of her leg.

Shit, what am I tied up in, some abandoned anchor line? Lacey thought. But that thought disappeared as quickly as it came. Rope wouldn't hurt like that. *Maybe a shark?* Somewhere way back in her mind, she thought she could hear some internal smartass let out a loud guffaw. But another part of her conjured up horror-movie images of scaly beasts with large teeth. That part of her was damned scared, and it wanted out of this mess RIGHT NOW.

Thinking back on years of swim lessons at the Y and with her teeth chattering, Lacey reluctantly relinquished her tenuous grip on the bulkhead. Instead, she began crisscrossing her arms in the frigid water before her and bicycle pumping her one free leg, doing a lame imitation of treading water.

Relax, she told herself. *Take time to think this through. There's something down there alright, but it's clearly not a damn shark or a killer snake. This isn't some fucking movie!*

"Help! Help! Help!" she started to scream, instantaneously ignoring her own advice.

"Fire! Fire!" Her automatic distress call finally was enough to make her actually laugh, and she managed to calm down. This was good, she thought, because her senseless flailing would do little to help and could potentially accelerate her drowning. Her mom had taught her when she was very small, that if she were ever really in danger and wanted to get people's attention quickly, calls of "fire" are far more effective than shouts of "help," which merely indicate that someone else is facing treachery.

Of course, in this case, getting someone's attention would require attracting either a random police officer driving around searching for looters or the aforementioned looters.

Lacey suddenly couldn't wait to tell her mom that even shouts of "fire" have little effect if no one else is currently living in your ZIP code.

As she treaded water, Lacey considered her options. Even though her swimming skills were excellent, she wouldn't be able to stay afloat that long in this cold. Also, no one was coming to help her, so waiting for a rescue seemed pointless. That left only one option. She would have to dive back under the surface to see what was gripping her leg.

Okay, count to 10, and then go under, she told herself. *One, two, three, four.* Then she went. She was too cold, scared and in too much pain to wait any longer.

Holding her breath, she opened her eyes but without effect. The ebony of the night sky was simply mirrored below the surface. Instead, Lacey climbed her hands down her own body, starting at her waist. At her left knee, she found what felt like a barbecue rack wedged against a really hard and immovable, twisted object. She fumbled around there for a few seconds then surfaced, gulping in air before plunging below once again.

Kicking with her right foot and pushing with both arms, she bent the rack up and finally freed her leg, which was throbbing. She was distracted momentarily by an absurd thought that was probably true, but useless nonetheless. *That couldn't have been a barbecue rack. You can't bend them by hand. An oven rack, maybe? Where the hell did that come from?*

Who gives a shit? screamed the part of her that was still scared to death. *Swim somewhere!* Lacey couldn't tell if she was bleeding, but that terrified voice in the back of her mind was trying to raise the alarm about how a shark might sense her injury and attack. There were no answering guffaws this time. This ship was going down and that inner voice had made a run for it.

Of course, Lacey knew sharks don't hang out in the bay. *Oh yeah, but wasn't Jaws based on some real idiots who got eaten at the Jersey Shore?*

"Focus," she told herself and the night air, as she took just one freestyle stroke and reached up to grab hold of the bulkhead to pull herself out.

"Oww," she cried as she tried to put weight against her left foot and climb out the way she had done dozens of times before. Even though the Rock Throwing Place was a posted No Swimming zone, Lacey and her friends had jumped in here more than a few times over the years, especially when the Snobs weren't home.

"Shit," Lacey said, lifting her head up to the heavens. "Really?"

She lay with her head resting on the street end for what seemed an eternity but was probably just a minute or two. It was clear she was not going to be able to pull herself out, not without further injuring her throbbing and painful left leg.

Lacey's teeth chattered, and she started worrying about hypothermia. How was she going to get out? The answer wasn't a good one. She would need shallow water and a sloping beach.

She slipped back into the icy water and started to breast stroke the block and half to the Beach Club. It was a good thing she would know the way in her sleep. There was no scoping out her surroundings or watching her path. Everything was black.

After a while, Lacey thought she must be approaching shore because she could hear the waves hitting the beach. This wasn't the ocean, of course, and to most people the sound of the bay water lapping up against the sand would be barely distinguishable from other night noises. But Lacey could hear it well enough. She had spent a lot of time sitting on that beach, looking at and listening to the water

That's good, I must be getting close to the floating dock, Lacey thought. Then she remembered that the dock, which she dove off so many times, had washed ashore during the storm and broken into pieces. *Shit,* she thought. *Of course.*

Well, I'm still close enough. I can make it. But with her one leg virtually useless, Lacey's shoulders ached from the long swim, and her lungs burned. Exercise hadn't been high on her personal agenda lately. Hell, it never was.

Exhaustion washed over her, and she began slipping further into the water with each stroke. But then, out of nowhere, she heard something different. *Is that barking? Yes, it is.* That scruffy-looking Golden Retriever she had played with on the first nice day of the year. *Where is he?* Somewhere on the beach, from the sound of it. Then it stopped suddenly. *That's right, run for help, Lassie!*

Timmy fell down the well, Lacey joked to herself grimly, then seriously wondered whether that little bit of dark humor would be her last. *That figures. No profound last words from Lacey Freshet,* she thought, as the last of her strength gave out.

Lacey felt herself slip beneath the surface. She wanted to fight harder, but she was so tired and her limbs just wouldn't obey her commands. *I'm going down,* she thought, too exhausted to feel anxious.

But then she felt the dog by her side and sinking his teeth into her shirt. He immediately reversed direction and started swimming for shore. Almost without realizing what was going on, Lacey wrapped her other arm around the dog's middle, which was swelling and contracting rapidly with the animal's exertions.

They reached the beach so quickly that Lacey was caught by surprise, and she was rewarded with a mouth full of sand when her knees hit bottom first, causing her to flop face-down on the shore. The dog made landfall much more elegantly, as its legs switched from swimming to walking without missing a beat. After shaking himself thoroughly, he came down to the water's edge to nuzzle Lacey. She wrapped her arms around his head and held on for a long minute. "Thank you," she said. "I don't know where you came from, but thank you."

Lacey then crawled all the way out of the water and collapsed on her back, sucking in large lungfuls of cool night air. *I almost died,* she realized. *How stupid would that be, drowning at the Beach Club, where I actually learned to swim?* Suddenly aware that she was cold, Lacey looked around to see that the dog was gone.

Chapter Thirty-Four:
1 a.m. Monday, April 8, 2013

"Thanks, Mom," Lacey said as Polly handed her a cardboard cup filled with hot chocolate. "What, no whipped cream?" she joked.

"Sorry. That isn't an option on the hospital vending machine."

"No, really, thanks Mom. I'm sorry about all this," Lacey said, taking in the sight of her mother with her hair thrown in a sloppy bun and no makeup on.

"Shhh. Not now, baby. I'm just glad you're going to be all right."

"We don't know that yet," Lacey cautioned.

"What do you mean?"

"The x-rays aren't back. My ankle still might be broken, and I'm pretty sure these 22 stitches are going to ruin any chances I have of being a runway model."

"Oh, honey, are the stitches really bothering you? Are you worried about the scar? Not that you're definitely going to have one. But, we could call in a plastic surgeon tomorrow or later. Whatever you want."

"You heard the doctor, Mom. That would not be covered by insurance and would likely cost thousands."

"Lacey, if a scar is really going to bother you, we could do that. The hell with the insurance. What's a few thousand dollars?" Polly said.

"Last I heard, it was the difference between putting the bathroom tile back the way we had it or painting the walls," Lacey said.

"Oh, stop, sweetheart. Besides you said you like the paint."

"I'm kidding, Mom. Kidding."

"No, really, if you're worried about a scar, we can have them call in a plastic surgeon right now."

"It's okay, Mom. I was just joking. Let it go. Hey, why don't you go home and get me some clothes. I'm not going to leave here in these hospital gowns. They're a little too revealing," Lacey joked.

"Count yourself lucky. They normally only give you one of those gowns, and it can get rather drafty," Polly said with a laugh. "Did I ever tell you about the time I had tests done at the Mayo Clinic in Minnesota?"

"No, Mom. Somehow, I missed that story."

"Well, that's because it was long before you were born. I was just out of law school, and I got horribly ill. My glands, my face and my neck were all terribly swollen, and no one could figure it out."

"Uh, huh."

"Anyway we had these friends who were millionaires and mega-donors to the Mayo Clinic, so after I had seen like twenty doctors and was still sick six months later, they set it up for me to be examined in Minnesota."

"Uh, huh."

"Well, the first set of doctors were still stumped, so they suggested I see this specialist and they sent me over to see him. So there I am in my slippers and robe – and thank God for that robe – and they send me over to this specialist, but they don't tell me they're putting me in a cab and sending me to a medical arts building a couple of blocks away, just a regular doctor's office."

"What?"

"Oh, yeah, so I'm there in this waiting room looking like some sort of mental patient while everyone else is fully dressed."

"You're kidding me. What did you do?"

"Nothing. Made no excuses. Never said a word. Just read a *People* magazine and pretended everyone dresses this way back where I come from. I was mortified, but in the long run, it gave me one of my favorite stories to tell. Life's like that you know."

"Yes, Mom, I know. Comedy is nothing more than tragedy plus time. You've told me."

"Yup, and life…

"Is messy," they said together, and both smiled.

A nurse came into the room carrying x-rays, which he left on the counter. "The doctor will be in in a minute," he said.

"Is it broken?" Lacey asked.

"I'm sorry the doctor will be in shortly to review the results."

"Just tell me if it's broken," Lacey said, earning silence as a reply.

"Pleassse…"

The dark-haired nurse who didn't look that much older than Lacey smiled. "I'm sorry. I'm not allowed to discuss patient x-rays," he said, adding, "That's above my pay grade."

But as he reasserted the hospital's policies, he shook his head no.

"Great," Lacey said. "Mom, why don't you go get my clothes so we can get out of here?"

"Oh, honey, I'm sorry. You're not being released tonight," the nurse said.

"Why not?" Lacey asked.

"They're holding you at least overnight for observation," he said, patting her arm gently. "I'll get the doctor."

A tall woman with curly red hair, wearing a white lab coat over a blue dress and with a stethoscope around her neck entered the room.

"Dr. Tompkins," Polly said, "I was going to get Lacey some clothes she can wear home."

"Whoa, slow down," the doctor said. "We're not there yet, Mrs. Freshet."

"Ms.," Polly mumbled half under her breath.

"What?" Dr. Tompkins asked as she placed Lacey's x-rays on the light board and turned on the light.

"Never mind," Polly said. "So, her ankle is all right? Right?"

"It appears to be a bad sprain. Of course, sprains can often be more painful than a break," the doctor said, pointing to the picture. "As you can see, there's a lot of inflammation. That will subside in a day or so. John, I mean Nurse Singh, will be back in shortly to wrap it."

"Okay," Polly said as the doctor turned to Lacey. "On a scale of one to ten, with ten being the most unbearable pain ever, how much does it hurt right now?"

"About a seven," Lacey said.

"We're going to hook you up to an IV, and we'll give you something for the pain," Dr. Tompkins said.

"IV? Wouldn't it be better to give her some pills or a shot, so I can get her home?" Polly asked.

"Mrs. Freshet," the doctor said, adopting a soothing tone. "Lacey still needs to be seen by another doctor."

"Another doctor?" Polly said. "Why? Is it because of the water? Are you worried about tetanus? What?"

"Tetanus? Mom, you're crazy," Lacey said.

"Actually, that's a valid concern, but your shots are up to date," Dr. Tompkins said, turning to give Lacey her full attention. "Lacey, before you fell into the water, were you feeling dizzy or faint?"

"I told you before," Lacey said. "I didn't fall into the bay. I stepped into it."

"You stepped in," the doctor said.

"What?" asked Polly. "You told me you fell in."

"No, Mom, I didn't. You just assumed that's what happened, and we were so busy wiping up the blood and wrapping me in blankets, that I never really had a chance to tell you," Lacey said as she twirled a strand of her hair around her left index finger.

"Tell me what?" Polly asked, staring right into her daughter's eyes.

"I didn't fall, Mom. I walked in."

"You mean you jumped?"

"Not exactly. I just, you know, walked off the bulkhead."

"But why?" Polly asked.

"Why were you trying to hurt yourself?" Dr. Tompkins asked.

"I wasn't trying to hurt myself!" Lacey said, as anger rose ever so slightly in her voice.

"Okay, then what?" asked the doctor. "Did you really want to take a swim?"

"Yes! No!" Lacey said. "It wasn't about going swimming. I just wanted to…I just wanted to….I don't know. I don't know."

"Lacey, did you want to drown?"

"That's ridiculous. I'm an excellent swimmer. The water there is only about four feet deep in low tide, six in high," Lacey said, color rising in her cheeks as she looked pleadingly at the doctor. "And I wasn't thinking about anything like that."

"Did you want to hurt yourself?"

"No! How was I supposed to know there was an oven down there? It wasn't there last summer. There's a lot of crazy stuff in the bay now, but I had forgotten about that."

"I understand," the doctor said.

"You do? What do you understand?" asked Polly. "I don't understand."

"Me neither," said Lacey quietly.

"What do you mean?" asked the doctor.

"I don't know why I stepped off the bulkhead."

"Are you sure you didn't fall?" Polly asked, hopefully.

"No, Mom," Lacey said. "I do remember deciding to walk off, but that's all I thought. I looked out at the water, which was hard to distinguish from the night sky, and I decided I wanted to go in. That's it."

"But, Lacey, you could have been hurt a lot worse than you were!" Polly said. "I could have lost you," Polly said, sinking into a chair at the bedside.

"I'm sorry, Mom. I guess I just wanted to feel. I wanted to feel… I wanted to feel…something, just something," Lacey said as tears fell down her cheeks and her mother reached over and wiped them away.

"Lately, I haven't felt anything. I guess I've just been kind of numb, like the world is going on behind a thick distorted glass window and I can't get to it. It doesn't look right, and I can't touch it. It's just way too far away. And I guess I just wanted to *feel* something."

"Mrs. Freshet, could you step out of the room for a minute while I talk to Lacey privately?"

Polly grabbed Lacey's hand, sending an unspoken message that she had no intention of leaving her baby's side.

But Lacey really liked the idea of talking to the doctor.

"Mom," she said, "why don't you go check on Jake over at Laura's and come back with some clothes?"

"Actually, Mrs. Freshet, why don't you go home for the night and bring Lacey back a few things in the morning. But don't bring any shoes with shoelaces or drawstring pants."

Stronger Than the Storm

"What?" Polly said. "Since when can't you have shoes with shoelaces? Wait. Dr. Tompkins? Dr. Tompkins, are you telling me that you're admitting Lacey to...?"

"We will be admitting Lacey for observation," Dr. Tompkins said. "If you wouldn't mind, I would like to talk to her alone for a few minutes now."

"Okay. I mean, if that's okay with Lacey," she said and left the room, looking back once at her daughter.

Chapter Thirty-Five:
Mid-day Tuesday, April 9, 2013

"Mom, I swear to you. I didn't try to kill myself. I don't do drugs. And I'm not flippin' depressed," Lacey said as she begged her mother to please take her home rather than sign her in for "voluntary" commitment in the psych ward.

Sitting next to her daughter's hospital bed, Polly took Lacey's hand. "Honey, I believe you. I know you don't do drugs and you weren't thinking about killing yourself when you jumped…"

"Stepped," Lacey corrected.

"Into the water," Polly continued. "But the doctors are right. You probably are depressed or suffering from…"

"I am not," Lacey growled through clenched teeth.

"From post-traumatic stress disorder."

"Mom, just use the initials! PTSD. And, come on, do I look like I just got back from Afghanistan?" Lacey asked.

"War isn't the only trauma in the world," Polly said.

"Mom, I want to go back to school. I want to hang out with my friends. Maybe I wasn't depressed when I got here, but I sure will be if you make me stay in a psych ward."

"Honey, it's not even up to me."

"Of course it is. You're the mom."

"The doctors said if I don't sign the forms, we would have to go before a judge. And I would have to convince him that I know better than the two children's psychologists and a psychiatrist who are recommending commit… that you stay."

"What?!" Lacey said. "But you're my legal guardian! How dare they make decisions for me?… All right, so we'll have to go to court. Why would you be afraid of court? You're a lawyer! I'm sure the judge will understand that my mother knows better than some strangers what's best for me!"

Polly started to speak but had to choke back tears.

"They said...that....they said. They said they would enter your school transcript into evidence and kept telling me..." She broke off and cried for a few moments.

Lacey sat silently and stared at her mother. Her stomach knotted as if her organs were fighting a war with her soul to determine if she would show concern for her mother or just continue to be furious with the world.

"They said if I take you home, there's a good chance...there's a good chance... There's a good chance you'll be dead within the month unless we have someone with you twenty-four hours a day."

Lacey watched as her mother began to shake and then hid her face in her hands. In a split second, the scene had gone from her mother holding her hand and comforting her to Lacey holding her mother, and the two rocking together.

"No, Mom. No, no, no. That will never happen," Lacey whispered to her mother.

As she cried, Lacey whispered in her mother's ear. "It's okay, Mom. It's okay, Mom. I'm sorry. They're wrong. They're really, really wrong, but I'll stay. I'm sorry. It's going to be all right."

Then, she pushed back her mother's hair, kissed her forehead and made an elaborate show of smiling, so that Polly would follow suit.

And that was that. Lacey voluntarily committed herself, on her mother's signature, to three to five days of short-term intensive, inpatient psychiatric care.

Polly didn't even have a second to click the pen's end to retract the ink cartridge before an orderly was whisking her daughter away in a wheelchair to "the secure floor."

While she had been allowed to sit with Lacey around the clock during her two-day, "temporary stay" in the emergency room, she was not welcome on the psych floor. There visits were limited to just forty-five minutes a day, from five-thirty to six-fifteen p.m.

Lacey was stunned that her mother wasn't allowed to go up with her to settle her into the new room. She was creeped out by the armed security guard stationed right outside the elevator and the triple-door, buzz-me-in system required for entrance to what she would learn was referred to only as "floor six."

"Tina, this is Lacey," the nurse said as they entered a room with beige walls covered with scuff marks and dirt.

Tina, a preppy-looking girl in sweat pants and a matching hot pink tank top, didn't look over. She just sat in a bedside chair and stared at the ceiling.

"Tina is the strong silent type," the nurse said, eliciting no response from the tiny blonde whose arms were covered with both track marks and scars from suicide attempts.

"There's no TV?" Lacey asked as she looked around the room.

"It's down the hall in the lounge. We encourage patients to walk around and socialize. Also, here's a notebook and a crayon in case you want to write or draw," the petite brunette nurse said, handing them to Lacey.

"Crayon? Don't you have a pencil or a pen?"

"No. They're not allowed," the woman said, then quickly continued on with patient orientation. "Now that you're on six, you can change into whatever street clothes you have. You'll have two hour-long sessions with the doctor each day and two groups," said the nurse, whose nametag read Cindy. "But therapy is done for today. You already had dinner right?"

"Yup, I had the emergency room's finest fare," Lacey said, trying to force a smile.

"Well, there's a movie down the hall at eight, about an hour from now. And, there's magazines and a few books down there, too. Can I get you anything else?"

"A weekend pass?" Lacey joked half-heartedly.

"Don't worry, sweetheart. It's not as bad as you think. A lot of patients even like it here," Cindy said, gently touching Lacey's arm.

When every cell in Lacey's body went rigid, the nurse pulled her hand back. "Okay, well, if you need anything, just come down to the nurse's station or press the button," Cindy said, walking out the door.

After changing in the adjacent bathroom and waiting about fifteen minutes for Tina to say something -- anything, Lacey headed down to the lounge to watch television. When she walked in to the small, industrial-looking room with two faded, green vinyl couches, a card table and four folding chairs, she saw two teen boys. One was olive skinned, generously proportioned, disheveled and sporting a dark brown man bun, and the other was short, pale and comically strutting around in what looked to be a smoking jacket, his ginger hair slicked back with every strand in place as if a photo shoot were about to begin.

The boys were tossing the remote control back and forth across the room.

"Hey, I don't care if you want to play catch, but could you put the TV on?" Lacey said to the pair after pushing the power button below the screen with no results.

"Around here, we introduce ourselves before we make demands," said the gent of the twosome, who was only about five feet tall.

"Oh, leave her alone," his much larger companion countered. "I'm Adam. He's Nick. And you are?"

"Lacey."

"Lazy? What a weird thing to say," Nick said with a laugh tossing the remote over Lacey's head and dropping it expertly into Adam's uplifted hand.

"No. *Lacey*," she said.

"Lazy. We heard," Nick repeated.

"Never mind," Lacey said, heading toward the doorway.

"No, no. Don't be like that. He's doesn't mean to be a dick. He just can't help himself around pretty girls," Adam said.

Lacey blushed, then asked again. "So, can you put the TV on?"

"Sorry, no can do," Nick said. "It's broken. Been that way for two months now."

"Oh," Lacey said. "You've been here two months?"

"A little judgmental, are we?" Nick said. "And no, I have not. This is my fourth visit in the last eight weeks."

"And, he's wrong. It was working on my second trip here, when my friend Nick was absent from our company," Adam clarified.

"Got it," Lacey said. "I guess I'll find a book then."

"Great. You've got a few good options, *Catcher in the Rye, One Flew Over the Cuckoo's Nest*."

"*The Perks of Being a Wallflower, Go Ask Alice*."

"Are you kidding me?" Lacey asked.

"Just a little. There are other choices, too. Those are just our favorites. You see there's not a lot of funding for the demented kids ward. They stock the shelves with whatever people leave behind," Adam said.

"And get this. Nobody bothers to review the titles," Nick said, chuckling.

"So we repeat offenders make it our mission to leave a legacy of irony," Adam said.

"Is that really irony?" Lacey said. "It just sounds kind of sad."

"Well, hey, it's not rain on your wedding day, but we get our kicks where we can," Nick said.

"Gotcha," Lacey said and headed once again for the door with her head hanging low.

"Lacey," Nick called to her back.

"You did catch my name," she said, spinning around.

"Of course. We're not daft," he joked. "Lacey, don't look so sad."

"I don't think she looks sad. I think she looks scared," Adam said.

"Hmm. Which is it Lacey?" Nick asked.

"A little of both, I guess," Lacey answered quietly.

"It's not that bad," Adam said.

"Don't say that, you condescending prick. You don't know what her problems are."

"I mean this place," Adam said, ignoring Nick. "It can actually be a big help, and three or four days go really fast."

"Sometimes too fast," Nick said. "Sometimes it seems like you're just starting to get to the answers when they kick you out."

"Hey, you want to play Monopoly?" Adam asked, motioning toward the card table.

"Too long," Nick complained. "How about Clue?"

"Actually, I like that game," Lacey said. "I mean sure."

Adam pulled the board game from out of a closet, and the three of them sat down to determine who committed the murder, in what room and with what weapon. As they played, they ignored the fact that they were wearing lace-less shoes and using crayons to mark their detectives' notebooks.

Chapter Thirty-Six:
Wednesday, April 10, 2013

"At the end of homeroom, would MacGyver Anderson please report to the main office."

MacGyver's stomach tightened when he heard his name. *This can't be good news*, he thought. *Dad's been getting restless. I hope he didn't do anything to hurt his back. Worse yet, Mom said Grandpa was going for more tests yesterday. I hope he's all right.*

When the bell rang, he hurried out of the classroom, wondering what new doom had befallen his family. For just a split second he allowed himself to wonder what it would be like to be a superhero whose powers were the ability to heal with a touch of his hand. That's probably better than flying, he thought, as he pushed open the office door.

"Can I help you?" asked a wrinkled, ancient-looking man in a shirt, tie and button-down gray sweater sitting behind a large metal desk near the counter.

This guy must be ninety years old, MacGyver thought. All the school offices in Jersey were always run by mom types who baked cookies and left them on the counter for anyone to take.

"I said, 'Can I help you?'" the elderly man said, slowly getting to his feet.

"Oh. Right. Sorry," MacGyver said.

"Yes?"

"I was called to the office," MacGyver said, trying to get the words out quickly enough so the old guy didn't feel the need to walk over to the counter. He wanted to get whatever message there was from home as quickly as possible.

"And you are?"

"Oh. Right. MacGyver. MacGyver Anderson."

The secretary, if that was his title, picked up a magnifying glass and slowly waved his arm over papers on the desk in front of him. "Oh, Ms. Khanna would like to speak with you. Have a seat, and I'll let her know you are here."

"Ms. Khanna? Really? Isn't she the SAC?" MacGyver asked, sure this old guy had gotten it wrong.

"She is one of our counselors. Yes," said Sweater Man, slowly lowering himself into his desk chair. "Have a seat," he said and then typed something into his computer.

MacGyver did as he was told, but he was sure it was a mistake. This old dude was clearly mixing up paperwork. From what MacGyver had heard Khanna was the SAC or Substance Abuse Counselor. *Whatever*, he thought, *Khanna will straighten it out.*

The phone on the man's desk rang. He answered it, then slowly replaced the receiver. "Mr. MacGyver," he called. Then, he corrected himself, "Mr. Anderson."

"Yeah," MacGyver said, rising from the chair on the other side of the counter.

"Interesting name," the older man noted.

"Thanks," MacGyver said, offering no additional information.

"Ms. Khanna will see you now. Come around and go right in to the center office."

"Okay. Thanks. I mean thank you," MacGyver said, making his way to the office he was sure he would soon be turned away from.

"Come in, MacGyver," said just about the most beautiful woman MacGyver had ever seen in real life. Ms. Khanna was a brown-skinned beauty with curly black hair that fell to her shoulders and large brown eyes that met MacGyver's without having to look up, a rarity for any woman considering his height.

As they shook hands, MacGyver's eyes slipped down the double-breasted red dress the counselor wore and fell upon the shapely brown legs that stood before him in three-inch heels.

Wow, he thought, *we don't have counselors like this in Jersey. It's a shame I don't need a drug counselor.*

"Have a seat," she said, smiling, as she settled herself behind her desk.

"Okay," MacGyver said. "I um don't really know why I'm here. I'm pretty sure it's a mistake."

"I see," Ms. Khanna said, a tiny diamond sparkling at the side of her nose.

"I mean you're the SAC. Right?"

"Yes," she said, tilting her head to indicate she didn't see a problem.

"Yeah, I don't do drugs," MacGyver blurted out.

"Excuse me?"

"I don't do drugs, so there's no reason for me to have to see the SAC. I mean you," MacGyver said, fumbling over his words.

"MacGyver, what do you think SAC stands for?"

"Substance abuse counselor. And, like I said, I don't do drugs. Not that there's anything wrong with that. I mean there is something wrong with that. I mean…"

"Actually, SAC means student assistance counselor," Ms. Khanna said, smiling. "It's all right, MacGyver. It's okay if I call you that, right?"

"Sure…What else would you call me?"

"I guess Mr. Anderson."

"No, that's my dad," MacGyver said. He could feel himself blushing as he started to think all of his answers thus far made him sound like an idiot or maybe even someone who *was* on drugs.

"Okay, MacGyver. The reason I called you to my office is because…" As she spoke, she opened a manila folder on her desk and took out something MacGyver hadn't seen in nearly two weeks, his algebra exam.

"Oh, so Delaney thought I was on drugs because of what I wrote on the test. I get it," MacGyver said.

"MacGyver, no one thinks you're on drugs."

"You're sure?"

"I'm sure."

"Okay, good. So why am I here?" MacGyver said, confused, pushing back a little in his chair. Part of him was still shaking off the worry that something was wrong at home, and another part was trying to comprehend what exactly Khanna wanted, not that he minded talking to her. He definitely would rather look at her than attend history class.

"MacGyver, we are concerned about what you wrote."

"Don't be. It was just a joke."

"A joke?"

"Right. I mean I was just coming up with my own word problem. That's all."

"Yes, but MacGyver, aside from the fact that you chose not to answer any of the test questions, your word problem discusses 'sparing' students' lives.' What exactly did you mean by that?"

"Oh my God, you think I'm a school shooter," MacGyver said, standing up as a line of sweat formed on his upper lip. "I'm not. I've never even held a gun. I mean not yet. Kevin was talking about taking me hunting with his dad, but we haven't gone. And that would be for rabbits. And I definitely wouldn't shoot any rabbits. My best friend would kill me. I mean she wouldn't really. It's just a figure of speech…"

"MacGyver, sit down. Please. Can I get you a bottle of water of something? You seem so upset."

"You'd be upset too if someone thought you were a terrorist or a school shooter or whatever," MacGyver said, lowering himself back into the chair.

"MacGyver," Ms. Khanna reached into a back corner of her office where there was a tiny refrigerator and handed him a bottle of water.

"Thank you."

"MacGyver, first, calm down and relax," she said.

"Okay," he said, twisting off the bottle cap and taking a small drink.

"Mrs. Delaney referred your test paper to me because she's concerned you might be depressed, and she's worried about you," Ms. Khanna said, leveling her gaze on him.

"Oh," said MacGyver. "No, I'm good."

"Really?" Ms. Khanna said. "She said you don't seem to have any friends, and you don't participate in class."

"Well, I just moved here," MacGyver said.

"Yes, we know," Ms. Khanna said. "You were affected by Hurricane Sandy weren't you? That can be a lot to handle."

"Yeah, sure. But, honestly, I'm good. I just don't like word problems."

"MacGyver, I'd really like to have your parents come in and talk with me. Perhaps we can set you up with some weekly counseling sessions. Depression is an illness, and if you are suffering from it, you need treatment. And we can help you feel a lot better."

"Ms. Khanna, please don't bother my parents. They have enough to deal with. Besides, it would just be my mother, really. My dad's in traction from a back injury, and my mother is working at this dry cleaner's near the house part time, but six days a week. They really don't need this. I was just being a wise guy. I'm not depressed. I'm fine. Please don't bother them."

Ms. Khanna sat back and considered. MacGyver struggled to contort his face into a look of concern but not depression. What exactly does that look like? He could see the counselor was concerned and that felt a little strange since lately he felt so much like an island no one cared to visit.

"Please," he said. "You'll see I'll get my grades up in math. Oh, and, like I was telling you, I've just started making friends. Y'know, Kevin."

"Well," Ms. Khanna said. "We don't have to involve your parents right now, but I would like you to stop by my office every couple of weeks and just talk for a few minutes."

"Great, thanks," MacGyver said, springing from his seat and heading toward the door.

"And MacGyver," she said.

"Yes?" he said, barely turning his head back to face the counselor.

"You can consider me another friend that you've made in Florida."

MacGyver couldn't help himself. Her kindness made him smile.

"Thank you," he said and quickly headed out of the office and back to class. He'd rather be in history class than give his parents anything more to worry about.

Chapter Thirty-Seven:
Saturday, April 13, 2013

"Lacey, it's so good to see you," Ashley said as she hugged her friend tightly and lifted her off the ground. "I missed you so much. I thought I'd go crazy without you. Shit! Sorry, I didn't mean anything…"

Laughing, Lacey disentangled herself from her friend. "It's okay. I'm really not that sensitive about it."

"Really?" Ashley said, hugging Lacey again before both girls moved in synchronicity toward the trampoline.

Ashley, who was about six inches taller than Lacey, turned her back to the trampoline's metal frame, placed her palms on the bar and scooted her butt up over the springs, gently lying on her back, looking up toward the clouds.

Lacey was not quite as graceful. She bent head first over the trampoline bed and pitched herself onto it with her feet kicking in the air, looking for all the world like a fish flopping around a dock.

Ashley watched as her friend rolled onto her back.

"Smooth," she said, stifling a giggle.

"Shut up," Lacey said, with a laugh. "You wouldn't think I've been playing on this damn thing for ten years," she said, panting just a bit.

"Yeah, but at MacGyver's house, we had those stairs."

"What? No."

"Yes, we did until about a year ago. There were three stairs, wooden stairs his father built that – hey, what happened to them?"

"Don't ask me. Remember I'm the one who forgot they even existed."

Ashley squinted as the sun peeked out from behind a cloud. "Oh, I remember, they floated off somewhere during Hurricane Irene. Remember?"

"Sort of," Lacey said. "That sounds familiar."

The two girls were silent for a few minutes. Then Ashley reached over and picked up her friend's wrist. "I think you can get rid of this now," she said, holding Lacey's arm up by the plastic-coated hospital bracelet that her friend had neglected to cut off.

"I don't know," Lacey said as her arm bounced twice on the trampoline top. "You never know when someone's going to need to know that I'm A positive or allergic to penicillin."

"You're A positive? I don't even know what blood type I am."

"You should find out. Mine's easy to remember. It's the only A-plus I've seen this school year," Lacey said as she tried to pull and then chew the stubborn bracelet off. "I'll cut if off when I go inside."

"Yeah, you don't want to go back to school with that thing on. Britt and I checked with Polly, and we told everyone else your aunt died in Indiana."

"Why Indiana? I don't even know anyone in Indiana."

"I had to think quickly when Rittenhouse asked where you'd been all week. Sorry. You know I'm not good on the spot like that."

"It figures Rittenhouse would miss me. Okay, Indiana it is," Lacey said. "Ever been there?"

"Nah."

"Me neither."

"Oh, sorry."

"No, don't worry about it. I've got this," Lacey said, as Ashley looked at her phone.

"So how are you? I mean really?" Ashley said as she slipped her Samsung droid into her pocket.

"Actually, I'm good."

"Good?"

"Yeah, it's weird. I think I kinda needed to be there."

"Really?"

"So, what exactly did Polly tell you?"

"She said you were tired, emotionally tired."

"Tired? That's what she said?"

"Well, no. What she literally said was, 'tired, emotionally tired.' I'm quoting here. And she said it in that lawyer way she has of telling you not to bother asking any follow-up questions because that's all she's going to say," Ashley said. "But, three days after you went in the hospital, Polly was at the Rock Throwing Place with that guy who dredges the boat slips. You know the one with the big crane or whatever that sometimes docks in the Yanatellis' slip."

"Steve?"

"Yeah, Steve, that's it. Kind of a hairy guy. I mean he's bald, but his arms and back look like a gorilla."

"Yeah, yeah, that's him. So what were they doing?"

"They pulled this big old TV and a refrigerator out of the water. Tyler and I were out on the Snobs' dock just watching them. I don't think they knew we were there."

"A refrigerator!" Lacey screamed and sat up, crossing her legs to sit criss-cross, applesauce. "Damn, I thought it was an oven."

"Yeah, a refrig…Wait, what?"

"Okay, so what you don't know is what happened the night I went into the hospital."

"Yeah, I do. Remember, you told me when you called last Tuesday night. By the way, I had never even heard of a collect call until then. Anyway, you said you fell and cut yourself down by the Beach Club and the only one who could help you was some dog."

"Right. But that's not the whole story."

Ashley sat up and mirrored her friend's posture, facing her as if the two were sitting at a campfire. "So what's the rest of it?"

"I kind of stepped – well they say jumped – in the bay."

"In the bay. But Lacey, I was talking to you on Facebook that night. It had to be after nine or ten."

"Yeah, it was and really, really freakin' dark."

"Wait, so wait. Were you trying to? Were you trying to…y'know?" Ashley stared at her friend, who was muttering, "a refrigerator."

"Lacey, were you? I mean were you really trying to…y'know? I mean, because, I know I'm not the best friend in the world, but I'm always here for you. Y'know."

"Yeah, I know," Lacey said and touched her friend's arm, which seemed like an odd thing to do, but she felt she needed to comfort Ashley in some way and a full hug seemed like overkill. "Okay, so what you need to know is, 'No, I wasn't trying to kill myself."

Ashley just stared at her.

"Honest."

Ashley continued to stare at her.

"Cross my heart," Lacey said, taking her right index finger and tracing an X over her heart. "That's the thing. At the hospital, everyone insisted I was trying to commit suicide or something. But, c'mon, jumping into the bay might be a good way to freeze my ass off, but it's not exactly a recipe for oblivion. I mean, c'mon, I can swim."

"Okay, so you jumped in. Why?"

"Well, that's just it. I didn't jump in. I stepped in. I just kind of wanted to feel something. You know?"

"Not really."

"It's just that ever since Sandy, or MacGyver moving, or whatever, I've just been walking around kind of like a zombie. Just going through the motions. And that night…"

"Lacey, you're finally back from Indiana," Tyler yelled over the fence as he pedaled the chopped-up piecemeal bicycle he was always building over to the driveway, dropped it and began walking over to the girls.

"Later, okay?" Lacey whispered.

"Okay," Ashley said and squeezed her friend's arm.

"Sorry for your loss," Tyler said.

"Huh?" Lacey said.

As Ashley nudged her friend trying to get her to recall the cover story. "Your aunt, right?" Tyler asked.

"Ah, yeah," Lacey said. "But, it's okay. She lived so far away."

Lacey stared over at Ashley and made eye contact. "It's like I didn't know her at all. I really just went there for Polly."

Remembering the bracelet that would give her lie away, Lacey awkwardly jumped down off the trampoline and ran toward the house. "I'll be right out. I have to pee."

Chapter Thirty-Eight:
Monday, April 15, 2012

As Lacey climbed down the school bus stairs, she glanced over at her front door and watched as her mother backed away from the frosted glass. The sight of her mom's quickly retreating black blouse with the bright-colored butterflies reminded Lacey of middle school.

Every day when she, Ashley and MacGyver got off the middle school bus, Polly would be waiting at the front door. In sixth and seventh grade, her mom would often be standing there calling them in for fresh-baked cookies or cupcakes. By eighth grade, Lacey had begun to find the ritual intrusive and suffocating, and during the second week of school, they had an all-out screaming fight about Lacey's right to live her own life "without being spied on."

Despite insisting that she was merely happy to see her daughter at the end of the day, Polly agreed not to watch for the bus any longer and to simply go about her day "like normal mothers."

But Polly never lived up to her promise. By mid-October of eighth grade, Lacey realized that even though her mom no longer greeted her at the door and was often upstairs or out in the yard when Lacey entered the house, at two-forty-five when the bus pulled parallel to their house on Silver Bay Road, Polly was almost always hiding behind the frosted window. She'd thought about telling Polly the ruse was up, that she knew she was still being watched. But instead, Lacey enjoyed watching the silly ways her mother always tried to look engaged when she came home. Sometimes, she'd be engrossed in a long telephone call. Others, she'd be in the middle of gardening or making a bed or doing laundry. And always, since the day of the fight, Polly was incredibly involved in what she was doing, and she'd inevitably say, "I didn't even realize what time it was."

Even though Polly now worked full time, today was no different.

As Lacey opened the front door, her mother yelled down from upstairs. "Is that you, Lacey? God, what time is it?"

"What are you doing home?" Lacey called up the stairs, her voice echoing through their freshly painted, but vacant, living room.

"What?"

"I said, 'What are you doing home?'" Lacey repeated, dropping her purple backpack at the foot of the stairs.

"I'm sorry. I couldn't hear you. I was just vacuuming," Polly said, quickly descending the stairs and elaborately hugging Lacey as if she'd returned from a war. "How was it, honey? Would you like something to eat? Maybe we should go for ice cream."

"It was fine, Mom. Just school."

"I know, but it was your first day back."

"So?"

"I didn't want...I was afraid… I worried that's all."

"Mom, nobody knows. They all think I was in Indiana. And, to tell you the truth, I really wouldn't care if they all knew I was in the psych ward."

"Oh, honey, that's good. I wouldn't want you to have to deal with that stigma or rumors or anything."

"Mom, you're the only one worried about that. I don't care. Honestly, I swear half my class has been to rehab or something. And you wouldn't be embarrassed to tell people I had pneumonia, chicken pox or cancer, would you?"

"No, of course not. But I don't want it to be harder on you than it already is. I mean, you were already having a tough time."

"Is this why you are home early?" Lacey asked, staring at her mother.

"No. I just finished with court and decided not to go back to the office."

"Right. Like that happens all the time. C'mon, Mom, you've got to stop worrying so much. I'm fine. I'm not going to have a rough day in school and jump out a window or something. Hey, where's Jake?"

"He had a play date after school. Want to go for some ice cream?"

"Maybe."

"Maybe?"

"Maybe we could go to that frozen yogurt place over at the Marshall's Plaza?"

"Why there?

"Well, you know what else is in the Marshall's Plaza?"

"The movie theater?"

"No. I mean, yeah, but that's not what I'm talking about."

"So what then?"

"Verizon. I thought maybe we could have some yogurt while we waited for them to activate my new phone."

Polly didn't say anything.

"Please."

As her mom stared at her, Lacey could literally see Polly's mind running through all the possible answers, which was strange because Lacey really thought the options were simply yes or no.

Finally, Polly blew out a breath through the left side of her mouth and blew back some of her side bangs. "Okay, bu…"

"Oh, thank you. Thank you. Thank you."

"But."

"But?"

"But, while we are devouring those delicious desserts, we will be negotiating a contract."

"A contract? With who?"

"With whom, and a contract between you and me about curfews and grades and leaving the house without permission."

"Wait. That's all restrictions on me. What do I get?"

"Um. The phone."

"Right."

"And they're not restrictions so much as boundaries."

"Okay."

"And one of those boundaries will be that you have to go to group every week, even when you don't want to."

"That's okay. I like group. I think it helps. I might even start going to another group."

"Another group? Why?"

"Neza said she has a separate group for just Sandy kids, and I think I might want to go to that."

"Okay," Polly said without enthusiasm. Then, she quickly added, "I mean, that's really good."

Despite what Lacey's doctors had told her, Polly had trouble understanding why her daughter was still so fixated on the storm. It wasn't as if Lacey and her friends had to fill out endless paperwork and fight with insurance companies, banks and builders the way their parents did.

Chapter Thirty-Nine:
Late afternoon, Monday, April 15, 2012

"Holy shit!"

Lacey was down at the Beach Club sprawled out in a peach Adirondack chair, her legs hanging over one arm, catching up on what seemed five years' worth of text messages on her first smart phone. The bright afternoon sun was the only break in an otherwise, bright blue sky; the kind of cloudless day her parents always referred to as a Sept. 11 sky.

When she saw it, she couldn't believe her eyes.

"What the…No way!" she yelled to the abandoned beach as tears slipped down her cheeks, burning a red path across her face.

"No way!"

But there it was, the picture she had begged MacGyver to send her, the one she demanded on penalty of excommunication, a selfie of MacGyver with his arms wrapped around some "ratchet" blonde and his mouth suctioned to the skank's lips.

"Why didn't someone tell me?" she demanded of the cosmos, but there was no reply.

"Shit. Just when things were starting to get better!" she yelled.

Lacey almost threw her brand new iPhone 5 down but stopped herself at the last moment. Cuckolded or not, she didn't want to be without a phone again.

It was funny. She had just started to share the great MacGyver love story with her group last night, but now she would have to go back and tell them it was all in her head. He'd not only moved, he'd moved on.

I wonder if it would have been different if I had been here when he came home for Spring Break, she thought. *If only, if only….*

Chapter Forty:
Friday, April 19, 2013

"MacGyver, nice job," Mrs. Delaney said, as she handed back his most recent algebra test.

Thank god, he thought. *This will keep Khanna from calling home and upsetting my mother. Maybe the hour of studying Tuesday night actually paid off.*

As he turned the paper over, he spotted the red 92 in the upper right hand corner, and he inadvertently called out, "Yes!"

Kevin kicked the back of his chair.

"Dude," he whispered. "What are you doing?"

"Oh, sorry," MacGyver said, as he turned toward Kevin. "Didn't realize I said that out loud."

"Yeah, well you did," whispered Kevin, adjusting his glasses and lowering his voice even more. "These kids are going to think you're a psycho. Trust me. None of them care much about grades."

MacGyver turned completely around. "Me neither. It's just this is going to keep me out of…"

"Gentlemen, would you like to step out in the hall and finish your conversation? I wouldn't want to interrupt you," Mrs. Delaney said.

"No, we're good. Thanks," MacGyver said, completely earnestly turning his attention toward the front of the room, and the class laughed.

"Well, that's nice," she said with a sarcastic edge, but she smiled, and then launched into the lesson.

When the bell rang, MacGyver grabbed his books and headed toward the door, eager for the weekend to begin – even though it meant two and a half days of vegging in his room, playing video games alone.

"Hey, Mac," MacGyver heard Kevin calling from behind him, and he slowed his pace.

"Oh, sorry," MacGyver said and fell into step with his classmate. "What's up?"

"So where you running off to this weekend? Paris?" Kevin asked, rolling up the sleeves of his gray flannel shirt, preparing for the day's heat.

"Huh? What are you talking about?" MacGyver said.

"Last time we were supposed to hang out, you gave me some lame excuse that you were jetting off to Jersey."

"What? It wasn't an excuse. I did go to Jersey," MacGyver said. Then he added, "Nobody jets off to Jersey."

"Oh, what did you do drive?"

"No, but I mean, nobody calls it jetting off to Jersey. I mean, jeez, I flew Spirit. It's a no-frills airline; it's not exactly Air Force One."

"So what? You used a prop plane?" Kevin said, adjusting his books so that he could carry them under his right arm.

"You're a little whacked," MacGyver said, and both boys laughed.

"Anyway, if you're not flying off somewhere this weekend, do you want to go hunting with me and my dad?"

"Um," MacGyver said.

"Oh, I get it. Never mind. See you around," Kevin said, and he picked up his pace toward the exit.

MacGyver reached over and touched Kevin's oversized shirt. "Dude, I just don't have a gun. I've never used one," he said.

The grim look on Kevin's face lightened. "Yeah, I know," he said. "We got you covered. If you want to come."

"Sounds good," MacGyver said. "Give me your phone. I'll put my number in it."

"I don't have one," Kevin said, writing down his address on a piece of paper. "This is my house," he said, pointing to the address he'd written down. "Be there at seven tomorrow morning. Okay?"

"Sounds good."

"There's no way I'm letting you go!" Dina Anderson shouted. "That's the end of it."

"Are you kidding me?" MacGyver said, raising his voice. "For months, you've been yelling at me to get out of the house. Go out and do something. And when I finally make some plans, you say no. This is ridiculous."

"I didn't tell you to start playing with guns."

"They're not playing, Mom. They're hunting. And I'm not even going to shoot at anything."

"Then why go?" she snapped.

"I can't not go. I don't even have any way to let him know I'm not coming."

"Call him."

"I can't. He doesn't have a phone."

"He doesn't have a phone? What kind of people are these?" Dina Anderson argued.

"I'm guessing poor people," MacGyver said. "You got something against poor people? Aren't we poor?"

"We're not poor," Dina Anderson said, anger flashing in her eyes.

"Oh really. Is that why we shop at a food pantry, why we're eating pasta three times a week and why we had to come live in your aunt's old winter house where the rent is free?" MacGyver shouted.

Dina Anderson's face turned bright red, and her body stiffened.

"Lower your voice," she hissed. "You want your father to hear this? Don't you think he feels bad enough? How dare you? I thought better of you than this." His mother turned and walked out on the lanai without another word.

MacGyver backhanded tears from his face. Stuck between fury and heartbreak, he sunk into a living room chair and stared at his hands. What the hell was happening to his family?

He wanted to get up and go talk to his mother, but he was too angry, too hurt. When he was younger, his parents were very authoritarian. They set a series of top-down rules for him to follow. As he got older, the family dynamic slowly shifted. Instead of no-questions-asked rules, there were responsibilities and consequences. As he reached his teen years, his parents still set strict guidelines for him to follow, such as curfews and grades he was expected to get, but the tone in the house changed again. Every issue they faced was a conversation, a discussion. No one ever raised their voice and decisions seemed to be mutually agreed upon.

Ever since the storm, his parents had reverted to treating him like a child. Do this. Do that. How was he supposed to react to this?

His mother's words, "I thought better of you than this," rang in his ears. In his mind, his stifled response was a mix between a mournful "I'm sorry" and a shouted "I don't know what you want from me!"

Eventually, he left the house. He thought perhaps a walk, even in the oppressive heat, would clear his head. He really wished he had his bike or at least could walk to the Rock Throwing Place. As he passed his mother, he considered mumbling, "I'm sorry" but he just couldn't. Instead, he grunted, "I'm going for a walk," and didn't even glance her way.

Chapter Forty-One:
Immediately following, Friday, April 19, 2013

MacGyver was walking about half an hour when he came to the local convenience store/gas station. Feeling a little thirsty, he reached into his pockets searching for enough change to buy a bottle of water, but he came up with just sixty-two cents.

Frustrated, he looked longingly toward the store window. What was he hoping for, a sign saying water was on sale for fifty cents? Of course there was none. But he did see something that made him think: Part-time help needed.

MacGyver paused for a moment and rolled the idea around in his mind. In two weeks, he would be seventeen. Maybe it was time for him to get a job.

What he liked about the idea is that he would be able to help his family. Maybe he could relieve some of his mother's stress, and things could move at least a little back toward normal.

What he hated about it was that it seemed so permanent. He shouldn't take a job unless he was planning to stay here. And he definitely wasn't planning to stay. This place, this town, this part of his life was just temporary, right? Still, how did he expect to get back to New Jersey? If he were going to do it alone, he would need money, right?

MacGyver stood there staring at the sign, but his mind was elsewhere, weighing the various pros and cons. He couldn't decide. As he paused there, an older African-American woman came out and lit a cigarette. "Can I help you?" said the slightly overweight woman wearing the store uniform that identified her both as Madge and Manager.

"No, I'm okay. Thank you," MacGyver responded.

"Are you waiting for someone?"

"No, I was just taking a walk and stopped for a minute," MacGyver said.

"It seemed to me you were looking at the help wanted sign. You need a job?"

"No. Yes. I don't know," he said.

"Well, you're the only one who can answer that," Madge said as she took a drag on her cigarette. "How old are you?"

"Sixteen, but I'll be seventeen on the thirtieth."

"Where do you go to school?"

MacGyver answered her, and they chatted for a short time about school, his family and even Blue, the car he had fixed up but lost in Sandy.

"You sound pretty responsible," Madge eventually said. "So have you decided if you are looking for a job?"

"I guess. Should we, um, set up a time for an interview?"

"This was the interview," Madge said. "If you want to work four days a week after school and some Sunday mornings, you've got the job."

"Okay, great. I mean thanks," MacGyver said.

"But, you can't start till after your birthday," she added.

"No problem," MacGyver said. "Well, I better head home. Thanks again."

He reached out and shook the manager's hand.

"Come by one day during the week to fill out the paperwork," she said, as she stepped on her cigarette butt, bent down and picked it up and put it in the pocket of her navy blue vest.

"Don't cringe," she said to MacGyver. "Keeping this place free of debris is going to be one of your jobs. You should thank me."

"I wasn't cringing in. I mean thank you," MacGyver said, and Madge smiled.

"See you around," she said, opening the store door. Once inside, Madge took down the Help Wanted sign.

###

As McGyver got closer to home, he considered how to approach his mother. He was completely over being angry, but he didn't know how to bridge the awkwardness that had grown between them.

When he entered the house, he smelled the unmistakable aroma of chocolate chip cookies baking. He walked into the kitchen, just as his mother was pulling a tray of slice-and-bake out of the oven.

"Hi, honey," she said. "Want one?"

"Wow. I didn't know cookie dough was for baking," he said, mocking his mother's obsession with eating the raw dough, especially when she was a little stressed out, which seemed to be all the time these days.

"Ha. Ha, very funny," she said, handing him a small plate with three cookies on it. "Be careful. They're hot."

"I'll bring these in to Dad," MacGyver said.

"No, MacGyver, don't. Sit down," his mother said. "I'm pretty sure he's sleeping, and he can wait."

"He can?" MacGyver said, instantly regretting his words.

"Sorry," he said, slipping into a chair at the kitchen table. "Sorry," he said again, this time meaning something completely different, more important.

His mother poured two glasses of milk and joined him at the table.

"I'm sorry, too. I should have never said that to you before. I didn't mean it," she said.

"Don't worry about it," MacGyver said. "Look, I've got something I have to tell you."

"Okay."

"I got a job."

"You got a job? When? Where?"

"Just now. Down at that place that's like a Wawa."

"Oh, MacGyver, honey. No. You didn't have to do that. That's not necessary."

"I wanted to," MacGyver said. "I want to help out around here."

"We didn't want to ask you to do that."

"You didn't. I did it on my own."

"Yeah, but it's because of what I said. I'm sorry. Please. You don't need to…"

"Mom, stop. I'm 17. I mean I will be. It's no big deal for me to get a part-time job."

"Wow, your first job. You're really growing up."

"That's something else I want to talk to you about, Mom," MacGyver said, taking a bite of a cookie. "Mmmm, these are good."

"What?"

"The cookies."

"No, what else did you want to talk about?"

MacGyver took a large gulp of milk and looked at his mother searching for a way to start.

"Mom, you've been really short-tempered lately. I know things kinda suck right now, but you can't keep snapping at me like I'm three. I mean, maybe sometimes, if you talked to me, I can help. I want to help. At least, I can listen."

"I'm sorry. It's just…"

"Please don't apologize, but, Mom, can we maybe try a little harder?"

"Of course. I have to remember you're almost a man," his mom reached over and touched his hand.

"And, about that. I have to go hunting tomorrow." His mom pulled back her hand, and her whole body stiffened.

"But, it's dan…"

"Dangerous. I know. But, I'll be careful, and I'm not even going to shoot. Think of it as a hike."

"A hike with guns. MacGyver you ca…"

"Can. Mom, you have to let me grow up."

His mom looked over at him and frowned. "Okay, but be careful."

"I will," he said. Standing up, he kissed his mother on the forehead before he took a small plate of cookies in to his father.

Chapter Forty-Two:
Sunday afternoon, April 21, 2013

"Okay. I'll pick you up in an hour," Polly told Lacey as she dropped her off at the local Baptist church, where her support group met.

"Make it 4:15," Lacey said. "They serve snacks and things after the meeting, and people hang out a few minutes."

"You want me to come at 4:30?" Polly asked.

"God, no. Not that long," Lacey said. "I don't want people to think I'm desperate for company."

"Okay, then," her mother said with a laugh. "Four-fifteen it is. I'll pick up Jake from T-ball practice and be back then."

Before she got out of the minivan Lacey's phone chirped, "You go Glenn Coco." She looked at it and said, "Brittney's parents are taking her car shopping!"

"Lacey, you need to turn that thing off during group."

"No kidding, Polly." When her mother frowned, Lacey added, "Thanks for the ride, Mom," reached across the car and kissed her mom's cheek.

As Lacey climbed down the stairs to the church basement, she considered how she would explain that everything she'd said about MacGyver the week before was wrong. There was no great lifelong romance. Instead, they had just been silly childhood crushes who would clearly have no impact on each other's adult lives.

As she pushed open one of the double doors, Lacey was surprised to see Adam and Nick seated in the circle of mismatched chairs along with three or four teens she had met two weeks earlier.

"Well, look who it is," said Nick, who once again had his ginger hair styled so not a strand was out of place.

"It's Lazy," Adam responded without a beat, as he refastened his man bun. "Fancy seeing you here. Come sit with us."

"Hi," she said as she took the offered seat. "I didn't know you guys came here. You weren't here the last two weeks."

"Yeah, well, Adam was on vacation. Myrtle Beach, right?" Nick said, and Adam nodded. "And I was...Let's just say, I was otherwise detained. By the way, the TV's fixed, but I wouldn't go back just for that. It's not that great a picture."

Lacey laughed, but then she paused and looked at Nick more closely, seriously. "Are you okay?"

"Actually, I think I am," Nick said, cracking his knuckles one at a time as he spoke. "I think we're finally getting somewhere. Pity, though, that Nurse Cindy is starting to crush on me something bad."

"All right then," Lacey said and turned her attention to Adam. "What about you? How was your vacation?"

"Absolutely grand. It was ten days at the beach with my grandmother, just about the only person on Earth who can witness this mountain of man in a swimsuit without getting all hot and bothered."

"Right. So I see you two haven't changed."

"Nope, don't see that happening any time soon," Nick agreed. "And how have you been?"

"Don't ask her that. We know she's been incredibly busy."

Nick looked at Adam. "We do? And how do we know that?"

"Clearly, her life has been a whirlwind of parties and drunken orgies."

"What?" Lacey said puzzled.

"Oh, yes. We know," Adam said.

"What are you talking about?" Lacey asked.

"I'm pretty sure we both politely provided you with our contact information when you left Floor Six. And since neither one of us has heard word one from you, I assume it's because your raucous return to freedom has just been too exhausting." He wiped his brow with the back of his right hand in a display of melodrama.

"As if," Lacey said. "I'm sorry. When I first got home I didn't have a phone, and then when I did get one, I kind of swore off using it. All it brought was bad news."

"See that's how it is, Adam," Nick said. "We're just more bad news. Perhaps, Lazy would rather sit over there, away from the bad news."

"Oh, c'mon. I've got enough problems without you guys giving me a hard time."

Nick started to answer but was interrupted by Neza, the therapist, gently clapping three times and taking her seat, her signal that group therapy was about to begin.

"Good afternoon, everybody. I'm so glad you could come today," Neza said, gesturing so that each of her arms wound up extended by her sides, palms up.

"She's always so dramatic," Adam whispered, but Lacey shushed him.

"Today, I would like to start with a discussion of loss," said the therapist, who was dressed in gold gladiator sandals, a black tank top and a colorful fabric, expertly draped into a floor-length dress.

"Does anyone have any tales of loss they'd like to share?"

When no one raised a hand, Lacey decided to break the silence. "There are posters all over Silverton for this dog someone lost."

Nick laughed, and Lacey looked at him, hurt and insulted.

"Do you see what you did there? Neza asked for a tale of loss, and you literally told her about a lost tail. That's funny."

Lacey glared at him, but Neza smiled benevolently.

"Lacey, what do you know about this lost dog?"

"Well, the reason the posters really got my attention is I've seen the dog. Twice. It's a golden retriever named Pyrite."

"I guess the owners are really missing him," Neza said.

"Her. The posters say it's a female dog, and they must. They're offering a $500 reward for her return."

"For $500 they can just get a new dog," said Jeff, a boy seated across the circle. Last week, when Jeff talked about having to testify in court against his stepfather for beating him, Lacey had really felt bad for him. But that comment erased any empathy she'd felt.

"That's not how loss works," Neza said. "It's like John Green wrote in *The Fault in Our Stars*, 'Pain demands to be felt.' Loss, too must be felt."

Neza paused, then she said, "Loss must be felt. What do you think that means?"

A girl seated on the other side of Nick raised her hand. "I guess it means that no matter what we do to distract ourselves, it's never going to work."

"Never?" Neza said.

Nick raised his hand and was acknowledged. "Not never. But it's like if we keep just ignoring our problems instead of facing them, we can't solve them."

"Yeah, they'll still be there, holding us down," Adam added. He was used to talking when Nick did and didn't see a need to be called on separately.

Lacey raised her hand and spoke when Neza nodded. "It's kind of like when someone dies. My friend's dad died a couple of years ago, and people kept telling her she had to go through all the stages of grief. What are there, seven or something?

"Five," Neza said. "Denial. Anger. Bargaining. Depression and acceptance. And they are each very important."

"So are you saying that's why we're here?" said a girl named Amanda, seated near Jeff. "Because I haven't lost anything, I'm just depressed."

"I would argue that all teens are in some way experiencing loss," Neza said. "Does anyone know what I mean?"

The group just looked at one another. Then Jeff said, "You mean 'cause we're losing our childhood?"

"Exactly," Neza said. "You each experience the excitement of new freedoms and responsibilities as you get older, but you also must give up many of your childhood pleasures, even simpler things like playing on a playground, or better yet, in a puddle."

"I used to love to play in puddles," Adam said.

"Used to?" Nick said, and everyone laughed.

"I'll let you all give that some thought, and we'll get back to it next week," Neza said. "Right now, I'd like to do highs, lows and more."

Highs, lows and more, Lacey had learned at her previous group sessions, was when each person in the circle talked about the best thing that had happened during the week and the worst, and if they wanted, they could tell "more" about either one and get advice from the group.

The ritual began, and Lacey tried to pay attention and offer support to the other group members. But, honestly, she was focused on what she would say when it got to her turn. When it did, she still wasn't ready but stumbled through.

"So my high this week was getting a new phone, an iPhone," she said and held it up. "My low was losing my best friend, and no, I don't want to say anything more."

Chapter Forty-Three:
Late afternoon, Tuesday, April 23, 2013

"Thanks for inviting me over," MacGyver said to Kevin as they snacked on popcorn at the counter in Kevin's avocado green kitchen in his tiny ranch house.

"No problem. So, Mac, I was thinking we could go out back, and I could teach you how to shoot. That way next time we go hunting, you can be more than a water boy."

"About that," MacGyver said. "I had a great time hanging out with you and your dad Saturday, but I don't think I could ever shoot anything."

"Sure, you could. It just takes a little practice. For starters, you actually have to try shooting the gun."

MacGyver frowned but said nothing. He just grabbed another handful of popcorn, but Kevin didn't notice. Instead, he launched into a long story about how he learned how to shoot a shotgun when he was twelve.

MacGyver didn't want to interrupt, but he had trouble listening to Kevin talk about shooting and cleaning a wild turkey. His stomach turned a little at the thought of killing something. His father didn't even like to kill insects. He promoted a "capture and release outdoors" policy even with flies and mosquitos.

"Then, this other time, when we went rabbit hunting," Kevin said as MacGyver tried to tune back in to the diatribe.

"Look, dude," MacGyver said, playing with a pile of popcorn on the counter in front of him as he searched for the words. "My best friend had a pet rabbit, a wild rabbit we raised from a baby. We had to feed it Pedialyte and Ensure with an eyedropper for weeks. There's no way I could kill a wild rabbit. I just couldn't. Besides, she'd kill me. And I don't really want to kill anything." Staring down at his popcorn, he added, "Sorry."

"What do you have to be sorry for?" Kevin said. "I guess I'm the one who should be sorry. I guess I should have asked before I invited you."

"No, no, dude. It's cool," MacGyver said.

"Well, listen, Mac. We have these cans set up in the back where we just shoot for the hell of it. I could still teach you how to shoot, if you're not afraid."

"I'm not afraid," MacGyver snapped, then slowed his speech. "Target practice sounds good."

"Cool. Let's finish this popcorn first. Then when we come back, we can reheat some leftover pizza we have in the freezer."

"Great," MacGyver said.

"Oh, but you'll have to take the pepperoni off it," Kevin said, drawing a quizzical stare, until he added. "You being a vegetarian and all."

"Right," MacGyver said. "Good thing I'm not vegan."

"Ever think about going vegan?" Kevin asked.

"Nah," MacGyver said. "I never even saw myself as a vegetarian. It just kind of happened suddenly."

Chapter Forty-Four:
7:30 p.m. Wednesday, April 24, 2013

Lacey had been attending the Coping with Depression support group on Sunday afternoons for a few weeks. She liked the meetings and thought they helped. But she was still very nervous when she headed down the stairs of the Baptist church for her first Sandy support group session.

The difference was pretty clear to her. The depression group was for all teens. Neza had even said that every teenager feels anxiety and loss. That was part of the natural order of things.

But attending a Sandy group was different. This meant labeling herself a victim, someone who is having trouble coping, someone with a problem. For Lacey, that distinction made deciding to attend the Sandy meeting a much more emotional decision. Did she want help badly enough to admit the storm had left her hurt and angry? Something about copping to those feelings made her feel vulnerable, exposed.

She almost turned around and headed back out, but she kept going down the stairs. After six months, she desperately wanted to feel better, to feel like herself. Maybe this would be a start.

As she stepped into the basement, Lacey heard a familiar voice.

"Lacey, come over here!" called Donovan, one of the twins from her neighborhood.

"Wow, I never expected to see you here," Donovan said, as he stood up and gave her a quick hug. "You never even want to talk about the storm."

"Yeah, well," Lacey said with a shrug as the two sat down. "Where's Michael?"

"Can't get him to come, but I wish he would. He's such a nasty pain in the butt these days, always grouchy."

"Common problem," Lacey said.

"Yeah, well, it's annoying, and *you* don't have to share a room with him."

"True," Lacey said as she played with a strand of her honey brown hair. "How long have you been coming here?"

"All my life. This is our church," Donovan said.

"No, I mean the support group."

"Since the beginning."

"Really?" Lacey said. "Don't you run out of stuff to say?"

"Not really," Donovan said. "Have *you* run out of Sandy stuff to complain about?"

"As if," Lacey said and slumped a little in her seat, getting comfortable. As she looked around the group of chairs, she saw a couple of kids she recognized from school but didn't know: Tiff, who came in and sat on the other side of Donovan, and a couple of kids she knew lived over on the barrier peninsula in Seaside Heights or Seaside Park.

Neza entered, wearing jeans and a pretty purple blouse. She gently clapped her hands three times and took her seat.

"Good evening, everybody. I'm so glad you could come tonight," Neza said, as always gesturing so that each of her arms wound up extended by her sides, palms up.

Lacey had heard pretty much the same words and seen the gesture several times at this point and wondered why she didn't think it was corny. Somehow Neza's calming presence made her feel welcomed and inclined to talk. She couldn't figure out why. She never had a teacher that exuded so much charisma and warmth, and Lacey believed it was all genuine. It was as if Neza felt their problems were the greatest concerns in the world. Her life must be so peaceful, Lacey thought.

"This evening we have a new member. At least, I hope she will become a new member, joining us. For those of you who don't know her, this is Lacey," Neza said, gesturing toward Lacey and indicating she should say something.

"Mmm. Hi. I live in Silverton," Lacey said, nodding at Neza as if to say, "I'm good. Please go on."

Donovan leaned in toward Lacey and whispered. "How does she know you?" But Lacey shushed him, mouthing "Tell you later."

"This evening," Neza continued. "I want to talk about recovery."

"Ha," said a boy, who looked to be about twelve, sitting across the room, and everyone laughed.

"Ha. What do you mean by ha, Greg?" Neza asked without a hint of mockery as she repeated his response.

"There is no recovery," Greg replied confidently. "It's just another day, another problem." Most of the group nodded.

"Do you all feel that way?" Neza asked, and almost everyone chimed in affirmatively.

"So are you saying there's been no progress since Sandy?" Neza asked.

"Exactly," said Donovan.

"Well, that's not completely true," said one of the teens who Lacey knew lived over in Seaside Heights. "I mean they fixed the gas lines, so we can go back and work on our house."

Neza nodded. "Is anything else better?" she asked the group.

"Some of the really messed up houses have been knocked down," Tiff said.

"That's true," Lacey said. "And some of the houses by me are almost done."

"We were almost done about a month ago," said another boy, who sported a beard and looked to Lacey to be a little too old to be there.

"Then what happened?" Neza asked, but Lacey could tell by the looks on the other faces that they knew the answer because they'd heard it more than once before.

"You know what happened. Now, we have to lift the house. That's another three to six months of living with my grandparents if we're lucky."

"I thought you liked living at your grandparents. You said they're a lot better cooks than your parents are," Greg said.

"Yeah, and your grandmother slips you money sometimes. Doesn't she, Nelson?" Tiff asked.

"You're right," Nelson said. "But this whole thing is just getting old, y'know? It's been six months, and I just want things to go back to normal."

"And I'm tired of grumpy parents," Tiff said.

"If there's one thing I'm sick of, it's hearing about the 'new normal,'" Donovan said. "That just means not normal."

"I understand, Donovan," Neza said. "But let's get back to the things that have gotten better. Do me a favor. Indulge me for a minute and close your eyes."

Lacey looked around to see how the group responded and was surprised that everyone heeded the request. This group was different from the other one, she thought, less combative. Everyone just takes turns talking. Neza doesn't even ask them to raise their hands. As if Neza's spell had worked its magic on her too, Lacey closed her eyes.

"Now, think back to the first few hours, first few days after the storm. And I'm sorry if this is painful for some of you, but try and stay with us," Neza said. "Think about your worries and concerns in the first few hours, first few days. Let's talk about those for a few minutes. Let's just go around the circle. You can open your eyes."

A pretty blonde girl sitting on Neza's right seemed to understand it was her turn to speak.

"Well, the first big problem I remember was worrying that the water would reach the outlets, and the house would go on fire."

"And did it, Lauren?" Neza asked.

"No, that's when the blackout hit, but my father turned off the breaker switch anyway."

"We lost all our food in the refrigerator, but my mother was amazed when she found out it was covered by insurance," Greg said.

"We had a tree down on our car," Donovan said. And when Neza nodded at him, he added. "We got a new car, well another used one, anyway, about two weeks later."

"This isn't about my house, so much as the neighborhood," Lacey said. "There were signs everywhere, all up and down the road for repairmen and contractors, even some freelance insurance adjustors. I remember my mother said it was like election season on steroids with all the little signs stuck on the sides of the road."

As Lacey finished her thought, Neza nodded at her. "Yeah, most of them, but not all, are gone."

"That's just like the white vans that were everywhere. Do you remember that?" Nelson asked. "They all had out-of-town plates and small magnetic signs saying they did hurricane repairs."

"Oh, I remember," Donovan said. "Believe it or not, FEMA warned us about that the day after the storm when they came to assess damage."

"FEMA came to your house the day after the storm?" Lauren asked. "How did you pull that off?"

"Easy. We had a tree go down on Sunday afternoon, so my dad made a really early claim, before the real damage came," Donovan said.

"You know what I remember right after the storm? All the looting," Nelson said.

"Right. And the signs people had on their lawns that said 'Looters will be shot.'"

"Well, people are still looting," Lacey said.

"Yeah, but it's much better now that there's the police hotline and neighborhood patrols," Donovan said.

"So you see," Neza said. "Even though the recovery has been slow, and I understand that, and I understand how frustrating that is. You all can see progress."

"I guess so," Nelson said. "But it still sucks."

"Agreed," Neza said. "Now, I want you all to close your eyes again and think about the progress you personally, in your own situation, have made. If you believe in God or a higher power, now might be a good time to give thanks. But once you've done that, focus on your current biggest challenge – and it doesn't have to be Sandy-related. Think about it for just a few seconds, and think about how you can help meet that challenge. If it seems insurmountable by yourself, where can you go for help?"

There was silence for a few moments, then Neza said, "You can open your eyes now. I'd like to start highs, lows and more."

As Lacey ascended the stairs at the end of the meeting, she was surprised to realize that she actually felt much better. How weird, she thought. Nothing is different. What is it about Neza that makes this nonsense work?

Chapter Forty-Five:
Saturday, April 27, 2013

"Come to the Beach Club."

Lacey's heart leaped when she got Ashley's text. It was so simple, so normal. Maybe, just maybe, this spring wasn't going to be a total disaster after all.

"Be right there," she texted then headed for the door. As she slipped on her flip-flops, Lacey remembered her contract with her mom and retraced her steps.

"Mom, Mom, Mom!" she called throughout the downstairs.

"She's upstairs," Jake yelled from the kitchen, which was now nearly finished except for final touches such as moldings and drawer pulls.

"Okay, thanks," Lacey said, heading for the stairs.

"Lacey, come here. I need help with this word," Jake called back from the table where he was playing a video game that featured pop-up dialogue.

"I'll be there in a minute," she said, heading toward the stairs.

"What's all the yelling down here," her mother said, emerging on the second-floor landing, vacuum in hand.

"We're not yelling. We're just talking," Lacey said, still raising her voice.

"Really. I thought we had a rule around here that you need to be in the same room as the person you're talking to," Polly said.

"Do we, Polly?" Lacey said. Then, realizing her sarcasm might not be well received, she said, "I'm going down to the Beach Club."

"Correct me if I'm wrong, but what I think I just heard was, 'Mother dearest, could I please have permission to walk down to the Beach Club?'" Polly teased.

"Oh, c'mon," Lacey said. "Mother dearest? Where did you get that from, the 1890's? So, I'm going. Okay?"

"'I'm going. Okay? is a far cry from asking permission," Polly said, looking down at Lacey with a disappointed look that Lacey couldn't figure out. Was her mom really agitated? Or was she just playing around? Lacey hated when she couldn't tell.

Lacey stared up at her mother. "Okay?" she asked.

"Yeah, okay," Polly said.

"Thanks, Mom," Lacey said and bolted toward the door. As she reached for the handle, she heard Jake call out.

"Lacey! Lacey!" he yelled like his arm was being cut off. "You said you would help me."

"I know, but I..."

"Lacey! Please!"

"But, Bud, I got to go," Lacey complained, taking a tentative step toward the kitchen and her plaintive brother.

"Go ahead," her mother said from behind her. "I'll help him."

With that Lacey was out the door. She knew if she hesitated, she would get drawn back in.

As she approached the Beach Club, Connor yelled out. "What took you so long? You missed everything."

"I had to...wait. What'd I miss?" Lacey called back, as she walked toward him.

"The police and an ambulance just left," Connor said. "You missed all the excitement."

As Lacey pushed up the solid metal U keeping the cyclone gate closed, Ashley called over. "Mrs. Kane fell."

"Oh, is she all right?" Lacey asked.

"A little bruised up, but she'll be okay," Connor said, "But that's not important."

"It's not important that Mrs. Kane fell and the police and an ambulance had to come?" Lacey said.

"No," he said emphatically. "We have a good chance of getting the five hundred dollars."

"What five hundred dollars? What are you talking about?" Lacey turned to Ashley, who had been standing with Connor the entire time, unable to get a word in. "What's he talking about?"

"Connor and I were hanging out by the picnic benches when that dog, the missing Golden Retriever, comes running over, barking his head off. He wouldn't shut up," Ashley explained.

"She wouldn't shut up," Lacey corrected.

"That's what I said," Ashley said, her blue eyes squinting in the midday sunlight.

"No, you said barking *his* head off. It's a female, Pyrite," Lacey said.

"Pyrite? What the heck does that mean?" Connor asked.

"I don't know," Lacey said. "I guess it's just its name."

"Anyway, we're wasting time," Connor said.

"Well let me finish telling her what happened," Ashley said.

"So what happened?" Lacey asked.

"Oh, right," Ashley said. "So the dog, Pyrite, grabs my hand and pulls me, not hard or anything, but really demanding, until we both started following her. And she brings us over to the Kanes' driveway, where Mrs. Kane is face down on the asphalt and her head's bleeding."

"Was she conscious?" Lacey said.

"Yeah, but she was all disoriented and couldn't get up on her own," Ashley said.

"What happened? Did the dog hurt her?" Lacey asked.

"No," Ashley said. "Mrs. Kane said she just fell getting the mail, and the dog was nowhere around when she fell.

"Anyway, we called 9-1-1, and two cop cars and an ambulance came. Honestly, it was a bit of overkill."

"Yeah, and we were so distracted helping Mrs. Kane that we forgot all about the dog," Ashley said. "But that's your dog, right?"

"My dog?" Lacey asked.

"The one that helped you, right?"

"Helped her when?" Connor asked.

"Never mind," both girls said simultaneously.

Connor was getting very impatient. "Well, anyway, it's the dog with the five hundred dollar reward, and it's got to be right around here somewhere. We just have to spread out and find him."

"Her," Lacey said.

"Whatever," Connor said, smiling, the sunlight glinting off his braces.

"We texted everyone to come help. But so far you're the only one who's shown up," Ashley said.

"And we've already wasted a lot of time," Connor said.

With that, Brittney pulled up driving her mom's Lexus with her mother in the passenger seat.

"What's up?" she called out.

"It's about time you answered," Ashley said.

"Answered what?" Brittney asked.

"My text," Ashley said, exasperated.

"Oh, I haven't gotten it. As you can see, I've been driving," she said, proud of her new status as a permitted driver.

"We saw that dog," Connor said.

"What dog?" Brittney asked.

"Pyrite," Lacey said, knowing Brittney would recognize the name as the two of them recently had a long conversation about the missing dog and what seemed like thousands of lost posters her owner had posted all over Silverton.

"Oh," Brittney said. "Where is she?"

"Gone," Ashley said.

"But she can't be far. She was just here," Connor said. "So keep your eyes open."

"I have to. I'm driving," Brittney said, laughing.

"Right," Connor said. "Anyway, it's agreed if any of us find her, at least today, we split the reward. Right?"

"Okay," Brittney said. "But, I have a better chance than any of you. I'm driving." With that she pulled away with a wave.

"Brat," Lacey said.

"Oh, she's just joking," Ashley said.

"I know. It's just…"

"It's just you people are wasting time," Connor said. "Now, Brittney headed west up Silver Bay, Lacey you go east, down Silver Bay, and I'll walk along Bay Breeze and down the dead ends. Okay?"

"What about me?" Ashley asked.

"You wait here in case the dog comes back."

"Okay," Ashley said, and the friends split up Scooby Doo-style in their pursuit.

Two hours later, all four teens were back at the Beach Club. No success.

"Damn, I could have really used that money," Connor said. "I must have spent it a hundred different ways in my mind while we were walking around."

"Me, too," said Ashley.

"I wasn't thinking about that," Lacey said. "I just wanted to find the dog for the owners."

"Yeah," agreed Brittney. "I bet they're really lonely without her."

Chapter Forty-Six:
Tuesday, April 30, 2013

"I'll take twenty dollars on pump three." MacGyver heard the words, but they didn't register at first.

"What?" he said to the petite brunette who looked to be about fifteen and reminded him of Lacey, but without the dimples. She stared at him as if he were a bit dense.

"I said I'm at pump three. Twenty dollars," the girl said, handing him a ten dollar bill, seven singles and three dollars in quarters. He quickly counted the money and placed it in the drawer in front of him before turning the pump on.

Even though this was only his first day, the job wasn't difficult. But MacGyver had trouble remembering that some of the convenience store customers were also there to buy gas, and he had to hit the switches to turn the pumps on and off. Back in New Jersey, there was no such thing as self-service gas stations. State law required a trained service station attendant carefully deliver fuel to avoid any dangerous mishaps. New Jersey drivers simply relaxed in the driver's seat when they fueled up, merely passing their payment through small openings in their windows trying to avoid any fluctuation in their climate control.

MacGyver had always assumed his first job would be pumping gas. This Florida equivalent of the same job seemed wrong, just like everything else here.

"What's going on, MacGyver?" Madge asked, approaching his counter and startling him as he stared out the window, lost in his thoughts.

"Huh," MacGyver said. "I mean, nothing. Everything is fine."

"Any questions?" she asked.

"Well, actually, yeah," MacGyver said. "I know I probably shouldn't ask this on my first day and all, but we never talked about when I get paid. I mean, is it every week or every other week?"

"I'm sorry," Madge said. "I should have gone over that with you. Pay day is every Friday, but we hold a week back."

"Hold a week back?" MacGyver said, not sure what the phrase meant.

"So you won't get a check this Friday. You'll get paid for everything up to this Friday, next Friday. You get it?"

MacGyver nodded, but he wasn't exactly sure. "Okay," he said. "So my first paycheck is next Friday."

"Exactly," Madge said. "Have you got big plans for it?"

"No," MacGyver said. "I was just curious."

"All right then," Madge said. "I'll be in the back. If you have any questions, just give a holler."

"Okay," he said and resumed looking out the window. While some drivers came in and paid, many used their debit or credit cards at the pumps and never entered the store. With few customers, the minutes passed slowly, and MacGyver wondered if he was going to like this job. So far, he thought, he'd rather be home playing Nintendo.

When he spotted a short guy in a wrinkled green flannel shirt heading his way, MacGyver knew immediately who it was. But when he entered the store, Kevin didn't come right to the counter. He went to one of the refrigerator cases and picked out a Red Bull.

"How's it going, Mac?" Kevin asked as he paid MacGyver.

"Not bad. Do you want a bag for that?"

"Nah. It's for you, dude. Happy birthday."

"How did you know it's my birthday?" MacGyver asked.

"Facebook, and man, you have a lot of friends back in Jersey. I went on your page just to make sure I had the date right and your Facebook is blowing up."

"Really?" MacGyver said. "I haven't talked to any of those people since I got back after Spring Break."

"Well, apparently you're some kind of hero, and your party last year was the bomb," Kevin said.

"Ah, it was pretty cool," MacGyver said. "Lacey, I've told you about her. Anyway, she threw me what she called a Mock Sweet 16. Her mom even opened their pool early and put the heater on, first swim of the season. We had a blast, and at night we had a fire and..."

The door opened, and a mom came in with two small children.

"Do you have a restroom?" she asked.

MacGyver pointed her in the right direction and turned his attention back to Kevin. "You better go, dude. I don't want to lose my job on the first day."

"No problem," Kevin said.

"And thanks for the Red Bull," MacGyver said.

"See ya later," Kevin said. "And happy birthday."

As MacGyver waited for his customer to return from the bathroom, he quickly pulled out his phone and checked his texts.

"Have a great first day," a text from his dad. That was it. If his friends missed him so much, why weren't they texting him? Shit, it's his birthday, shouldn't someone have Facetimed him? And so what if they were messaging him on Facebook. Isn't that what you did with "online friends," people you barely knew? Did he already mean so little to them?

###

MacGyver's birthday, Lacey thought. What was she supposed to do about that? Could she really call him? Text? They hadn't communicated in more than a month, not since she got that disgusting picture of him with that ratchet blonde, whoever she was.

But it's MacGyver's birthday, she argued with herself again. Could she really do *nothing*? Shit, last year she threw him a party.

Still, hadn't he made his position clear? He sent that picture and then nothing else. Obviously, he didn't want to hear from her. He wants to make a fresh start in the Sunshine State, Lacey thought.

She sat at her kitchen table, wondering when her mother was going to put their artwork back up, like the picture of *The Last Supper*, and considering what to do. She wanted to reach out, but then she decided that it wasn't fair to MacGyver. Even though she and the rest of the Silverton Crew were stuck in some type of time warp where they had to suffer the effects of the storm every day, MacGyver was free to move on and be happy, and she had to let him. That was the right thing to do. Wasn't it?

Although she was pleased that she'd made a mature decision, Lacey put her head down and cried. But even privacy was hard to come by these days, and Jake quickly interrupted her.

"What's wrong Lacey? Did you get hurt?"

"No. Yes. Never mind. You wouldn't understand," Lacey grumbled, wiping the tears off her face.

"Sure I would. I'm not a baby," Jake said, sitting down on the chair next to her and looking up at her with genuine concern.

Lacey chuckled a little. She wanted to tell him to bug off, but he seemed so sincere that she couldn't do it.

"I'm just a little sad," she said. Then, she made the big admission. "I'm missing someone."

"Is it Daddy?" Jake said, resting his hand on Lacey's arm and slipping his thumb into his mouth. "I miss him, too."

Her baby brother's gentle touch and deep concern melted something in Lacey.

"You do?" she asked. "When?"

"All the time, but mostly on Sunday nights. Remember we used to always have family movie night, and Daddy would make popcorn? We haven't done that since he left."

"We haven't?" she asked. "I guess you're right. We probably haven't. Well, I'll tell you what, we can do that this week. What movie do you want to watch?"

"*Lion King*," he said.

"I should have known," Lacey said. "We'll watch it this Sunday, and I'll make the popcorn."

"Don't we have to ask, Mom?" Jake asked.

"Trust me. She'll be thrilled."

Chapter Forty-Seven:
Sunday, May 5, 2013

"The worst thing about this, about being diagnosed with depression is what I overhear my mother saying about me. All my life, until now, if I came into a room and she'd been talking about me, I would always be embarrassed because she was blowing some little accomplishment out of proportion like it was a big deal. 'Oh, Mom, I wish you could have been at the chorus concert. Lacey had a solo. It was absolutely wonderful.'

"She wouldn't say it was just one line. Or, it would be, 'It's such a shame her father wasn't here to see her win the county spelling contest,' as if that really mattered. But now when I enter a room, whether she's on the phone or talking to someone in person, her voice drops to a whisper, and she paints on a fake smile. Or even worse, I'll hear, 'I have to go now. Lacey just came home,' which is clearly code for my daughter's a basket case, and I now have to watch her every second of the day. Otherwise, you never know, she might off herself or something."

Lacey fidgeted in her chair at her depression support group meeting and considered ending her diatribe there, but Adam patted her arm, and Neza smiled at her.

"Lacey, this is wonderful," Neza said, looking Lacey in the eyes.

"It's wonderful that my mother thinks I'm a mess?" Lacey asked.

"No, no," Neza said. "I feel as if this is really the first time you're opening up. Thank you so much for trusting us."

Neza's appreciation was so sincere, Lacey couldn't help but wonder how happy she must get when someone gives her a present. *Imagine what she'd be like if someone gave her a new car or a cool trip,* Lacey thought, *she'd probably spontaneously combust.*

"Lacey, dear, please go on," Neza said.

"No, that's all right. I think I've said enough. Let someone else have a chance," Lacey said, her left hand reaching up for a plait of hair to twirl around her fingers.

"Go ahead," Nick said, reaching across Adam and patting her knee. "What else bothers you?"

"Well," she said, and gave Nick a half smile. "Since you asked, I wish there was a blood test or a piss test or something that you could take and prove this is a real diagnosis, a chemical imbalance, and not just me being overdramatic. And even though Dr. Walsh – my psychiatrist – and I agree that I don't need drugs -- I mean as long as I come to group -- I think about getting a script anyway because I think maybe then my mother would be less embarrassed. I mean she was never ashamed of me when I got the flu or a virus," Lacey said.

"Now, wait a minute," Adam said as he pushed his chair back and stood up. His formidable presence made some of the group members shift a little awkwardly in their seats.

"Adam, don't you think we should let Lacey finish what she was saying?" Neza said.

"Oh no, I'm not going to sit here and listen to her talk shit about her mother. Polly, that's her mom, drove me home from here twice, and she is the sweetest, most sincere lady. She shows up with cold water bottles and offers to stop at Wawa or McDonalds. Lazy, honey, I love you, but you can't go acting like she's some kind of monster. It just ain't true."

As Adam spoke, he looked around the room, playing to his audience.

"Adam," Neza said, "You know none of us knows what goes on behind the scenes in any home."

"Sure, that's true," Adam said, slowly sitting back down. "But I'm telling you this is just a sweet lady."

"I agree. I'm not arguing," Lacey said. "But, she's too sweet. Too caring. She acts like caring about us – my brother and me – is the only thing she has to do in the world. And now, now that I have her afraid, she barely lets me breathe without 'checking in' with me. It's like being slowly smothered," Lacey said and slumped back in her chair, hoping to indicate she was done talking and it was time to move the discussion along.

"Smothered?" Nick said. "I would love smothered. You know how my dad has dealt with my depression, after three suicide attempts? He told me last week that I need to, and this is a quote, 'Knock it off. You're upsetting your mom.'"

Neza turned the radiance of her smile toward Nick, asking him questions about his situation. Lacey played with her hair and literally thanked god – with a silent prayer – that the focus in the meeting had moved on.

When the meeting ended, she couldn't wait to get home, make popcorn and watch *Lion King*. It felt good knowing how happy Jake would be.

Chapter Forty-Eight:
Tuesday, May 14, 2013

MacGyver considered purchasing a box of Marlboros, but the idea of giving up six dollars and twenty-nine cents just didn't sit right with him. He was struggling to quit or at least cut down. Knowing that he had to spend an hour stocking shelves or ringing up customers to clear enough for a pack could sometimes make the decision a little easier. *Who wants to light their money on fire?*

Instead, he rolled a dollar bill into a cylinder shape and shoved the mock cigarette in his mouth.

"Gross, man," Kevin yelled over as MacGyver stepped out of the In and Out at the end of his shift.

"What?"

"Freakin' get the money out of your mouth. That stuff is filthy. Mr. Flores, the biology teacher, said a dollar bill carries more germs than a public toilet bowl. What you're doing is like licking a toilet, Mac."

"Oh, c'mon, you're exaggerating," MacGyver said.

"No, really, dude. They've done tests that show the flu virus can live for almost three weeks and infect more than sixty people on a single dollar bill," Kevin said.

"You're shitting me. Right?" MacGyver said.

"No," Kevin said with a smirk. "And that's such a weird expression. Kind of gross."

"Listen to the princess," MacGyver teased as the two fell into step alongside one another.

"Look I support your trying to quit, but find another way, man. That's nasty," Kevin said, grabbing the dollar out of his mouth and handing it to him.

It had become the daily ritual for Kevin to meet "Mac" after work and then the two of them would hang out for the night at either of their homes and play video games.

"Hey, you know that girl Hannah?"

"The one with the braces?" MacGyver asked.

"Yeah, her," Kevin said.

"What about her?"

"She's been asking a lot of questions about you. I think she's into you."

"Really?"

"Yeah."

"Well, of course," MacGyver said, subconsciously straightening up and walking a little taller.

"So?" Kevin asked.

"So," MacGyver answered, and when Kevin didn't say anything, he added, "So, what?"

"What do you think?"

"About what?"

"What do you mean about what? About Hannah."

"She's kind of hot. I mean, I don't really like girls with big teeth, but yeah, she's hot."

"Big teeth?" Kevin asked.

"Yeah, you never noticed?"

"Her big teeth?"

"Yeah."

"No, dude. I look at her big bazoombas, like normal guys."

"Bazoombas?" MacGyver said, cracking up. "Bazoombas? Yeah, that's exactly what a 'normal' guy would say."

Kevin ignored this and plowed on. "So, you gonna ask her out?"

"No. You should ask her out."

"Me? Why would I ask her out? I just told you, she likes you."

"That just means she's available," MacGyver said. "I'm sure you could win her over with your Southern-boy charm." As he finished his sentence, MacGyver elbowed Kevin in the stomach.

"So you're not interested in her? Not even just to mess around with?" Kevin asked.

"Nah. I told you I don't have time right now, what with work and my dad and all."

"Liar."

"What do you mean, liar?"

"I mean you're full of shit. You're not too busy. You're just still hung up on that girl, Lacey."

"Nah," MacGyver said. "We were just friends, and besides, we don't even talk anymore."

"Bullshit," Kevin said.

"Ah, shut up," MacGyver said. "You know what? I could really go for a pie."

"A pie? Who suddenly starts craving pie?" Kevin asked.

"Huh?"

"Why are you thinking about pie?"

"Pizza, you moron. There are no good pizza places around here," MacGyver said.

"What are you talking about? We've got both a Dominos and a Pizza Hut."

"Chain store pizza. That's just pizza for people who don't like pizza. Back home, a pizza slice is as big as your face. You have to fold it over to eat it, and you know it's going to be good before you even bite into it when the grease runs out the bottom of the slice and burns your hand."

"You've got to stop saying that, Mac," Kevin said.

"That I like pizza?"

"Home. You keep calling Jersey home. You live here now, dude," Kevin said.

MacGyver looked at his friend and considered, but before he could answer a Jeep covered in mud drove by filled with three of their classmates. The kid in the shotgun seat lowered the window and shouted over to them.

"Enjoy your walk, losers," and then the Jeep sped off.

"Assholes," MacGyver said. "What's that about?"

"Nothing personal," Kevin said. "They're just jerks. They treat everybody like that. They've been that way since, like, third grade."

"Great," MacGyver said. "What really gets me is I never thought I'd be seventeen and not have a car."

"That's where I'm different. I always knew I'd be seventeen and not have a car," Kevin said.

"No, seriously," MacGyver said. "I was only fourteen, just about to turn fifteen, when the motor blew on Lacey's dad's car. It was an electric-blue PT Cruiser, and they were going to junk it. So I begged my dad to let me buy it for one hundred dollars. I had the money because I used to mow lawns."

"Why did you want a car with no motor?"

"It didn't matter. In Jersey, you can't get your license until you're seventeen, so I had plenty of time to get it back on the road."

"So, what, your Dad was good at fixing cars or something?"

"That's just it. My dad's always been very good at stuff around the house, but he never really worked on cars. But I wanted to learn, and he was willing. So between a Chilton's we bought and Youtube videos, we were able to rebuild the engine. Then, about two weeks after I got my permit, the trans went, and we had to rebuild that too," MacGyver said.

"Sounds like all you ever did was work on the car."

"We spent a lot of time on it, pretty much every weekend morning. But, she was running well and sounding great by last September."

"Couldn't you have just fixed it up again? Y'know, after Sandy?"

"Nah, man. She was completely under water. Even if I could get her running, all of the wiring would have been shot from saltwater intrusion. I'd have to rewire the whole thing."

"Sorry, dude. But, hey, with this new job, you should be able to get something soon. Right?"

"Nah, I just keep a couple of bucks for myself and give the rest to my folks. They kind of need it right now. It's all right."

"Sorry, dude."

"Sorry? You will be when I kick your butt at Mario Kart," MacGyver said, expertly changing the subject.

"Oh, we'll just see about that," Kevin countered.

"Yeah, we will," MacGyver said as they turned the corner onto his block. "So about that pizza. I think we have DiGiorno in the freezer. You up for it?"

"You have to ask?"

Chapter Forty-Nine:
Wednesday, May 15, 2013

Lacey, Donovan and Tiff settled into their seats at the Sandy support group meeting. Now that Donovan had his license, he picked Lacey and Tiff up on the way to group, even though state law required that new drivers take no more than one passenger.

"I want to see the cop who'd give me a ticket for driving my friends to support group," Donovan had said when Lacey argued that Polly could still drive her.

As Lauren, Nelson, Greg and a few others filled in the seats around the circle, Neza took her place near the front of the room quietly and clapped three times.

"I am so pleased that you could all be here this evening," Neza said as she sat down.

"Why is it I always believe her?" Lacey said, leaning over and whispering to Donovan, who shrugged.

"She's just so freakin' nice," Tiff said, leaning across Donovan to answer Lacey.

"Today, I want to spend a little time talking about anger," Neza said. "As I've said before, your emotions, all of them, demand your attention. Trying to bury them is not only unhealthy, but also unproductive. You must acknowledge them. For many of us, anger is one of the most difficult emotions to accept. Why is that?" Neza asked, her eyes searching the group for someone who would like to speak.

"I don't know about that," Nelson said. "I have no trouble with anger."

"What do you mean? How do you express it?" Neza asked.

"I yell. I throw things. I mean, not at anybody or anything," he said. "At least, not usually." The group laughed a little uncomfortably.

"That's okay," Neza said. "You're right. Sometimes your body and your mind both need a release. It's all right to throw things, even healthy, as long as you're not throwing them at people or damaging someone's property. Your ability to express your anger is a very healthy sign, Nelson. But not everyone can do that. Does anyone here have trouble with anger?"

"I do," Lacey said. "A lot of times when I get really mad, instead of yelling or screaming. I just start to cry."

"My dad," said Lauren. "He's like the mellowest, most easy-going guy. He never gets mad at anyone, lets everything slide. But then something small will tick him off, and he just explodes. But once it's over, he apologizes and it's done. Like this one time, a couple of days after the storm, when all the stores and restaurants were still closed, and we were still in the middle of the blackout, we were standing in line at Burger King. They were the only place open for miles, and the line was about an hour long. And we're standing there waiting, and this guy behind us starts complaining loudly that life is so horrible without electricity, and he can't find anywhere to charge his phone.

This went on for about thirty minutes, then my dad turns around and starts yelling at the guy to shut the fuck up. Literally that's what he said, and my dad never curses. Then he starts telling the guy off, that there are people on this line who lost their homes, and they don't need to be listening to his baby whining about his cellphone. Now, it was my whole family on the line -- me, my dad, my mom and my brother -- and my mom turns to the man and apologizes and says we're leaving and orders us all into the car."

"Wow," Donovan said. "That must have been awful."

"Yeah, it was," Lauren said. "But not the way you think. Once we got into the car, my dad cracks some stupid joke, and everybody was fine. He apologized to us and said he just needed to put that guy in his place. He even said he wasn't really mad for himself but for anyone else in the line who had to listen to the guy."

"That's pretty chill," Donovan said.

"Yeah, but there were no other restaurants to go to. The grocery stores were still closed, and we were out of real food. So it was peanut butter again that night, not even sandwiches. We were out of bread," Lauren said.

After hearing Lauren's story, Lacey surprised herself when she said, "I did something just like that" and told a story about her recent trip to Disney World that she hadn't shared with anyone.

"We were getting off Pirates of the Caribbean, and my little brother Jake was laughing and pretending he had a sword and saying stupid stuff like 'Aye,' when all of a sudden he just shut down. His expression changed, and he looked like he was going to cry," Lacey said. "My grandmother was busy trying to navigate the escalator that leads off the ride, so she didn't notice. But I was all confused until I started to hear the conversation of the people behind us.

"This old couple, who didn't have kids with them or anything, are talking about how tired they are about hearing about Sandy and how it's so ridiculous because it was nothing like Katrina. The woman even said, 'It's not like a lot of people even died or anything.'

"So we get upstairs into the gift shop. All the good rides dump you out in a gift shop. I handed my grandmother twenty dollars my mother had given us for souvenirs and told her to get Jake a sword while I went to find a bathroom. But, I didn't go to the bathroom. I followed these people till they were out of my grandmother's sight and then I laid into them. 'First of all, a lot of people did die. They not only died when the storm hit, they've been dying from staph infections from the water. They died from strokes from the stress. They died of heart attacks when they got frustrated and tried to do the rebuilding themselves. They died from the weekly fires that the Jersey Shore has had ever since Sandy corrupted all our wiring.

"And they committed suicide from depression. So I just wanted to say I'm really sorry that Sandy didn't live up to your sadistic fantasies of what a killer storm looks like, but you should know a lot of people died. Oh, and by the way, my six-year-old brother overheard your conversation, so thanks so much for ruining a trip that was supposed to give him just a few days of normal. We really appreciate that."

"What did the people say?" asked Neza, smiling.

"The lady was like, 'Well, I never.' But her husband was cool, he was all apologies. The thing is I don't normally do things like that. I mean I never do things like that. I try to not even fight with my friends, but when I saw that look on my brother's face, something inside me broke. You know?"

"I do know," Neza said. "I actually have a small stuffed doll that I sometimes yell at or throw at a wall."

"You do?" Lacey asked. "You're kidding."

"Lacey, why do you find that so hard to believe?" Neza asked.

"I don't know. You are always so calm, so peaceful. I can't imagine you getting angry at anyone."

Neza smiled.

"Sometimes anger and outrage are the only appropriate response," she said. "Other times, you have to do everything you can, like you did, Lacey, to try to make others see how their behavior hurts people.

"Now, let's do highs, lows and more," Neza said, and the meeting fell into the ritual that somehow helped everyone face the week ahead.

Chapter Fifty:
Friday, May 24, 2013

Summer school. The words played over and over in Lacey's mind and despite the alliteration, there was nothing pleasant about combining those polar opposites.

Here it was the Friday before Memorial Day weekend, the unofficial start of summer, and instead of figuring out which beach to go to tomorrow, she was searching for a way to tell her mom that she would have to go to summer school. Ms. Jones told her today that even though her midterm grades in the fourth marking period were pretty damn good, B-pluses to high A's, she would still end the year failing both chemistry and geometry. Her counselor actually had the nerve to suggest Lacey "take the summer off, get some rest" and return in September as a super sophomore.

No thank you, Lacey thought. I'll just suck it up.

When Brittney dropped Lacey off, Lacey slowly walked to her front door as if she were heading to her own execution, but her somber steps were quickly impeded by Jake springing all around her on a pogo stick.

"Look what I got! Look what I got! I won it at school in the coloring contest," Jake told her, nearly bouncing on her toe.

"Hey, watch it," she said.

"Why so grumpy?" her mother asked standing up from her seat on the front stairs.

"Oh, hi, Mom," Lacey said.

"Oh, hi yourself," her mother said with a smile.

"I've got to talk to you," Lacey said.

"Can it wait? I was just about to take Jake over to the playground. He's doing so much better. I don't think I've seen him suck his thumb in weeks," Polly said.

"Yeah, that was weird," Lacey said. "He hadn't done that in years."

"The doctor said it was completely normal after a trauma," Polly said.

"Look, I've got to talk to you," Lacey said.

"When I get back from the park, okay?"

"I have to go to summer school," Lacey blurted out as tears rolled down her face.

"Oh." Polly stepped to her daughter and hugged her. "It's all right. We knew this might happen. We'll just have to deal with it, like everything else. We're good at that. Right?"

"I really tried, Mom," Lacey said. She started to dig her left thumbnail into her ring finger, caught herself and shoved her hand in her pocket.

"I know, honey," her mother said, wiping away Lacey's tears. "It will be all right."

"Will it?"

"Sure it will. It's like I tell you all the time, sometimes you just have to accept life's obstacles and figure out a way around them. This is just a detour."

"More like a sinkhole."

"Really? Honey, it's a nice day. Do you want to come over to the park with us?"

"No thanks. It's not a great day for me," Lacey said. "I'll stay here."

"All right," Polly said. "Well, you might want to sign yourself up online for the classes you need. I understand the summer courses fill up quickly. Figure out how much it'll be, and I'll send in a check, but you'll have to pay me back."

"A check?" Lacey asked.

"For your classes," Polly explained.

"Mom, it's public school. Isn't it free?"

"First of all, 'free' just means you pay for it through your taxes. Nothing is really free," Polly corrected. "Also, summer classes are four hundred dollars each. How many do you have to take?"

"Two," Lacey said. "But, mom, I only have eight hundred and thirty-five dollars, and that's to get a car."

"Well," Polly said. "You could just stay back a year. It's up to you."

"Shit," Lacey said.

"Lacey cursed," Jake said.

"I know," their mother said. "That's not right, is it, Jake?"

"Nope," he said. "Can we go?"

"One minute," Polly said, and Jake went back to bouncing.

"Grandpa Freshet is thinking about getting a new car next year. He said you could have his car," Polly said.

"Mom," Lacey whined. "It's not a car, it's a minivan, and it's puke green."

"I know it's a minivan. I think it's a Plymouth Voyager, and you should be very grateful that he's willing to give it to you."

"I know. I know. It's just...never mind," Lacey said. "Enjoy the park. I'll sign up for classes. Thanks, Mom."

Lacey trudged into the house and up to her room. She opened her laptop and navigated to the school website. "Shit," she yelled, when she pulled up the school calendar. The last day of regular classes is Friday, June 28, and the first day of summer school is Monday, July 1.

Why is it, she thought, in all the other years, all the ones where she didn't have to go, there's always been a break between the end of classes and the start of summer school. Of course, she realized, the answer to every problem was the same: Sandy. In the wake of the storm, schools had been closed for two weeks during the blackout and while flood refugees took shelter in the government buildings.

Lacey signed up for geometry from eight a.m. to noon and chemistry from twelve-thirty to four-thirty every day throughout all of July and the first week of August.

Getting a summer job would be impossible. On Saturdays, Polly needed her to watch Jake. On Sunday afternoons and Wednesday nights, she had group, and on other nights, she'd likely have homework.

I'm doomed to a summer of poverty and solitary confinement, she thought, sinking both into her air mattress and the depths of depression.

She allowed herself a small pity party while she stared at her ceiling and let her tears fall freely. Then, she sat up, wiped her eyes and made a decision.

I'm only going to complain in group, she promised herself. There's no point in wasting the little time I have with my friends bitching and moaning.

She pushed herself to her feet, looked out the window at the still beautiful spring day and decided to go for a bike ride. When she realized she no longer owned a bike, she refused to let that get her down and instead walked to the Beach Club.

Chapter Fifty-One:
Monday, June 10, 2013

Despite the state's insistence that all schools make up the extra days that they shut down when the hurricane hit, by the first week of June, temperatures were soaring into the high nineties and conditions in many unair-conditioned school buildings were stifling and unhealthy. Emergency half days were called, and many parents kept their children home anyway.

This is going to be great, Lacey thought, knowing those same conditions were never enough to end summer classes early.

Lacey was rinsing dinner dishes and placing them in the brand-new dishwasher when she heard the soothingly nostalgic sounds of "Turkey in the Straw" getting louder.

"Mom!" she yelled. "Mom!"

"What is it?" Polly said, padding into the newly remodeled kitchen in her bare feet.

"Wow," Lacey said. "I haven't seen those in a while."

"What?" her mother said. "My jean shorts?"

"No, your bare feet."

Polly laughed. "Isn't it great? With the tile in, no more worrying about splinters."

"I never worried about them in the first place."

"I know, but that didn't keep you from getting them. Did it?"

"I like going barefoot. It's just one thing I had control over."

"And you chose getting splinters. Great move."

"Whatever. Hey, Mom. Listen."

"What?"

"No, I mean really listen. We haven't heard that in a long time," As the sounds of the folk classic filled the kitchen, they both grinned like six-year-olds. Lacey asked, "Can we get ice cream?"

"Sure. What do you want?"

"A chocolate Chipwich."

Polly reached into her pocket and handed her daughter a ten dollar bill. "And I'll have the same. You go get it. I'll finish up here."

As Lacey headed for the door, she called back. "What about Jake?"

"Grandma won't be bringing him back till later."

"Got it," Lacey said running out the door and dashing into the bright sun. Running in front of folk-tune playing trucks is a very strange ritual, Lacey thought.

"Hey, Joe," she called out to the ice cream truck driver. "You're starting awfully late in the season this year."

"Lacey, oh my God. You're all grown up. What a difference a year makes," the middle-age, beer-bellied man Lacey had known all her life responded, and then whistled at her.

"Joe," Lacey said with a laugh and even though the flirting was just play-acting, Lacey blushed. "Where have you been since April?"

"Sorry, honey," Joe said, shaking his head. "I had to change the route this year. Not enough people living here right now."

"Oh," she said. "Two chocolate Chipwiches."

"How are you guys doing? Did you have much water?"

"Four feet."

"I'm sorry, kiddo," Joe said, handing over the ice cream.

"Nah, we're good now," Lacey said. "The builder is supposed to be done on Friday. A bunch of new furniture is coming next week. Then, we only have to deal with the landscaping and the pool."

"Oh, that's great, honey. I drive by so many blocks where the houses all have to be torn down, and it's taking so long. I just feel sorry for all these people. I mean I've known them all for years. It's like family."

"Are you going to start coming over this way again?" Lacey said with a hopeful smile.

"Yeah, hon, I figure with summer here, whether they're living here or not, people will still be at the Beach Club. Right?"

"I hope so, Joe. I hope so. Have a good night," Lacey said and took the ice cream in to her mom.

Chapter Fifty-Two:
11 a.m. Friday, June 28, 2013

"Last one to the diving dock buys the beer," Tyler said, running across the Beach Club sand, trailed by Ashley, Brittney, Lacey, and about a half dozen other friends.

As they ran past another group of girls they knew from school, they tore off and abandoned clothing until each was appropriately attired by the time they reached the shoreline and plunged into the water.

Lacey pulled herself onto the new dock, very similar to the old one -- except that this 12-by-20-foot floating platform at the outer edge of the swimming area, was built with synthetic deck boards instead of wood. *No more splinters,* Lacey thought.

Not that splinters were ever much of a deterrent. Once they became good enough swimmers to reach the dock, Lacey and her friends would stake it out as their virtual home on most summer days. It was like a private oasis just for them, right there in plain sight of the entire neighborhood. Many secrets and more than a few dirty jokes had been shared out here, even on crowded beach-party days, when adults stayed under their umbrellas and younger kids floundered around in the shallows near the water's edge.

"Suckers," Lacey said triumphantly as she looked at her friends.

"What do you mean, suckers?" asked Tyler, who sported a pair of black board shorts with Harry Potter images, such as glasses, a lightning bolt and the number nine and three-quarters. "You were last. You're buying."

"No can do, pal. I've got nada. You guys are out of luck."

"Wait. That's not fair," Tyler said, hip-checking her back into the water.

As Lacey emerged, he reached out his hand to pull her back up.

"No way. I can't trust you," Lacey said, swimming around to the ladder on the other side.

"It is so nice to finally be out of school," Brittney said.

"Yeah, I thought this year would never end," Ashley agreed.

"Hey, speak for yourself. This is just another weekend for me," Lacey said, readjusting her red bikini top. "No last day of school here."

Ashley patted her back. "It won't be that bad. We've still got nights and weekends."

"So, where are we going tonight?"

"The twins' place," Brittney said.

"Really," Lacey groaned. "Their window is so freakin' high."

"It's all right. We left your stepladder there last Saturday. Remember?"

"Oh, yeah. Still, I miss Ashley's and just using the key."

"Sorry," Donovan said. "My parents thought boarding up the front door would keep the lowlifes out."

"Little did they know their sons and their friends are the lowlifes," Lacey said.

"No, we're not," Brittney said, standing up with her jet black hair shining in the sun. She cleared her throat as if she were about to make some dramatic point but instead did a flip into the bay.

Donovan's twin, Michael, chimed in. "Yeah, the lowlifes are those assholes who are breaking into other people's houses and partying. We only go in our own houses."

"Yeah, that just makes me sick," Lacey said. "Those North Dover and South kids don't belong here. It's so flippin' disrespectful, messing up people's homes when we're already going through all this crap."

"Yeah. You know the kid with the uni-brow who's always in rehab," Donovan said.

"Trevor?"

"Yeah, him. Anyway, he was living in the Farino house for like two weeks, and he was so stoned out of his mind he actually wrote his name in feces on the bathroom wall."

"No way," Ashley said.

"You're making that up," Brittney said, folding her arms in front of her as if she were cold, even though she wasn't.

"No, really. Mr. Farino had to get in there for the deed or something, and he found it. The old man was actually crying when he told my mom," Michael said.

"Those people are in their eighties. They don't need to deal with all this shit," Donovan said.

"Literally," Lacey said.

"What?" Donovan asked.

"Shit. You said shit. That's what they literally had to deal with," Lacey said with a snicker. But no one else seemed to think it was funny. As the group talked, the boys took turns diving off the dock while the girls stretched out on their backs to enjoy the sun.

"Yeah, Officer Cheng said they're putting on more Silverton shifts this summer to try and deter the break-ins, but there's only so much they can do," Connor said.

"Some of those assholes are having keggers and leaving all their garbage and crap just thrown around like these aren't people's homes," Tyler said.

"Yeah, Yanni and his buds are actually posting it on Facebook," Brittney said.

"No way," Ashley said.

"Yup," Brittney said.

"I haven't seen that."

"You probably have. You just don't know what you're looking at."

"Are you calling me stupid?" Ashley said, narrowing her blue eyes.

"No, you idiot. They post it in code," Brittney said.

"Damn, if I had my phone, I'd just call it up for you. Did you ever see how some of their posts will end with something like, 'See ya later B104 L10?'" Connor asked.

"No."

"I have," Ashley said. "They've been doing that for a couple of months now. I figured it had something to do with video games."

"Video games? Why video games?" Tyler asked.

"I don't know. I don't know anything about video games, and it made no sense to me, so I just put two and two together," Ashley said.

"Brilliant," Tyler said.

"Why? Am I right?"

"No," Connor said. "You know how the tax maps have all been posted online while people file all their paperwork with FEMA?"

"No."

"Yeah, my mother said it makes her life a lot easier because a lot of court records are identified by block and lot rather than street addresses," Lacey said.

"Right," Brittney said. "Well, that's what those idiots are using to announce their hangouts."

"Really?"

"I wouldn't think they were smart enough for that," Ashley said.

"Yeah, well, Yanni's dad is a builder," Donovan said.

"And Corky's dad's a surveyor," Tyler added.

"Damn," Ashley said.

"Still, I wouldn't have thought that crew would have been beyond yelling addresses across the cafeteria," Lacey said.

"That's so last year," Tyler said.

"What?"

"No, literally, last year," Tyler said.

"Don't you remember? Corky yelled across the cafeteria," Connor said.

"Hey, Bri, meet us at the yacht club. We'll bring the Molly,'" Donovan, Michael and Tyler said in unison.

"No way," Lacey said, surprised she had never heard this story.

"No, really," Connor said.

"But isn't Officer Cheng always in the cafeteria during lunch?" Brittney asked.

"Oh, yeah," Tyler said.

"Didn't he say anything?" Ashley asked.

"Nope, he just sent his buddies over to the yacht club that night," Donovan said.

"Oh, right, that's when Jamie got sent to juvie," Brittney said. Her jade green eyes lit up once she understood how this story fit into the history she knew.

"Hey, Lacey, isn't that your mom's minivan?" Tyler asked.

"Oh," Lacey said, sitting up and squinting into the sun to see. "Yeah."

"Are you in trouble?" Connor asked.

"No, I don't get in..."

Beep. Beeeeep. Beeeeeeeeeeeeep.

"Okay, Mom, we hear you," Lacey called over. "What's up? And why are you home so early?"

"I'm not. I was just driving back from a deposition in Brick and stopped to pick up three pizzas."

With that the boys all dove from the platform and did their best impression of an Olympic trial.

Tyler arrived at the car first and gratefully took the three flat boxes Polly offered through her open window.

"Thank you so much," Tyler said.

"Don't mention it. I thought it would be a nice last-day-of-school treat."

"You're the best," Connor said, smiling wide so the purple bands in his braces showed.

Brittney and Ashley dried themselves on the beach and yelled over in spontaneous sing-song, "Thanks, Polly."

Just as Polly reached to shift back into drive, Lacey arrived at her mother's open window, dripping wet.

"I'd hug you, but...," Lacey said as drops of water pinged onto Polly's side-view mirror.

"That's all right," Polly said with a laugh.

"You didn't have to do this."

"I know. I wanted to."

Lacey smiled broadly.

"Now, that's why I do it."

"Huh?" Lacey asked.

"That smile. I'd do just about anything in the world to see that smile. I gotta go back to work. See you later. Love you."

"Love you, too," Lacey said, walking back toward the Beach Club in bare feet. Her mother was so thoughtful. She wanted to be thankful, but mostly she just felt spied on.

Chapter Fifty-Three:
Early afternoon, Friday, June 28, 2013

"Things seem good between you and your mom," Ashley said as she and Lacey walked the pizza boxes over to the recycling bin on the side of the Beach Club building.

"You think so? Don't you think that it's weird her showing up here like this? She's afraid every time I'm out of her sight."

"Umm. No offense, but you can't blame her... To be honest, I kinda feel that way, too."

"Oh, come on, Ash, you know I'm fine."

"I know. You seem fine. But..."

"But?" Lacey demanded, color rising in her cheeks.

"Well, you seemed fine before, too. You know."

"Oh, so you both think if you don't babysit me I'm going to go off myself or something," Lacey said, searching Ashley's eyes.

"No, no. It's not like that. It's just...I worry... Honestly, Lace, I don't think I can do this without you."

"Do what?"

"All of this, y'know? It's always been like that, at least for me. You've always had MacGyver, but I really only have you. You're the only one who gets me. Y'know?"

"Don't even mention his name," Lacey said as she lifted the bright blue recycling can lid, tossed the boxes in and slammed the lid shut.

"MacGyver? Why?"

"Never mind."

"No, why? You're not still mad that he didn't tell you he was coming home over Spring Break. Are you?"

"No. No, I mean that sucked and all, but I get it. I don't know....In therapy, Neza tells us to focus on the positive things in our life and build upon those."

"So, wait. MacGyver's what? Something negative in your life?"

"Well, no, not exactly. He's just, let's face it, not in my life," Lacey said, kicking up some sand as the two turned toward Brittney and Connor, who were headed toward them and about twenty feet away.

"Geez, I hope I never move," Ashley said, earning a very brief death stare just before Lacey picked up a cardboard packet of pills in the sand and started waving it around. "Whose is this?" she shouted somewhat excitedly.

"Someone's going to need these," she said raising her voice to gain the attention of the group of girls from school tanning nearby. But Ashley's hand shot up in a flash and grabbed the item from Lacey.

"They're mine," Ashley said with a growl. Then softer, "Let it go."

"I got them for cramps," Ashley added, quickly bending over and stuffing the pills into the pocket of her discarded jean shorts laying nearby on the beach.

"Got what for cramps?" Brittney asked as she joined them.

"Midol," Lacey said quickly. For some reason, she felt a sudden need to provide Ashley with some rare privacy.

"Where'd everyone else go?" Ashley asked, straightening up and trying not to look startled.

"Fishing," Brittney said. "You know the boys. They're always trying to snag something."

"Hey!" Connor said.

"Tell me that's not true," Lacey countered.

"You want to go back out to the dock?" Brittney asked.

"Nah, I'm going to wash off. I don't like the feel of the salt water on my skin. It's always so dry," Ashley said.

"Dry? The water is dry?" Brittney asked with a small laugh.

"I don't know, tight or something," Ashley said.

"I don't know about that, but whenever we go in the bay, I feel like I smell like fish," Brittney said.

"What? Eww," Lacey said. "But you can't wash up down here. They haven't rebuilt the outdoor shower. We can go to my house if you want."

"Okay."

"I'm going to check out the fishing," Connor said and wandered off.

"Sounds good. Let me just grab my clothes," Brittney said.

"Actually," Lacey said, staring up at her gorgeous, long-legged friend. "You might want to put them on."

"Just to walk to your house?"

"What the hell for?" Ashley said.

"It's just that there's a lot of strangers – umm workers – in the neighborhood, and well they're not used to seeing three hot mamas walking down the street in bikinis."

"Lacey, you're starting to sound like your mother."

"No, really, they can be a little creepy," Lacey said.

"Uggh."

So the girls fumbled awkwardly into their clothes to walk the four doors down to Lacey's. Brittney arrived at the chain-link gate first and held it open for her friends.

"Ouch," Lacey said. "I didn't expect the asphalt to be so hot. It's usually not this hot on the last day of school."

"It's usually not July on the last day of school," Brittney said.

"It's not…"

"Practically is."

"Yeah."

"Lacey, when are you opening your pool?" Ashley asked.

"Not anytime soon."

"Why? I thought you just needed a new liner and a couple of other parts," Brittney said.

"Yeah, that's what we thought. That's what they told us in November."

"But?"

"But when the guy came back last week, he said the uprights rusted out over the winter, and now we need a new pool."

"Y'know, you wouldn't think the flood would have killed the pool. I mean it's a pool. It's made for water," Ashley said.

"Yeah, well, you didn't see it the first day Polly and I came back here. The water in the backyard was six feet up. It went right over the top of the pool. It was like the pool was just some play toy in the middle of a lake or something."

"Geez."

"Inside the house, the water was still up to my waist. Get this, lately Polly keeps complaining that she's always wanted an indoor pool and the one chance we had to swim in our house she didn't take it."

"We went swimming in your house!" Ashley practically screamed.

"What? You weren't here," Lacey said.

"No, no when you were five – no six! Your kindergarten birthday party."

"Oh my god, you're right," Brittney said.

"Oh, that party," Lacey said.

"Yeah, the Miss America party. That was sooo much fun," Brittney said.

"That was insane."

"Oh, it was so cool. We arrived in our formal wear for tea in your living room, complete with miniature sandwiches and companion seats for our dolls."

"Then, it was time for the swimwear portion," Lacey said.

"And your mother dramatically pulls down the tarp she had taped up."

"Nailed up," Lacey said.

"Covering your dining room. And there's an entire indoor beach with two plastic swimming pools, one with a slide and sand everywhere."

"Don't forget she jacked the temperature up to eighty-eight degrees and covered the wall with that giant poster of the sun and palm trees."

"That was amazing."

"So much fun," Lacey said. "My parents spent months trying to get all the sand out of the house. My mom thought it would all stay on this blue tarp, but it ripped when they were trying to clean up. My dad was so mad. He kept saying, 'I told you this was a bad idea.'"

"Ouch," said Ashley.

"Ahh, they were fighting all the time back them. That party was amazing, but it was classic Polly. I complained that other kids get to have pool parties and it wasn't fair that because my birthday is in March, I couldn't," Lacey said.

"She's always tried to fix everything for you," Ashley said.

"Yeah, but then she yells at me for not being able to accept change and disappointment. How could I? She's never prepared me," Lacey said. "Anyway, about the pool, Polly's not sure we'll be able to get one this summer. Apparently it's not covered by insurance, and it's like five thousand dollars."

"For an above ground pool?" Brittney said.

"Yeah, but it's huge," Ashley pointed out. "What is it, 15 by 30 feet?"

"Actually, it's 18 by 36 feet," Lacey said. "I know because my mom always reminds me when I tell her I'm going swimming in someone's in-ground pool."

"Our pool is just as big as anyone's in-ground pool," Ashley said, mocking Polly the way Lacey always did.

"Yeah, except no diving," Lacey said.

"Who needs diving? That slide is amazing," Brittney said. "Oh, are you going to be able to save it?"

"We think so, but we really haven't gotten there yet. Mom doesn't want to spend the money on the pool until we're completely done with the house stuff and the landscaping. Nothing fancy, just getting a front lawn back."

"Should be a lot easier without all your trees. Why did you take them down anyway?"

"They were dying."

"Saltwater intrusion," Ashley said.

"I miss the tree with our tire swing," Brittney said.

"Me, too," Lacey said. "Hey, you guys better clean up. Everyone's going to wonder where we are."

Chapter Fifty-Four:
Tuesday, July 2, 2013

Hey

Lacey deleted the text. Two months had passed since MacGyver sent that vile picture, and in that time, she'd managed to keep herself from texting, Facebooking or calling him. Why would she respond to him now? Better question, why was he even texting her? He should be somewhere making out with his blonde in beautiful Florida. Meanwhile, she needed to focus on this stupid geometry class and earning her junior status. It would really blow if all her friends were upperclassmen, and she was stuck in the cafeteria during every lunch period.

She slipped her phone back into her pocket and set about proving why angle CAB and angle DEF are equal. *Who flippin' cares?* she thought as sweat dripped from her forehead onto the paper, staining the page with a peach-colored smudge.

I must have put on too much makeup, Lacey thought as she tried to dry the splotch with her equally moist hand. *How is anyone supposed to put proper makeup on at seven in the morning?*

Most of her classmates in the morning class showed up in shorts and flip-flops, hair barely combed, looking like they'd be more comfortable on a camping trip or at least back in bed. But Lacey learned right away yesterday that she and Corine didn't have that luxury.

Corine, a kid from the south end of town whom Lacey had never met before, was the only other girl who was taking two classes. They were the only a.m. students who had to worry about their appearance. That's because half the afternoon students came in made-up like they were headed to prom. It was as if since they couldn't do anything fun in the morning – 'cause they'd have to cut it short and go to summer school – they spent the entire time grooming.

Lacey had been surprised by how many kids joined her during these high-temperature torture sessions. Her high school was huge, with hundreds of students in each year's graduating class. But it was just one of three that served the school district, so many of the other summer scholars were teens she'd never met.

"This is a good opportunity to meet new friends," Polly had said.

But Lacey told her, "I don't need to make the acquaintance of summer school losers."

"Remember, you're one of those summer school los... students," Polly said.

Lacey laughed.

"And you're not a loser," her mother said.

"Okay, right. You almost just called me one."

"Did not."

"Did too. What were you going to say then, summer school lovers?"

"Hmm, maybe that's an idea," her mother countered. "Maybe you'll meet a new love, some hot boy."

"Don't say hot, Mom. You sound ridiculous."

"What? You can say hot, but I can't?"

"No, not at all. Feel free to tell Jake, 'Don't touch the stove; it's hot.' Or if we're having chili or wings, please, by all means, remind me they're hot. But not when we're talking about guys. In fact, better yet, here's some advice, and I'm not trying to be mean, but honestly, Polly, we should not be talking about boys. I mean, c'mon, if the wrong people heard you talking about sixteen-year-old boys and calling them hot, you could probably be arrested for pedophilia or something."

"Very funny," her mother had said that day and shoved her nose back into some FEMA or insurance paperwork. Too bad, Lacey had thought, we were kind of having fun there for a minute. It's like we never have a minute to just talk and joke around.

"Lacey. Lacey."

Lacey looked up from her geometry proof and stared blankly at the teacher, whose name escaped her. "Ah, huh," she croaked.

"Where are you?"

"Oh, I'm sorry. I'm still working on this proof. I didn't even realize we were going over it."

"Try and pay attention," said the teacher, who hadn't broken a sweat even though he was dressed in khakis, a long-sleeve blue shirt and a tie in the 100-degree heat.

"Ah, huh," Lacey said. "Yes, sorry."

"I don't really care, but I'm guessing you don't want to give up your summer and still have to repeat, what is it, freshman year?"

"Sophomore," Lacey snapped.

"Exactly," he said, returning to the white board and picking up a purple dry-erase marker.

Mr. Whatever probably thinks he's giving constructive advice, but goddamn it, Lacey thought, teachers are supposed to care. It's one of the main characteristics of a good teacher, isn't it?

"I don't really care," the words played over and over in Lacey's mind and made her boil so that there was no way she could concentrate on what Mr. What's-his-face was writing. She simply got up and headed to the bathroom. This was the one and only good thing about summer school, she thought. Throughout the year, any student experiencing a bathroom emergency, no matter how urgent, was required to raise their hand, get recognized and ask for a bathroom pass.

Lacey knew from experience that sometimes, that's the last thing you want to do. Take, for example, the day she started to realize she'd gotten her period unexpectedly. There she was sitting in class wearing a white skirt. She definitely didn't want to draw attention to herself and have everyone watch her walk out the door. In fact, that day, she just stayed in her seat until everyone left, then asked Miss Koch if she had a sweater or something to help her out.

But, here in summer school, bathroom use was simply on a need-to-go basis. You could just get up and leave the room the way you would if you were anywhere else in the world instead of one of the prisons we call schools, Lacey thought as she walked out.

In the girls' room, Lacey splashed cold water on her face. She looked at the hand dryer, but more hot air didn't seem like a great idea on this triple-digit day. Instead, she wadded up some toilet paper, lightly patted her face dry and wiped off her hands. She looked around for a garbage can, but finding none, she tried to toss the clumpy mess from the sink area, beyond a stall door and into a toilet. Not surprisingly, she missed.

Lacey stared at the small white mess about a foot from a toilet and considered picking it up. *Ah, screw it*, she thought and instead locked the stall door and sat down, fully dressed on the toilet.

Then, she pulled out her phone.

There it was again: *Hey*

I thought I erased that text, Lacey thought as she stared at yet another shout-out from MacGyver. She glared at it, then checked the time. Crap, he'd just sent this one. Now what. She sat there in the tan-tiled room thinking. *What do you mean, now what? Don't answer him. That's done. He's done. You made a decision.*

A text from Ashley appeared, saying, "We miss you," along with a picture of her and Britt at the waterpark.

Yeah right, Lacey thought. *No one misses me*, but just as she thought those words, her phone shook just a bit and a new text from MacGyver appeared: *Hey, why are you ignoring me?*

Damn, she thought, *leave me alone.* But the hits just kept coming. *I miss you.*

I miss you, too, her thumbs typed and hit send practically without her consent. *Look, I'm in summer school. I have to go.*

Then, Lacey did the unthinkable. She turned off her phone. I'm not going to repeat sophomore year, she thought. She headed back to class, where she actually paid full attention.

Chapter Fifty-Five:
Wednesday, July 3, 2013

Climbing down from Corine's white SUV around five p.m., Lacey thanked the girl profusely for the ride. "See you Friday," she called as she slammed the door.

As she approached the side door of her house, Lacey noticed a large brown basket blocking her front door and headed that way instead.

A gift, she thought. *Flowers?*

Is Mom finally seeing someone, and without telling me? Hey, maybe it's for me, some secret admirer. She closed the short distance to the door.

The basket was huge, about two feet long and nearly a foot deep and a foot wide. It was covered in a weird purple, plastic wrap generally reserved for Easter baskets. Inside were towels, face cloths, sponges, earth-friendly cleaning supplies and a set of queen-size sheets in a yellow-and-red-plaid design.

Lacey sat down on her front porch and examined the contents without unwrapping anything. Then, she spotted the card. "For Our Friends in Toms River," was carefully written across an envelope neatly punctuated with a small cross and the words First Christian Church of Ohio in the upper left-hand corner.

"No way!" Lacey said. She ran down the stairs and halfway down the block toward the Beach Club, looking to see if she could find the culprits who had dropped this off. But there was no one.

She did a quick about-face and ran to the corner, looking first left, then right. Eventually, she spotted a group of teenagers about three blocks away, all wearing shorts and the same orange tee-shirt.

Lacey forgot how tired she had been after chemistry and sprinted down the street, stopping at each street corner to yell, "Hey!" or "Hey, wait a minute!"

Finally, she caught up with the small posse of six teenagers, who looked like a television ad for diversity, including one in a wheelchair. Two middle-age women, wearing the same tee-shirt, which read Crusaders for Christ, accompanied them.

"Hey," Lacey said, as she encountered the two older group members, who each were dragging large, gardening-type wagons filled with baskets just like the one she had found on her doorstep.

"Well, hello there," said one of the women, with a big cheery smile.

"Awfully hot to be running," said the other. "Can I offer you a cold bottle of water?"

"No," Lacey snapped. "No thank you. Look," Lacey said as she overheard the teens on the porch explaining they were a youth group from Ohio on a serving trip.

"Look," Lacey said. "You left a basket on my door and..."

"Oh, that was so nice of you to come find us and thank us. But that wasn't necessary," the more pudgy and older of the women said.

"No, I didn't come to," Lacey started, just as the younger, taller woman said, "When we saw what you were going through last November on the news, we decided right then and there we had to come here this summer and do whatever we can. Did you have water in your house? Well, of course you did. How much did you get?"

"Four feet."

"Oh my, we're so sorry," said the taller woman. "It must have been awful."

"It was. Look, it's just that we don't..."

"Our youth group raised money for six months, and the local hardware store donated all the cleaning supplies. We are just so glad to help. Well, here, we'll let the kids tell you themselves," said the pudgy one, as the teens started heading over.

Lacey watched as the ragtag charity team approached looking tired, extremely sweaty, yet very happy. She thought back to the two serving trips her own youth group had made to New Orleans after Katrina and lowered her head. She had run down here to yell at these people, to tell them she didn't need their charity, and their efforts were misguided and insulting. But she couldn't do it.

She smiled at one short blonde girl with glasses and braids and then walked up to her and shook her hand.

"I just want to thank you so much for coming all this way to help us. We really appreciate it," she said. "Most of my neighbors aren't home, so I just wanted to find you guys and let you know how much all this means."

The girl beamed.

"Well, I gotta go," Lacey said and quickly turned and headed home. She knew Polly wouldn't keep the basket because they didn't need it. Instead, her mother would bring it down to the People's Pantry, a food bank the school district had opened immediately after the storm to provide whatever basic necessities they could.

When she got back to her driveway, Jake was riding the new royal blue bicycle their grandparents had bought him, and Polly was sitting on a lawn chair, watching him.

"Where've you been?" her mother asked. "That's not the direction of school."

"Nah, I was just talking to some people."

"Sounds mysterious. Are these people boys?"

"God, Mom, you've got a one-track mind."

"That doesn't sound like a no."

"Actually, Mom, did you see the gift basket by the front…Where is it?"

"Oh, I brought it inside, and obviously, yes. An awfully nice gift."

"I know. Right? Anyway, I was down Silver Bay Road thanking the youth group that dropped it off.

"You were? That doesn't sound like you."

"Well, remember when you insisted we go to the Elks Club Christmas party and holiday dinner?

"Yeah."

"I think I get it."

"Get what?"

"Why you made us go."

"Oh."

"It's a lot easier to give other people help than it is to take it."

"It can be."

"On all those serving trips you made me go on every summer."

"I never made you."

Lacey tilted her head and mock frowned at her mother.

"You strongly suggested I go on. Anyway, it was so easy. You see someone who needs help, and you give it to them. I never really thought about what it felt like on their end. I just figured they were happy to get some assistance."

"Oh," Polly said. "It's just that it's…"

"Complicated," she and her mom said together.

"Yeah, I get that now," Lacey said. "It's like you always say, 'life's messy.'"

"That it is," Polly said. "Jake, watch out! There's a car coming," Polly yelled down the street.

"Speaking of cars. When can I get my permit?" Lacey asked, plopping herself on the ground next to her mother's chair.

"About that. I've got good news, and I've got bad news."

"The good news is that we've won the lottery and you're going to buy me a brand new red Mustang."

"Red Mustang. Really?"

"Yeah, why?"

"Oh, it's just funny. I always wanted a red Mustang."

"Did you ever have one?"

"No, closest I ever got was a green Pinto."

"Pinto. What's that?"

"Oh, they were great little cars – unless they got hit from behind."

"What happened then?"

"They'd explode. But only if the left blinker was on. Or something like that."

"Really?"

"Lacey, I've told you a million times. I don't lie to you. Anyway, the good news is we can call tonight and set up your six hours."

"Really?"

"Things are getting pretty settled around here now. I can swing the three hundred bucks for the driving school."

"That's great, Mom," Lacey said, jumping up and hugging her mom. "Thanks, Mom. I love you."

"Hold that thought," Polly said.

"Huh," Lacey said and then remembered there was more information coming. "And the bad news..."

"It's pretty bad."

Lacey frowned and sat back down. Then, she got seriously worried, "You're not putting me back in the hospital are you?"

"No, of course not. You're doing well. You seem to be doing okay. You are okay, aren't you?"

"Yes, Mom. I'm fine. So what's the bad news?"

"Well, nobody's dying."

"Shit."

"Lacey!"

"Sorry, but that's how you start conversations that end with things like, 'Dad's moved out.'"

"Well, you're on the right track. And, I'm sorry. I'm really sorry."

"What?! C'mon, Polly, just spit it out."

"Jake, stay off that property. There are probably nails all over there."

"Mom."

"Sorry. Honey, I just got the final paperwork from the insurance company and the township."

"That's good, right? I mean we have our CEO now, right?

"CO. A CEO is the head of a big company. A CO is a Certificate of Occupancy. And, yes, we passed all the inspections, and we have our CO."

"So all we have to do now is the landscaping and the pool, right?"

"Well, that's what I thought, but it turns out…"

"What? We're not going to be able to afford the pool? Crap. I thought we were okay. I thought…"

"No, Lacey, honey. I'm sorry, but we have to move out again."

"But, you just said," Lacey was up on her feet and yelling now. "You said we have our CEO, CO, whatever."

"Baby, we have to lift our house."

"What? No!" Tears began to fall down Lacey's face. "But you said we didn't have to! Shit! We just got all new furniture! I finally got my bed back!"

Polly began to cry, too. "I know. I know," she said, as she stood and hugged her daughter. "I'm sorry. I'm so sorry. I keep trying to make things better for you. I keep..."

Lacey's mom abruptly left the embrace and ran down the street. "Don't cry, Jake. I'll be right there. I'm sure you're okay, baby. It's just a fall. Mommy's coming."

"Yeah, but don't let her fool you. She can't fix everything," Lacey mumbled as she folded up her mom's chair, tossed it into the garage and headed inside.

Chapter Fifty-Six:
Fourth of July, 2013

"Lacey, are you coming in the pool?"

Ha, she sounds like it's any normal Fourth of July, Lacey thought as she rolled over and finally decided to get up around twelve-thirty. It was so nice to linger in her own bed after so many months on what she had come to call, "the raft."

"I told you before," Lacey yelled into the hall, hoping her voice would travel through the upstairs hallway and down the stairs.

"Lacey, how many times have I told you. You have to be…"

"In the same room with the person you are speaking to," they finished in unison as Lacey got to the top of the stairs.

"There you are. You are looking particularly cheery this morning," Polly said, staring up at her sleepy-eyed daughter in her "Will Trade Virginity for Concert Tickets" night shirt.

"Do I?"

"No," Polly said and laughed. "Jake and I are going in the pool. Do you want to come?"

"Polly, I've told you before that is not a pool. It's a puddle," Lacey retorted.

"Don't be so spoiled, and don't call me Polly," Polly scolded. "I've told *you* before it's a standard five-foot pool."

"It's two feet deep."

"Two and a half. But it is five foot in diameter," Polly countered. "Besides it's better than those jellyfish in the bay."

"Ahh, pft. They don't really bother me. Besides, Mom, it'd be pretty embarrassing swimming around in a baby pool on my front lawn."

"Lawn, what lawn?" Polly said with a good-natured laugh.

"Okay, on our front dirt."

"Honey, I understand, but honestly you need to start embracing the life you have instead of worrying about the one you lost. I know it's taking a while, but all this is just temporary."

"So are my teen years."

"Oh come on, it's hot. You might like it."

Lacey and her mother stared at each other for a moment. Then, Polly sighed.

"Okay, okay. I won't push it. Your loss," Polly said. "Come on, Jake. Let's go."

"Have fun," Lacey called down to them and headed back to her room.

Last night, after her big reveal that they would be homeless again just in time for the new school year, Polly rushed out to Walmart for the splash pool "to make the best of things." She also tried to cheer Lacey up with the news that they didn't have to move out again until the end of August.

Of course, Polly's idea of making the best of things meant total humiliation for Lacey. Instead of simply suffering through a summer without a pool, Polly insisted on turning their front lawn into some odd cityscape with a barbecue, lawn chairs, the splash pool and even a porch swing.

Lacey couldn't believe how excited her mother had been with her purchases, especially with the pool, which she bragged "came with a filter and everything."

Honestly, with temperatures spiking in the high fever area, Lacey totally understood the need for a small pool, especially for Jake. And she would even have splashed around in it herself if Polly had put it in the backyard, like normal people.

Lacey had lived much of her life secluded from neighbors and passing cars by a six-foot-high wooden back fence. They were the standard in Silverton. In fact, many people had long ago forsaken their wooden fences for the easy maintenance of the white plastic-looking fences, but Polly said they were too expensive.

With towering border walls in place, kids like Lacey could yell and scream, run around, jump on trampolines and even play fetch with MacGyver's barking dog without disturbing a living soul or inviting unwelcomed thoughts, comments and suggestions. She definitely wasn't used to having her summer days scrutinized by passing strangers. Also, she wasn't used to seeing passing strangers, who seemed to be everywhere these days.

Lacey had begged her mother to remove the skeletal structure of her beloved pool and move Tiny Pool into the back. But, Polly explained that the now useless pool had to stay because it had taken months to get the original permits, and she didn't want to start over again.

"Why would you have to start over?"

"Because if we no longer have a pool, we will have to start from scratch and ask permission to build one."

"Whose permission do you need? We own the property, don't we? Can't we just do what we want?"

"I'm afraid it doesn't work that way. Pools require building, electrical and fence inspections, not to mention gas for the heater."

"Who inspects them?"

"The town."

"The mayor?"

"No, they have professionals come out and make sure all the laws are being followed."

"That's stupid."

"You'd think so, but how would you feel if the whole block exploded because someone had the natural gas line for their pool heater installed by a handyman who didn't know what he was doing?"

"That happens?"

"It happens."

"Okay, but I still don't get it. Why can't we just tear down this pool and get another one?"

"Because the approvals are only good for the first pool. That's why we're going to *repair* this one, rather than get another one, even if we are replacing nearly every piece."

After a while, Lacey had zoned out. Just because Polly had to know all this technical stuff about laws and variances didn't mean Lacey did. In fact, she couldn't care less. For her, the only significant thing was that for this summer her backyard would remain off limits, her front yard would be treated like her backyard, and Tiny Pool would remain a silent sentinel until they moved out again on Aug. 31.

Chapter Fifty-Seven:
Immediately after, Thursday, July 4, 2013

Lacey texted Ashley to determine what their holiday plans would be.

L: *Hey*

A: *Hey*

L: *Want to hang out?*

A: *Sure.*

L: *Where?*

A: *Beach?*

L: *OK*

A: *Wait, do you mean beach? The Beach Club or the beach beach?*

L: *The real beach.*

A: *Yes!*

L: *Can you get us a ride?*

A: *I think so.*

L: *Great. Go ask.*

A: *…*

L: *…?*

A: *Not home right now, but I will be soon.*

L: *Soon?*

A: *Less than an hour.*

L: *OK*

###

Getting into the back of Ashley's mom's forest green Subaru Outback, Lacey didn't hesitate to ask, "Where were you before?"

"Umm," Ashley said, flashing her eyes toward her mom and then back at Lacey.

"Uh, oh," Lacey said.

"Ashley was at the People's Pantry. She spends a lot of time there these days. She's been volunteering since... What was it, April or May?

"April," Ashley said in a sort-of soft growl.

"She doesn't like to talk about it, but she's there so much it's practically a full-time job," Mrs. Peterson said proudly.

"A lot of kids help out there, sorting donations and helping shoppers," Lacey said. "When we used to go there, the first couple of weeks after the storm, they were always asking me if I wanted to volunteer."

"Me too," Ashley said.

"My mom said I was pretty rude, but I didn't mean to be. It's just this one woman was so insistent. I swear she worked on human commission, so finally, I said to her, 'Well, the only way I could spend time helping out here is if one of you guys sorted through all my stuff figuring out what to throw out and helped tear down our Sheetrock.'"

"Oh," said Ashley's mom. "Most of the volunteers are very nice. They're trying to help."

"I know," Lacey said. "I was always in a pretty bad mood back then."

"And now?" Laura Peterson asked, her voice suddenly heavy with concern.

"Mom," Ashley scolded in a sharp, quiet voice.

"It's okay," Lacey said. "I'm doing pretty well. Thanks for asking. They say I have PTSD, but so far I don't need meds or anything, and I'm really feeling a lot better."

"That's good to hear," Laura Peterson said.

"Mom," Ashley growled again and groaned.

"It's all right, Ash, your mom's just concerned about me," Lacey said, adding in a slightly teasing voice, "You know, the way you must feel about all the people who use the pantry… It's great that you're spending so much time there."

Before Ashley could respond, the Subaru pulled up next to the twenty-dollars-for-beach-parking sign in a dirt lot across from the Seaside Heights Boardwalk. "I'll pick you girls up at six-thirty. Okay?"

"That's great. Thank you," Lacey said, getting out and pulling her Hello Kitty towel from the back seat.

"Okay, Mom. Thanks," Ashley said and pushed the door shut. As she straightened, she looked into Lacey's glaring brown eyes.

"You've been volunteering at the pantry since April?" Lacey bellowed loud enough to make a few of the young mothers heading home from the beach with toddlers turn and look.

"Not exactly."

"But we hate that place. All those cloying do-gooders."

"Actually, they're not that bad."

Lacey stared at her.

"I mean once you get to know them."

"I can't believe this. Why do you keep lying to me?" Lacey demanded.

"Lying? I wasn't lying. I just never told you."

"That's called lying, a lie of omission."

"Oh, come on, now you sound like your mother."

"Well, she's right."

"Look, if it makes you feel any better, I've only really been going there for a few days. Y'know, since you started summer school. And, to be honest, I kind of like it."

"Ugggh," Lacey groaned.

"No, really. It feels good, helping out, y'know? And at least it's doing something, rather than sitting around feeling sorry for ourselves."

Lacey breathed in deeply and blew out the air. "I guess," she said. "But, wait a minute, why does your mom think you've been going there since April."

"Well, I've kind of used the pantry as an excuse."

"An excuse? An excuse for what?"

"Well, y'know how they were always asking us to volunteer? And we went there a lot longer than you did. Anyway, I told my mom that I was going to do it and then…"

"And then?"

"Tyler and I would go to my house pretty much every day."

"Yeah, so?"

The girls just looked at each other.

"Lacey, my house, not the apartment."

"What for?" Lacey asked, wondering why Ashley's cheeks and ears were starting to flush.

"Y'know," Ashley said.

"I know…? Oh!" Lacey said. "Every day?"

"Practically."

"Oh. Hey, do you have a beach badge or do you have to get a day badge?"

"Neither."

"What?"

"It's one of the great things about getting up so late. They're supposed to check beach badges till six, but after three, they usually don't even bother."

"Cool. Then I've got some money for Curley fries."

"Awesome."

The girls simultaneously reached down to pull off their flip-flops and slipped right past the beach badge hut onto the sand. Then they spread out their towels to take in some rays.

As Lacey laid there with the hot sun beating down on her, she wondered if she should say something more to Ashley, whether she should ask her something, but she just didn't know.

She wasn't shocked that her friend was now "active" or even that she hadn't told Lacey, but it kind of bothered her that Ashley and Tyler weren't a couple. Most of the kids in school didn't even know the two were hooking up. Was that the way things were supposed to go? Maybe all this secrecy was just part of being mature, Lacey thought. But then again, maybe not.

Chapter Fifty-Eight:
Saturday, July 13, 2013

Because of summer school, Lacey's time was really limited, so her mother arranged for her to do the whole six hours of driving school at once.

When she'd heard she'd be spending a summer day driving all over the Jersey Shore, Lacey let her imagination run wild. She thought of all the Springsteen songs her parents used to sing with the car windows open and the radio blasting. This was going to be fun!

Early that morning, Lacey anxiously paced outside her house in denim shorts and an orange tank top. She remembered this one day when she was walking down Silver Bay Road and this kid Jason passed her driving a bright yellow Mustang with black stripes.

They had been in many classes together in elementary and middle school, so Lacey was a bit pissed when he didn't beep or wave. Then she noticed the lettering on the back bumper, LEARN IN STYLE. Apparently, this driver's education school in Brick, the next town over, sold all of their regular cars and picked up three hot rods and were charging more than twice the price of most schools for the driving lessons needed in New Jersey to get your permit before age seventeen. Rumor had it they were even in the process of restoring an old DeLorean, so new drivers would be able to spend their first legal hours on the road going *Back to the Future.*

The whole idea totally captured Lacey's imagination, and she daydreamed of hitting that magic number eighty-eight in a DeLorean during her very first driving lesson. Of course, she knew she wouldn't time travel, but hey, *what if?* When she'd asked her mother if she could do her six hours with them, she had said yes –

with a catch. Of course, she did; Polly wasn't like a lot of parents who say no when they think their kid's ideas are dumb or too costly. Instead, she almost always said yes but often with restrictions.

This time, her mother said she wouldn't pay a penny more for the flashy vehicles, but Lacey was welcome to use her own money to make up the difference. So, they looked into it. The cost was crazy high.

Still, Lacey knew she wouldn't be getting a Mustang or a DeLorean as her main drive, so she decided it was worth it to her to start her driving career with class. But then Sandy hit – and summer school.

When Polly finally gave the green light to set up driving lessons, Lacey called around, compared prices and hired Go-Pro Driving School. Despite the cheesy name, Lacey was optimistic as she paced her driveway. That was until a filthy, navy blue Ford Focus pulled alongside her mailbox and what looked like an octogenarian woman with glasses hanging from ruby-colored beads around her neck stepped out wearing what Lacey assumed is what people meant by the term muumuu. It was a strapless, bright yellow and green affair that stopped at her knees and was bunched at the bodice.

MacGyver used to tell her that guys never get tired of looking at cleavage, but this lady and her parrot outfit probably was not what he had in mind, Lacey thought as she stared at the woman, who was getting out of the car and approaching her.

"I'm Mrs. Peter Johnson," she said, reaching out to shake Lacey's hand.

"Hi," Lacey said, as the woman's clammy hand grasped her own dry one. *Is this woman's name really Peter?* Lacey thought.

The first twenty minutes of the lesson extinguished any thoughts Lacey had that this was going to be a fun day. They sat in the car at the edge of her driveway "reviewing" where everything was, and they did this on a ninety-degree day without turning the car on – meaning without any air conditioning.

Lacey tried to concentrate, but she could feel the sweat dripping from what had to be every single pore on her body – all five million of them or at least the 20,000 on her face. *Why can't chemistry be more relatable?* she thought. *I still remember those statistics from freshman year!*

As she felt the moisture on her hands, Lacey started to panic just a little. *My hands are going to be too slippery to grip the wheel! I'm going to crash before I even get off my own block!*

Eventually, she was allowed to start the car and put it in drive. The air conditioning kicked in and slowly the temperature became comfortable.

The first two hours were uneventful, driving up and down Silverton streets in a random fashion, make a left here, a right there with no destination in mind.

As they drove, Lacey found it difficult to relax. Mrs. Johnson seemed to spend every minute staring at her. *Why doesn't she look at the road!* Lacey thought. *Doesn't she realize I have no idea what I'm doing? If all she's going to do is stare at me, we could have saved a few hundred bucks.*

As they drove down blocks Lacey normally had no reason to travel, she was struck by the randomness of the storm damage. One or two blocks were uniform with every house gutted, lifted, under construction or just gone. But most streets were so haphazard, one house raised, another still decorated for Halloween and clearly untouched and the next, brand new and ready for an open house. For-sale signs, in-window permits and builder signs were everywhere.

Two signs, John and Sons Home Building and Fox Builders of Pennsylvania dominated the scene, and Lacey hoped the owners were honest people. Every day, Polly came home with a new story about someone being "bilked out of their life's savings." The phrase made Lacey think. What exactly is a life's savings? Would the thirty-five dollars she had left in her savings account be called her life's savings? And how was anyone supposed to generate any sort of nest egg when everything in the world was so expensive?

"Left at the next corner. Lacey, slow down. Lacey. Lacey! Stop! That was a stop sign!" Mrs. Peter Johnson shrieked. "Pull over to the curb."

After pulling over and putting the car in park, Lacey stared straight out, directly in front of her. Mrs. Johnson turned to her and demanded her attention, glowering at Lacey until she met her gaze.

"Where are you? You can't drive if you're not going to pay attention. No daydreaming," Mrs. Peter Johnson said sternly.

"I'm sorry, but I wasn't daydreaming," Lacey said. *No one would daydream looking at this landscape,* she thought. Then, she realized she sounded rude. "I'm sorry. I was just thinking. I'll pay more attention."

Lacey breathed a sigh of relief when "Peter" told her to pull away from the curb. This earned her a nasty look but no further lecture.

For the most part, the next hour or so was uneventful. Lacey simply listened and did as she was told. This formula changed only once. When a black cat darted out in front of the moving car, Lacey slammed on the brakes, coming to a stop just a foot or two away from the feline. The cat screeched and ran away.

"Are you okay?" she asked her instructor, bracing herself for another lecture. Instead the old lady readjusted herself in the seat and nodded, adding, "good reflexes."

Shortly past the three-hour mark, Mrs. Johnson said it was time for Lacey to leave town, and she laughed. Lacey smiled even though she wasn't sure what the big joke was.

As they finally moved from a twenty-five mile-per-hour road to a forty mile-per-hour zone, Mrs. Johnson asked if Lacey minded if she put the radio on. Lacey's heart leapt as she enthusiastically encouraged her instructor to crank some tunes. But that's not what happened.

Mrs. Johnson turned on a talk radio station. *I have no desire to listen to a bunch of talking heads*, Lacey thought. But, hey, be careful what you wish for. It wasn't talk radio at all. It was a radio preacher with a polished and gentlemanly voice forecasting Lacey's – and pretty much everyone else's – damnation.

Within thirty minutes, Lacey had been enlightened that the only way to avoid the eternal fires of hell was to be saved.

"Are you a Christian?" Mrs. Johnson asked.

"I was baptized Catholic," Lacey said.

"Oh," "Peter" said, not at all hiding her disappointment. "You need to give your life to the Lord. Stop here. Make a left. Turn away from sin."

"Which way is sin?" Lacey said, trying to be what Polly would call a wise ass.

"It is all around us, my dear," Mrs. Johnson said.

"Oh, I don't think I'm allowed to talk to you about this," Lacey said.

"Why not, dear? I'm just spreading the good word."

"Well, like I said, I was born Catholic, but we're now Satan followers, and our pastors, these two guys who are married to each other, a real cute couple. Anyway, they said we really shouldn't speak to heretics about the, um, freedoms only sinners have the power to release."

"Excuse me?"

"Yeah, my mom started taking my brother and me to these meetings in the woods about three years ago. At first, we thought it was just open to biker families, but it turns out anyone can join. We, um, sing songs and talk about the devil. Oh, and at the end of the service, they set off fireworks. It's a lot more fun than going to Mass."

"Dear, if you are trying to be funny, I don't think this is a topic you should be joking about. Head east on Route Seventy and see if you can follow the signs to the Parkway."

"East? Is that left or right?"

"Peter" sighed heavily. "Bear right."

"Okay, and I wasn't trying to be funny. You can come with us sometime if you like. We go on Wednesday nights."

"I might just do that," "Peter" said, turning off the radio. The next two hours were conducted in silence except for the occasional driving direction.

When Lacey finally got out of the car, having survived her six hours, she was tired and frustrated. *At least I have my permit now,* she thought. *I wonder if Mom will let me take her somewhere.*

Chapter Fifty-Nine:
Tuesday, July 30, 2013

Hey.

Hey, yourself. Lacey typed.

You in a bad mood or something? MacGyver asked.

I guess, Lacey replied.

Text silence. About five minutes passed. *Great,* Lacey thought, *I haven't heard from him in four weeks and now this BS.* Not in the mood to play the waiting game, Lacey decided to bridge the void.

L: *What's up?*

M: *I'm coming up there.*

L: *You're coming home? When?*

M: *This weekend.*

L: *Are you staying with your aunt?*

M: *Yup. But I thought…*

L: *You want to stay here?*

M: *For two nights. If it's OK*

L: *I don't know.*

M: *You don't know?*

L: *Well, we're mostly packed up.*

M: *You're moving?*

L: *Yeah, before Labor Day.*

M: *Wait. Why? Where?*

L: *We're not really going anywhere.*

M: *What?*

L: *You ask a lot of questions.*

M: *Lacey, what's going on? I thought you just got settled back in. I heard the trailer is gone, and your room is even back to normal.*

L: *Oh, right…Turns out that was a mistake; we could have used the trailer. Oh, and it's back to the air mattress for me. This time in the living room.*

M: *What?*

L: *We are raising the house six feet. We're moving to the apartments off Kettle Creek Road for about three months.*

M: *That sucks.*

L: *You're telling me. Jake and Mom are sharing a bedroom. I'm in the living room.*

M: *I'm sorry.*

L: *Me, too.*

Another two minutes of silence passed between them. Lacey sat in her room and stared at her phone.

This time MacGyver reached out.

M: *My plane lands at 3 Friday.*

L: *That's great. Why are you coming up?*

M: *My grandfather is sick.*

L: *I'm sorry.*

M: *Me too.*

L: *Is it bad?*

M: *Not really sure, but bad enough for them to fly me up.*

L: *Shit.*

M: *I know. I go back next Tuesday.*

L: *Damn. So short.*

M: *Better than nothing.*

L: *Definitely.*

M: *I think I have to do family stuff Friday and Saturday, but if it's OK with Polly, I can probably stay by you Sunday and Monday.*

L: *I'll check.*

M: *OK.*

L: *I'll text you later.*

M: *Alright.*

Rather than put the phone down, she immediately called Ashley.

"Hey, girl, hey," Ashley answered the phone.

"You're in a good mood."

"Yup. Been hanging out with Tyler most of the day."

"Oh."

"What do you mean, 'Oh?'"

"Uh, nothing. I just don't want to bother you if you're busy."

"I'm not."

"I thought you were with Tyler."

"Not anymore. So what's up?"

"MacGyver is coming home this weekend."

"Really? Cool. He can come to the party Saturday at that new house they're building over on Aldo. It's all closed in now, but no Sheetrock is up, and it's really big, so it's like walking through a giant maze. And Tyler said the bathtub and showers are in now, so we can just bring ice. We don't have to bother with coolers."

"Sounds great. But, I'm a little confused."

"About what?"

"I thought the GES Club only met in our own homes. Doesn't this make us just as bad as those kids from North?"

"Absolutely not."

"Okay, but why not?"

"First, of all, we'd still be going to my house if it was standing."

"Right, but we're not."

"Yes, but the rule is we don't trespass."

"But..."

"Let me finish."

"Okay."

"In someone's home."

"This house on Aldo is going to be someone's home."

"You're right. But, and this is a big but, it's not now. It has a for-sale sign out front. It has never been anyone's home. It's owned by a builder, a speculator. If it makes you feel better, my mother calls them carpetbaggers. There is no way we have to show those people respect. They are making money off our misery."

"Okay, now you are going a little over the top, don't you think?"

"Nope. That's my opinion, and I'm sticking to it. Besides, it's going to be so nice having parties in new houses instead of gutted ones."

"That's true. Is it easy to get in?"

"Yeah, someone just has to climb in the second-story window. Then, we can walk right in on the first floor."

"That's perfect. I won't even need my stepladder. But I don't think MacGyver will be able to come."

"Why not?"

"Grandpa Anderson is sick. He has to visit him first. He's coming over Sunday."

"Is he in the hospital?"

"I don't know. MacGyver didn't say."

"You still mad at him?"

"No…Yeah…No…I don't know."

"I'm so glad we cleared that up."

"I mean there's no point. He and I are just friends. Why would I be mad?"

"Right."

"What do you mean, 'Right?'"

"Nothing. I mean, you're right. It's just that…"

"It's just that what?"

"Well, and I don't want you to be mad at me or anything. But, for two best friends, you spend an awful lot of time being mad at each other. Y'know?"

"It's complicated."

"Okay, but I'm just glad we're not like that. You and me, I mean. I wouldn't be able to stand it if we were on-again, off-again all the time. I'd feel so... I don't know."

"Insecure."

"Yeah, insecure, like our friendship was always balancing on a ledge or something. I really couldn't take that."

"Yeah, I get it. It's just different with MacGyver. I'd explain it to you, but then I'd have to understand it myself." Lacey sighed and added, "Life's messy."

Chapter Sixty:
Saturday, Aug. 3, 2013

"I can't believe those a-holes," Ashley said, as she looked out the third-story window of their new party digs. "They're making a mess in the Krug house. Come here guys. Take a look."

"Wow, what a nice view. Look at the Seaside bridge from here," Brittney said, seeing her hometown from a new altitude.

Until Sandy hit, homes in the town's Silverton section were limited to two stories high, but the township changed the rules to make it possible for residents to lift their homes as required by their flood insurance. Now, even new buildings, like the one Lacey and her friends were claiming squatters' rights to, were allowed to build to the new three-story height maximum.

"Brittney, I didn't call you over here for sightseeing. Look at the crap they're pulling over there," Ashley scolded her friend and pointed to the Krug house about a block away, where through a picture window, the girls could see Corky and Yanni and some other North students building a Budweiser can pyramid, while others tossed around what looked like Mrs. Krug's Lladro collection.

"Shit, that's not right," Brittney said.

"I've got this," Connor said, taking out his phone. "I've got an e-mail account I use for just these times."

"What?" Ashley asked.

"Oh, yeah, I'm Silverton's Spiderman. I fight crime and stop assholes. Only I don't really do anything."

"What?" Lacey asked as she watched a figurine of a mother and child being passed around like a Nerf football.

"You know that special e-mail they set up to report looting and vandalism?"

"No," came the choral response.

"Well, trust me, they set up a special e-mail and phone number for reporting looting and vandalism."

"But, Connor, you can't e-mail something like this. What if the police don't check the e-mail account for a couple hours or even days?"

"Ye of little faith," said the broad-shouldered football player. "Watch and learn."

He e-mailed a message to the police from his phone and then looked at his friends. "In about ten minutes, we need to turn off the flashlights and someone has to check that the door downstairs is shut," he said.

"Yeah, right, the police are going to be here in ten minutes," Tyler scoffed.

"You'll see."

So they waited. Lacey and Ashley checked the front door, which was a good thing, because someone had left it standing wide open. When eight minutes had passed, Connor urged them all to be quiet, so they were. And they gathered by the window, mostly expecting to see nothing. Soon red and blue lights swirled around the room as two patrol cars came down the street with their lights flashing but sirens off. About fifteen minutes later, the neighborhood had returned to complete quiet.

"I told you I was Spiderman," Connor said. "I do it all the time.

"I first started reporting things a few days after Sandy, the day after the Kanes' TV got stolen. I couldn't believe anyone had the balls to come down here and take things when they had to go through an armed National Guard checkpoint just to get into Silverton. I don't know about you guys but having to pass those soldiers with their high-powered rifles gave me the willies."

"Me, too," Lacey said. "But my mother made conversation every time we went through there. Once Dunkin' Donuts opened again, she would bring them a Box of Joe and donuts each time."

"Your mother would," Ashley said.

"She did," Lacey agreed. "A couple of weeks later when the Guard was replaced by township police and you still had to show your license to get in, Polly started giving this one cop the third degree. 'You don't really know if I live in Silverton,' she said. 'All you can tell is that I have a Toms River address.'"

"Did she really?" Brittney said, her jade green eyes growing wide.

"Oh, yeah, but this guy got her good. 'No, ma'am,' he said. 'Everyone on guard detail has special experience in the Silverton area. Most of us grew up here. I lived on Cedar Tree across from Silver Bay School until I was fourteen.'"

"Actually, my mother asked one of the police officers about that, too. He said those who didn't know the area were paired with volunteer firefighters who did."

"I hate to admit it, but you really have to give those volunteer firefighters a lot of credit," Lacey said, stuffing her hands into her pockets to avoid jabbing her nail into her finger.

"Yeah, we used to go over to the firehouse every couple of days to pick up water and other supplies. The firefighters were always there helping out, even though most of them lost their houses, too."

"So, wait a minute," Tyler said to Connor. "Why do you get to be Harry? Anybody could do that."

"Okay," Connor said. "You're right, but so far I'm the one doing it. Hey, you know what, from here, we can see a good part of Silverton. Each time we come, I'll bring my binoculars and we'll surveil the area. Then, we'll party."

"Surveil? Is that even a word?" Lacey said.

"I don't think so," Brittney said.

"Sure it is. It's the root word for surveillance," Connor said.

"Ashley, look it up on your phone," Lacey ordered, but she didn't mean to. It was just that Ashley had her phone out.

"I will, but if it is a word, Lacey, you have to chug a beer. And if it's not, Connor does."

"Yeah," the others agreed.

"You're going down," Lacey said, comically standing toe-to-toe with Connor, staring up at him.

"'Fraid not, Lacey," Ashley said. "You lose. Chug."

"Chug it. Chug it," the group chanted.

Lacey walked through what would one day be a wall and reached into a bathtub filled with ice for an Angry Orchard.

"I said beer," Ashley said.

"What's the difference?" Lacey said, as she grabbed a bottle opener.

"The difference is the beer is mine," Tyler said. "Let her drink the Angry Orchard."

Lacey downed the "hard cider" without a pause.

"Hey, let's play. Never Have I Ever," Tyler suggested.

Chapter Sixty-One:
Immediately following, Saturday, Aug. 3, 2013

Ashley went first because her mom had picked her up early the last time they played. "Never Have I Ever failed a test," she said.

"Lame," Tyler said as he and most of their friends drank.

"Wait a minute, Britt. Why are you drinking? You get straight A's," Ashley asked.

"Uh, my driving test," Brittney said. "Remember?"

"Geez, I forgot about that," Lacey said.

"Well, I never will," Brittney said.

"But, Britt, you've been driving illegally for three years. Your dad always used to let you drive, even when we were in middle school," Tyler said. "How did you fail the test?"

"Yeah, and why won't you tell us what happened that day?" Lacey asked.

"All right, you really want to hear this?" Brittney said. Everyone shouted out a chorus of yeses and yeahs. "Well, then I need to drink more first."

She tried to down an Angry Orchard but stopped halfway through. "Lacey, how do you do that?"

Lacey shrugged her shoulders. "Skills," she said with a smile.

"C'mon, you're stalling," Ashley said.

"All right, so I'm going to start this story the way every good story starts, at the end," Brittney said.

"What?" Tyler said.

"You'll see. So when the test is just about over, I pull back up to the stop sign where we started, and the instructor tells me to put the car in park, and at this point, I'm so excited."

"Excited, didn't you know you failed?" Tyler asked.

"I would have been crying," Ashley said.

"If you people want to hear this story, you're going to have to shut up," Brittney said, looking around her circle of friends and making eye contact with each, one at a time. "Anyway, like I was saying, I was so excited. Here I am in my brand-new Jeep Wrangler, and I just freakin' passed my driver's test. No mistakes."

"No mistakes, but," Lacey said.

"Lacey, shut up. Like I was saying, I was really excited. I mean I'm flying. And the guy looks at me over the top of his glasses, not through them. I mean what's up with that? And he says, with no inflection at all, 'Please put the car in park.' And I can't contain myself. I practically shout at him, I'm so excited, 'I passed, right? I didn't make any mistakes. Did you see how well I parallel parked? I gotta tell you yesterday, I was practicing, and I was like three feet away from the curb almost every time. But just now, wow, what was that, like three inches.'"

"I hate parallel parking," Ashley said.

Brittney shot her a look, and Ashley stopped speaking.

"So the guy says to me, 'Miss,' and his face has no expression at all – like a blank piece of paper, and I'm not even that worried because everyone makes fun of Motor Vehicle types. All the comedians do, right? They're supposed to be humorless. But, he says, 'Miss, while your driving in many areas was more than satisfactory, I'm afraid you did not pass,' and he hands me a slip of paper and starts talking about going online and making an appointment and tells me I can make it as early as two weeks from that day. And this is why I've never told you the story," Brittney said and took a large gulp of the Angry Orchard.

"I lost it. I clicked out of the seatbelt, so I could comfortably face him and screamed in his face, 'You just said my driving was more than satisfactory. What the fuck did I do wrong? Is this because I showed up in a brand-new car with the dealer's sticker still on the window? My friends said you guys are tougher on kids when you think we're spoiled rich kids. Y'know, 'cause you guys did say that, and I'm screaming, 'Is that what this is about?'"

"Oh my God," Lacey said and scooted her butt a little closer to Brittney, trying to give her friend moral support as she told this embarrassing story.

"I'm freakin' screaming right in his face, and his expression doesn't change. He just reaches up to the steering column and starts tapping the directional. 'Do you know what this is, Miss?' 'What? Yeah, it's the turn signal? Why?' 'Good,' he says, and stares into my eyes like he's going to tell me what Eve learned when she bit into the apple. 'In two weeks, I suggest you use it.'

"He was so freakin' condescending I just couldn't help myself. I started screaming at him. 'What the fuck are you talking about?'"

"Oh shit," Connor said, and Lacey lightly put her hand on her friend's back.

"What did he do?" Ashley asked, softly.

"He's like, 'Young Lady, I understand you are upset, but please watch your language. During the entire test, you didn't signal, not even once. I'm sure you were just nervous. It happens, but I even had you make a few extra turns to see if you would remember and, well...just make an appointment. There's no backlog right now, which is good, so we'll see you in two weeks.'"

"No big deal. We all make stupid mistakes," Lacey said, thinking that was the whole story.

"That's when I *really* lost it. I started bawling like some little kid who's peed his pants in kindergarten, and I'm screaming and begging. 'No, please, please. Did I fail anything else?' And he shakes his head. So I'm just sitting there crying and yelling! 'So I didn't fail any actual driving things. I'm a good, safe driver. I mean I just didn't signal. Please. You don't understand. Please!

"And that's when my mother opened the car door and starts apologizing to the guy, and he says he understands. But I can't help myself. I start grabbing his arm and screaming over and over."

Ashley covered her mouth. It was a gesture that seemed to say, "It's okay, you don't have to tell us anymore. We understand."

"There I am, begging and crying, 'But, I'm a good driver.' And he says something to my mother about a restraining order, but I think he said it as a joke. I don't know. And he stands up to get out of the car, and I'm still holding onto his sleeve, and then my mother just said my name, but you know, not just my name, my whole name: Brittney Maria Consuela Martinez. Just like that, I snapped out of it. And I just look at the guy, who's walking to the next car but looking over his shoulder like he's still worried he should be calling the police or something, and I mouth, 'I'm sorry.'"

"Holy crap. I'm so sorry, Brittney," Lacey said and gently rubbed her friend's back.

"Oh, that's not the end of it," Brittney said.

"There's more?" Ashley said, her blue eyes widening.

"Oh yeah," Brittney said. "We – my mom and me – went to Burger King then because all my plans of picking up you guys and going to Taco Bell were shot to hell, and my mother called my father. But it's the middle of the workday, so my dad wasn't paying any attention to her. So she handed me the phone and he was like. 'Congratulations, Brittney. I knew you wouldn't have any problem. Enjoy the Jeep!'"

"You're kidding," Tyler said, but Ashley and Lacey shot him a look that said, "Yeah, that's the kind of crap that's been going on there."

"And now I was in Burger King, and I was screaming at him on the phone. 'Congratulations for what? I failed, and you would have known that if you had listened to Mommy.' Yeah, I said

Mommy, I still do that sometimes. 'I failed. I failed. I failed. I totally fucked up.' And I was screaming this in the Burger King. And that guy who graduated last year, the one who used to go out with Olivia, he's like the manager there or something, and he was staring over at me. But he didn't make a move, and my mother begged me to sit down and be quiet. And my father said something like I should go buy myself something pretty, and I started screaming at him, 'You can't buy your way out of everything,' and I threw the phone down."

"That sucks," Tyler said. "Parents can be such dicks."

Ashley looked at him as if to say, "You're making it worse."

"Then, I walked out and walked around the Burger King, like, three times, while my mother ordered food inside," Brittney said. "She's seen me act like this before, and eventually, I just went back inside, sat down and ate fries, and we talked about this episode of *Family Guy* my mother had seen me watching the night before, the one where Stewie and Brian go to alternate worlds."

"That's a good one," Connor said.

"It is. It's one of my favorites," Brittney said. "Anyway, for two weeks, I honestly felt as if everybody in the whole fucking world was staring at me and whispering about what a loser I am, and I did badly on tests in school because failures fail. That's what they do."

"You failed tests?" Ashley asked.

"I got Cs."

The group collectively gasped, mockingly, but Brittney continued.

"And I thought I would feel that way forever, and I'd always be the loser who can't even drive. Then exactly two weeks later, I took the test, and it was as if the last two weeks didn't even happen."

"Yeah, I had even forgotten you failed the first time," Ashley said.

"Yeah, it's just great that one of us drives," Connor said.

"Hey, I drive," Tyler said, sounding just a tiny bit hurt.

"And has a car," Connor added, smiling wide, his braces showing.

"So I guess this just proves that no matter how bad things seem, it's probably not that bad," Lacey said.

Tyler threw his jacket at Lacey, yelling, "Give me a break."

"He's right. You sound just like Polly," Ashley said.

Brittney drained her Angry Orchard and grabbed another one, and the game moved to the next person.

Chapter Sixty-Two:
Sunday, Aug. 4, 2013

"Wow, your house looks great!"

"Polly thinks so. I liked the old furniture," Lacey said as she ushered MacGyver into the living room on Sunday afternoon.

"Yeah, I miss the love seat that used to be by the door."

"Me too. Polly promised she would replace it with one that was equally flop-able, but eventually, I told her not to worry about it."

"You used to fall into that every day as soon as you got off the bus."

"Me. Umm. Excuse me, but I usually wasn't alone."

"I remember when I saw it on top of the Dumpster the day after Sandy. I admit it. I cried."

"Baby," Lacey said and went to punch him in the arm. But MacGyver grabbed her wrist, spun her around and pulled her into a familiar wrestling hold they had practiced over more than a decade.

"No fair!" Lacey said.

"Really," he said, holding her tight with just his left arm across the front of her while his right hand reached down to her abdomen and tickled her. "Then, you won't think this is either."

Lacey wiggled and squirmed and wriggled out of his hold. She took two steps away and faced her childhood friend. They stared at each other for a moment, seeing one another for the first time in months and after so many things had changed and admissions had been made.

Lacey bit her bottom lip, and MacGyver took a step closer to her. "Hey, where's the love?" he said, holding out both his arms. "You didn't even hug me when I got out of the car."

"Sorry," she said, but told him with her eyes that she didn't really mean it. Things were not right between them, and they both knew it. Lacey quickly flung her arms around his neck and gave him the type of embrace she normally reserved for her disgusting uncle who hits on her and pinches her butt every time he gets drunk at family parties, the cursory cuddle designed to keep her parents from asking why she is so rude to Uncle Mike.

"Okay, then," MacGyver said and reached into his pocket for cigarettes and a lighter. "I'm going to take a walk."

"A walk? Going for some fresh air?" Lacey mocked.

"Something like that," he said. "Want to come?"

"Tell you what. Take your walk first," Lacey said, nodding toward the Marlboro Black pack in his hands.

"Don't judge me," MacGyver said. "I haven't had many this month. Being here though. It's tough."

"Yeah, I get it. Hanging out with me can be stressful," Lacey said.

"Oh, c'mon, you know what I mean," MacGyver said.

"Look," Lacey said, "take your walk. Then come back and get me, and we can go to the Rock Throwing Place."

"Perfect," he said. "I think I'll go check out my house."

"Sounds good, but you'll have to go around. We took the gate out."

"That was cold."

"Yeah, well," Lacey said with a shrug. "See you in a few."

"Um. Before I go, where should I leave my backpack?"

"You mean vacation valise," Lacey said with a smile.

"Oh, God, not that again."

"You remember?" she said with a laugh, then added, "Just leave it by the dining room table for now."

"Okay. I'll be right back."

Watching MacGyver walk out her front door seemed so normal and natural, yet so strange. It had only been a few months since they had seen one another and yet he seemed older. His shoulders seemed broader and there was a quietness about him. And while Lacey's friends had told her that MacGyver smoked now, it was one thing to know about it and another to see it. Lacey thought the world had inflicted enough damage on their lives without helping it along on its course of destruction.

He's here, she texted Ashley.

A: *Who's where?*

L: *Are you kidding?*

A: *No, why?*

L: *Did you really forget?*

A: *Forget what?*

L: *Who. Not what.*

A: *What?*

L: *…*

A: *Lacey, what the hell?*

L: *MacGyver's here.*

A: *Oh, wow. I forgot.*

L: *You want to meet us at the Rock Throwing Place?*

A: *I'm kind of busy right now. Why don't we meet at the Aldo house at 9?*

L: *OK.*

A: *See you later.*

L: *See ya.*

When MacGyver returned, he let himself into the house and began shouting, "Lucy, I'm home."

"Oh, Ricky, darling," Lacey replied, mocking the "I Love Lucy" reruns they used to watch on snow days. MacGyver's mom was a huge slapstick comedy fan and had tons of VCR tapes of "I Love Lucy" and "Three's Company." Lacey couldn't remember how they got into the habit of watching those shows only on snow days, but somehow it had become a longstanding tradition. In fact, when she got off school for a storm last February, Lacey flipped around the channels totally dissatisfied until she found an old "Gilligan's Island" episode on some obscure channel. It was a snow day, one of God's perfect gifts to school kids, and she couldn't find happiness without MacGyver's stash of sitcoms.

"How's your grandfather?" Lacey asked as they walked toward the bay and their favorite spot.

"Not good."

"Did you see him?"

"Yeah."

"He must have been happy to see you."

"If he was, I couldn't tell. He's on a respirator and can't talk. But he did kind of smile."

"Well, that's good," Lacey said, twirling her hair around her left index finger.

"Yeah, Aunt Susan announced me to him like he wouldn't know who I was if they didn't tell him."

"Geez."

"And what was worse is they didn't even use my name. She just said, 'Here's Richard's son. Like that's all I am, the only thing that matters.'"

"I'm sure that's not what she meant."

"I don't know, maybe. But the whole time I was at the hospital, both times, I just felt like I was some ambassador for the ailing Richard Anderson. I think my parents sent me up here just in case Grandpa dies, so that my father made some sort of appearance, by proxy or something."

"What? I'm sure that's not what they were doing."

"No? Lacey, they're flat broke. We're even using an EBT card for groceries."

"A what?"

"An EBT card. It's food stamps."

"Oh."

"Anyway, I know they couldn't afford to send me here. My dad only did it out of guilt because he can't come up himself."

"Well, that's nothing to feel guilty for. How is he, anyway?'

"Miserable."

"I meant, how is his health?"

"Not great. He's still in traction, and he's so friggin' grumpy all the time. I can't stand it."

"I'm sorry."

"Not your fault."

"Yeah, but I'm still sorry."

MacGyver picked up a rock and skipped it across the water's surface. It jumped seven times.

"I hate you," Lacey said.

MacGyver grinned. "Me, too... I guess we have to head over to the party."

"Not yet. Let's just look at the water."

The two stared out at the quiet bay and across to the county park that forever mocked their youth and inability to get around town without a parent driving. The distance between the two friends as they stood next to each other, not touching, was like Silverton and the park's shoreline, so tiny and yet completely insurmountable.

Chapter Sixty-Three:
Monday, Aug. 5, 2013

On Monday night, the GES Club, which they were now fond of calling themselves, met at the newly constructed house on Aldo for what was becoming their nearly daily party. But this one was special, because MacGyver was there for the second night in a row, and it was the last night of his visit. Even though it was a weeknight, their parents let them all hang out until midnight, so they could soak up as many minutes of being together as they could.

Everyone lied and picked a different friend's house to say they were at. Everyone, that is, except Brittney, whose parents went to bed at nine o'clock because work was so busy, and never checked to see what time their daughter got home.

In past years, such deception would not have been possible. Their parents all ran into one another in the neighborhood and made small talk, but now they were scattered. Even when their parents encountered one another at the Wawa convenience store or elsewhere, their conversations were consumed by discussions of insurance, FEMA and rebuilding. Their talks with one another no longer centered on their children, and neither did their lives.

Lacey and her friends were kind of buzzed, but no one was drunk when the alcohol ran out. They sat around and talked about things they'd all shared, telling stories that really didn't need to be told, since they all knew how they went. But somehow the reminiscing made everyone happy.

"This is what I miss," MacGyver said.

"Running out of beer and sitting around being bored?" Tyler said.

"I'm not bored," Ashley said pointedly.

"Me, neither," added Lacey.

"Don't twist your wand into knots. I was kidding," Tyler said.

"What does that even mean?" Brittney said.

"Nerd," Ashley said, mocking him.

"See? Now this is what I'm talking about," MacGyver said.

"Stupid arguing?" Lacey asked.

"Yeah. No. I mean yeah, kind of. It's just we're all so comfortable with each other."

"Too comfortable," Ashley said with a look at Tyler who was sitting across the circle from her.

"What?" MacGyver asked.

"Just go ahead. What were you saying?" Ashley said.

"I miss this. Having real friends," MacGyver said.

"Don't you have friends in Florida?" Brittney said.

"No, not really. There I just have..."

"A girlfriend," Lacey said.

"What? No," MacGyver said.

"Oh c'mon. Yes, you do," Lacey said, staring at him.

"Is she hot?" Tyler asked.

"She's nonexistent," MacGyver said.

"Did you break up?" Lacey asked, hating how concerned she genuinely was.

"You can't break up with someone who doesn't exist," MacGyver said.

"So you didn't have a girlfriend?" Ashley asked.

"Nope. I have one friend. It's a guy, and I'm kind of friends with his dad, too, if that counts. We all hang out a lot together and do stuff, like hunting."

"You hunt?" Lacey asked, stunned.

"Not really. They hunt. I just go along for the walk in the woods. It gets me out."

"Do they kill things?" Ashley asked.

"That's sort of what hunting is," MacGyver said.

"Eww," said Lacey and Ashley together.

"It's okay. I guess. They only shoot what they'll eat, and they *are* kind of poor, so I think it helps them out a lot."

"Do you eat it, too?" Lacey asked.

"Nah," MacGyver said and kind of smirked. "I told them I'm a vegetarian."

They all laughed.

"You?" Tyler said practically bent over in pain, he was laughing so hard.

"The cheeseburger king of the world," Brittney said.

"Well, it was either that or eat rabbit with them," he said, looking uncomfortably toward Lacey. "I couldn't do that."

They nodded, and MacGyver said. "The worst part is now when we get pizza – even at my house, we have to get it without pepperoni."

Everyone laughed, but Lacey, who was looking through her phone.

"Well, who is she?" she said, shoving her phone in his face.

MacGyver blinked and then focused, and then he laughed as he saw the picture of him embracing a wavy-haired blonde.

"You don't know who that is?" he asked and laughed harder. Then, he grabbed the phone and passed it around the circle and after a second, everyone laughed, except Lacey and Ashley.

"What's so funny?" Lacey asked.

"You don't recognize the girl?" Brittney said.

"No," Lacey and Ashley responded in unison.

"Do you think she's pretty?" Brittney asked while her eyes darted around the group demanding quiet.

"Shut up," Ashley warned.

"No," Lacey said firmly.

"You don't think she's pretty?" Ashley asked.

"No," Lacey said. Then, feeling all the eyes on her, she added, "I don't know. It's just the back of her head. Why?"

"You jerk. It's Ashley," Brittney said.

"No, it's not," Ashley said.

"Sure it is," Brittney answered.

"Oh, crap! It is you," Lacey said.

Lacey pulled her phone out of Brittney's hands and stared at the photo.

"It is you," Lacey said, confused and upset. "What? Wait. You guys hooked up over Spring Break?"

"Did you?" Tyler asked.

"Eww. No," Ashley said quickly, eyes darting back and forth between Lacey and Tyler. Then, a second later she remembered MacGyver and looked at him. "No offense."

"None taken," MacGyver said with a smile.

Ashley was on her feet with her hands on her hips now.

"MacGyver, when you asked me to take the picture, you said you wanted it to make some girl at home jealous," she shouted.

Everyone looked at him.

"*This* is home," he said.

Chapter Sixty-Four:
Just before midnight, Monday, Aug. 5, 2013

"You are such a jerk," Lacey said as she and MacGyver walked back to Lacey's house under a dark, moonless sky.

"Why do you say that?"

"You had me pissed off at you for months."

"Why?"

"What do you mean why? You know why."

"No, I don't. I did exactly what you told me to do. You said you wouldn't text me unless I sent you a picture of me kissing a girl."

"I know what I said, but Ashley is not a girl."

"What? I think you should look again."

"You know what I mean."

"No, I don't. And I don't know why you stopped texting me when I did what you wanted."

"I guess I was upset."

"Because I did what you wanted?"

"No. I don't know. Maybe. But you didn't do what I wanted."

"And you proved you didn't really want me to."

"How did I prove that?"

"Because you got mad when I sent the picture."

For a few minutes they walked in silence.

"Mom said we can watch movies in the living room when we get back."

MacGyver slipped his arm around Lacey's shoulders. "You sure you don't want to watch sitcoms?"

"It's not a snow day. But, we could watch *Edward Scissorhands*."

"I don't think so. No storm."

"True."

"What do you want to watch?"

"How about *Ghosts of Girlfriends Past*?"

"Are you trying to tell me I'm a jerk?"

"No."

"That I remind you of Matthew McConaughey?"

"I don't think so. Do I remind you of Jennifer Garner?"

"Nah, Emma Stone."

"Yeah, right."

"No, really."

As they reached Lacey's house, she started to think about the supplies they would need for a successful movie night.

"Okay, I'll make some popcorn and get some soda. You can grab a couple of pillows out of my room. Oh, and get the DVD from the shelf over my desk."

Lacey was about to turn the doorknob and head inside, but MacGyver put his hand over hers and looked into her eyes. He was smiling down at her, and she felt a gentle fluttering in her stomach, a feeling that signaled something wonderful was happening.

The smell of Budweiser, which Lacey would normally consider sour and pretty disgusting, washed over her. This time the scent was intoxicating. She looked straight into the brown of his eyes and expected MacGyver to kiss her. But he didn't. He just stood there.

"Before we go in. There's something I have to tell you."

"What?"

"I've told you before but only by text."

"Ah huh."

"Lacey Haley Freshet, not a day goes by when I don't think of you, your smile, your gorgeous eyes and the way you make me feel."

"You've told me this?"

He put two fingers to her lips to hush her. "Lacey, I love you."

She wanted to say it back or kiss him or something, anything. But she didn't. They just stood there and stared at one another for what seemed like an eternity.

Then, he took his fingers from her lips and kissed them, while gently turning the doorknob with his other hand.

Chapter Sixty-Five:
Just after midnight, Tuesday, Aug. 6, 2013

As MacGyver was retrieving the movie, Polly stepped out into the hall in sweat pants and a tee-shirt, calling softly, "Lacey?"

"I'm sorry, Polly. I was just getting some stuff from Lacey's room. She, um, said it was okay if we sat up and watched a movie for a while. That's okay, right?"

Polly yawned. "Oh, MacGyver. Sure. Just keep it down. I have to work in the morning, and I don't want you guys to wake up Jake."

"Right. I mean thank you, no problem. Thank you."

"Oh, and MacGyver," Polly said as she headed back into her room. "It's been really nice having you here. Once we get back home again, we'll have to arrange it so that you come up every few months or so."

"Thanks. I'd really like that. Thank you," MacGyver said, grinning. "Good night."

In the past when Lacey and MacGyver watched a movie, she almost always rested her head on a pillow on MacGyver's lap. But this time, they sat really quietly next to each other holding hands and leaving the snacks untouched on the coffee table.

About an hour into the film, MacGyver reached over with the same two fingers he had shushed her with earlier and touched them to Lacey's lips again.

"Shh."

"I've barely said a word the whole movie."

"No, I wasn't telling you to be quiet. I was kissing you."

"What?"

"You see, I was thinking earlier I kissed my fingers because they touched your lips. Right?"

Lacey nodded.

"Now they're touching your lips again. It's like we've kissed."

"Cheesy," Lacey said, laughing, but McGyver looked hurt.

"Hey," she said to draw his downcast eyes back to her own. "There's a better way to do that." Surprised at her boldness, Lacey slid over so that she was now sitting on MacGyver's lap, lowered her head so their noses almost touched, then tilted just enough so their lips met.

At first, she looked directly into his eyes until they both giggled and pulled away.

"That is better," MacGyver said.

The pair had kissed many times before, but not in a few years. And those middle school slobbers had always been awkward, with the feeling of playing at being grown-up. This was different. When their mouths met again, their lips parted, their tongues touched, and a new excitement shot through them both.

"Umm. I don't want to wake your mother up," MacGyver said, pulling away.

"She sleeps like she's in hibernation."

"Okay, but..." MacGyver started to protest but then got caught up in the delight of her hands on his cheek and his neck.

As they kissed and their fingers trailed across each other's faces, arms and backs, they shifted positions. It was as if they weren't just trying to be comfortable; a force outside of themselves, or at least their conscious thought, was trying to make them one.

They shifted so that Lacey was lying flat on her back, and MacGyver was lying pressed against her. They kissed and touched and rubbed against each other, and before they realized it their pelvises were moving in rhythmic convulsions and their breathing had become nothing more than attempts to gasp and catch their breaths.

Lacey was terrified when she heard MacGyver cry out in what sounded like terrible pain. What had she done? How was she hurting him? What had she done so terribly wrong that MacGyver was no longer worried about waking her mother or Jake?

"Are you all right?" she asked. "I'm so sorry I hurt you."

"No, I'm sorry. I'm so sorry," he said and ran to the bathroom.

"Why?" she called after him, but he didn't answer. She just heard the bathroom door shut.

Lacey slumped back into the couch and closed her eyes. She felt great. She felt terrible. She didn't know what she felt. Slowly, she caught her breath, struggled to a sitting position and straightened her clothes. She grabbed her cup of soda and took a long drink. Then, she snatched up the popcorn bowl, placed it on her lap and returned her attention to the movie.

When MacGyver came in a few minutes later, he sat next to her without a word, and they quietly ate popcorn and pretended to focus on the movie, neither looking at the other.

Lacey fell asleep, and MacGyver gently moved her legs onto the couch where he had been sitting, brought the snacks into the kitchen, covered Lacey with a blanket and turned off the TV. He stood there for a few moments watching her. Then he lightly kissed her forehead and headed upstairs to the air mattress that had been placed in the empty guest room.

Chapter Sixty-Six:
Tuesday, Aug. 6, 2013

When Lacey awoke, she was confused until she realized the sun was streaming in the window. She looked around the living room for MacGyver, and when she didn't find him, she headed upstairs to the bathroom. Once she glanced in the mirror and saw her hair pointing in every direction, she was grateful MacGyver hadn't been by her side when she woke up.

She took one of the quickest showers of her life, because somehow, it felt weird being naked when she knew her childhood friend had to be somewhere nearby. After retrieving clean shorts and a red tank top, Lacey towel-dried her hair and headed downstairs to the kitchen.

She was pretty excited, knowing that her mom said she could stay home from summer school today. There were only four days left, and since she hadn't missed a day yet, taking off would be no big deal. When she got to the kitchen, she found a note on the table.

"I know how much you two like making breakfast, so there's bacon, pork roll, eggs, pancake mix and chocolate chips. You can make whatever you want, but you have to clean up. Jake is at Kyle's house and will be home around 1."

Polly signed her note as she always did with the drawing of an eye, one of a heart and the letter U. She had started doing this when Lacey was in preschool, too young to read, and the tradition stuck.

Lacey glanced at the teapot-shaped clock on the kitchen wall. It was already ten-thirty. MacGyver's aunt would be picking him up for the airport in two hours.

She grabbed her mother's big red mixing bowl and dumped a bunch of Aunt Jemima Complete into it without measuring. Then she dragged the bowl under the kitchen faucet and splashed in some cold water. She plopped the bowl back on the table and stirred with a fork until she realized the thin concoction was way too watery to make pancakes. She reached for the Complete and added more flour.

When the texture was finally right, Lacey pulled out a frying pan, sprayed it with Pam and poured out five silver-dollar-sized pancakes.

Hmmph, she thought to herself. He's going to complain that he prefers larger, fluffier pancakes, but I'll just tell him he should have gotten his lazy butt out of bed and made them himself.

There was something about the Freshet house and the way scent traveled. No one could ever cook secretly downstairs. Within two minutes, any aroma filled every nook and cranny of upstairs even while people sitting in the living and dining rooms smelled nothing.

This fact had been true Lacey's whole life, and no amount of renovations was going to change it. At least, Lacey hoped not. The truth was Lacey wasn't really cooking to be nice to MacGyver: She wanted Aunt Jemima to wake him up.

As Lacey flipped the pancakes, she realized she hadn't put the chocolate chips in yet and headed to the pantry to find them. MacGyver always preferred to put them in the batter, but Lacey liked the pancakes better if the chocolate was a little less melted.

As she looked around for the chips, Lacey heard the familiar, "Lucy, I'm home" and then "Holy crap! What are you trying to do, burn the place down? Where are you?"

Lacey popped her head back into the kitchen to find the room had filled with smoke, and MacGyver was running the hot frying pan under cold water. As the pan sizzled, a loud beep-beep-

beep began, and then there were beeping sounds throughout the house, none of them in synch.

"Crap!" Lacey said. "That's the new smoke alarm system."

"Really? I never would have guessed," MacGyver said with a smirk.

"Quick! Go wave something in front of the sensor at the top of the stairs, and I'll do this one. If we don't get the alarm to turn off in two minutes, it sends a signal to the fire department, and it's like a two hundred dollar fine for a false alarm or something. At least that's what Polly says."

"Really?" MacGyver said.

"No time to talk. Go," Lacey said, dragging a chair under the kitchen smoke alarm. She climbed up on the chair, realized she had forgotten the dish cloth and scrambled down to get it. Then, she returned to her post and started fanning the sensor.

When she heard her alarm stop, she jumped down from the chair and sank into it, only to hear it begin screaming again for help.

Then she and MacGyver both started to hear the alarm upstairs shouting with a deep voice, "Fire, exit the building immediately. Fire, exit the building immediately."

Lacey scrambled back up on the chair swatted at the alarm, then removed the battery. To her amazement, battery-removal did not stop the alarm from sounding.

But soon the house quieted down. Lacey jumped off the chair and headed through the mild haze to the sink. MacGyver returned at that moment and boomed, "Good morning."

Lacey held up some charred and soggy pancake bits and said, "Tradition," and they laughed.

"Wish we were going to a dance," MacGyver said, moving to the kitchen table. "Just rinse that out. I'll make some more batter."

"Okay," she said and did what he asked. Despite her earlier clumsiness in the kitchen, the two fell into a familiar pattern, deftly moving around one another, until they were each seated before a pile of fluffy large, chocolate chip pancakes.

As they took their seats at the table, Lacey teasingly complained, "You know I like the smaller pancakes."

"At least these aren't burnt," MacGyver said.

"Fair enough," she said and put the first forkful in her mouth. "They're good."

"Of course," he said, taking his own first bite. "Mmmm. You're right."

"I can't believe you're leaving in an hour."

"I know," he said, not meeting her eyes.

"It sucks."

"I know."

They ate for about five minutes in silence.

"You're leaving, and we're going to waste the few minutes we have together not talking," Lacey said, pushing back her chair.

"Well, you're not talking, either."

"I know."

Then the silence fell again.

"Lacey," MacGyver finally said. "I'm sorry about last night."

"No, I'm sorry."

"You're sorry. What are you sorry for?"

"I don't know. Did I hurt you?"

"What?"

"Last night, did I hurt you or something? I know I must have done something wrong."

MacGyver laughed so hard he doubled over.

"Don't laugh at me."

MacGyver put down his fork, pushed out his chair and walked behind Lacey. Then, he hugged her and kissed the top of her head.

"Silly," he said.

"What? What's silly?"

"Now," he said. "Don't laugh at me, but you did everything right. Too right. Almost too right." He leaned over to look at her face. "Do you know what I mean?"

"Oh," she said, then more strongly, "OH!"

Now it was Lacey's turn to laugh. As she did, MacGyver turned bright red and slumped back into his seat. Lacey moved to his lap and smiled at him.

"You really do like me. Don't you?" she said, leaning in for a kiss.

They kissed for a few minutes, then Lacey accidentally put her hand in some pancake syrup.

"Uggh," she said and went off to wash her hand.

MacGyver followed her to the sink. "Before I came up here, my mother made me promise not to do this."

"Do what?"

"'Go there and mess with that girl's head,'" he said in a voice that Lacey recognized was his Mrs. Anderson impression.

"Oh," she said. "Look, I understand. You live in Florida now, and I live here. There's nothing we can do about it. There's no point in even trying. But wait. What if you lived with us? Polly really likes you. You're practically her second son."

"What's not to like?" MacGyver said and smiled. "Lacey, even if your mother said yes, I couldn't."

"Well, what about your aunt? You could live with them."

"I probably could. But the thing is I can't."

"You mean you don't want to," Lacey said, angrily.

"No. I mean I can't. When I go back home, I'm going to start working full time at the In and Out, this store by my house. My parents really need the money."

"Don't lie to me. You're just a teenager. You don't have to worry about your parents' bills," Lacey said. "You just don't want to be here anymore. I'm so stupid."

"Lacey, that's not true. It's just…"

With that the doorbell rang. MacGyver's aunt was at the door more than a half hour early.

"Oh my goodness, Lacey. You are such a beautiful young woman now," MacGyver's Aunt Susan said. "Isn't she beautiful?" she said to MacGyver.

"Always was," he mumbled.

"Do you have everything you need?" she asked.

"No, but I have everything I brought with me," MacGyver said. "I'm ready."

"Well, I'll let you say your goodbyes," his aunt said. "I'll be in the car, MacGyver."

"No need. I'm ready. We're done here," he said.

"Right," Lacey said. "Goodbye." And she closed her front door.

Chapter Sixty-Seven:
11 a.m. Tuesday, Aug. 20, 2013

Lacey was lying face up on the beach with her eyes closed, trying to make up for all those rays she'd missed going to summer school, when her phone chirped, "You go, Glen Coco."

She was hoping it was Brittney or Ashley, who were supposed to meet her here "first thing in the morning," but likely wouldn't show up before noon.

She rolled over and grabbed her phone and was surprised to see it was a group chat from Nick to her and Adam.

N: *I need to see both of you IMMEDIATELY.*

Lacey flipped around on her blanket and sat up. Outside of support group, she never talked to Adam and Nick aside from an occasional joke text. Lacey pushed back and leaned her back against the Adirondack chair behind her. She searched through her backpack for her beach towel and threw it over her head, so she could concentrate on texts without the glare of the sun.

L: *Is everything all right?*

N: *Fine. But there's something I have to show you.*

A: *At work. Can't talk.*

N: *Noooo*

L: *Can it wait till he gets off work?*

N: *No!*

L: *Do you want me to meet you somewhere?*

N: *What time do you get off work?*

L: *If it's important, I can meet you now-ish. I'm just at the beach.*

N: *What a princess. Nothing better to do than spend the day at the beach?*

L: *Back off. I spent most of the summer in summer school. Don't judge me.*

A: *She's right. Don't judge her.*

N: *This you can respond to, but you STILL HAVEN'T SAID WHEN YOU GET OFF WORK*

A: *Calm down. 5*

L: *Can this hold till then? Or should I meet you now?*

A: *That's right just cut me out.*

N: *I guess it can wait. Shit.*

L: *Are you sure?*

N: *Yes, dear. No worries.*

A: *Any hints?*

N: *No.*

N: *Lacey, where do you live again?*

L: *And you say no one pays attention to you.*

N: *Sorry, love. Toms River? Right?*

L: *Silverton*

N: *That's where the McDonald's is on Brick Blvd. Right?*

L: *It's Hooper Avenue in Toms River.*

N: *What is?*

L: *Brick Boulevard. It's called Hooper Avenue in Toms River.*

N: *Right.*

N: *How 'bout we pick you up at your house when Adam gets off work?*

A: *You're picking me up?*

N: *I just said that.*

L: *OK.*

L: *Wait. I'll meet you at the Dunkin Donuts.*

N: *See, I told you she was embarrassed by us.*

L: *What?*

N: *Never mind. Where's the DD?*

L: *Across from McDonald's.*

N: *5:15*

A: *God, give me a minute to change out of this stupid uniform.*

N: *5:20*

A: *That's really tight.*

N: *Would you go back to work!*

A: *Fine. May I take your order?*

L: *Haha*

N: *You're going to get fired. You already have two warnings.*

A: *You're right. See you later.*

L: *You sure you're OK till then?*

N: *Yes, yes, love.*

N: *See you at 5:20 at DD?*

L: *OK But, you're sure it can wait?*

N: *You worry too much. It's very sweet.*

A: *A minute ago you said she was embarrassed by us, now she's sweet.*

L: *LOL*

N: *Go back to work!*

L: *See you guys later.*

N: *Till then.*

And that was that. The texts stopped coming. Lacey removed the towel from her head and stared out at the horizon. Since it was a weekday, there were only two boats gliding across the bay between the Beach Club and the county park a mile away.

Most of the time when Lacey sat on the beach, she was content to enjoy the beautiful view, but sometimes, like now, being surrounded by water was kind of imprisonment. Everyone she knew owned a car, or at least their family did, but the water could only be navigated by that much smaller percentage of people who owned a boat, something that Polly said was very expensive.

Maybe someday, she thought, then wondered about the strange conversation she just had. Nick and Adam had never included her in anything outside of support group before. Why now? She hoped, even prayed, Nick hadn't done something stupid. She threw the towel back over her head and reread their conversation. Nick had started out by saying he had to show them something. He wasn't a cutter, so that's probably not it. A tattoo? A haircut? Hair dye? Although she mostly preferred texting to talking on the phone, at times like this she wished she had something more to go on than cold, hard words on a screen, no inflection, no way to judge if this "something" Nick had to show them was good or bad.

Not for the first time, she thought Dr. Seuss was definitely right. The waiting place sucks.

Chapter Sixty-Eight:
5:15 p.m. Tuesday, Aug. 20, 2013

Although she'd enjoyed a fun afternoon on the beach with Brittney and Ashley, and later Michael and Donovan, Lacey had really never left that waiting place. A part of her spent the entire day contemplating what had Nick so agitated.

She was five minutes early, but Lacey still paced back and forth in front of Dunkin' Donuts, checking her phone repeatedly, but the digits never seemed to change.

When it was finally five-twenty, she searched the parking lot. What type of car did Nick drive? She'd never seen his car, but he had mentioned it once or twice in group; hadn't he? The only thing she thought she remembered was that it was yellow. At least, she thought it was.

At five-twenty-two a bright yellow Monte Carlo pulled into the lot, and Lacey could definitely see the boys riding around in that. But, nope, it was some old lady with a gray pony tail. The car was so bright, she considered texting "Yellow" to MacGyver, but they had not spoken since he left two weeks ago. And she wasn't going to text first.

Five-twenty-three. Damn. Where are they?

At five-twenty-four, Lacey wondered if the boys were playing a trick on her. Were they yanking her chain? Maybe they didn't plan to show up.

At five-twenty-six, Lacey considered exactly how long she should wait for them. What was the appropriate amount of time? She knew it was definitely longer than six minutes, but exactly how many more? Brittney's rule, she knew, was no one was late unless they were at least fifteen minutes late. But could she stand here looking like an idiot for another nine minutes?

As Lacey paced, a short school bus swung into the parking space right outside the main entrance. *Geez, this is going to block my view. Do I stand here blindsided? Or do I change where I'm standing? Maybe I should just go in and get a coffee and wait at a table.*

Lacey was dumbfounded when Adam and Nick piled out of the bus.

"Sorry we're late, love," Nick said, as Adam hugged her.

"Girl, close your mouth. And don't go making any jokes about Phyllis," Adam said, swinging his right arm around her shoulder while pretending to close her mouth with his left hand.

Lacey hugged Adam, then Nick, then pulled away. "Phyllis?"

"That's what I call her," Nick said, pointing to the bus, which had Shalom painted on it along with some other words that had been painted over with bright green splotches.

"It used to say Shalom Country Day School. I got a real steal on the bus 'cause my mother used to drive for them," Nick said.

"Why Phyllis?" Lacey asked.

"Because I figure I always want to keep it filled with us," Nick said, and Lacey nodded her head, not sure she got it.

"I told him it was dumb," Adam said.

"This is your warning," Nick said. "Make fun of Phyllis, and you walk. You know the rules."

Nick held open the DD door for Lacey and Adam, and walked to the counter.

"I've been waiting all day to hear what's going on," Adam said. "What is it?"

"Don't be so uncouth," Nick said. "First, get yourself a donut or a croissant or some such thing and a cup of coffee. Then we'll talk at the table."

They ordered and found their way to the furthest table from the counter.

"All right, now," Adam said. "What's up?

"Neza."

"What about her?"

"She's not who we think she is."

"What do you mean?" Lacey said.

"Read this," Nick pushed his phone across the table to Lacey.

"Now, wait a minute. She doesn't get to see it first," Adam said, pushing back his chair and walking to the other side of the table, where he sat down next to Lacey.

"Suspected Rwandan Genocide Commander on Trial in Boston. What the hell does this have to do with Neza?" Adam said.

"Just read," Nick said, drinking his coffee and eating his Boston cream donut.

Adam and Lacey read. After the first minute, both looked up for more explanation, but Nick said, "Keep reading."

About five minutes later, Lacey blinked back tears and muttered, "This is horrible."

"Awful," Adam agreed. "But also irrelevant. There's nothing about Neza here."

"Keep reading," Nick growled, as he balled up his napkin and tossed it into his empty coffee cup.

"I don't know if I can," Lacey said. "It's talking about some horrible woman ordering rapes and murdering nuns. I don't want to read this."

"Me neither," Adam said.

"Keep reading," Nick said. "You're almost there. I've been waiting all day to talk about this."

So they kept reading about the genocide that had taken place in the spring and summer of 1994 over one hundred days in Rwanda, Central Africa, just three years before Lacey was born. Lacey had heard about the mass murders of the Tutsis once in a history class but not in the graphic details used in this article. The magazine story Nick had called up on his phone gave personal stories about how nearly one million people were murdered by their neighbors, most by machete. Suddenly, the word genocide sounded so sanitized in comparison to the horrific mass murders described.

The article mainly focused on a woman named Betty Ntahoboli, who witnesses claimed was a "commando" responsible for many grisly deaths. Ntahoboli fled to the United States in 1995, swearing her country was unsafe and that she was a victim of the genocide, not a perpetrator.

After she became an American citizen, Betty began talking about the Holocaust-like horrors of the Rwandan genocide. In public speeches, she would say she was a victim who would always do whatever was necessary to survive.

It was news accounts of these talks at schools and in libraries that drew the attention of other Rwandan refugees, including one who recognized Betty and knew her story was a ruse. This refugee, a woman, contacted the U.S. Department of Justice Office of Special Investigations, which eventually tried Ntahoboli in the United States for crimes against humanity. But it was too hard to prove murder cases that took place years earlier and thousands of miles away.

Even after the unsuccessful trial, the Rwandan refugee worked with investigators to build a case against Ntahoboli. And earlier this year, in February, the government tried Betty Ntahoboli again, but his time for lying on immigration forms and her citizenship application. With the witness's help, the federal court convicted Betty. Her American citizenship was revoked, and she was sentenced to ten years in a U.S. prison.

Adam and Lacey finally got to the important line in the story at precisely the same time: The witness was Neza Magambo.

They looked up at Nick.

"Are you kidding me?" Adam asked.

"Don't stop now. Finish reading," Nick said. "You're almost done."

The reporter had spoken to Neza, who told how she had hidden with five other women inside a secret closet, for about three months. This was after she'd seen Ntahoboli murder dozens of people simply because they were members of the country's Tutsi minority group and not the Hutu majority.

"I was just twenty years old at the time," Neza said in the story. "When the killing was over, I was only sixty-five pounds, and very quickly, I discovered my grandfather, parents and fifteen-year-old brother had all been slaughtered by machete at the hands of one of our neighbors. My whole family was gone, and I had nowhere to go."

As they came to the end of the story, Adam let go of Nick's phone, leaving it solely in Lacey's hand. He looked across at his friend.

"Shit," he said and then looked out the window.

Tears rolled down Lacey's cheeks. When she finished reading, she scrolled back up and reread everything related to Neza.

"While your stunned silence is appropriate," Nick said rather abruptly, grabbing his phone and putting it in his pocket. "This really sucks."

"Okay. That's an understatement," Adam said.

Lacey took in a deep breath and blew it out. "Of course it does. Poor Neza."

"Yeah," Adam said.

"Poor Neza?" Nick complained. "Don't you get it? She's a liar."

"What?!" Lacey screamed. Then she lowered her voice, "What? What are you talking about? Ntahaboli is the one who lied."

"In court, right," Nick said. "But to us, Neza is the liar."

"Huh?" Adam said. His shock over what he had read had left him a bit inarticulate.

"Don't you see? She sits there week after week acting like our problems are the most horrific thing she's ever heard, and we believe her."

Lacey and Adam stared silently at Nick and then each other.

A few quiet moments passed, as they each considered the situation.

"He's right," Lacey said, as she slumped in her seat, color draining from her face. She started pulling apart the donut she'd purchased with no intention of eating any of it. "She is kind of lying to us. I mean she's never even said she's Rwandan."

"Yeah, I always thought she was Jamaican," Adam said.

"I assumed she was from Haiti," Nick said. "But the thing is, she's not who she claims to be. She's always like, so you didn't make the football team. I understand. That's awful. It really hurts."

"The football team?" Adam said and laughed.

"Yeah, when did you ever try out for a sports team?" Lacey said.

"You're missing the point. She's a fraud. How could she possibly give a crap about all our nonsense?"

"I see your point," Lacey said.

"I don't know," Adam said. "Maybe."

"We have to confront her," Nick said. "Right now."

"Oooookay," Lacey said. "How do you suppose we do that? Do you know where she lives?"

"No," Nick admitted. "But I think we really need to talk to her."

"Agreed, but I guess it has to wait until Sunday," Adam said.

"No, it doesn't," Lacey said. "I have Sandy group with her tomorrow."

"You do?" Adam said. "Why don't you tell us anything?"

Lacey ignored the comment. "Tell you what. Can you guys meet me at the church at eight-thirty tomorrow night? We can talk to Neza then.

"I don't know," Nick said. "She owes us an explanation, but I don't even know if I care. Maybe I'll just stop going to group."

"What?" Lacey asked.

"I mean if we can't trust her," Nick said.

"Oh, stop being a drama queen," Adam said. "We need to talk to her."

"I guess," Nick said. "Lacey, you want a ride home?"

"Wasn't planning on going home," she said. "Do you want to come meet my friends?"

"Wow, Lacey's friends," Nick mocked.

"Oh, yes," Adam said. "I would love to meet Lacey's friends."

The trio threw out their garbage and headed to Nick's little school bus. While they tried to keep the mood light, each was weighed down contemplating Neza's past.

She must think I'm the biggest crybaby, Lacey thought as they headed down Silver Bay Road. To lighten the mood, she asked, "Do you have to sing class trip songs when you're in this thing? You know, like One Hundred Bottles of Beer on the Wall?"

"One hundred..." Adam started, and Lacey and Nick joined in.

Chapter Sixty-Nine:
Wednesday, Aug. 21, 2013

"So why is it you don't need a ride home?" Donovan asked as support group came to an end for the night and participants headed over to the refreshment table to grab some iced tea and cookies.

"I've just become super religious. Thought I'd stick around for Mass," Lacey said.

"Cute," Donovan said. "We don't have Mass. But, it's cool as long as you're not going to get stuck here without a ride."

"No, I'm..." Before Lacey could say "good," Nick and Adam burst into the room with all the subtlety of a tsunami.

"Lacey!" Adam called out to her.

"Where is she?" Nick demanded.

"I'm over here," Lacey said, taking a step toward them.

"Oh, I got it. You've got a new boyfriend?" Donovan said.

Lacey turned her head back. "No, they're friends."

"Right," he said, as Adam enveloped her in a hug.

"Are you denying our love affair, sugar?" Adam said, teasing.

"Your affair?" Nick said, pulling Lacey away and into his embrace. "You know she's mine."

Donovan shook his head. "I guess you're in good hands then."

"Oh yes," Adam said, holding up his hands. "I could be a quarterback."

"I think you mean a wide receiver," Nick said.

"Is that a crack about my weight?" Adam complained.

"Don't mind them. They're always like this," Lacey said as Donovan stepped away, mumbling, "Well, nice to meet you."

"Where is she?" Nick asked Lacey, scanning the room for Neza.

"Wait till everyone leaves," Lacey insisted. "I want to talk to her alone."

"More waiting," Nick said.

"Just a few minutes," Adam said and motioned them toward the empty circle of chairs. Lacey sat down and immediately began twirling some of her hair. Adam plopped down next to her, but Nick chose a seat across from them and pulled a red bean bag out of his pocket.

At first, he threw the tiny sack up in the air and caught it a few times. Then, without any warning Lacey could discern, he either threw it at or to Adam, Lacey wasn't quite sure which one.

"Got it," Adam said, snagging the flying rectangle out of the air. "Hey, where'd you get this?" he asked as he flung it back across the room.

"Toss Across," Nick said. "I was playing with my sister before I picked you up."

"How is Katy?"

"Annoying."

"His little sister is so adorable," Adam told Lacey as he threw the bean bag. "She's seven and missing both front teeth."

"She's..." Before Nick could say anything more, Neza stepped into the circle of chairs, and Lacey realized it was just the four of them left in the room.

"Adam, Nick, it's wonderful to see you, but is everything all right?" Neza said, taking a seat two away from Adam.

"No," Nick said and walked across the room to stand in front of her.

"What's wrong? How can I help?" Neza said, rising and immediately reaching to give Nick a hug.

"Don't," he said with a coldness that froze her in her steps.

"Neza," Lacey said. "The boys and I wanted to ask you about something."

"Of course, dear, anything," Neza said.

"Why are you such a phony?" Nick demanded.

"Wait a minute!" Adam said. "Back off a bit. I didn't sign up for this. I thought we were just going to talk to her. Sit down, Nick."

Lacey was surprised by the way Adam barked the order, but she was shocked when Nick didn't argue and sat down next to Lacey.

"What is all this about?" Neza said. "I can tell something is really bothering you. I want to help."

"Do you?" Lacey said. "Why?"

"What do you mean?" Neza said, confused.

"Why do you want to help us?" Lacey asked again.

"That's what I do," Neza said. "I don't understand."

"Neza, no matter what we tell you, you always seem so concerned, so interested," Adam said. "Why?"

"Because I care about you," Neza said, opening her arms to indicate each of them.

"But why?" Nick said, his voice almost a growl.

"I don't know what you're getting at," Neza said calmly, pausing a moment. "But I will tell you that when my brother was your age..." Neza stopped again, cleared her throat and looked searchingly around the room before she continued. "I was only five years older than him, but it seemed such a wide chasm. He wanted my help all the time. Help with homework, advice about girls, assistance with his chores and negotiating with our parents. It seemed such a burden at the time. I often said no."

She closed her eyes and was silent for a long moment.

Adam reached over and briefly touched Neza's hand. She looked at him and smiled.

"I never wanted to help him," she said, then stopped speaking, as if this should answer all of their questions.

"What happened to your brother?" Nick asked.

"He's gone home, far too soon," Neza said. "He's with God again."

Lacey was struck by the serenity with which Neza spoke of her murdered brother.

"Neza, we read a story about you in a Massachusetts magazine."

"Oh," Neza said. Then, Lacey's meaning struck a chord. "Oh."

"Right," Nick said. "So we know you can't really give a crap about our stupid problems. Why do you pretend to?"

"Why do you say that?" Neza asked patiently.

"We read the article," Nick said angrily.

"I feel like such a stupid crybaby. Boohoo, my house got wet," Lacey said. She choked back tears and surprised herself when she added, "Do you go home and laugh at us or tell your friends what little spoiled brats we are?"

"Nooo," Neza said, quickly moving from her chair to Lacey's side and hugging her. "I would never."

They held one another for a few minutes before Lacey pushed back, and Neza retook her chair.

"We're hurt," Lacey said. "We feel like you let us make fools of ourselves in front of you."

"And we want to know why," Adam said.

"That's what they want," Nick said. "I don't think I care. I think I just wanted to come and tell you your secret is out, and you can't use us for your amusement anymore. At least, not me. I won't be back."

"I see," Neza said, and there was silence as they looked around at one another.

351

After a few minutes, Neza said, "My brother was just about your age when he was murdered. For years, when I thought about him, I was overwhelmed with grief and angry not with our neighbor who slit his throat, but with myself. I had the power to make the life he had, short as it was, better, and I did not. I was too selfish. I found him annoying, and now he was gone.

"All of my anger was focused on me, and it took me years to overcome that. When I came to the United States, I got therapy, and it helped me so very much. I decided I wanted to be that help for other people, but not just anybody, teenagers. I vowed to help as many teenagers as I could because I did not always help the one I should have."

"But when you've seen your neighbors get murdered and lost your whole family, you must look at someone like me and think, 'What do you have to be depressed about? Get over yourself,'" Nick challenged.

"Nicholas, when I speak to you, and you tell me how you've been struggling with depression, I think, 'How can I find a way to help?' That's all. 'How can I do some small thing in this world to make someone else's, your, life better?'"

"But you've got to admit our problems are ridiculous in comparison to genocide," Adam said.

"No one's problems should ever be compared to someone else's," Neza said. "My suffering does not make yours any less potent. Who would tell a mother crying at her baby's grave, 'You have no right to cry. Some mothers have lost several children'?"

Neza looked at each of their faces. "Pain is like love. It cannot be measured, weighed and compared. It must simply be accepted and experienced. Do you understand?"

"But still," Lacey said. "Pretty much all we talk about in group, both groups, are just so First World problems."

Neza laughed.

"No," she said. "People who come here…When each of you come here, your problems are all pushing you down like weights on your shoulders. My job, at least, what I think my job is, is to relieve just some of that pressure, to help you feel as if you can carry your load. And, if you're a person of faith, perhaps help you see there is someone there to help you. But if not, show you that there is, at the very least, a community that will help. That's what I try to do. Do I succeed?"

They each nodded.

Neza paused for a moment, then, she said, "Rather than make me bitter, my experiences have taught me to love and appreciate life. I've learned how strong we can be and that there is always, even at the darkest moments, reason for hope. Do you understand?"

Again, they nodded, but very slowly.

"Then, I would like to continue this journey together," Neza said. "I must tell you. I have never had clients who learned of my past before. I would never have expected your reaction. You've given me a lot to think about."

"It's just, and don't take this the wrong way," Adam said. "We sort of felt lied to, like you weren't being honest with us."

Neza nodded. "I see that now. I may have to change what I share with my groups. Thank you," she said. "Are we okay?"

"Yes," answered Lacey and Adam immediately.

"I don't know," Nick said. "I'm not sure I'll feel as comfortable as I did."

"Would you be willing to try?" Neza asked.

"I guess," he said.

"That's all I can ask."

Neza stood and opened her arms, and without words, the group hugged one another, holding tightly for just a few moments. Then, they broke away. Neza turned off the lights. The boys began tossing the bean bag once more, and they all headed for the parking lot.

Chapter Seventy:
Saturday, Aug. 31, 2013

"Well, that's the last blue container," Polly said as Ashley placed a Rubbermaid tote into the tiny room that would serve as both Lacey's bedroom and the Freshet living room for the next three or more months.

"This one's not blue," Ashley said.

"What?" Lacey asked.

"It's not blue. It's green."

"Oh, yeah, we know," Lacey said. Then feeling Ashley's eyes on her, she added, "We just call them that."

"What?"

"Well, we used to only have blue ones, so that's what we called them."

"But since Sandy and all this moving, we've got them in a rainbow assortment," Polly added. "Tan, purple, red, even orange."

"After we move back home, if I ever see another one, I swear I'll kill someone," Lacey said.

"Well, you're going to see them, Lacey. We must have fifty or sixty of them," Polly said.

"Yeah, but once we're home, they won't have to be our chairs, closets, dressers and tables. We can just put them away in the garage or something."

"True," said Polly. "I am tired of the constant moving and compromising. It would be nice to put something away and have it stay there for a long time. When my mother decides where to put a lamp or a chair, that's it. It stays there for decades."

"Yeah, well, that's a problem, too," Lacey said.

"Hey, at least you know your house will eventually be okay. We still haven't gotten a building permit. Now, my mom cries that she shouldn't have knocked down the house. She should have fixed it."

"I'm sorry, Ashley. That must be terrible," Polly said. "I remember when we got the letter from the town offering to demolish our home, free of charge."

"And this was right after we pretty much had everything up and working again," Lacey said.

"Yeah, but when the total cost of the restoration went over fifty percent of the property value, then we were eligible," Polly said, explaining why the township sent its well-meaning letter.

"What were we over by like two thousand dollars? Right?" Lacey asked.

"Just one thousand, nine hundred and eighty-five," Polly said. "I called the adjuster and asked him if there is any way he could lower the pay out, just knock off two thousand dollars. He not only told me that was unethical, but he said in twenty-eight years of working in the insurance business, he had never heard of anyone begging to lower their adjustment."

"Mom, I'm hungry. Can we go to McDonald's?" Jake asked, running in with mud covering the front of his jeans.

"Where have you been?" Polly asked.

"Down by the pond," Jake said happily. "There's these tiny fish there."

"That's a drainage basin and those fish are mosquito larvae. Stay away from there. Besides, when I say stay in front of the apartment, I mean right out front, not a block away."

"But you always said it was all right as long as I can see the front door."

"That's at home."

"But this is home now," Jake whined.

"Mom, just take him for McDonald's. We'll finish up here," Lacey said.

"Are you sure?"

"Yeah."

"Do you want me to bring you guys back anything?"

"Chicken Selects."

"They don't have those anymore."

"I *know* that, but you asked what I wanted, and that's what I want."

"Ashley, can I bring you back something from McDonald's?"

"No, thanks, Polly. I think Brittney is coming by and taking us to Taco Bell."

"Oh, really. I don't remember anyone asking about..."

"Mom, can we go? I'm hungry," Jake complained.

"Well, go wash your hands," Polly said. "Lacey, you know even though some of your friends have their licenses now, you still have to ask permission before leaving the house."

"I know, Mom. I was going to tell you."

"Tell me?"

"Ask you."

"All clean. Can we go?" Jake said, holding up his hands as if he were a victim in a bank robbery.

"You better go, Mom," Lacey said. "And Taco Bell with Brittney is okay, right?"

"Yeah. Let's go, Jake." Polly took Jake by the hand and headed for the door, but he pulled away.

"Are your hands clean?" Jake asked. "'Cause mine are clean, and I don't want you to get them dirty."

"It starts so soon," Polly mumbled as she grabbed the doorknob. Turning back, she yelled toward the girls, "Be careful, and don't distract Brittney when she's driving."

"Thanks, Polly," Lacey called. "If you hadn't said that we would have been totally reckless. But now we'll be careful."

Ashley giggled. Polly frowned. Jake pulled on his mother's hand, insisting they hurry up and get his Happy Meal.

"You're lucky I love you," Polly said.

"I am. You're right," Lacey said. "Don't forget the Chicken Selects."

"That's your problem, Lacey. You have trouble accepting any change."

"C'mon, Mom," Jake complained.

"Well, maybe if some of it was for the better," Lacey said. "You better go. I think your favorite child is hungry."

"Mom, please," Jake practically sang.

"You're not fair," Polly called into the apartment as she closed the door, but she was happy when she heard Lacey call back, "Love you."

Polly cracked the door open again. "Love you more."

"Oh, Mom, not this. It takes all day," Jake said.

"More," Lacey called.

"More," Polly said and shut the door, and though they couldn't hear each other, both Freshet women whispered, "More."

"Thanks for helping us move," Lacey said as she turned her attention to Ashley.

"No problem. I don't have much else to do anyway."

"Aren't you still helping out at the People's Pantry?"

"Yeah, but just two days. I really like it there. It makes you feel like you're... I don't know, not to be corny or anything, but like you're making a difference. Y'know?"

Lacey nodded as she sorted the containers into stacks four high.

"Like this one mother comes in all the time with her three-year-old son. She not only lost her house in Silverton, her job was at this insurance agency in Sea Bright and all of the businesses there were affected. Her husband is in Afghanistan, and well, it just feels good to be able to help her. The boy, Aiden, really likes this cereal. It's some off brand we get in once in a while, but when I see it. I hide two boxes 'cause it makes him smile. You should really think about com…"

The cold stare Lacey shot her friend was enough to stop Ashley midsentence. She knew Lacey wanted nothing to do with the scores of charitable organizations that had set up shop around town since Sandy.

"You said you have nothing to do besides volunteering. Where's Tyler? Did you break up?"

"Great choice of words, Lace. Y'know we couldn't break up. We were never going out."

"Okay, so you've decided to…"

"I decided nothing. I guess I kind of ruined things."

"What do you mean?"

"Well, with school starting next week, I was thinking a lot about Tyler and me and what it was going to be like."

"Yeah, sure, that makes sense."

"So, I asked him if he was going to sit with us at lunch."

"Sure. I mean you've been, um, hanging out all summer."

"Well, that's what I thought. But, he's like, nah."

"So, what'd you say?"

"Like, y'know. At first, nothing."

"Nothing."

"Yeah, it's his life. If he doesn't want to sit with us, whatever. But then we were like…Y'know. We were fooling around, and after, I was like, you're going to stop by my locker and walk me to classes sometimes. Right?"

Ashley started to cry. Lacey sat next to her on two blue containers, one purple/one green, stacked on top of each other.

"What did he say?"

"He said," Ashley's voice broke off, and she sobbed heavily.

"Yeah?"

"There I am lying in this bathtub with him over in the new Aldo house, and he looks at me and says. 'Those are things a boyfriend does. You know I'm not your boyfriend. Right?'"

"I'm sorry," Lacey said, holding her friend while she cried.

"That's not the worse part."

"Oh."

"So I get up. First, I trip on this sleeping bag we've got half under us, half over us and I chipped my tooth on the bathtub. See," she pointed to the tooth next to her left front tooth, which was now visibly shorter than it should be. "At this point, I'm crying and I'm screaming, 'Well, this is something a girlfriend does and that doesn't seem to bother you.' And he's like, 'Ashley, be quiet. There are people working in the house next door.' And I'm yelling, 'No, I won't be quiet. What do you think I am, your whore? Is that what you think?!'"

"I'm sorry," Lacey whispered, not knowing what else to do or say.

Ashley pushed out of her friend's embrace and got up and started pacing. "So now he gets up. And he's standing in the bathtub, naked, screaming. 'You said this is what you want. You said this is what you want.' And I start screaming back, 'Well, it's not what I want. Okay. It's just not!'

"Then we hear a knocking on the door downstairs, but they don't wait for us to answer. And these two guys come in, workers from the house next door. They clearly don't speak much English, but they see us standing there, me in just my thong and a tank top. And they come in and just stare at me. 'You okay? You okay?' they say. I'm pretty sure they couldn't speak English.

"So I nod, but they're not sure what to do. Tyler meanwhile puts his pants on and tosses me my shorts. So they're still there staring. 'Call police? Call police?' they keep asking maybe seven or eight times. Once I get my shorts on, I go over to the guys, and I'm like, 'It's okay. Thank you. It's okay.' And they're nodding.

And Tyler tries to talk to them, but the one guy just says, "Sali! Sali!' Then the other one yelled, 'Get Out.' And Tyler gets the hint and runs out. And well, that was two days ago, and we haven't spoken or texted since."

Chapter Seventy-One:
Tuesday, Sept. 3, 2013

"We've finally arrived," Brittney said as she, Ashley and Lacey climbed out of her Jeep in the dirt lot that served as the juniors' parking lot.

"At school? Wow, that's exciting," Lacey said as she adjusted the safety-pin seams she had installed in her jeans.

"Yeah, this is much better than hanging out on the beach," Ashley said.

"Ha. Ha. Jerks," Brittney said. "At least this year, we're driving to school. C'mon, we've wanted to be upperclassmen since kindergarten. This is our year."

As the girls walked from the dirt onto the asphalt where the seniors parked, two popular senior girls passed in front of them, hips swaying, hair blowing in the wind and the scent of Japanese Cherry Blossom wafting around them.

"Nope. I think it's their year," Lacey said, as she looked down at her jeans and tee-shirt. *Maybe, I should have dressed up.*

"Oh, c'mon, this year is going to be great," Brittney said, her long black hair swinging freely for the first time in weeks, no ponytail today. "No school buses, and we can go out at lunch."

"You're right," Ashley conceded. "You just have to remember that you're the only one who has a license, so it's not the same for us."

"Yeah. I don't get my license until next spring," Lacey said. "And, oh my God, I didn't tell you guys. My mother wanted me to take the bus this morning."

"What?"

"Why?"

"Well, apparently in the letter with the bus pass, there's a note that asks us to please use the bus the first day so that they can establish who is supposed to be on the route. Polly was like, 'It wouldn't kill you for one day. Then, you can go with Brittney.' And I was like, 'No way.'"

"Did you even change your address, Lace?" Ashley asked.

"No. I would have had to get up half an hour earlier and let Polly drive me to our house, so I can take a bus I'm never going to ride from a place where I don't live."

"Geez," Ashley said.

"But you'll never have to take the bus. I got this covered," Brittney said.

"Yeah, well, I said that, and Polly was like, 'Well, what about when Brittney is out sick or something? You can't be handing in your bus pass in November. The bus driver won't know who you are.'"

"Well, I'll have my license by November," Ashley said, practically. "If Brittney is sick, I can drive us."

"Will you have a car?" Brittney asked.

"Oh, yeah, I don't know. I have a couple hundred put aside, but Mom's like, 'Anything you can get for that money won't be safe.'"

"And besides, there are other costs, like gas and insurance," Lacey said in her Polly voice.

"So you've heard it, too?" Ashley said.

"Daily," Lacey groaned.

"Damn," Brittney said. "Maybe I should stop complaining that my folks don't even look at my credit card charges."

"Yeah, maybe you should," Ashley said pointedly.

"You think?" Lacey asked with a chuckle.

"So who are you guys going to go to Homecoming with?"

"Ashley, school just started," Brittney said.

"It hasn't even started. We haven't even gotten to the door yet," Lacey said. "Don't you think you could wait at least a few days before you start worrying about Homecoming?"

"No," Ashley said. "Dances are the only good thing about school."

"Well, not the only good thing," Lacey said.

"Oh yeah, what else is there?" Brittney said. As she did this, a good-looking guy with light brown hair, wide shoulders, and tight buns who the girls had never seen before passed in front of them.

"Him," Ashley said, running her fingers through the blonde hair she'd spent an hour straightening. "Wow! Where'd he come from?"

"Don't know."

"Hope he's in some of our classes."

"What are the odds?"

"Not great, but hey, you never know," Lacey said as she pulled open the door to the school.

The dim fluorescent lighting and crowded, claustrophobic halls were a polar opposite to the beautiful day outside. The building had a fresh-paint smell about it that assaulted them immediately.

"Here we go again," Ashley said as they headed for their lockers.

"You realize this is the first school year we've ever started without MacGyver," Lacey said.

"Here we go again," Brittney said, rolling her eyes over Lacey's observation.

"Give her a break," Ashley said. "It's hard."

"Everything's hard," Lacey said.

"Everything?" Brittney said with a tone that made it clear that she was employing the humor generally reserved for twelve-year-old boys.

"Gross," Lacey said.

"Is it now?" Brittney joked, continuing down the same path.

The bell rang, which was quite a misnomer, as it was more of an electronic beep.

"See you guys at lunch," Ashley said, heading off to her physics class as Brittney and Lacey headed to the chorus room.

Chapter Seventy-Two:
About 4 p.m. Thursday, Sept. 12, 2013

Lacey heard Ashley arriving at the Beach Club but didn't turn her head to see her friend's bicycle heading down the street toward the waterfront.

"I've gotta feeling. That tonight's gonna be a good night. That tonight's..."

Because her attention was riveted to the horizon, Lacey didn't bother getting visual confirmation that the Black Eyed Peas lyrics were coming from Ashley's iPod.

"Come over here quick," Lacey called out as Ashley dumped her bike against the fence and slogged across the sand.

"I knew you'd be here. It's still summer, right? We've got like ten days left, right?"

"Yeah, tell that to all the freakin' leaves piling up," Lacey scoffed. "Check this out," she said, pointing to her left and the distant horizon, where black smoke was filling the sky.

"Is that where the bridge is?" Ashley asked.

"Right about there," Lacey responded, her eyes fixed to the ever-blackening sky.

"Shit," Ashley said. "I knew I smelled something. Do you think the bridge is burning?"

"Nah, but something over there is."

"How long have you been watching it?"

"About half an hour. Where've you been?" Lacey asked.

"Yeah, sorry about that," Ashley said. "I was up at the pantry. I was locking the door when this woman approached me and asked if she could please run in and grab a few items. Y'know, I say woman but she was really just a kid, maybe a year or two older than us. Anyway, she was begging me to let her a grab a few things because she had no food in her apartment for Jeffrey and the baby, like I knew who they were."

"What'd you do?"

"I let them in. I mean, who could say no?"

"I could."

"Yeah, sure you could. Anyway, it didn't take her long to get a few things."

"Since when do you lock up?"

"Oh, I don't normally. The manager, Cassie, had to leave early because her son fell at school and either broke or sprained his arm."

"And she trusted you to run the place? That's kind of cool."

"Yeah, at first I thought, 'Awesome, I got this whole store to myself.' As soon as she left, I cranked up the radio, put my feet up on the counter. But, you know, after a while I realized the time went faster when I was actually working, so I went back to shelving the canned beans."

"Lame," Lacey said.

"I guess," Ashley said. "I can't believe all the smoke."

"I know. Instead of dying down, it just gets thicker and thicker."

"We should go over there," Ashley said.

"How?"

"When Brittney gets here, let's skip Taco Bell and go over to Seaside."

"She doesn't get off work for another hour. By then, there probably won't be anything to see."

"True. Can't wait till I get my license."

"Me neither."

Chapter Seventy-Three:
About 5 p.m. Thursday, Sept. 12, 2013

"I don't know why we had to stop at Taco Bell. The fire will probably be out by the time we get over there," Ashley complained as they sped down Route 37 headed east toward the Mathis Bridge to Seaside Heights on the barrier peninsula.

"Because I was hungry," Brittney said.

"So am I," Lacey said, scarfing down nachos. "Besides, you know nothing's open over the bridge now that the Bennies have gone home."

"I hate that word," Ashley said.

"Bennies?" Brittney asked. "Why?"

"Well for one thing, we don't even know what it means."

"Yes, we do. It means out-of-towners or tourists," Brittney said.

"Tourists, really?" Lacey asked. "I'm with Ashley. Nobody tours the Jersey Shore. It's not like anyone comes and takes a bus trip to explore local history."

"Sure, they do," Brittney said. "Lots of people take tours of the Jersey Shore House."

"Great," Lacey and Ashley said together.

"That's what we want to be known for, a drunken reality TV cast," Lacey complained.

"Have you ever even seen the show?" Brittney asked.

"No."

"Once, just part of one," Ashley said. "I can't believe that people think that's how people at the Shore are. Those people aren't even from here."

"Ashley, take the food bags on your side quick and get me a napkin. And, Lacey, put your seatbelt on," Brittney snapped as they approached the base of the bridge, where a patrol car was parked sideways across the lanes with its lights on.

Ashley handed her a paper napkin and grabbed the bags to place in the well near her feet. As Brittney wiped her mouth and then her steering wheel, she slowed the Jeep to a stop even though the light was green and tapped the button to bring down her window. Meanwhile Lacey scooted over from rear seat center to sitting directly behind the driver's seat and buckled up.

"Hi, officer, is there a problem?" Brittney said.

The police officer ignored the question and waved through two fire engines, both from towns more than half an hour away.

"Where are you ladies headed?" he asked when he turned back around.

"Over to Seaside," Brittney said as she watched what seemed an endless and growing plume of smoke blowing from south to north in the distance ahead of her.

"Do you live over there?" asked the officer.

"No, sir," said Brittney, surprised that she suddenly sounded like a military recruit.

"Well, then I'm afraid you're going to have to turn around. We've got a major fire we're battling, and we closed the bridge to any unnecessary traffic," he said, stepping away from the car.

"Wait," Brittney called.

"Where's the fire?" Lacey yelled out the window.

"What's burning?" Ashley said.

"Is the Boardwalk on fire?" Brittney asked.

"Honestly, ladies, I haven't been over there, but I'm pretty sure it is up on the Boardwalk," he said and again stepped away.

"Wait."

"Is it in Seaside Heights or Seaside Park?"

"Has anyone been hurt?"

Debbie Mura

The girls continued to call out questions, but the officer ignored them.

"I suggest you head home and turn on the news," he said. Then, he actually tipped his hat and made what looked like a whoopee sign, circling the air with the index finger of his right hand, demanding they turn around and head back into Toms River.

"This must be some fire," Lacey said.

"Yeah, I really wanted to see it," Ashley said.

"Oh, we're still going," Brittney said.

"Oh, really," Lacey countered. "What are you going to do? Run him over?"

"I don't think we have to run him over," Ashley said. "You can probably just drive past him. What's he going to do? Shoot out your tires?"

"Yeah, I don't think he's going to shoot at three teenage girls," Brittney said.

"You never know," Lacey said. "I don't think we should chance it."

As they talked, Brittney turned the Jeep northwest on Fischer Boulevard.

"You're going home? I thought you had a plan?" Lacey complained, recognizing the familiar path toward Silverton.

"I'm not headed home," Brittney said.

"Yes, you are. Even with my bad sense of direction, I know the way home," Ashley said.

"No. I mean yes. I mean I am headed in the same direction as Silverton, but I'm driving up to Brick."

"Why?"

"Because there's no way they closed the Mantoloking Bridge."

"Sweet," Lacey said. "But won't the fire be out by the time we get there?"

"Lacey, did you see that smoke? Whatever's burning over there is going to be burning for a long time."

"I don't know about you guys, but this feels a little creepy to me," Ashley said.

"Why?"

"Well, yesterday, all my teachers took up at least part of their classes talking about what it was like to watch the World Trade Center burn 12 years ago."

"I don't think this is a terrorist attack. Terrorists wouldn't even be able to find Seaside."

"Still those documentaries really make you think."

"Yeah, I didn't expect one of the privileges of being an upperclassmen would be that we'd have to watch documentaries and delve more deeply into 9/11."

"Oh, did you see the one Smith showed from CBS news?" Lacey asked.

"No, Calcagno had one done by Fox News. The one Rodriguez showed had video of people jumping from the towers, and you could see their faces and all. How awful that must be for their families."

"Okay, that's enough," Brittney said.

"I liked it better when all we had to do on 9/11 was have a moment of silence," Lacey said.

"Ms. DiStefano said it was ridiculous that we are only being taught this stuff now. She just moved here from Iowa, and she said students all over the country learn a lot more about the attacks than we do here in New York and New Jersey."

"That's because no one in Iowa lost a family member at the Trade Center," Brittney said, reminding her friends with her tone that her aunt – her father's sister – had died there.

"Do you not want to go?" Lacey asked Ashley, not that she had any control at all over where Brittney drove.

"Nah, I'm okay," Ashley said. "How about you?" she asked Brittney.

"I'm good. We don't even know what's on fire," Brittney said. "For all we know, it's a controlled burn that got a little out of control."

Ashley pointed out the window at the smoke that was clearly visible ten miles away. "That's no controlled burn."

"Yeah," Lacey agreed. "But I want to see it anyway."

"Me too," her friends answered in chorus.

Then, Ashley pulled her phone out and said, "Siri, play 'Burning Down the House.'"

"No," Lacey and Brittney shut her down. Instead, they turned up Cee Lo Green's "Forget You" on Brittney's stereo and headed south on Route 35 toward Seaside with tunes blaring. They knew they were going to what could be a deadly fire, but it was still an adventure.

Chapter Seventy-Four:
About 5:30 p.m. Thursday, Sept. 12, 2013

"It's like driving in a thunderstorm," Brittney said as she turned her lights on.

"Maybe we should go back," Ashley suggested.

"No way," Brittney said.

"I can't believe the amount of ash that's falling."

"I can't believe we can't even see where it's coming from anymore. Do you think it's right here?" Lacey asked as they left Ortley Beach and entered Seaside Heights.

"I don't think so. Even though the smoke is thick here, it still looks thicker up ahead."

"Make a left and go down to the Boulevard or Central," Ashley suggested.

"Yeah, maybe we can go up on the Boardwalk and see where this is coming from," Lacey said.

Brittney drove by the waterpark and headed down one of the dead-end streets to get as close to the Boardwalk as possible.

Smoke enveloped the girls as they scrambled out of the Jeep and up the ramp onto the Boardwalk that had only been rebuilt about eight weeks ago.

"Oh, my god," Lacey said.

"Holy shit," Brittney echoed, as Ashley stared.

From their new vantage point, they could finally see what was burning. The Funtown amusement pier and the businesses that stood on it were engulfed in flames that shot high into the air and looked like giant red and yellow skyscrapers.

Although they were about a mile away, the Boardwalk where they were was completely immersed in smoke. Their eyes watered and they coughed, breathing the foul air, and a strong south-to-north wind whipped the smoke past them.

"Let's get back in the car and try to get closer," Brittney said, herding her friends off the boards.

As they crawled down Central Avenue, they started to see and hear firetrucks coming from all directions. Brittney had to pull over a few times to let the emergency workers by, but no one stopped her progress until they were about two blocks from the burning amusement pier.

At that point, they parked Brittney's Jeep at the curb, walked a block west of the Boardwalk, then continued on foot to get as close as they could.

They found a crowd forming in a parking lot on Ocean Avenue, just across the street from the Boardwalk, right in line with the amusement pier that for decades had jutted into the ocean. Flames danced in every direction, and smoke strangled the breathable air.

"They just built this," Ashley said with tears rolling down her cheeks, as the girls found a place in the crowd.

"I can't believe it," Brittney said, openly sobbing.

"At least," Lacey said, choking back tears. "At least, it's the Funtown Pier and not Casino."

"What?" Ashley said.

"Why?" Brittney said.

"Well," Lacey said logically, trying as best as she could to summon the optimism Polly had always taught her. "Most of Funtown was closed this year. They hadn't really started to rebuild from Sandy yet."

"I guess," Brittney said.

The girls stood there as a crowd of about two hundred people slowly gathered around them. Most people said little to nothing. It was hot from the fire, and the smoke made it more and more difficult to breathe. But it was the enormity of this tragedy less than a year after Sandy that made it impossible to talk or even think.

They watched as firefighters blasted water at a blaze with a voracious appetite. By the time, the girls had arrived, the fire had jumped from the original cluster of buildings near the base of the pier across the Boardwalk to buildings on the street side.

Police moved the crowd further west twice as the fire moved to a row of small businesses across the street, while it simultaneously continued its unrelenting race down the boards from Seaside Park north to Seaside Heights.

At one point, firefighters did the unthinkable. Using construction equipment, they tore up the brand new Boardwalk to create a firebreak and stop the fire.

"I can't believe they are doing that," Lacey said. "They just built it. They just built it."

Brittney slipped her arm around Lacey's shoulders. "I know," she said. "I know."

Facts, rumors and ridiculous stories floated through the crowd along with the ash that fell all around them. The prevailing story was that the fire had started at a closed custard store on the pier.

The onlookers gasped in unison as the pier collapsed, sending the few rides, including an antique carousel that had been spared from Sandy's wrath, into the ocean. About an hour after the firefighters had created the firebreak, word spread through the crowd that it hadn't worked. Although it seemed as if every fire company in New Jersey and beyond had sent assistance, the blaze had all the advantages. The wind was sweeping hot embers from building to building, so that the fires weren't even all connected. The firestorm jumped from structure to structure and across conjoined rooftops but also under the Boardwalk, erupting through the gaps and licking at new buildings until they surrendered.

When the firebreak failed, a new team of firefighters mounted construction equipment and again tore up a twenty-five-foot swath of brand new boards. After that, they brought in sand and built a temporary dune to try and battle the ever-surging fire, desperately trying to save newly refurbished buildings and the second amusement ride pier.

The girls eventually moved a few blocks north into Seaside Heights. The fire was a block south of their new vantage point, but this parking lot was full of people, mostly firefighters and local residents, anxious to see if their rebuilding efforts would be turned into a pile of ash. They didn't speak to each other, only watched and listened.

Around seven o'clock, a woman who looked to be in her forties came running down the center of the street dressed in heels and business clothes, like she had just gotten off work in the city. "My building! My building!" she screamed and dropped to her knees, arms stretched out at her sides, palms skyward, staring up at the sky and screeching, "God, why do you hate us?" Many averted their eyes.

Chapter Seventy-Five:
About 7:15 p.m. Thursday, Sept. 12, 2013

"I need to take a walk, get away for just a few minutes," Ashley said.

"I'll go with you," Brittney said, then turning to Lacey. "You coming?"

"I'm good here, if it's okay," Lacey said, as she stared at the inferno.

"Okay, we'll be right back," Ashley said. Then, she and Brittney headed west, away from the oceanfront Boardwalk and toward the bay.

As her friends receded from view, Lacey heard a man's voice shout out from the other side of the parking lot. "Hey, anybody want to give me a hand? I need help over here."

She averted her eyes from the fire, expecting to see firefighters calling out to one another for assistance with equipment. Instead, she saw an older man, probably in his seventies or eighties, unloading folding chairs and a few tables from a beat-up minivan at the curb. She joined a dozen or so people who worked as an assembly line unloading about two hundred chairs and setting them up throughout the lot.

"I grabbed these from the VFW," the man who originally called out said to no one in particular.

After they set up about ten tables, they unloaded several cases of water and a few cases of assorted chip bags.

"It's not much, but it's what we had," the man said.

"Thank you so much," said a woman, who wore a navy windbreaker with the emblem for the local fire company auxiliary. "We're having trouble getting enough drinking water, and these guys are getting hungry. Not much is really open. We've already emptied the local convenience stores."

"How long have they been here?" asked the man.

"Since it started around two-thirty," she said, as the sun was starting to set behind her. "Some of these firefighters have been here for five hours. They're hot and exhausted, but you can't convince any of them to take a break."

"I understand. I used to be a volunteer myself," the man said.

"Some of these people have had to be dragged away from the line. They need to stop and eat, or it's going to get really dangerous for everyone," she said.

As Lacey walked back toward the front of the gawking crowd, she noticed all of the water and snacks were already gone. She passed exhausted firefighters resting momentarily on the provided chairs and noticed how each seemed anxious to get back in the fight.

"Any more chips?" she heard one firefighter ask another.

"Nope. They're out."

"Damn. That's all I've had to eat all day. Never mind, ready to suit up?"

She watched as they returned to the blaze. While she stared at the smoke and flames, she heard the most incongruous laughter. *Show a little respect,* she thought. *What's wrong with people?*

Just as she turned her head, Lacey recognized the irreverent giggles behind her. Ashley and Brittney were all smiles as they approached her.

"Remember that guy we saw the first day of school?" Ashley asked as she popped a piece of gum into her mouth.

"No."

"Sure you do. The really buff new kid you were drooling over just before we got to the door on the first day," Brittney said, brushing her long black hair.

"Me? Ashley was the one drooling," Lacey said, turning her back to the fire and giving her friends her full attention.

"His name's Jagger, and he's got the most intense green eyes," Ashley said.

"How do you know that?" Lacey asked.

"We just saw him," Britt said, bending over to brush the underside of her hair.

"He lives down the block on the bayside, next door to Josh Brown. We just ran into them and they're having some people over – Josh Hamilton, Amber Burzinski and Scarlet Scott. They're all Seaside people. They figure if the bridge is closed they won't have school tomorrow so they're taking over Jagger's dad's tiki bar. Apparently his parents are at their old house in New York finishing up with the move."

"Yeah, you're lucky we love you. We could have just stayed there, but we told them we'd come get you and be right back," Brittney said, putting her brush in her pocketbook.

"We don't really know those guys," Lacey said.

"So what?" Brittney asked.

"Jagger, the new kid, seems really nice, and besides what better time to get to know them? With the fire, we won't even need to find stuff to talk about," Ashley said.

"Besides if we turn them down this time, you know we'll never get asked again," Britt said.

Lacey looked from Ashley, who was practically bouncing in place, to Brittney, who was applying lip gloss. "You're right. What are we really doing here anyway?" she said.

Without looking back at the fire, Lacey added, "Let's go."

We're going to a party! she wanted to yell, but restrained herself as they headed toward the bay.

"Hey, did you see the governor?" Brittney asked.

"What? No," Lacey said.

"He's here, y'know," Ashley said.

"Now, he shows up," Lacey complained.

"What?" Brittney asked.

"Never mind," Lacey said.

"Anyway, we were talking to a couple of firemen on our way back, and they said there are more than four hundred firefighters here. And they think this might take days to put out," Ashley said.

"Shit," Lacey said.

"But the good thing is we can tell our parents we got stuck over here when the bridge closed and hang out for hours," Brittney said, smiling.

As the girls talked and walked, a small black car pulled up along the curb ahead of them. Two women got out and ran to the corner convenience store. When they got to the door and realized it was locked, they both began cursing, quickly returned to the car and sped away.

When Lacey noticed the fire auxiliary bumper sticker on the back of the car, she stopped in her tracks.

"What?" Ashley asked, tugging Lacey's arm.

"We can't do this," Lacey said as much to herself as her friends.

"If this is about MacGyver, I'm going to lose it," Britt complained.

"Yeah, right," Lacey said. "Look. We can't just go to a party and forget what's happening."

"Why not? What else are we going to do?" Brittney asked.

"I don't know. Something. We've got to do something," Lacey said.

"Like what?" Ashley asked.

"We can't just go hang out with some strange guy. We need to help out," Lacey said.

"Jagger," Ashley said.

"What do you suppose we do? Grab a hose?" Brittney said, looking at Lacey as if she had lost her mind.

"No, listen," Lacey said. "When you were on your walk, I helped unload some water and snacks."

"So?" Brittney asked.

"Listen to me. The firefighters are hungry and need water."

"Again, so?" Brittney asked.

"I'm thinking maybe we should go home and get all the water we can and make some sandwiches and bring them back."

"Really? Instead of hanging out?" Ashley asked.

"Lacey, what's wrong with you?" Brittney said. "Even if we got a couple of cases of water, that's not going to go very far among hundreds of firefighters.

"Well, do you have any better ideas?" Lacey said. "It just doesn't feel right to do nothing when we could help, at least a little."

Brittney and Ashley looked at Lacey, and then each other.

"You're right," Ashley said, disappointed.

"Well," Brittney said, weighing her options then sighing. "My dad does have at least ten cases of water in the garage that he has the crews bring to construction sites.

"Great," Lacey said. "Let's go get it."

"Yeah!" Ashley said, getting into the spirit.

"Okay," said Brittney. "Head to the car. Let's hope they'll let us get back there. When we left the Jeep, it was a few blocks north of the fire. Now, the fire's blocks past there."

Chapter Seventy-Six:
Immediately following, Thursday, Sept. 12, 2013

"I know what we can do!" Ashley excitedly yelled from the shotgun seat of Brittney's Jeep.

"I thought we already knew what we're going to do," Lacey said.

"I've got an even better idea!"

"What?" Brittney asked.

"Who's more prepared to feed four hundred people?"

"I don't know. Lacey's mom on a summer afternoon when she plans a backyard barbecue?"

"You're not wrong," Lacey said.

"No. No. Think," Ashley demanded.

"The school cafeteria?" Brittney asked.

"Eww," Ashley said. "And besides, they're not open."

"We give up," Lacey said. "Who?"

"The pantry!"

"Yeah, but they're not open, either," Brittney said.

Ashley pulled out her keys.

"How are your house keys going to help us?" Brittney said, getting a little tired of the conversation.

"I've got the key to the pantry," Ashley said.

"You do? Since when?" Brittney said.

"Today. It's a long story, but the bottom line is I've got the keys. We've got plenty of cases of water and granola bars and stuff."

"That's brilliant," Brittney said.

"I don't know," Lacey said. "That stuff is for people who need it. People who have nowhere else to go."

"Sounds like the firefighters. Doesn't it?" Ashley said.

"Well, call your boss and ask what we should do," Lacey suggested.

"She's not my boss," Ashley said. "It's a volunteer position."

"So what is she then?"

"My supervisor."

"Whatever. Get her on the phone," Brittney said.

"She didn't answer. I'm texting her now," Ashley said.

"What are we going to do if she doesn't answer? Is there anyone else you can ask?" Lacey said.

"I'm texting her and the lady who asked me to volunteer," Ashley said.

"Okay, I'll head to my house first for the water. Hopefully, by the time we get that, you'll have an answer," Brittney said.

"No need," Ashley said. "We have plenty of water at the pantry."

"Yeah, but we might not be able to take any of it," Lacey said.

"No, we will. Don't worry," Ashley said.

When they arrived in the parking lot of the People's Pantry, Ashley still hadn't gotten any answers.

"What do we do?" Lacey said.

"We're doing this," Ashley said and opened the car door.

"We're doing this," Brittney said with a shrug, stripping off her pink hoodie as if hard work required short sleeves. Slamming the Jeep doors behind them, the girls joined Ashley at the pantry door.

"See," Ashley said, showing the girls a storeroom filled with off-brand water cases.

"Holy crap," Brittney said. "Everybody get out your phones and post that we need kids with cars to come help us out."

By the time the three of them were done posting, two senior guys they barely knew were there packing their SUVs with supplies. Just as they were about to start loading water into Brittney's Jeep, four more kids pulled up. These were people they'd previously reported for vandalizing Sandy homes. Lacey visibly stiffened, but Brittney pulled her aside.

"Look, if they're going to help, we have to let them," Brittney told Lacey.

"But, how do we know they're even going to bring it over to the fire?"

"Because it's not beer," Brittney said. "C'mon, Lacey, we have to trust them."

"Okay," she agreed reluctantly.

The first six cars had been packed and left, and three more cars were waiting when a fourth vehicle sped into the parking lot. Lacey was using a hand truck to pull three cases of water to a waiting car when a woman stepped directly in front of her.

"Hey, I don't have time to play," Lacey said before she looked up from the dark pants and saw the badge.

"Can I ask what you're doing?" a tall blonde female police officer in her twenties asked.

"Ummm, loading water to take to the firefighters," Lacey said.

"Loading or looting?" the officer said.

"Excuse me?" Lacey said.

"Who's in charge here?" the officer asked.

"Ashley!" Lacey yelled. "Ashley, can you come over here?"

Ashley walked over but only her eyes and the top of her head were visible as she was carrying three cases of granola bars.

"What's up?" she said. Then, spotting the police officer, she put down her load and asked, "Can I help you, officer?"

"Are you the supervisor here?" the officer asked.

"No, I'm just a volunteer," Ashley said. "But I have the key," she said for no reason at all.

"Did someone authorize you to pack up this food and water and send it over to Seaside?" the officer asked.

"I don't know," Ashley said. "Let me check my phone."

"All right. All right," the officer said. "Everyone put down whatever you have."

"You two," she called over to two boys from school waiting to have their cars packed. "Do you have any food or water in your car?"

"No, sir. I mean, no, ma'am," a senior Ashley recognized from math class stumbled. "Well, I have my own bottle of water. But nothing else," he added.

"And you?" the officer asked the other teen.

"No. Not yet," he answered.

"Then you two can go," the officer said.

"But we wanted to help bring supplies over to the fire," Ashley's classmate said.

"I said you can go," the officer repeated.

"Thank you, sir...ma'am."

Both drivers pulled away.

Ashley looked up from her phone. "No," she said to the officer.

"No what?"

"No, ma'am?" she said hesitantly.

"What?" the officer asked. "What are you saying no to?"

"You asked if someone authorized this. The answer is no," she said.

"I know," the officer said. "That would explain the burglary alarm."

"I didn't hear anything," Lacey said.

"Me neither," Brittney said.

"It's silent," Ashley said.

"So you know about the alarm?" the officer said.

"Yeah," Ashley said. "But when we came in, I forgot about it."

"Officer, we were only trying to help," Lacey said.

"Yeah, you see, we were over at the fire, and we realized they didn't have enough food or water," Brittney said.

"So we were going home to get stuff," Lacey said.

"But then I realized I had the key to the pantry, and we thought that would be faster. And well," Ashley said.

"All right, ladies. Bring this stuff back inside and wait there. I'll be right back," the officer said and headed toward her car.

"Are you going to arrest us?" Lacey asked.

"Just wait here," the officer said.

"Crap," Lacey said. "This was supposed to be my year to turn things around. Sophomore year I failed and needed summer school. I figured junior year I could maybe make high honor roll, or at least not get arrested."

"My mother is going to freak out," Ashley said.

"I wonder if I'll even be able to reach my parents to bail me out," Brittney pondered aloud. With that, the door opened and the officer they'd been talking to came in followed by six other uniformed officers.

"There they are," she said, pointing in the direction of the girls.

"Oh my God," Ashley said. "Look, we're sorry. We'll pay for everything we took….somehow."

"No problem. We can pay for the food and make a donation to the pantry," Brittney jumped in.

Lacey stood there and cried. "We're sorry. Please don't handcuff us."

Without a word, the officers picked up the cases of granola bars and water and carried them out the door.

"You're not getting arrested," the young officer they'd originally spoken to said. "I called the chief, and he called the mayor, who confirmed your story about the shortage over in Seaside. These officers are here in their patrol cars to bring over the needed supplies."

"Well, we can help," Brittney said. "My Jeep is right out front."

"No need. We have this under control. I suggest you girls head home," the officer said. The girls didn't want to wait for her to change her mind and quickly scurried toward the door. "And ladies."

"Yes," they said in unison, turning to face her.

"Nice job," she said.

"Thank you," they responded, relieved.

Once home, despite being exhausted, Lacey couldn't stop checking the news and Facebook on her laptop for information about the fire.

I'm so tired, she thought, *but I need to know. Did they stop it? Was anyone hurt?*

Just before 11 p.m. she shouted, "Yes!" after seeing on Facebook that the firefighters had stopped the blaze from continuing its march down the Seaside Heights Boardwalk. *Yes!* she thought. Finally she could close her laptop, and her eyes, and go to sleep in her new living room/bedroom.

Chapter Seventy-Seven:
Monday, Sept. 16, 2013

On Monday morning during the general announcements, Lacey, Ashley and Brittney were mortified when their names were read off as this week's "everyday heroes, for their quick thinking in a time of crisis."

"Great. This was everything I never wanted," Lacey said as the girls enjoyed being out of the building at lunchtime and grabbing pizza at Vesuvius.

"I know. I actually laughed when I heard your name being called this morning," Ashley said.

"Your name was announced, too," Lacey said.

"Yeah, but I never pledged to kill, and I quote, 'every single one of those lowlife everyday heroes.'"

Brittney cracked up. "Oh my god, she did say that. And, wait, she also said, 'They're only looking to pad their college applications.'"

"Is that what you were doing, Lacey?" Ashley teased.

"Knock it off," Lacey complained. "Look, I wasn't trying to be a do-gooder. It's just when I saw all those firefighters needing help and realized we could do something. How could we not? I mean you both agreed."

"I know," Brittney said. "But don't you think it's possible, just maybe a little possible, that some of the other 'everyday heroes' felt that way too?"

"No way," Ashley said.

"Don't be stupid," Lacey said, taking a bite of her pizza.

"Yeah, you're right," Brittney agreed and turned her attention to her slice of Sicilian. "I almost forgot to tell you guys. My dad is working with the township to hold a Stronger than the

Storm party for all the Silverton Sandy victims next month for the one-year anniversary."

"Ewww," Ashley and Lacey said simultaneously.

"Oh, c'mon," Brittney said. "My dad's donating all this money for the food, and some old-people band is playing during the afternoon, and Harborland is playing at night."

"I do like Harborland," Lacey said. "But I'm not going."

"Me neither," Ashley said.

"Oh, c'mon, I have to go," Brittney said.

"Have fun," Lacey said.

"See ya,'" Ashley added.

"Well, then I guess you're both walking back to school," Brittney said.

"Not funny," Lacey said.

"Don't worry. You're everyday heroes. You probably can't get in any trouble today."

"Very funny," Lacey said in a monotone.

"Look, we'll consider going," Ashley said as they cleared their table and threw out their grease-stained paper plates.

"What?" asked Lacey. "No, we won't."

"C'mon, Lacey," Ashley said. "You do like Harborland."

"Sure, but not enough to label myself a victim again."

"What?" asked Brittney, holding the door open for her friends.

"Bye." "Thank you." "Have a nice day," the girls called back to the owner standing behind the counter as they exited.

"How does going to a party make you a victim?" Brittney said as they stepped outside.

"You just said it's for Sandy victims. I don't want to be a victim anymore. I'm tired of that. It's almost a year," Lacey said, climbing back into the shotgun seat in the Jeep.

"Think of it this way. It's for Silverton residents affected by Sandy, not victims," Brittney said as she put her key in the ignition.

"Oh, then all *your* neighbors will be coming, too?" Ashley asked, more curious than accusingly.

"What, my neighbors? No, no one up by me flooded," Brittney said.

"You said it's for everyone affected by the storm," Lacey said. "I would argue that everyone in Silverton was 'affected' whether they flooded or not. Sandy changed the whole area."

"She's right," Ashley said.

"Sure, but I told you my dad's company is paying for most of the food. He can't buy food for all of Silverton."

"I get that, but honestly, I would think it makes more sense to have a Silverton Strong party rather than a Stronger than the Storm party."

"What's the difference?" Brittney said, as she pulled back onto the school property.

"There's a big difference," Lacey said.

"Slogans like Restore the Shore and Stronger than the Storm are about all of us as victims," Lacey said.

"Silverton Strong is about our hometown, where we live. It's about everyone – not just the people who flooded. It's about how Silverton is working together to get everyone home."

"I see what you're saying, but I don't think my dad is going to want to buy food for the whole town."

"He doesn't have to," Ashley said.

"Yeah, at my church any time they tell people to bring a tray of food, we wind up with way more than we need."

"Besides, if it's a party for everyone, then it's more of a celebration that the worst is over, not another gathering of people asking, 'So how much water did you have?'"

"Jerk!" Brittney screamed.

"What?" Ashley said, feeling the jolt as Brittney slammed on the brakes.

"Watch out!" Lacey yelled.

"I was looking at my phone. What just happened?" Ashley asked.

"Some senior..."

"It was Gordon Simsek."

"Okay, Gordon Simsek just walked out right in front of me," Brittney complained as she parked the Jeep.

"He was walking and texting and not looking at all," Lacey said.

"Oh, he was probably hitting on that freshman he likes, Erica Ramirez."

"Really. I know Erica," Brittney said as the girls got out of the SUV and headed toward the building. "Her mother will never let her date a senior."

"Who said she was going to tell her mother?" Ashley said. The three friends laughed. They could each remember times they "forgot" to reveal dating details to their parents.

Chapter Seventy-Eight:
Tuesday, September 17, 2013

As soon as Ashley got into the Jeep the next morning, Brittney cut Lacey off right in the middle of a story about some judge hitting on her mother.

"My father said it's a good idea."

"What?" Lacey said.

"Great. What's a good idea?" Ashley said.

"Calling it a Silverton Strong party and inviting everyone."

"Cool," Lacey said. "So anyway, Ashley, I was just telling Britt about this judge in Brick, who after Polly won her case before him had the nerve to ask her…"

"I'm sorry, Lacey, but before I forget, my dad wants all of us to work on the party planning committee."

"Uh, no," Lacey said.

"Yeah, not my thing, either," Ashley said.

"Oh, c'mon, it might be fun," Brittney said.

"Brittney, planning a party celebrating being hit by a hurricane is not my idea of a good time," Lacey said. "Isn't it enough that we've agreed to come to this thing?"

Brittney was uncharacteristically silent.

"Brittney, what gives?" Lacey said. "When did you become Silverton's top party planner?"

"Shut up," Brittney snapped. "Sorry. Never mind."

"Never mind what?" Ashley asked. "You're acting really weird."

"It's just that my father's in charge of this thing, and he actually asked me for help," Brittney said. "He came to my room, sat down and talked to me about it and asked for my ideas. It's the first time since, since I don't know when."

Lacey and Ashley exchanged glances. "We do," they said together.

"What?"

"Since Sandy."

"Huh?"

"You're just like us," Lacey said. "Your dad hasn't had any time since Sandy."

"No," Brittney said, pulling into the school parking lot. "Since his business got busy."

"And it got busy because of?"

"Sandy," Brittney said grumpily.

"Think of it this way. Now you get to use the Sandy card," Ashley said. "And, yeah, I'll help you work on the party."

Lacey rolled her eyes and sighed. "I will, too."

"Check this out," Brittney said instead of responding. She pointed to a silver pickup truck in the senior parking lot where Gordon Simsek and Erica Ramirez were making out.

"Good for them," Lacey said.

"Yeah, at least Erica will have a fairytale high school romance story."

"What?"

"You know, crush on the senior football player that turns into the love of your life."

"Gordon's not on the football team. He's not on any team."

"He's on the debate team."

"Nobody fantasizes about dating the captain of the debate team."

"Whatever. We better hurry up. The bell's about to ring."

Chapter Seventy-Nine:
About 9 p.m. Saturday, September 28, 2013

"I don't think I'll ever get used to this view," Lacey told Ashley and Brittney as she stared out her real bedroom window down toward the Beach Club.

"Is it that different?" Brittney asked.

"Come take a look," Lacey said. "I can see so much more of the bay now."

"Wow, it's amazing what just a few feet can do," Ashley said. "This is a much better view than you had before."

"Yeah, but I miss my old one," Lacey said.

"Your old view was of that tree," Brittney said, pointing below them.

"Yeah, but I kind of communed with the squirrels every day. Darth Vader would chase them, and they would scamper up here and chatter outside my window."

"Oh, brother," Brittney said. "Did you ever think that maybe, just maybe, you're a little too nostalgic?"

"Nope, not really," Lacey said. "I like it when things don't change."

"Well, one good change you've made is that you're not so afraid of heights anymore," Ashley said.

"You climbed up that ladder and into this house like it was perfectly normal to go into your house when it's six feet off the ground," Brittney said.

"Isn't it?" Lacey said with a laugh. "It's just nicer hanging out here than it is in the apartment."

"If your mother finds out we're here, she's going to have a fit," Ashley said.

"She won't find out. Yours never did," Lacey reminded her.

"But my mom's a basket case. Polly's more on top of her game," Ashley said.

"You think so, but this crap is wearing on her. Lately, whenever I walk in a room she's on the phone crying to my grandmother in Arizona. Like Mom-Mom can help her from all the way out there."

"That sucks," Ashley said.

"Yeah, and the crazy thing is she doesn't think I know. She keeps trying to act like she's fine."

"What do you do?" Brittney asked.

"Nothing really," Lacey said. "I try to let her have privacy, which is hard when we're living on top each other over there. And, I guess, I try to help out a little more with Jake."

"Do you smell that?" Ashley said.

"Smell what?" Brittney said.

"Wow, yeah," Lacey said, turning on her cellphone flashlight. "I'll check the house."

"What is it?" Brittney asked Ashley as Lacey headed out of the room.

"Smells like smoke," Ashley said.

"Oh, geez, not again," Brittney said.

"Guys, c'mon down here," Lacey called from the first floor, which technically was now where the second floor used to be.

Ashley and Brittney ran to and down the stairs. Ashley tripped and almost fell halfway down but caught herself.

"God, this is hard in the dark," she said.

"Come here quick!" Lacey said from the living room window.

Across the street, flames shot out on the roof of the Allens' house.

"Should we call…" Brittney started to say when a police car followed by two firetrucks pulled up. The firefighters started to connect to the fire hydrant outside Lacey's house.

"We better get down there," Lacey said. "Make sure you take your stuff."

"I gotta go back upstairs and grab my purse," Ashley said.

"Grab my backpack," Brittney called after her.

Outside, the girls joined a small crowd watching as the firefighters battled the blaze.

"Thank god, Mrs. Allen wasn't there," Lacey said as they watched.

"She's been staying with her son since the storm," Ashley said.

"Yeah, I know," Brittney said. "That's one of my father's jobs. It was almost done."

"Shh," Lacey said.

"Why?" Brittney said.

"Shh," Lacey repeated, then hissed, "Listen."

Behind the girls in the crowd were Corky and Yanni, two of the boys who arranged the parties in the vacant Silverton homes.

"I can't believe we fell asleep," Yanni said.

"Yeah, if that Golden Retriever hadn't been barking outside, we would have been toast," Corky said.

"I know," Yanni said. "I think you must have knocked over your kerosene lantern."

"No, I'm pretty sure you did," Corky said.

"Whatever," Yanni said. "If that dog wasn't barking its head off. I don't think we would have woken up."

"I know. It's kind of crazy. You think we would have woken up from the heat."

"Nah, we were too drunk."

Ashley, Brittney and Lacey exchanged looks. Brittney started to speak, but Lacey shot a look her way that said, "You'd better shut up now."

"There she is," Yanni said. And Lacey turned her head hoping to find Pyrite, but it was just some girl in a blue pickup truck.

"What about our cars?" Corky asked, indicating parking spots down the street near the Boat Slips.

"We'll get them later."

As the boys pulled away in the pickup truck, Lacey exploded. "This is the last straw!"

"Shut up," Ashley said.

"Let's take a walk," Brittney said, and they escorted their friend away from the crowd.

The girls climbed around the Beach Club fence and found their way to the Adirondack chairs.

"Those assholes!" Lacey shouted. "They burnt down Mrs. Allen's house!"

"Well, not exactly burned down, although there does seem to be heavy structural damage," Brittney said.

"Stop talking like a builder," Ashley snapped.

"Sorry."

"Yeah, and I can't believe Pyrite helped them," Lacey said.

"Wait, what?" Ashley asked.

"Pyrite, the missing Golden Retriever," Lacey said. "Corky said if Pyrite wasn't barking like crazy outside the house, they probably wouldn't have gotten out."

"Okay, I got that," Ashley said. "But why does that bother you? You wouldn't want them to die. Would you?"

"Well?" Lacey said. "No, I guess not. But, I just thought... It's just that up to now the dog always seemed to be, y'know, one of the good guys. Now she's helping them."

"You're upset about what side you think the dog is taking?" Brittney asked.

"No, I guess not. Never mind," Lacey said. "We need to report them."

"What for?" Ashley said.

"What do you mean what for?" Brittney asked.

"Their dads are mega rich. They'll just pay their way out of this, too. They only got fines for the damage over on Aldo," Ashley said.

"Well, we can't just let them get away with it," Lacey argued.

"What are we going to do?" Brittney asked.

"I don't know," Lacey said. "Something."

As they contemplated their next move over the next couple of hours, they saw the firetrucks pull away, and the crowd disperse.

"I've got it," Brittney said. "Let's use my Jeep and push their cars into the bay."

"I don't think so," Ashley said. "Lacey and I don't have rich dads who can buy our way out of juvie. And I want my next institution to be college, not the state pen."

"I don't know. She may be on to something," Lacey said.

"Lacey," Ashley said in a commanding tone.

"I kind of like the idea of their cars being flooded. That way they get a little taste of what we went through," Lacey said.

"Yeah, but if we push their cars into the bay, we'll face all kinds of charges, even state environmental crimes for polluting the bay," Ashley said.

"How do you know that?" Brittney said.

"Eighth-grade earth science class," Ashley said.

"All right, so how else can we flood their cars?" Lacey asked.

"What about just using one of the hoses over by the Boat Slips?" Brittney said.

"That won't have nearly the same impact. It's fresh water," Lacey said.

"What about your sump pump?" Ashley asked.

"What about it?" Lacey asked.

"We can take the sump pump from under your house. Plug it in at one of the slips, use one of the hoses there, and pump bay water into their cars."

"Brilliant," Brittney said. "Ashley, Lacey, you guys get the sump pump, and I'll undo one of the hoses down there. But we have to be quick, we're supposed to be back at my house by midnight. We've got about thirty minutes."

Chapter Eighty:
11:30 p.m. Saturday, September 28, 2013

Brittney unscrewed a hose from the slip in front of Corky's 2012 Mitsubishi Eclipse. Then, she checked out the car. Fortunately, Corky had left the driver's window half open, and even better, the back floor was filled with school books and folders.

When Lacey and Ashley got there they attached the hose to the pump, plugged it in and began pumping bay water into the car.

Yanni's SUV presented more of a challenge. All the windows and doors were locked. The girls considered their situation.

"I've got it," Brittney said. "Let me handle this while you guys go back to the Beach Club shed and grab two buckets or pails, fill them with sand and bring them over here."

Brittney set off to work removing the spare tire from the back door. Then, she went to her own car and grabbed a screwdriver and started unscrewing the tire bracket on the SUV.

"What are you doing?" Lacey asked.

"If I can get this off, if it's anything like my car, there's a small hole that should be just big enough for the hose."

"What do you want us to do with the sand?" Ashley asked.

"Dump it on Corky's hood and get more.

"What?" Ashley asked.

"You'll see," Brittney said, and Lacey and Ashley did as they were told. When they came back, Brittney complained that she couldn't get the screw out. Lacey gave it a shot while Brittney took a sand run with Ashley.

When they got back, Lacey held up a screw and the tire bracket. "I got it. I'm the king of the world," she said.

"No time to gloat," Brittney said. "Switch the hose over to Yanni's car and start putting some sand on his hood.

"Damn, it's 11:55," Brittney said. "We better wrap this up. My mom said we needed to be back by midnight. We'll be late, but not too bad."

"I liked it better when your parents were never home," Ashley said.

"I didn't," Brittney admitted. "They're actually trying to make an effort to stay home on weekends and make meals and things once in a while now. It's kind of nice."

"Britt, why the sand on the hoods?" Lacey asked.

"Well, you know how they're not too bright," Brittney said. "I think if we want to send them a message, we better spell it out. Put some water on that sand so it's sticky."

Once the sand was moist, Brittney wrote with her finger in the sand on Corky's hood. "Stay out of Silverton."

"I've got Yanni's," Lacey said. And she scrawled, "I know what you did last summer."

"There," Lacey said, stepping back to admire her message.

"We gotta get going," Brittney said.

"I'm way ahead of you," Ashley said, unplugging the sump pump while Lacey undid the hose.

"I'll reconnect the hose at the slip, you guys bring the sump pump back, and I'll pick you up in front of Lacey's," Brittney said.

Before going to pick up Lacey and Ashley, Brittney inspected their handiwork. Both cars had water over the seats, with bits of notebook paper and fast-food wrappers floating around. There must have been a box of condoms hidden under one of the front seats in the SUV, because now at least half a dozen individually wrapped foil packages were floating near the dashboard.

When they were all in the Jeep, Lacey asked Brittney if anyone spotted her after she and Ashley left the scene of the crime

"No. I don't think anyone will notice anything until the boys get back. The water level in the cars is going down really fast," Brittney said, disappointed.

"It's pouring out the bottom of the doors, right?" Lacey said.

"Yes, exactly," Brittney said.

"No problem. That might be even better!" Ashley said. "Since it's dark, they might not even notice how wet the cars are inside until they go to get in and sit down. They'll be too busy bitching about the sand on the outside."

"Wet butt!" the other two girls said in unison. "Ewwwww."

"Mission accomplished," Lacey said, after the three of them got their laughter under control. "Now let's get the hell out of here."

Chapter Eighty-One:
Wednesday, Oct. 2, 2013

Lacey couldn't help laughing when Donovan shared his high at support group.

"There's this kid, Corky, in my history class, who shows up Monday without the paper that was due, and he's all like, 'You don't understand. Something happened to my car,'" Donovan said. "Then, he holds up his history book which is all blown up and won't close, and the pages are all wavy like it's been dropped in a bathtub. And he holds up what he says is his history paper, only it's just soggy paper with the words all washed off it. The teacher wasn't having it. He's yelling at Corky that if this was some sort of joke, it was in very poor taste, and Corky argued back that it wasn't a joke and his laptop was ruined. Then, he got sent to the principal's office. And the thing is, Corky's really a jerk, and I couldn't help but think it serves him right."

Neza cut her eyes to where Lacey was laughing. "I guess you agree?" she said.

"Definitely," Lacey said. "It's sweet revenge for all the crap he puts other people through."

"I take it you know him?" Neza asked.

"Yeah, he's one of the kids who's been breaking into the vacant houses and trashing them."

"Well, I don't want to get into that. We don't want to slander anyone, but let's talk about what you said. Is it sweet revenge?"

"Oh yeah," Lacey said.

"Let me ask you something? What is revenge? Or rather, what is the difference between revenge and justice?"

"Revenge is about getting even," Donovan said. "Justice is about getting what's fair, returning power to people who don't have it."

"Exactly," Neza agreed. She paused for a moment, looked over at Lacey and smiled. "For the last few years, I have been involved in something that I have kept very quiet because I wasn't completely comfortable with myself and my actions. I feared I was seeking revenge, but I've been thinking a lot about this, especially after some friends have talked to me. I want to share more about myself with you all because I, too, have realized the difference between revenge and justice."

Neza then told the story of her own history and surviving the Rwandan genocide. She explained that while she continued to testify both in the U.S. and abroad about things she witnessed she worried that she was indulging an evil need for revenge.

"Today, I realize that it is not revenge I seek but just a small amount of justice for those so savagely taken from us," Neza said.

The room was silent. No one knew what to say. Lacey made eye contact with Neza and casually flashed her a thumbs up.

"I am telling you, and all of my clients now, because I want you to understand that my experiences do not in any way diminish yours. We are all part of a global community that shares one another's joys and our heartbreaks.

"I believe I understand your situations more because of what I've lived through, not in spite of it. In some ways, I see my past as a gift, though not one that anyone would ever want, that I must share," Neza said. "I hope you will agree. If any of you have questions, feel free to ask them."

Neza spent the next several minutes answering questions that ranged from where exactly is Rwanda to how she survived in hiding. Eventually, Tiff asked Neza if what happened made her hate Hutus, the group that perpetrated the genocide. Neza's answer surprised them.

"I don't think I hate anyone," Neza said. "I couldn't hate all Hutus because it was a Hutu pastor who hid us and risked his own life sneaking us food for three months."

"Don't you hate the neighbor who killed your family?"

"I did, but not anymore. Now I hate the circumstances that caused him to pick up his knife. You must remember that if you were to come to Rwanda, you would not be able to tell the difference between a Tutsi and a Hutu. We share the same race, religion and culture. Yet, because different countries colonized parts of Rwanda, we found a way to see one another as 'other.' Whenever that happens, it leads to pain and suffering. Yet it keeps happening all over the globe.

"Part of what you all have been experiencing is because teenagers in your schools have made you into 'other' simply because your houses flooded. That's what they did when they labeled you GES," Neza said. "This is part of the human experience, but it is one we can change if we work hard enough."

As the group broke for snacks, Lacey approached Neza and gave her a warm hug.

"Thank you," Neza said. "You and the boys helped me see I needed to share this. See, you think group therapy is just for you, but it helps me, too."

As she emerged from the church with Donovan and Tiff, Lacey was surprised to see her mother parked out front. She said good-bye to her friends and headed over to the minivan.

"What are you doing here?" Lacey asked.

"I had to work late, so Grandma is home with Jake. I thought you might like some ice cream."

"Am I in trouble?"

"Lacey, I ask you if you want ice cream and you think you're in trouble?"

"You have to admit this is suspicious. Do you really want ice cream or do you need to talk to me? 'Cause I haven't done anything."

"You know, I am your mother. Can't I just want to spend time with you without an agenda?"

"I guess."

"Good, because when I realized we could grab a minute alone, I went for it," Polly said, smiling over at Lacey.

As Polly put the car in drive, Lacey considered. "Mom, can you imagine if our neighbors killed me and Jake with a machete?"

"What?!"

"That's what happened to Neza's family," Lacey said.

"You must have something wrong."

"No, she's from Rwanda."

"Oh," Polly said. "That's awful, but I thought this group was supposed to be about Sandy?"

"It's about all of us," Lacey said, "and how it all fits together. I don't think even you realized how right you are when you say, 'Life's messy.'"

"Probably not," Polly said. "Did Neza upset you? What happened in Rwanda was pretty awful, not that it was covered much at the time. What was it, 1996?"

"I think she said ninety-four. Neza didn't mean to, but she made me realize there are a lot worse things than, say, a mother who wants to buy you ice cream," Lacey said.

"I can't argue with that. So, you want Friendly's?"

"Actually, there's a new place over on Route 9 I like."

"A new place? Really?"

"You know, Mom, not all change is bad."

"You don't say."

Chapter Eighty-Two:
Saturday, Oct. 26, 2013

"This is such a beautiful place for a party," Ashley said, as she adjusted a banner that read, "Silverton Strong," hung between two pine trees in the county park.

"I've always loved Cattus Island, but I've never been to a party here. A couple of field trips, but never a party," Brittney said.

"Well, it's a wildlife preserve. They don't like to disturb the animals," Lacey said, adjusting her self-designed, sleeveless top, which had been a navy and white striped, long-sleeved shirt that Lacey had turned upside down so that the top part of the shirt and the sleeves were now tied as a belt. "I still think we should have held this in Silverton."

"We've been all over that! The fire department's parking lot wasn't big enough. Besides, Silverton is right there," she said, pointing a mile across the Silver Bay to the Rock Throwing Place.

"You know, this is kind of funny," Lacey said. "We always feel so private and secluded at the Rock Throwing Place. But from here you can see everything that goes on there."

"You're right," Ashley said. "It kind of creeps me out a little."

"Why? What were you doing at the Rock Throwing Place?" Brittney asked curiously.

"Never mind," Ashley said. "I mean nothing."

"Hmmm. Mmm," Brittney said and smirked.

"It was nice of the parks department to donate the use of Cattus," Lacey said, purposely changing the subject.

"Well, yeah, but remember, they also have an ulterior motive."

"What do you mean?" Ashley asked.

"Half this park is still destroyed," Lacey said. "They've got miles of trails to rebuild, not to mention the environmental center."

"Yeah, they thought if we had the party here they could remind people there's still so much work left to do. My dad said this way people remember to donate to the park or volunteer some time. Besides it's just gorgeous here," Brittney said.

"We better go back where they're setting up the food and see if they need any help," Lacey said.

"Did you see how much food there is?" Brittney said. "I swear, every restaurant in town donated.

"And all those food trucks," Ashley said. "I can't believe they're all giving away their hot dogs and ice cream for free."

"I know when Tyler and the boys get here, they're going to have a field day," Ashley said.

"How are things?" Lacey asked.

"Fine," Ashley said. "We're starting to get back to normal now. And you won't believe this. I can't believe I forgot to tell you guys. Tyler asked me to Homecoming. Well, actually he invited me to the Hogwarts Feast, but he meant Homecoming."

"Oh," Brittney said. "What did you say?"

"I told him I'd think about it," Ashley said.

"Good," Lacey said.

"Always keep them guessing," Brittney said.

The girls busied themselves helping to fill coolers and put out garbage cans. The rangers were very specific in their directions: Every garbage can had to have a cover on it at all times. The park is home to numerous wildlife species and open garbage cans are seen by everything from chipmunks to deer as an invitation to dinner.

"Brittney, come here," her father yelled over to her while he was in a conversation with the mayor and his wife.

As Brittney walked about a dozen feet over to where her father was, Lacey could hear him talking about how proud he is of his daughter and how much work she and her friends did organizing the party.

"I still can't believe neither of us are back home yet," Lacey said.

"I know. When I heard a storm was coming last year, I never would have thought it could do all this," Ashley said. "But, hey we have a building permit now."

"That's great," Lacey said and hugged her friend. "Now we can race to see who gets back in first."

"Not much of a race. It's supposed to take six to nine months for the builders to finish ours. You only have, what, another month?"

"Yeah, but by now, our house was supposed to be back down on the foundation and it's not. The first house that we saw being raised last January, still isn't done," Lacey reminded her friend. "But, whatever happens, at least now we know we can deal with it."

"Look at this. You're even talking about the storm," Ashley said.

"Sandy," Lacey said. "You can say it."

They both laughed. As Brittney turned toward them, she added, "Let's go check out the band. They're doing Beatles covers."

Chapter Eighty-Three:
Immediately following, Saturday, Oct. 26, 2013

It surprised no one when the Yellow Submarine cover band opened with "Here Comes the Sun" and got the whole crowd to sing along, "It's All Right."

"Lacey, darling, so nice of you to invite us," said Nick as Adam hugged her from behind and literally lifted her off her feet.

"Glad you can make it," she said. "My friends really like it when you guys come around."

"We are the life of the party," Adam said with a smirk.

Soon Tyler, Connor, Donovan, Michael and Tiff joined their group, and they were all having a great time shouting out the words to "Help" along with hundreds of their neighbors. Then the band suddenly stopped playing mid chorus.

While the lead singer, trailed off at, "Help, I need someone. Help not just...," the crowd continued with "Anyone." But then the music, even the drums, dropped out.

"Weird song to do a cappella," Brittney said.

"Shh, shh. Everybody, you can't see what I'm seeing from up here on stage. You're not going to believe this," said the guy covering the Paul McCartney part.

The crowd mumbled and turned around to look where the singer was gazing, but the trees were in the way of their view.

"I'll be Damn...Yankees," the singer said. "There's a guy paddling what looks like two coolers and an American flag sail, heading this way from Silverton. It's the craziest-looking thing!" he said, staring out in amazement. "So, I think the band's going to take a little break right now, so we can head down to the water and check this out. You probably don't want to miss it, either. On the other hand, the food lines will probably be pretty short while we're down there, so do whatever makes you happy. We'll be back in about fifteen."

"You want to get some food?" Lacey asked, ignoring the excitement.

"Yes! But not food – ice cream," Ashley said.

"That sounds good," Brittney said, brushing her hair. The trio headed to the Pied Piper truck, while the rest of their friends headed to the waterfront to check out the spectacle.

When they had gotten their treats, they moved to the waterfront, where most of the crowd had migrated.

"Oh my God, look at that thing!" Ashley said as they reached the beachfront.

"I don't believe it," Brittney said.

"Now that the excitement is over, we're gonna head on back to Strawberry Fields," the lead singer of the band called out without the assistance of a PA system, as he and the band, followed by much of the crowd, passed Lacey and her friends and headed back to the stage.

"That's insanity," Ashley said.

Brittney finally got close enough to walk around the contraption. "Nope. It's a surfboard, two coolers, an American flag and part of a bicycle."

"Did someone really paddle over from Silverton on that?" Lacey said, getting closer to the contraption.

"Not somebody. Me!" came a very familiar voice from behind her.

Spinning around on the sand, Lacey turned to face the pioneer.

"MacGyver!" she screeched, bear-hugging her friend and ignoring the bay water that dripped from his clothes.

"So this is MacGyver," Adam said.

"What an entrance," Nick added, clearly impressed.

"Yup," MacGyver said, smirking and then opening his arms for warm hugs from Ashley and Brittney.

"What the heck?" Lacey said. "What are you doing here?"

"My grandfather's funeral was yesterday."

"Oh."

"I'm so sorry."

"He was a great guy."

"Really funny."

"He loved you a lot," Lacey said.

"I know. Thanks," MacGyver said quietly. "Anyway, my aunt dropped me off in Silverton this morning, but no one was there. I mean pretty much no one at all."

"Well, yeah, everyone's here," Brittney said.

"I can see that," MacGyver said. "The only one in the whole neighborhood, except for some workers, was Mrs. Connors, across from the Beach Club."

"Yeah, she hasn't been feeling well," Ashley said.

"She told me," MacGyver said. "Then she told me about the party, but I had no way to get here."

"So I figured I'd just sit at the Beach Club and wait till someone came home. Then, I started to think about how we always wanted to figure out a way to get over here."

"You mean when we were kids?" Ashley asked.

"Exactly," MacGyver said. "Anyway, I looked around the shed at the Beach Club, and I found a bike, and I thought okay, it's a few miles, but I can do that."

"But?" Lacey said.

"It had two flats."

"Dry rot. That's been like that forever," Ashley said. "We should really fix that."

"I don't think we can now. Look," Lacey said, pointing at MacGyver's homemade raft, boat or whatever it was.

"Yeah," MacGyver said. "I thought maybe I could make a pedal boat, like they have at some parks. But that didn't work. I wound up just using part of the frame and the seat."

"I took everything I could find that would float and a bunch of line that was hanging around. Tied it all together and went bon voyage."

"You paddled all the way over here?" Ashley said.

"When I got out in the middle, a fishing boat came by and this guy asked me if I needed help. I told him what I was trying to do, and he threw me a line and towed me till the water was too shallow for his boat.

"I was so grateful, and I thanked the guy profusely, but he kept saying, 'Don't thank me; it's the law.' He said he's required to help boaters in distress, and he'd rather be home cleaning his fish. I mean he was grumpy and all, kept shaking his head at me, but he helped get me here."

"Bet his buddies will think he's telling fish tales," Ashley said.

"What?" Brittney said.

"You know, fish tales. Stories out of school," Ashley clarified.

"What?" asked Brittney again.

"Fake stories," Lacey said.

"Oh," said Brittney. "Hey, MacGyver, I guess you finally earned your name."

"True! I hadn't thought of that," MacGyver said, clearly impressed with himself. "Do they have food here?"

"Plenty."

"Does anyone have any money they can lend me?"

"It's all free."

"Free! Then what are we waiting for?" MacGyver said, crossing the sand and heading into the depths of the park.

Chapter Eighty-Four:
Around 9 p.m. Saturday, Oct. 26, 2013

"I can't believe people made such a fuss over the raft," MacGyver said as he sat with Lacey on her front steps, which remained on the ground while her house loomed over them more than six feet above their heads.

"Well, you could have killed yourself."

"How?"

"You could have drowned."

"Most of the bay isn't that deep. And I can swim."

"Some of it is. Besides, you could have exhausted yourself and been too tired to swim, and the bay's cold this time of year."

"I was on the raft the entire time."

"Well, something could have happened."

"I guess."

"I'm sorry about your grandfather. I really liked him."

"I know you did. Enough to talk to me."

"Oh, c'mon, I would have talked to you today no matter what."

"Really?"

"Yes, really. I was so excited to see you."

"It's been two months since I left, and you haven't texted me once."

"Neither have you."

"You were pretty mad at me."

"I'm sorry."

"Don't be."

"So how's the job?"

"It's all right, but Dad's starting to get better. He's moving around some, and he's supposed to be able to start working next month."

"That's great!"

"And with the holidays coming up, he'll definitely be able to find something, at least for a while."

"I'm sure he will. It must be driving him crazy not being able to work. He's always been so active."

"Just like me."

"Yeah, right."

"Lacey."

"Yeah?"

"After Christmas, if things work out, my mom said I can move in with my aunt if I really want to."

"Really?"

He nodded his head and stared down at his hands.

"Is that what you want to do?"

"Mostly."

"What about the other part?"

"It's hard, you know. They still kind of need me."

"And you'd miss them."

"I would, but I really miss you, too," he said, looking directly into her brown eyes.

Lacey's phone chirped, "You go Glenn Coco," and she reached into her pocket and without looking, turned her phone to silent. *What could be more important?*

"MacGyver, do you know why I never said yes when you'd ask me out?"

"You did when we were younger."

"I know, but I mean since then."

"No, not really."

"I've been saving you."

"Saving me?"

"Yeah."

"From what?"

"Not from what, for what."

They sat quietly for a moment. Then Lacey added, "You know how high school romances never work out?"

"Almost never," MacGyver corrected hopefully.

"Right. Almost never."

"So?"

"When the time is right. Let's face it, *if* the time is ever right..."

"Yeah?"

"I want us to work out."

"Huh?"

"If you and I are going to try this someday, I want to give it our best shot."

MacGyver said nothing.

"You see what I mean?"

"So you *don't* want me to move in with my aunt?"

"It's not that."

"Then what?"

"I don't think it's our time yet. Do you? I mean really?"

He put his arm around her, leaned in and kissed her. The kiss seemed to go on forever, but when they finally pulled away. MacGyver grinned and said, "Feels right."

She smiled and kissed him again. "You could convince me."

They hugged for a long time, not saying a word.

"I know you're right, but this sucks," MacGyver said.

"I know," she said and leaned her head against his shoulder. "But we'll get through this storm."

"Oh, right," he said holding her close. "We're ...

"Stronger than the storm," they said in unison and laughed. As they held each other, Pyrite came running around the corner and licked Lacey's hand.

Lacey grabbed the dog gently around the neck and pulled her close. Then, she took out her phone to find a picture of the wanted posters that had been hung around the neighborhood.

She entered the phone number and handed the phone to MacGyver. Then, she turned her attention to Pyrite. She petted and poured out all her welled-up affection on the Golden Retriever.

Lacey was only vaguely surprised when she heard MacGyver say, "No, we couldn't take the reward. From what I've heard, in some ways, we'll never be able to pay *you* back."

MacGyver pushed the button to end the call, and Lacey slipped the phone into her pocket. He put his arm around her shoulder and looked down at Lacey and the dog snuggling in his arms.

Lacey took in the scene and thought they made a perfect nuclear family. MacGyver kissed the top of her head, pulled her close and said, "Maybe someday."

ACKNOWLEDGMENTS

This book would not have been possible without the help and support of many, many people, including my first readers, Daniel Holt, Amanda Kovaleski, P.J. Mura and Amber Nigro, my dear friends, editors, and personal cheerleaders Anne Medeiros and Bobbi Seidel, my husband and rewrite editor Bob Mura, and the therapist who saw me through post-Sandy PTSD and got me back on the right track, Phyllis Alongi. Special thanks to my tea lady support group, Patti Rezac, Janet Ritchey and Marsha Tatarian, who fill my world with laughter, and to Bonnie Frizziola for the warm socks and so much more.

It literally took the hard work of hundreds of people just to get my own family of four back home after Sandy. I want to thank all my family, friends, coworkers, neighbors, students, etc. My family is especially grateful for my brother-in-law and builder, Al Trudeau, my uncle/painter/builder/and all-around amazing guy, Larry Borja, my father and the hardest worker I'll ever know, Marc Borja, and my sister-in-law Tricia Nigro and her family who housed us for many months. Thanks, too, to the Maddalena family for fostering our pet bunny and much more and our always thoughtful friend, Lisa Fobian. I must also thank our church, Holy Cross Lutheran Church, Toms River, and every community organization, church group, local, state or federal organization that helped us following the storm.

For those who have never lived through a natural disaster, I urge you to try to remember the real people behind the headlines immediately following an event and in the days, weeks, months and even years after the media has moved on. Please make a commitment to help out in any way you can. You have no idea how much even a cup of hot chocolate can mean!

"The aftermath of Sandy revealed a previously hidden struggle in Ocean County. Over 79,000 people are struggling with food insecurity, or lack of access to a consistent food source, the breadth and extent of damage finally made people, Sandy affected or not, feel comfortable asking for help," according to The People's Pantry, a nonprofit organization that continues to fill that need today. To donate: send to The People's Pantry, 1769 Hooper Avenue, Toms River, NJ 08753.

ABOUT THE AUTHOR

Debbie Mura has been a working journalist for about 40 years. A playwright and founder of the former Shooting Stars Theater Company, Debbie is an associate professor at Brookdale Community College currently teaching journalism, communications and English classes, always focusing on teaching students to become global citizens. A Toms River resident, Debbie and her family (and thousands of others) lived through the devastation of Superstorm Sandy. This is her first novel.

35397013R00253

Made in the USA
Middletown, DE
10 February 2019